Beyond Demon Belief: Anastasis Dunamis

Written By: Ray Korban

xulon PRESS

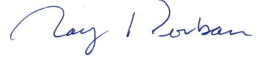

Anastasis Dunamis
by Ray Korban

Printed in the United States of America

ISBN 1-60034-811-4

www.xulonpress.com

INTRODUCTION

The source for the term BEYOND DEMON BELIEF comes from: James 2:19
"You believe that there is one God. Good! Even the demons believe that—and shudder."

James presents this as a challenge for us to have faith beyond that of mere idle acknowledgement. Maturing beyond demon faith to a position of authority is the duty of all Christians. Our call is to be part of the kingdom of God and as Paul plainly tells us in 1 Corinthians 4:20 ***"For the kingdom of God is not a matter of talk but of power."***

But "power" is not what most of us have been taught. I wrote this book to change my own mindset—to grow beyond the doctrines and limitations I was taught.

How did I do that? How can you do that? We have to read the Word of God for what it really says. We're handicapped in doing this by the English language. So many versions of the Bible try to put into modern words an approximate meaning so that we get the gist of what the Bible is trying to tell us. But, we don't get the whole idea. Words express ideas and to get only part of an idea is like hearing almost the right beat from the drums in an orchestra— what you hear is not what the composer meant and the experience is compromised if not painful.

There is a great source for anyone with an internet connection: **http://www.blueletterbible.org**. Develop your study skills to look up the original language and what it means. With the Holy Spirit's revelation, your understanding and appreciation of the Lord will grow as has mine.

The characters in this book are fictional but occasionally based on similar people in my life. No character is solely based on one individual, however.

Many of the things in this book have also happened in my life to one degree or another. That doesn't mean all of these things have happened—after all, this is fiction.

What is not fiction are the Bible quotes themselves. If not designated otherwise, all the quotes are from the New International Version. Occasionally I quote from the King James or other versions that bring out the original idea better and tell you which version is referred.

The geographical places in Oregon and Washington are real including Stonehenge. Sam Hill, a colorful turn-of-the-century northwest investor built Stonehenge and he is often the west coast source of the term, "What in the Sam Hill are you up to?" In respect to Stonehenge, it's an appropriate question with it isolated in the desert end of the Columbia Gorge where it stands as a full scale replica of the original.

Last but most important, I want to dedicate this book to some important people in my life: my great love, Cindy Dawn; my daughter and editor, Eden Dawn Harrington; and my son, Eli Killen. Nita Vining, Don and Dalene Cobine made this venture financially feasible—thank you.

INDEX

PROLOGUE

Exodus 13:21
By day the LORD went ahead of them in a pillar of cloud to guide them on their way and by night in a pillar of fire to give them light, so that they could travel by day or night.

The cloud on Dawn hides the light…it's suffocating. Maybe it's more like a burial shroud…it's been a long time since she's really lived. Sometimes she feels it isolates her, other times it's her companion. Its presence is strong in the most unlikely places. Or, maybe those places aren't what they appear? Is she the only one struggling?

No, there are others. Some in her own family, some she has yet to meet. Will their lives be entwined under the same fog or under a light so bright it's impossible to imagine?

Doom or life, die or grow, that's the extremes before them all. With unrelenting force, whatever it is drives them person-to-person and step-by-step into a new spiritual awareness unlike any "church" experience. But, with every step comes an attack.

And around every attack lurks a dark stranger. Is he helping or hurting? Where does he come from? It's a mystery of vital importance.

Whatever may come, the forces that draw them are like a black hole, relentlessly pulling them in. The light they thought they had disappears into a new power and who they are, or better said-- who they *were*, disappears into that same power: The power of Anastasis Dunamis.

PART I

CLOUD AND SHADOWS

1
CONTROL

I WAKE, STARTLED, AND MORE FEEL THAN SEE IT. A dark cloud descends from the ceiling onto our bed. On to me, really. And with the cloud comes the hate. The cloud controls how I feel and what I feel now is loathing for Joshua.

I lay here stewing in my emotions looking at the man I married. "My pain in the ass." For short, "Josh P.I.A."

The loathing I feel towards him must be obvious to everyone it seems except for him. Look at him sleeping as if everything in his world is OK! It's not. I'm not OK.

My sister, Dusky, is normally someone I would trust and talk to about this stuff. "Dusky," I almost mannishly snort. Even after all these long years I snort thinking how my parents named me, the first born, "Dawn" and her, the last born, "Dusky". Guess it's a good thing we didn't have another sister or brother—would have been hard for them to go through life as "Twilight."

For a year now Dusky said many times that I act as if I were lost in a fog. It would be more difficult to explain beyond that. It's as if I were so confused in every part of my body and mind that I didn't know what to do and couldn't remember at the end of a day if I had done anything. I have no control or will of my own, the cloud owns me.

Yesterday Ray, my son, called me at Dusky's and said he and my daughter Julienne, but we call her Jules, were waiting for me to pick them up at the mall. They had waited two hours and all the while I talked to Dusky about nothing without a hint anywhere in my mind that I had left them behind. Sister seized the mistake and convinced me something is wrong.

Now this cloud confirms it. It is so thick upon me that I can't even see my husband. I can almost hear Martha Stewart say, "And that's a good thing."

I turn on the TV as I always do when I can't sleep or the sex was too good keeping me awake. Not that I had experienced that kind of wakefulness for a long time now. It's been a little over a year since we last had sex.

The pompadour healer-pastor was on. It seems like they round up every trashy trailer park person for each program. Some grandma drenched with runny make-up is literally grabbing the microphone, blubbering about how she was healed of something when you know if she'd just lose the weight she'd have been healed long ago. The poor old lady stumbles over trying to pronounce the impossible to say diagnosis pompadour-pastor asks for and as she stammers I want to scream at her, "tell him what you really have--Twinkie-idiocy."

I was feeling a malicious spirit in me and refer to this as the "mean Dawn." Usually, I feel guilty about indulging the "mean Dawn" and then feel isolated as if I were the only mean spirited-acid-mouthed person in the world. Not now. It's almost like the dark cloud cuddles up to me in comfort assuring me that such attacks are good, necessary and have their place. What is this thing and why isn't it threatened by pompadour-healer-pastor when every other person on his stage is flying backwards into a heap on the floor? Maybe clouds don't heap.

A bird calls outside my window and I turn off the TV to listen. I only hear that bird before it gets light but can't remember what it's called. Maybe I'll rename it the Dawn Alarm.

I stretch out under the cloud and start to sleep as it rises from me. I replace the cloud with my blanket.

"Tomorrow," I say to no one in particular, "I've got to figure out what's going on. I can't go through life hiding in this bedroom under that dark cloud." But I feel almost lonesome as the cloud draws away and the blanket doesn't replace that comfort.

❖

I think I'm awake…it's like being in a fog on the water and not sure where you are…the kid's voices are downstairs, the front door shuts. Someone comes up the stairs. Who would dare ascend into my dark cloud?

"Crap, is Joshua still here?" I whisper in dread.

"Dawn-dawn the little lost fawn. I bring you coffee." Dusky sings out to me as she opens the door with one hand and somehow holds on to two coffee mugs with the other. "Dawn-dawn the little lost fawn" has survived since we saw Bambi as kids. I was almost six years old and she thought she was a clever four-year old. She thought wrong then and the error is now compounded.

Dusky's husband is out of town for the week and I suspect she's here to take care of me in the interim. Thankfully she hands me the coffee and waits for the caffeine to replenish me before poking me to respond. After a few minutes of blissful silence the unwanted poking begins.

"A psychiatrist?" she asks expecting me to know she means as an answer to my dark-cloud out-of-control problem.

Without saying a word, I started giving the come on wave with my left hand as if asking for more. Dusky knew I meant more suggestions…almost like you would to a waiter who had memorized the whole menu.

"A celibate monk who has a 12 hour release from his vows," she answered in Jeopardy game-show-quick response knowing this to be a jab at Thorn Birds, my favorite novel.

I shake my head. As sex hungry as a celibate monk may be, my deficit cravings are an equal and opposite reaction.

"A yoga who can teach you enlightenment in 29 minutes while permanently adjusting that crick in your neck?"

I shake my head. Although a permanent neck crick fix is an enticing consideration.

"Grandma returned from the dead to bake her "wicked apple" pie and home made ice cream?"

I shake my head again but not too quickly—Grandma's wicked apple pie is still seriously missed in my family for many years. We call it "wicked apple" because of the story of Adam and Eve and the forbidden fruit which we had been taught is an apple. Somehow that "wicked" label just seemed to add to the delightful taste. Once Dusky and I ate a piece for breakfast before church…we could hardly contain our giggles throughout the sermon knowing we had eaten the wicked forbidden fruit. We were sure our Sunday school classmates smelled it on our breath and would at any moment take us for a good dunking in the baptismal tank.

Dusky looks me eye-to-eye knowing I like this game that ends right now: "Tom Fogel."

I've never told anyone else this, but while most affectionately call him TF, I secretly make TF stand for "Turd Fogel". The few times I've met him he just seems to crap on my parade. Now she expects for me to agree to visit TF. I sip my coffee thinking this over.

Dusky wasn't through and I had yet to respond verbally to her.

"You know," she says in her sing-song soft voice, "it's worth a shot, won't cost a penny, and what you tell Josh is up to you."

She gets up and starts pulling clothes out of my dresser drawers and now disappears into my closet. Emerging with jeans and my favorite Donna Karen blouse she says, "You're on your own picking your shoes. I got dizzy looking at the shoe shrine in your closet." This too is an old but true joke.

After laying the clothes beside me on the bed, she takes my coffee cup and then grabs my hands and pulling me to my feet. I follow her to the bathroom shower. It takes less effort to go along than to resist.

As I finish toweling off but before the hair dryer drowns her out, Dusky calls out, "Hurry, we don't want to be late."

"We, Tonto?" So there really isn't any need to speak to Dusky about this because she's already arranged it. We are going to visit TF. Half of "we" doesn't know for sure if she wants to do this. What I do know is that I don't want to stay lost in this depressing fog covering my life.

I drift back thinking of the first time I met TF. It was a potluck after church service. The man likes to talk and coincidently, people like to listen to him. It's discouraging how encouraged he is by other people listening. I regret to admit it but it's not just his voice, as sonorous as it is. TF really thinks through things and has a provocative way of engaging people. Simply put, he will not be ignored.

I'm just one of the many people whose toes TF stepped on. Some would say that metaphorically, but at that potluck he was so wound up when he was talking that he turned and literally stepped on my left big toe. And, he did it twice. I couldn't walk without pain for a week. Regardless, I am thankful for many of the things he's brought up. Even begrudging that he has something to say, his propensity to talk, talk, talk makes me want to scream, scream, scream.

Lost in my thoughts, I'm not sure how we transitioned to Dusky's car and are on the way.

Portland is one of Oregon's gems. I read that somewhere. But it seems true as we zip down Barbur Boulevard towards our church and TF's office. The Willamette River is quite broad on our left. In a few miles it joins the Columbia River. We have a boat and in years past, we would have been out on the river right now. That was before the cloud took control. I forget what all the cloud has taken away. The main loss is my memory.

Dusky and I have the kind of relationship where we don't have to talk when we're together. In fact, I still haven't said a word to her this morning. Not talking this long is a bit unusual. "She is good to me," I think as we park the car in the church parking lot. I'm sure she would enthusiastically agree.

Oregonians are used to rain and all types of clouds except the cloud I've been under. Today is filled with sunshine and my soul soars in the light…usually. Instead, I feel the cloud's weight on me and there is no soul-soaring. Not today. It's almost as if Dusky is leading me down a dark tunnel and if it weren't for her, I would not be able to find my way.

We walk down the stairs away from the main entrance and to the side offices for the pastoral staff. I didn't realize how many positions this church had until I saw the row of offices. I read as we walk by the doors and find that the titles designate increasing authority as we pass each door. "A mile south to the right must be God's office," I stifled the temptation to say out loud. "Now that's a place I would rather go," and my sigh is genuine.

I had never believed much in church authority. It could be that I came of age in the 70's and who from then does believe in authority? Or, and I hope this is the case, there's something more than church structure, church spirit, and church living. "How long had I thought that?" I ask myself.

Thankfully I didn't have time to start conversing with myself since here we are in TF's office.

Dusky leads the way into the office and shakes TF's hand in a nice way while rolling her eyes at me to make-nice as well. I do make nice but still feel somewhat reluctant to proceed. How do you start talking with a stranger about your home life when in fact, you feel a bit put off by the stranger's character? "At least I won't care what he thinks about it," but not sure if I were looking on the bright or dark side of it.

TF walks back behind his desk and while sitting waves at us to sit down. There were three chairs—a test I thought. Who's right-brain, who's left brain, who's the oldest child? "Who cares, I like the blue one," I think as I sit down with an empty chair between Dusky and I.

Taking a deep breath I get ready to launch into a mini-explanation, self analysis, and kum-ba-yah spiritual experience. Except good old TF has his right hand raised in a STOP position. Figures he would want to be the first to talk… or is he supposed to pray?

"I suppose you want to pray," I said breaking my long silence. I expect this would be the right thing to do and feel it would be hypocritical to be here in the associate pastor's office seeking insight and not pray about it. In fact, maybe I am sinning just for not praying first.

TF astounds me with his announcement.

"I'm not sure you want my opinion or my prayers. You see, today I, uh, resigned my position and by the end of the day, I'm out of here."

"Sure you 'uh' resigned," I nod silently in my best impression of caring and signaling for him to proceed.

"Just being seen here with me now may cause problems for you with the church hierarchy. If you want to remain members in good standing here, you should leave right now."

Dusky got up but instead I stay seated and stare at TF. This is better than anything on TV back home in the cloud. Instead of wondering to myself, I ask aloud, "Why are they so threatened?" Taking this as a cue, Dusky sits back down.

"Two months ago," TF begins, "I went on a 40 day fast. It wasn't easy but it wasn't as hard as you'd think. Partly because for me it wasn't about going without food."

I'm suckered completely into the story, "What was it about?"

TF picked up from his desk a well worn Bible and reads, "John 14:12 'I tell you the truth, anyone who has faith in me will do what I have been doing. He will do even greater things than these, because I am going to the Father.'"

"Five years ago," TF goes on, "I was trained to cast out demons." He sees the contortion in my facial response and adds, "I don't believe in Hollywood-style possession as in ownership of a person, but I do believe demons exert demands, limit control, harass, discourage and cause diseases and disorders. It's almost as if there were a dark shroud on people's lives or a shadow...maybe even from generations passed."

"That's what's happening in my life," I sputter out looking at Dusky more than TF. But it's TF who responds.

"Huh?" he stares at me. His eyes move back and forth as people do when they search their memory. "OK, we'll get back to you in a second-- IF you still want. Let me finish explaining where I'm coming from."

"I've seen successful events where demons leave and they always take with them some disease, discouragement or disorder so that the people going through this are healed. I checked this out in the Bible and here is what I found—"

He lays down the first Bible and picks up a second, "King James," he winks—must be a pastor-thing. "Mark 9:29, 'And he said unto them, This kind can come forth by nothing, but by prayer and fasting.'"

"So, what I saw is that Jesus expects us to do what He did, and, one of the ways to get that faith is through fasting. I don't know why. I'm just doing what He said to do and it works."

"What do you mean?" I ask. Dusky turns to me in surprise at how verbal I've gotten. She does her bobble-head shake like she does anytime I say something that surprises her.

"Remember Glenda the church organist who had to stop playing because of her arthritis?" asked TF.

That stirs up the mean Dawn in me. Not only do I remember her but I thanked God when she stopped playing. Every song had the same lingering sad notes manipulated from the pipes of the organ as if someone, probably Glenda herself after secretly getting liquored up on the sacrificial wine, were strangling the windpipe of a person. I bet Dusky one time that we could sing all three stanzas of the verses before Glenda played the first stanza through. And we indeed sang all three stanzas with time to spare. There must be a point beyond Glenda to this story so I just nod and let the story go on.

"Have you noticed that she's playing again?"

This time it is Dusky who responds and giggles. TF turns his attention to her appreciating what she's laughing about.

"OK, I didn't say she was a great organist, I just asked if you noticed that she's playing again. And, I see by the dread on your face that you've realized that." He laughs without giving away the mystery of how Glenda got to be the church organists.

"Well, you might not appreciate it in this instance, but after my fast I prayed over her and while holding her hands felt the arthritis leave. I truly believe power came about because of the fasting and praying just like Jesus said it would."

"Hmmm," I slowly ponder. "And because you proved that Jesus is right..?"

"No, that's not what got me fired. What got me fired, only I fired myself," he corrects, "is the first corollary principle I found in the Bible."

"Principle," I wonder, "when did this church start teaching principle?"

I thought back to a joke that Dusky's friend Sam told me. It's probably been passed around many denominations, but what I heard is, "One of two Evangeline (our church) business partners was over paid 100 dollars by a customer. He turned to the Bible to find a verse to say what he should do with it. When he couldn't find a Bible verse, he realized that he would have to try and make his own ethical decision. Should he or shouldn't he... share it with his partner?"

"That is our practical principles here," I think to myself.

Dusky tries to follow TF's conversation, "If that's the first principle, what's the second?"

"It has to do with spiritual authority," TF turns his head at the sound of a commotion outside coming towards the door. It seems like he is in a hurry now.

"Jesus said call no man "Father", "Teacher", "Reverend," or "Pastor"...He actually said "Shepherd" but you know "Pastor" and "Shepherd" is the same thing. Our only authority is to the Father and His spirit in us. Jesus restored the direct authority of God over us and we're not supposed to allow any person spiritual control in any way. When we do put a person in authority of us, we can only tap into that person's authority instead of the power God has given us through Jesus."

This is the kind of information that topples denominations... maybe even changes governments. I am startled and see rows of dominoes tipping over. I feel this more than see it. "Wow." What else could I say? I feel the dark cloud dissolving as one of the dominoes tipped over. Am I "wowing" to what TF said or to the dark power over me diminishing?

Although TF had already identified and reacted to it by hurrying through explanation number two, neither Dusky nor I are prepared or suspect what's happening.

Unannounced and without knocking, the office door violently flings open. If it were a Hollywood movie, there would be diabolical laughter and lightening behind him.

Instead of Lon Chaney it's Pastor Bill. Oops, he's wearing his priestly overcoat and with it demands we call him Reverend Senior Pastor William. His arm stretches out like Moses parting the sea, his finger points directly at TF, and in his most God-like authority says, "Tom Fogel, you are a corruption on God's church. You are not to talk to these women or any other members. I will defend God against you and will have you arrested if you are not gone within 20 minutes."

Reverend Senior Pastor William turns to us and points first to Dusky, then to me, and saying nothing but jabbing his thumb outward and we know he means to leave with him.

TF is in shock.

We're not sure what to do but years of church authority kicks in and we meekly follow the pastor outside.

Reverend Senior Pastor William, who also used to be our friend Bill but who now by godly authority verified by his formal overcoat transcended friendship put his finger in my face and said, "You are forbidden to talk to this man ever again." Crossing his finger over to Dusky he shakes it in her face to emphasize that she's included in this mandate.

We stumble to our car and Dusky drives home in silence. What could we say? What did it all mean? She looks to me as if I have the answer. She moves me by her awkward questions and somewhat motivates me to say something.

I open my mouth to say that something, still not sure what to say, but all that comes out is laughter. From teh-heh to belly shaking and it keeps building to an opera-like crescendo. I can't stop.

I wheeze for air. Head back laughing, head ducking down between my legs wheezing, head back laughing, I look like I escaped from a mental hospital.

Dusky looks shocked, "What are you laughing at?"

I can't stop. This is not hysterical. It's not even comedic…even though in a way, we just witnessed something mighty peculiar. No, this gut-wrenching-out-of-control dangerously close to pee-provoking laughter is sheer joy.

"Isn't life grand?" I say in my best Bette Davis voice between the diminished but continuing rolls of laughter.

Dusky goes from shock to scare. "Hey, you ok?"

Alright, I admit I don't do a great impression of Bette Davis but that's not what this is about.

How do I explain the different feelings all happening at once?

My mind attempts to define it: No dark cloud, no doomsday fear, no unidentifiable pain, I want to see my children; I want to make love to my husband—am I ok? The dark cloud control leaves and my life's urge return. Is it really that simple?

"Never better," is all I say but I really, really mean it.

2
FREEDOM

I DO WONDER WHAT JOSH WILL SAY ABOUT TF'S CONFRONTATION. That's the first time in over a year I wondered how Josh would feel about anything. He is an "elder" on the church Elder Board and by now he should have heard about TF and maybe even about Dusky and I being there.

Josh has his own construction company. He specializes in building senior housing from nursing homes to retirement apartments. He partners with a large management company and the agreement is we get a percentage of ownership as well as construction fees for each building. It requires long hours and lots of demands but Josh is good at what he does.

Like a lot of people who are good at what they do, when things started getting uncomfortable here at home, Josh focused on work. Here he is repugnant to me but at work he is the great Josh-Wonder Boy. He is as adored at work as if he were the champion high school quarterback. I often told Dusky that he didn't have time for another woman because he was so wrapped up in work. Work is his affair. Although for the last year I didn't care if he were with another woman or at work, as long as I didn't have to look at him.

Now I know it was not I but the cloud that hated him. When the cloud left, so did the hate.

A list of good things comes to mind. I hadn't been able to think of anything good about him for a long time. But, he is handsome, tall enough, a little plump but sweet, charming, patient. A great father. What in the hell have I been thinking? Where's the loathsome in any of this?

As I started dialing him at his office I question, "I haven't called him in over a year. I wonder what he'll even think about me calling?"

On the third ring a woman's voice answers. Is that his secretary? Confused I stammer, "This is Dawn. Have Josh call."

I'm surprised at how much I care and how much I hurt at the possibility that he may be with another woman. I have no reason to believe he is but who needs reason when you have overwhelming fear?

As I run back through my mind the secretary's "hello", I picture a bleach blonde, early thirties, huge boobs, undeniably a nymphomaniac who literally had him tied up where he couldn't even answer his own phone.

This jealousy is very contrary to my morning revulsion. Josh is officially no longer of P.I.A. status and I welcome that while worrying about our relationship for the first time in a long while.

The sounds of Josh parking in the driveway interrupt and put an end to such wasteful jealousy nonsense.

He approaches the house but stops to answer his cell phone. "I'm home now. Really, she called?"

Incredulously Josh looks over to the house as if were the Bates Hotel. Even from here I see the dread on his face. He asks again, "Dawn called *me*?" Why would he believe it?

He hangs up and stands there alone in the driveway staring first at his feet, then the house, he looks up at the bedroom window where he knows there's no welcome mat out for his feet...or any other part of his anatomy.

As I had wasted time imagining the nymphomaniac-vampire woman who answered the phone, now Josh stood in the driveway with his imaginations.

I guess, "He probably thinks I've got my bags packed, divorce filed, and ready to leave with the kids."

Oh, my God. I've been that horrible of a witch to live with for the last year. No wonder he's trembling.

I feel a shadow of the dark cloud at my feet. "He's not trembling; he's relieved that you'll be gone. He can do better without us." Us? "We can all do better without you," I verbally say, "dark cloud of control, I am under the authority of God alone and I command in that authority for you to leave me."

The cloud's shadow releases and I feel its control is broken forever.

My feet warm up and unfreeze from their place and I run outside to Josh. I clasp onto him but he isn't sure whether to duck or defend himself. After a brief hesitation he allows me to grab him. "Am I glad to see you." That's a statement, not a question. I am glad and he relaxes into me as he feels it.

As little as I talked this morning I now make up for.

I watch Josh's face as I tell him about the dark cloud, the year long fog, and of being under control. These were all things he knew but didn't know if I was aware. Does it make a difference or has it caused too much damage?

I search his face as I ask, "Did you call Dusky to come over this morning?" He starts to nod but withholds actual confession. Regardless, I disregard the unconfirmed silence and the pause gives me the starting point I need to talk again.

"She suckered me with the 'Dawn-dawn the little lost fawn' routine and much needed coffee," I start and don't end until TF's office and the cloud losing power over me during the conversation on authority. Now it was Josh's turn to talk even though I'm not sure I want to hear what he has to say.

"I didn't know you knew about the cloud," he says, "but I felt it several months ago.

Come to think of it, he was the first to call our situation confusing and described it back then as a dark cloud. Was that at Christmas? I just remember at the being mad at him calling it "our situation"—it was <u>my</u> situation and in my anger I wouldn't let go of it even to share.

Thankfully, I don't feel that way anymore.

"If you remember, I suggested counseling and even lined up a couple of meetings?"

This was a question and I do remember it now. We have good insurance and it was a reasonable thing to suggest. But at the time I didn't feel reasonable. What I remember feeling the day of the first appointment was "you better bolt now before you end up in the medical insurance databank permanently labeled a lunatic."

I've had friends cyber-branded in the national insurance database and wherever they move, their past files follow. So, I purposefully avoided that round up and held it against Josh. When I refused to go to the second appointment, he asked me to call the shrink and cancel it so we wouldn't be charged.

"Did you ever go there?" I ask Josh.

Nodding his head he tells me, "Yep. I went to the first appointment when you skipped out. It's that six story building across from Pioneer Park with the huge brass elevator. His office is on the fourth floor overlooking the park. You would have appreciated the décor in the reception area. I was told the doctor would be 'right on time'. I turned to grab a magazine before sitting wondering if 'right on time' meant three or five magazines? Remember how our family doctor is a three-magazine-on-time but the allergist I saw last year was a seven-magazine-on-time guy?"

We both knew there was no such thing as on-time time—the lost Einstein theory of magazine-time relativity in doctors' offices is a many years old inside joke between us. I love that I remember that. We secretly believe Einstein has lost theories that explain everything.

"Before I could sit down with my five magazines in hand, Ramona Johnson came out of the doc's office. You know how she likes to stand up front at church to read the announcements and ramrod every committee she can? This time she didn't want to be seen. She looked at me, I stared back, and we both were totally embarrassed. I remember how you called the process 'cyber branding' and wondered about her brand and if I were at risk from her seeing me.

She's always seemed threatening to me. I wondered if the doc had to call down to the doorman to give him a heads up and protect the public from her dominating attitude. Instead the doc called for me—can you believe a no-magazine wait?"

"He's not a bad guy but in the stage lights of the drama of life, he's the dim bulb. I'm not trying to be mean but he first started telling me what my problem is before asking me. He told me about certain age-related issues, how some people use affairs to make the transition, etc. So much for the psychic psychiatrist because he just didn't know what he was talking about. I told him so. Then I left and never returned."

"That's not to say I haven't tried other things," Josh continues. "The last month I've been meeting with Tom Fogel. You forget that you told me your version of TF and I knew you wouldn't have approved."

He's right, I wouldn't have approved only now I don't know what I really think of TF.

"Besides, it's not all about you. I've been under my own cloud."

I hadn't thought of that—Josh owned or was owned by his own cloud.

"Was I supposed to blame you, confront you, or do I attack my own issues first?" Josh continues obviously unsure of the answers, "So I contacted TF to discuss it with him."

"We had an Elder board meeting scheduled last Wednesday and TF said to save time afterward. You probably didn't even notice I stayed late with him."

"TF was the topic of the Elder board by his choice. He laid out for us the fantastic healings going on...do you know about Glenda?"

I nod instead of saying anything. We don't need to go there. Talent challenged church organists are beyond the scope of this discussion...maybe beyond any kind of polite discussion.

"No one could ignore the miraculous healing of Glenda. She was there and held her hands up for the board members to see. Bible-Bob Sully was there and he kept insisting that we get a full medical report. No one needed a medical report to see how her hands had changed. We'd all seen her hands gnarl up into the shape of an old dried apple. But now, she could flex all of her fingers, individually, and I almost expected her to flex her middle one to Bob Sully."

I laugh. Bible-Bob Sully got his nickname because he has a Bible quote for every situation. There is not a man who more desperately needs to be flipped off than Bible-Bob and the Elder board would have been the best place to do it. Bet he wouldn't have a Bible quote for that!

Josh's eyes dance in the light of my laughter. How many dark nights has he spent cut off and alone while I was lost in despair? I feel a lump forming in my throat as I think of the loneliness and grief he went through. Tears fill my eyes. I forgot how they can sting it's been so long since I've felt like this.

I start to tell him how I feel when we hear the front door open and know the kids are coming back down the hall to us in the kitchen. What teenager doesn't first come home to the kitchen?

Josh eyes connect with mine and I know he's happy to see to see me back, emotionally connected, and caring for him. He winks and says, "More to come later."

Ray and Jules stop in their tracks. "Uh, Mom?" Ray says. Looking to their Dad then back to me, finally Jules asks, "How are you feeling?" Obviously it had been a long time since they had seen me out of my bedroom, even longer since they had seen me in the kitchen.

"No gourmet meal," I answer the unspoken 'am I cooking' question. "But how about some macaroni and cheese?"

To my kids, this is a gourmet meal. I could tell by their face that they knew Mom was back. How long have they been suffering? It must have been for a long time judging by their response to macaroni and cheese. I'll have to add some sliced up Costco kosher dogs. For them, that's the only way to improve an otherwise perfect meal.

That lump is rising in my throat again after seeing how happy my children are for getting the slightest bit of nurturing. I try to swallow it down knowing the time for feeling sad is done. They've seen enough sadness. Now it's time for joy even if it's a simple meal at least it's together as a family.

Josh clears his throat in an attempt to get attention.

"There's a lot going on in the church right now. Tonight is Wednesday and the usual prayer meeting has been changed to a church membership emergency meeting. We all need to go. Actually, Pastor Bill called and said we have to be there in particular."

That's the first demand performance we've ever had. It doesn't sound good so everyone turns to look at me. "Sure," I nod. You couldn't keep me away I want to add but don't.

"Kids," I tell them, "you go get ready and I'll have dinner waiting as soon as you're done." I'm not sure what the grocery status is but wouldn't be surprised if Dusky had already taken care of things. I look through the refrigerator and cabinets as I talk. My assumptions are confirmed and I start grabbing food. "Everything is here. So hurry off."

The kids take off upstairs to get ready. Josh walks over and says, "I haven't had a chance to tell you how the Elder board exploded over the healing. Basically, TF said he heals by throwing out demons just like Jesus did."

"Yeah?" I offer thinking how cool it is. People are getting healed…wonder if there's hope for Glenda's talent as well? If so, how about Josh's singing…that healing would be a terrible test of God's ability. I smile not meaning to be sacrilegious. Instead of my recent disgust, I remember now how I love his inability to carry a tune.

"It took them until this afternoon to figure out what healing means. Dawn, the Evangeline Church has a doctrine that says once you're saved, demons can't possess you.

While TF argued about the word possession with Bill today..."

I interrupt Josh, "You mean Reverend Senior Pastor William?"

"Oh, no, he didn't pull that on you?" pleads Josh.

"In full vestal array," my eyes lock with Josh's.

I nod and he continues visibly upset about fully arrayed in pastoral vestal clothes Reverend Senior Pastor William.

"So, that's what's got everyone in an uproar. To heal like Jesus did means throwing out or cutting off a demon. Our church doesn't believe you can have a demon. Therefore TF came to the conclusion that the board was really saying there can be no healing at Evangeline without being in violation of church doctrine."

I mutter under my breath, "Like that movie Catch-22".

He picks up on my muttering, "Exactly. We have a church who says it lives according to the Bible yet we know half the Elder Board men are in constant lawsuits and the other half are going through divorces. I've been out many times with the other Elders pouring oil on people's foreheads praying for them to be healed, all done according to the directions in the book of James, and the first miraculous healing and they call it 'undoctrine.'"

"What's going to happen tonight?"

Josh looks at me and says, "All hell is going to break loose."

The cloud is gone but a wall of diversion goes up. We both think of ways to get out of this but can't. Josh was told we had to be there and as an Elder, he feels it necessary. After this afternoon, I know I better be there.

Hearing the kids finish up and start coming down the stairs I ask, "What is this going to do to them?"

As we sit around the dinner table enjoying the "gourmet" macaroni and cheese with kosher dog slices, it's Ray who brings it up.

"Dad," he turns to Josh. And as he gets serious and starts to ask his question, Jules reaches over quickly with her fork and starts stealing Ray's kosher dog slices all the while smiling at me. This was a move she perfected when she was nine. She's good at it and her brother has never caught her.

Without a clue about Jules, Ray finally finds the right words, "in our church youth group I told everybody what Glenda said about her hands. I thought it was something exciting. Instead, Miss Jackson told me to stop talking and said if we knew the real power behind this fake healing we'd be angry."

"You want me to tell you what's going on?" Josh thought about it a moment before saying, "I've talked a lot to TF— Pastor Fogel. I'll tell you more about it after our meeting tonight. All I can tell you right now is Pastor Bill is very upset and that's what tonight's agenda is all about."

Hmmm, Josh wants them to make up their own mind. That's pretty clever. I'm interested in their thinking as well. But is it fair to throw them into a hubbub without warning? Are they mature enough to handle the immaturity of church politics?

Both our kids have always been spiritual. Josh and I grew up in churches and according to church doctrine. Unfortunately for us it was different churches and different doctrines. Our compromise was to try and not teach our kids any doctrine and just stick to the Bible.

I used to accuse Josh of practicing his religion like he works—according to specifications, rules, guidelines and generally accepted practices. No heart, all rules. Truth is I do the same thing. To me, that's what church doctrine is—something that removes the heart of Christianity to conform all the brains and actions to some kind of uniformity.

When Josh became a church Elder, he stated clearly that while he believes in church unity, he could not accept any actions to enforce uniformity. I don't think anyone really understood what he was saying.

It's been surprising to both of us that our kids really have grown up without paying much attention to church doctrine. At least until tonight.

After tonight they may well understand what mis-thinking motivated the 4th Crusade into destroying a fellow Christian empire.

I smile as I comprehend that my memory is returning. My senior college paper was on the Byzantine Empire and I remember that ugly Christian versus Christian campaign that burned down half or more of ancient Constantinople. Doctrinal differences cause the worst wars. Every side claims God is for them which they use as an excuse to act most ungodly.

Done eating, it's now my turn to go get ready and change my clothes. I motion to Josh to take care of the dishes.

Just before leaving the kitchen I turn, "Would you please call Dusky and tell her your TF scheme worked and warn her about tonight?"

He hadn't yet confessed that he designed today's trip with Dusky but it is obvious now who the instigator was. And, he was right; Dusky was the only one who could have got me there.

Determined not to be the one who made everyone late, I jump every other stair step to go get ready. What is this energy that drives me? Freedom from my dark cloud?

3
SHADOW STRANGER

JOSH IGNORES THE SOUNDS OF THE KIDS COMING FROM THE KITCHEN. He is totally focused on something outside the house. I stop halfway down the stairs and observe him watching a shadow of a man close to the front of the house.

Josh sees me watching the shadow as well. Motioning me to stand back, Josh grabs the club he keeps in the front closet. We don't believe in having guns in the house but we do believe in discouraging anyone who would think of bringing harm to anyone of us. We decided long ago that a metal baseball bat would be proper discouragement. If called for, this would be the first time to use it.

I'm on edge as much as he is. I watch Josh silently count to three before opening the front door and running out after the shadow.

I run downstairs to the front door and follow.

No one is outside, not even a shadow.

Josh just stands there looking left and right up and down the empty sidewalks. The fact that the sidewalks are empty is unsettling of itself. We always have people out walking on our street.

Now what is Josh looking at?

There is a pole stuck in our planter. Not a big pole. It's almost as if someone cut off a rake handle and stuck it upright to the left side of the front door in the bamboo planter.

I'm closer to it than him but I'm not about to touch it and leave it for him.

Josh reaches for a scroll tied to the end of the pole by an old yellow lace ribbon.

This is weird. I search Josh's face for fear, relief, anything. All I see is confusion.

"Dawn," he reads from the scroll now, "This says:

`Fear Not'

Pausing, he waits for me to understand that the next sentence is a separate thought.

"Have The Faith Of God"

This time no pause.

"And All Things Are Possible."

I ask, "Do you think it's a warning about tonight?"

He nods, "But this doesn't seem like a threat. It's almost like a promise."

"I don't know, with all that's been going on today, this is no random coincidence."

Josh agrees but just shrugs "who knows?"

That is what I'd like to know, "Exactly who does know?"

Ray comes out the kitchen door and looks at us from the driveway, "What's up?" Josh holds out the scroll and he comes to take it.

"Ray," he looks at me, "where's your sister?"

"Bathroom," is the one word reply.

I go inside and leave Josh to tell Ray what's going on. Not that he can say much beyond handing him the scroll. Before I step inside I do think of one thing, "Ray, be sure to bring your multi-version Bible in the car. Maybe you can figure out what verses are being quoted in that thing."

Inside I turn and lock the front door. I hear Ray say, "Weird."

Back in the kitchen I grab my purse and set the alarm before joining Jules standing on the backdoor step. There are just too many things going on to not be suspicious. Although we probably haven't set the alarm for two years now and who knows if it really even works?

Just a few steps to the van but Jules already senses something and is eager to ask questions but doesn't want to interrupt.

Ray, who did not go back into the house to get his Bible is in the car booting up his laptop already. "I'm using QuickVerse," he explains to everyone.

"I'm searching the New International Version. Wow." That "Wow" sounds like a caricature of my voice but I let it pass. The kids do annoyingly good impressions of me. The van backs up and we're off to something different.

"There's only one place that the Bible says 'Fear Not'. It's partly through Isaiah 43:1 to partly through Isaiah 43:3.

'1 Fear not, for I have redeemed you; I have summoned you by name; you are mine.

2 When you pass through the waters, I will be with you; and when you pass through the rivers, they will not sweep over you. When you walk through the fire, you will not be burned; the flames will not set you ablaze.

3 For I am the LORD, your God, the Holy One of Israel, your Savior;'"

"Wow" this time it's my 'wow'. I thought the warning was about don't be afraid tonight. Really, I took it as you'll survive tonight. More like "by the skin of your teeth you'll survive a brutal beating," but I don't say that part out loud. Clearly, this 'Fear Not' verse is a promise beyond just tonight.

Jules asks, "Is this new to you, Mom?" She sees me nodding. "Dad?" She looks forward checking in with him and sees his nod.

She pauses getting her thoughts together.

Josh looks in his rearview mirror at her and I turn and stare.

"Ray and I have certain Bible verses we read every day as proclamations over our lives. We took a Bible study once that taught us to make proclamations from Bible promises... it's kind of similar to how Muslims proclaim four times a day that there is no god but Allah. We proclaim Jesus and His promises into our lives. This is one of our proclamations. We include you two when we proclaim this."

Josh turns to see the tears in my eyes and I see the tears in his eyes. How could these kids be so mature?

"What about the other two statements?" I turn to Ray.

"Have The Faith Of God," he says as he types in his search.

We wait. Josh drives in silence.

"Let me try another version," Ray offers shaking his head.

"How many versions do you have in that thing?" Josh tilts his head back and searches for Ray in his mirror.

"Four. Let's see, 'Have The Faith Of God.'" Again we wait.

"Another version." We wait. Josh drives. The sun has just set but twilight lasts long in the Oregon summer.

Josh just shakes his head as he opens up the last version.

"No luck. It sounds like a verse but I can't find it. Maybe I should ask Pastor Bill?" We're not sure if he's serious or joking but we hope he's joking. His smile now tells us that's the case.

We pull into the parking lot beside Dusky's car where she stands outside waiting for us.

"I'll have to get out my Bibles at home tomorrow," Ray promises.

4
SANCTITY

TOO MUCH HAD HAPPENED SINCE I LAST SAW DUSKY. I don't know where to begin nor do I want to concern her about our warning. Instead I decided to tell her everything later including about the note. Who knows what she's going to endure with us in the next hour?

"Did you get a command appearance invitation," Josh asks Dusky.

She nods but there are too many people coming up behind who can hear us as we walk towards the church. I suggest, "Let's talk about it later when we get more of the missing pieces of the puzzle."

Dusky was OK with that...she suspects that I am putting her off. She's my sister so it's her duty to be suspicious anyway. However, we have enough to worry about right now. I don't know yet if she knows all the TF business that Josh knows, but anyone can feel the tension in the air around us. Most of the people in the parking lot seem to be purposefully ignoring us.

Bible-Bob Sully is pointing at Dusky and me from beside his car. His wife follows his direction and stares. I step aside and turn lifting my finger and pointing at Dusky silently as if collaboration. Now I pretend to be part of the Bible-Bob triad conspiracy.

Dusky laughs, "No immunity for rescuing a dark cloud member today?" I slowly turn my head "no.".

We laugh and then turn and point at Bible-Bob Sully laughing and feeling as naughty as the day we ate "wicked apple" pie before church.

Ray and Jules are appalled. Josh shakes his head. We know this is no time to get comedic but it's like getting the giggles at a funeral. That literally happened to us at Uncle Virgil's funeral. The whole church condemned us then. Luckily it wasn't this church so we maybe we still have a chance tonight?

It was close to 9 PM but in Oregon, the summer twilight is still bright. The last glow of sunlight bounces off of the church spire. Proud and erect it stands but again my knowledge of history returns. While I'm sure for some people it's inspiring, all I could think about is "didn't the spire design come from the Egyptian obelisk?"

"I wonder if God looks down and sees these church spires as the severed penis of Osiris?" Geez, that comment could have come out of the black cloud but I wasn't in that cloud anymore. Yes, obelisks represent the severed penis of Osiris and I've always wondered why there's one in the middle of the Vatican. Maybe that's why they call it St. Peter's Square? I shake off the giddiness with Dusky and pull myself together before I start saying things like that out loud. Besides, church is no place to be thinking of severed penises.

Josh holds my hand as we cross through the golden colored massive doors propped open for us attendees. Yesterday I would have dreaded holding hands. Today my husband on one side and sister on the other and every dread is gone. Why isn't one of these church members praising God for that? Oh, yeah, I am one of those members. "Praise God," I say out loud. Both Josh and Dusky smile at me.

The kids disappear to their group and we walk into church.

Pastor Bill, excuse me, Reverend Senior Pastor William climbs the short stairs to the pulpit. Again today he is wearing the formal vestal robe usually reserved for Holy Days—wonder what's up with formality? The pulpit is raised ornately holding him several feet in the air so everyone can easily see him. We all talked about how well trained his voice is…he could recite a potato chip commercial in that voice and make it sound as if it were a holy pronouncement...probably even move most into giving an offering.

I wonder how my old black cloud had felt so comfortable sitting here on the same pew we always sat at. In fact, it felt more comfortable here than at home. Isn't that strange? And, while I'm not sure what Reverend Senior Pastor William had said for the last year, it was nothing that threatened my old dark cloud.

This morning I would have thrown up if Josh had grabbed my hand as he did now. Instead I find his touch reassuring for what I'm sure is not going to be a pleasant event. In fact I remember last Sunday when Josh took my hand—I shook my head and pretended that he was interrupting Pastor Bill. Piety is such a great way to not deal with someone. But I knew Pastor Bill would never stop whether I caused a raucous or not. Pastor Bill would never let anyone distract him from the Pastor Bill show.

I look around and wonder how many other black clouds sit comfortably in their pews? I look up in the dark recess of the vaulted beams above me—are those dark areas filled with clouds?

Without even thinking about it I whisper loud enough for Dusky and Josh to hear, "Lord, take away the dark clouds, bless us with understanding, and change our lives to really know you."

Dusky and Josh together said, "Amen."

Silently accusing someone, the right Reverend Senior Pastor William points past the rows to the entry door. We all watch his hand go up. We watch his arm stretch out. We watch the finger point, the finger that Dusky and I know well from earlier today. We follow the direction and there stands Ray and Jules delivered to the middle of the main doorway by Miss Jackson who now slinks away.

"First," he says in his most impressive pulpit voice, "I want you to know that as God's mouthpiece, I have to do the will of Him. And the first thing God told me to do was get rid of Tom Fogel."

He never drops his hand from pointing at Ray and Jules. I stand, turn and walk to them so quickly that Josh doesn't know what I'm doing. I see that Jules has tears in her eyes and Ray is angry. He's shaking, red, and ready to punch someone. "What the hell?" I say to no one but loud enough for the whole church to hear as they watch me go to my kids.

"Second, it was revealed to me that Josh and his family have been corrupted by Tom Fogel. Ray and Jules spread demonic lies in the youth group. Josh has had secret meetings with the heretic Fogel. And Dawn and Dusky were being trained in Fogel's dark arts this afternoon when I put an end to that." Smugness drips like acid from the tone of the not so good Reverend's voice.

From my half-turned head I see the finger pointing to Josh, then Dusky and it stays on my back as I race towards my kids. I feel it on me the whole way but don't bother to turn to see it.

"You have all been expelled in front of the church according to the Bible's admonishment to take someone before the entire church." Pastor Bill nods to Bible-Bob Sully for that little paraphrase that is not very complete but provides the sanctimonious crutch these pretenders need.

I'm more than halfway to my kids and that crazy Bible-Bob Sully is coming out into the aisle as if to provide Christian consolation. What mockery! I'm not the one who claims to be an Elder or any other church position. Fully convinced of my moral immunity I reach over and grab his poor secret of a toupee and fling it backwards towards the pulpit. If it were a poodle, it would look better and would have the decency to hide from the embarrassing display Bible-Bob bears now.

Jules's tears turned to laughter and Ray looks jealous. He so urgently wants to do something. Young men lack verbal skills and what I did expressed his anger better than anything he could say. "Careful, son," is all I muster.

With my arms around my kids I turn for Josh and Dusky who are there beside me now. Both of them laughing as well.

Now Josh turns into the smart ass, "Thanks for the soiree kids. It's been a blast. When hells fire is all over your ass, Bill, we'll be the ones laughing." He turns to Ray as if giving a cue.

Before I could say, "no", Ray takes the unintended cue and flips them all off. Hands straight up, bent at the elbow facing outward, middle fingers fully extended as if it were an honorable salute, Ray turns to face every corner. About a third of the church laughs—a third now all high on the list of heretical suspects. Some catcalls and a few whistles. No telling where this spiritual blood bath will lead.

Ray has never been one to seek public attention. It's going to his head. The third of the congregation laughing look to him for more. And, they're getting what they've provoked.

Jules, Dusky, Josh and I suck in our breaths in unbelief. Ray is standing on a pew mooning the church shouting as he slaps his bare rear end, "I've got your right-Reverend Senior Pastor William right here."

Now half the church is laughing. Not just a half-assed laugh but belly laughs. No one understands what Pastor Bill screams from the pulpit. Bible-Bob Sully is swearing on his hands and knees still trying to find the toupee that Josh kicked under the pews. Whatever else was on the agenda is surely cancelled.

Josh grabs Ray off the pew and literally carries him out. I watch as Ray reaches behind Josh and grabs one of the sacrificial wine bottles off the "Remembrance Table" beside the door. Josh lowers him off his shoulder now that we're outside.

We run to the parking lot.

The stars are coming out. A summer's wind blows cool air on us. We look at each other. Tears, laughter, and every other emotion drain us. With little energy we look at each other.

Jules breaks the momentary silence, "pizza." She nods her head in my face until I nod back. Then from me she goes to her aunt Dusky. The two of them are so alike. "Pizza." Dusky immediately nods back.

"Shotgun," Jules cries out running for Dusky's car.

The girls drive off as we still head towards our car. The commotion from inside the church heats up again. Josh can't help it, "Ray, better put that ass away."

Please, no more cues or encouragement—let the kids keep his pants up. But, no, that's not what happens. Ray jumps up on the car trunk and starts to moon again.

We can't even talk on the drive or one of us starts laughing.

At the pizza parlor we walk in to find Dusky and Jules talking with Isaac Hope. Isaac's wife ran off with another woman last year. Isaac was another of Evangeline's fine elders until about a month ago.

Josh nods to me, "Isaac was the first one who researched everything that TF said. Isaac even fasted with him the last two weeks."

There are no secrets now so I get to the point. "Isaac, we just got excommunicated."

Isaac laughed, "protestants don't excommunicate but I bet if feels that way. Has the church heard about it yet?"

"Heard about it?" I said while everyone else laughs. "We were the first thing on the church menu tonight—it was done in front of the whole church."

Isaac looks pained. "Are you OK? Can you deal with that? That's awful."

Josh offers, "We're OK. Except Ray made an ass of himself?"

"Not true," defends Ray while we all laugh. "Baring one's ass is not the same as being an ass."

"Profound," mocks Dusky.

I've never really liked Isaac before but tonight we all felt connected. Isaac obviously wants to hear the whole story and we tell him as we eat our pizza.

"What are you going to do now?"

Josh answers Isaac, "I don't know. Pray for us. Pray for my son's ass." He stops the foolishness for a second, "Do you have a suggestion?"

"Sure, come to my house Sunday. There are a few us that meet and really study the Bible. But, I warn you," Isaac gets our attention with that, "TF leads out the study time."

Isaac turns to me as he says that. I wonder if everyone knows what TF stands for to me?

I make the commitment on everyone's behalf. "Call and tell me the time and directions. We'll be there but ONLY if TF will be there."

Looking serious Isaac lowers his voice to Josh but I hear him say, "Pastor Bill is mean. Don't assume this is over."

The ride home is quiet and I appreciate it. I look out the right side of my window and see across the east side of Portland. It really is a beautiful city.

As we turn down our block we see police lights. The lights are coming from a cop car parked in front of the neighbors.

"Oh, oh. The second car is parked in our driveway," I announce.

Without a doubt this is a continuation from the church commotion.

Wade Freeman, a detective and someone we know fairly well is talking to the officers with the car lights going. "You're not needed. Turn the lights on and get back to work." Those guys don't look happy but do as they're told.

Wade waves as he walks over. "Busy night?" I swear he's smirking. He motions for the kids to follow us with little doubt meaning as to right now.

Josh takes them through the front door while I go through the kitchen door and release the alarm. Before meeting up with them in the living room I cry out, "Wade, want some coffee?"

"No, thanks. Do you have anything cold?"

"Beer or bottled water."

"Water".

Of course 'water', I was just kidding about the beer.

I come in, hand Wade a cold bottle of water and sit down beside Josh on the love seat. The kids are on the sofa. Wade is in the Lazy-Boy. Our eyes are on Wade.

"Sorry about the squad car and the light show for the neighbors," Wade sounds genuinely sorry. "The call came over the radio at first that there had been an assault at the church. Officers were nearby and responded but after interviewing conflicting testimonies decided that the wig incident was not an assault, that it must have been accidental?" He looks at me nodding his head and I follow the nod of his head.

"The squad car was dispatched here before the assault was discovered to be false. Good thing you weren't here five minutes earlier or you would have been cuffed and taken downtown for booking." We're not sure if he's talking to Ray, Josh or me.

I'm still nodding my head to his question about the wig being an accident. "Good, glad to have the accident confirmed." I guess that means I can stop nodding.

Now he turns to Ray. "Here's the mean accusation." He's reading from his notes now. "Reverend Senior Pastor William wants you charged with a sex crime for exposing yourself to the congregation."

We gasp.

"Conviction of such crime would be a minimum six months in jail and you would have to register as a sex offender the rest of your life."

We all talk at once but Wade just sits back staring at Ray.

"What's that bottle in your hand?" Wade asks.

Oh, my God. Ray's holding onto the sacrificial wine bottle he grabbed on the way out. On top of everything else, will he be charged as a minor in possession of alcohol?

"You can't blame him for that," Josh shouts. I know how he feels.

Not another crime...they're ruining Ray's life for not rolling over and letting them ruin his church life without resistance. What's wrong with these people? They're more demonic than demons or at least equal to them.

Wade reaches over and grabs the bottle, takes a tiny tasting sip and then says, "Sacrificial wine."

Unbelievably Wade winks at Josh then me.

"It's illegal to serve a minor alcohol. According to the report I write up, all blame for all actions belong to the church and their liquor handling license will be suspended. If they fight it, their liquor license bond will be recalled and the process will take up to a year. It would take me that long to interview every person in attendance tonight. Especially since this case is such a low priority. Meanwhile, I'm sure the threat of a lawsuit from you for allowing them to serve an under age drinker will discourage them even more."

"What?" We all say that together.

Wade just hands us a great counter offense strategy, one we would never imagine on our own. Since our minds don't work that way, it's literally a gift for our salvation against their evil intent.

"Your Reverend Senior Pastor William some years back seduced a talented young organist. She was my niece. The good reverend kept it secret from most everyone but his wife found out. The organist was expelled from the congregation after the good Reverend and Senior Elder Bible-Bob Sully agreed to pay her way through college to keep her quiet."

"That explains the current organist," I smile. No one would be tempted to seduce Glenda.

"Then last year one of the Sunday School teachers was caught molesting a non-member's child off the church grounds. I went and had a talk with the Reverend and he threatened my job and to sue if we made any links to the church. Do you remember who suddenly quit church last year and shortly thereafter got arrested?"

We do remember. The rumor was he was backsliding, quit church, and without the guidance of the good Reverend committed a horrible crime.

"Did anyone interview the church kids to make sure nothing happened to them?" I remember several parents in the past year having problems with their kids acting in strange ways. At the time we all thought drugs, but now?

Wade sighs, "No. We need the Reverend's support for that and he refused. Without definite leads, we can't just go randomly ask kids those kinds of questions."

"Wade," Josh asks, "where do you go to church?"

"They're all the same—a political-social club with reverend holier-than-thou screwing things up. I guess a more interesting question is where will you be going to church?"

I answer Wade, "This coming Sunday we're going to a study group at Tom Fogel's house. Know who he is?"

Wade responds, "The only pastor I ever respected. Do you want company?"

This is what most people would call a strange turn of events. Josh closes the door behind Wade and locks up for the night.

We all look at each other and watch as extreme exhaustion falls across our faces.

Josh steps up the first stair and holds his left hand backward to mine. I hold on and allow him to pull me up one step. Now I hold out a hand to Jules. Josh pulls us up another step. Jules holds out her hand to Ray. Josh pulls us all to the top of the stairs.

No TV, no dark cloud, just the irresistible exhaustion pulls me into an immediate sleep.

"Why a yellow lacey ribbon?" I whisper barely able to complete my sentence.

Is Josh answering me? Tell me in the morning.

5
CLOUD NINE

THURSDAY MORNING AND I FIND THE LIVING ROOM COVERED WITH BIBLES, ALL OPEN SITTING ON EVERY PIECE OF FURNITURE. I look at Ray going back and forth between them like a hen in the barnyard scratching for food. A good simile I decide because this boy has a hunger.

"I promised you I'd look up 'The Faith Of God,'" he says without even looking up. "One little preposition change and the meaning is lost." Now he's mumbling to himself.

I recall my grammar school teacher saying, "A preposition is what a plane does to a cloud—it goes through, under, over, out of, into..." Of course she was totally nuts in her real life but we kids loved her. So did her 20 cats.

Over the years when it comes to spiritual studies, I tend to mix up my prepositions. If you start using theological terms like "indwelling" and "outpouring" then I get confused quickly. Do I love Jesus or do I have the love of Jesus? Prepositions are what lead us to the medieval argument of how many angels can dance on the point of a needle. I find prepositions suspicious. In spiritual terms, I'm not sure prepositions even apply.

That is so profound it surprises me. I've got to remember to bring that up for discussion at TF's house: the evil of prepositions.

Josh comes out of the kitchen to greet me, "Hey, sleepy head. Would you like some eggs?"

"Eggs?" It's been a year since I last ate breakfast. "Sure—over hard." Runny eggs give me the creeps. It's like the embryo is still trying to get away.

Jules comes down the stairs with her cell phone to her ears. "That's not what happened!" Her eyes roll upward and back down locking on Ray. She rushes down the stairs to make sure we hear the conversation.

"No, he didn't strip and run around the pews." Close enough to hear, Ray laughs at that.

Jules catches my eye, "That wasn't Ray, it was my mother!"

"You brat!" I shout laughing somewhat nervous over who may be on the other end of that phone.

"Stephie says she believes you did," Jules passes on what her long-time friend giggles. Josh always calls Stephie his auxiliary daughter—if Jules cannot for any reason fulfill her regular duties, then Stephie takes over. While that may work for Miss America, so far, this hasn't worked with cleaning rooms, dishes or helping with the laundry. Evidently, auxiliary daughters do not take their duties very seriously.

Ray's cell phone rings. He always has his phone on him somewhere but never remembers which pocket. So, each time the phone rings he slaps all his pockets in search of it like some kind of folk dance. Without bragging, it's an easy bet that it's one of his many girl friends. Sometimes these calls are relentless. We've often begged him to turn his phone off in the evening so we can finish a TV show.

"Thanks," is all Ray says. Whether overly sincere or sarcastic, I can't tell but will ask him.

Then his phone rings again.

Now our phone is ringing. Josh picks it up in the kitchen. "That's hysterical," he chortles but it's Josh's laugh that's hysterical.

Jules's phone is ringing now. She's laughing.

What's going on?

Are all these calls about last night?

Of course they are. If it had happened to anyone else, I would have thought it all hilarious. Shoot, I do think it hilarious.

Now Ray and Jules hold their phones to their ears as they stare at me and the belly laughs from yesterday return. Unstoppable, I just give in and join them as we collapse on the floor rolling side to side.

Josh must have heard it too because he's now above me with laugh tears streaming from his eyes. He is trying to say something but all that comes out is a cartoon-like laugh--- "buwh-ha-ha-ha."

Ray goes into the fetal position laughing even harder now in reaction to his father's laugh.

Jules jumps part way up, runs bent over, laughing hard, on her way to the bathroom. We're all hoping she makes it.

The phones keep ringing and we all keep laughing.

Finally, I prop myself up crawl over and take Ray's phone turning it off. Laughing, I continue on my knees over to Jules' phone on the coffee table and turn it off.

Ray sees what I'm up to and he goes and unplugs the living room phone and is now heading back to do the same to the kitchen phone.

The phones are silenced but we're still not in control.

A pack of hyenas can not compete with our wild laughter. Yet, this is such a terrific feeling. It's sheer joy.

Instead of under a dark cloud, we're together on top of Cloud Nine.

6
THE SHADOW

SOMEONE IS ALWAYS WALKING ON MY SIDEWALK. Maybe it's the mature trees covering the sidewalks with their shade and noticeably cooler shadows. Or, maybe it's the neighbors with all the varied age groups: kids and their summer games, seniors doing their mid-morning strolls, deliveries mid-day, after work yard care, etc. There's almost always someone on the sidewalk in front of my house. And, that never bothered me until now. Today is creepy feeling even for a Friday.

On the way to get the mail I stop halfway between my door and the mailbox feeling mesmerized.

By the mailbox the long stretched black car, not from an American maker, almost hovers. The mirrored windows only reflect what can be seen outside. It just looks sneaky as if built to prey.

The engine lopes lazily which is only possible in a big engine capable of high speed.

And the man outside the car? How do you describe such a man? I can't because I've never seen anyone like him. Actually, I still haven't got a clear look at his face. High collar, big hat, all dressed in black. I'm guessing leather pants but can't tell for sure. The boots are either anachronistic or avant-garde. The whole effect comes across as if I were looking at a shadow.

"Who dresses like that on a sunny day?" My church training kicked in and I almost ask, "Is that you, Satan?"

Yet at the same time I feel very confused and can't tell if I am in the presence of evil or what? My increasingly reliable instinct kicks in, "You're in the presence of power. Not used to that, huh?"

This power isn't like Reverend Senior Pastor William's priestly vest and attitude. I feel real power coming this man. I just can't sense if it's good or evil power.

He looks at me with what seems to be incredible insight. Smiling, I wave back feeling half-assed. "Nice day," I offer to Satan or whoever this power-being is.

He says something, almost a whisper but it carries loud enough on the air. Was it Russian or Greek?

"Dunamis" is all I get clearly. I assume it must be his name. I try to say my name but he enters the now open backseat door. As quickly as light makes a shadow disappear, the car is gone.

I intend to finish my interrupted mail trip. Still wondering about the Shadow Man, I find an old lacey yellow ribbon on my mailbox. "OK, he's declared who he is." I feel relief about knowing who the Shadow is...maybe not exactly knowing but being able to identify him.

An electric bill is the only mail worth keeping. The rest are coupons for things I never buy. No more scrolls.

As I return to the house I look again at the old yellow ribbon. This is very old. In fact, I'd bet the ribbon itself was white before it turned this pale yellow.

The feel is not satin but it almost glistens like that. Maybe it's old silk? It's something very tightly hand woven, more like delicate cords or some very fine lace than a ribbon.

And, it's long. Maybe almost three feet? The previous ribbon is less than a foot. I wonder if the total length means anything?

This time I see the fine hand printed notation and read, "It's not in a version; it's in the translation. Search for the original Greek."

The phones have rung constantly for the last couple of days and I hear it ringing now as I walk through the front door.

The people calling are appalled at what they saw in church. Many don't want to go back. Others are afraid of being next on the hit list. I always tell those afraid to stay home—be a martyr for Jesus but not for that church.

I answer the phone and it's Isaac. "Sure, 2 PM tomorrow is fine, we'll be there. I'm not very good with directions so please give them to me slowly."

"Will TF have any answers tomorrow?" I wonder too softly to be heard.

Speaking up louder, "Isaac, we've had maybe a 100 phone calls and they all want out of that church. So far, I've only invited Wade."

He says to hold off inviting anyone else until we have our first meeting and get our feet under us.

"No problem. Is it just us or do you sense this is the beginning of something bigger?"

Isaac's answer is just laughter. Provoking laughter. The kind of laughter that turns back thunder clouds and chases off shadows.

Now I start laughing and hang up.

Jules hears me all the way upstairs and starts laughing.

Soon Ray is laughing.

"Not again," I say between laugh tears.

Josh drives up and I see him laughing.

It's just hilarious whatever "it" is.

Wait, I know what it is: "John 10:10 'The thief comes only to steal and kill and destroy; I have come that they may have life, and have it to the full.'" We're experiencing a more abundant, fuller life even in the middle of church persecution.

No more shadows and dark clouds with thieves, now we're in the light of abundance.

We get kicked out of church to have something spiritual that makes us joyous—that's not hysterical, that's hilarious.

PART II

THE GATHERING

7
SHARING

TF's SPRAWLING HOME IS ON THE HILL ABOVE THE PEARL DISTRICT FACING EAST TOWARDS THE WILLAMETTE RIVER. Other than watching out for the one way streets which seem to logically be going the wrong way, it wasn't too hard for us to find it. Josh seems surprised that I got the directions right as we pull into the driveway. Actually, I'm a little surprised myself. Tell me go north or go east and I won't go anywhere. I need to know what landmarks to use and if it's related to a restaurant or a special boutique, so much the better.

The circular drive allows for multiple cars with six already here. As Josh opens his door a hand reaches out from behind and grabs his elbow hard as a prank to startle him. "Hey, it's Josh and Dawn Brawler," the joke being funnier to Detective Wade than to us. I do wonder if we should just change our last name to "Brawler".

Dusky's car is coming up the drive. I see her husband, John is driving. We haven't seen John in a week since he had to fly to Germany for Hewlett Packard—or "HP" as he says it. John is an electronics engineer. I wonder what he thinks of all that has gone on in his absence? No time to find out now.

Wade and Josh motion for John to step over and shake his hand.

"You've missed a lot of fun," Josh dead pans.

"And I hope you've got a good alibi, mister," Wade adds. The problem is, John doesn't really know Wade and doesn't know if he should be afraid, forewarned, or if he should just laugh.

One of the many things I like about John is his willingness to let things play out. He is very mellow but he isn't anyone's push around either. When Dusky found out she couldn't have children, it was John who got her through it. All of my support sounded kind of hollow due to the fact that I have kids. Quoting Elkanah to Hannah before she finally gave birth to Samuel, John would ask Dusky, "Don't I mean more to you than ten sons?" And, in fact, he did.

Many of the HP engineers loved their trips to Palo Alto, California or to Germany. They loved getting away from the conflict in their home. They loved going places where people respectfully called them "Mister" and treated them special, something not found at home. John hates every minute away from Dusky.

John flies red-eye flights to get back sooner to Dusky. He will travel straight to and from but never stays to play golf the next day. He also never arrives a day early to go out drinking with the boys like so many of them do. John just didn't have much in common with the people he works with. In fact, he doesn't in any way want to be like them. He simply feels deprived every second away from Dusky and keeps that as his focus.

"He's a good man," I say to no one while watching him smile at Dusky.

I catch up with Dusky. "Who else is here?" she asks as if I knew.

Jules and Ray come up to us and ask, "Auntie, is it true that Pastor Bill is here?" Dusky doesn't see the laughter hiding in Ray's eyes.

Gasping she says to Jules, "Tell me he's joking."

Jules turns her head side to side as if saying "no" but at the same time says, "It's true... he is joking."

We never had a brother and Dusky will never get used to this relentless teasing. It's even worse when both kids team up on her. But, they love Dusky and never get mean about it. At least not as much as to make her suspect so.

TF is holding open the door and nods to me as we approach. Whatever differences we had in the past are long forgotten. He holds onto Ray's arm for just a second.

"My furniture isn't nearly as strong as the church pews, just in case you are moved to demonstrate your feelings." Of course Ray loves the attention. I need to remember to explain 'negative reinforcement' to TF.

I move over to allow Dusky in before me which makes me the last person. Except another car drives up and a gorgeous young lady, maybe 24, gets out hurriedly.

Since I don't know her, I leave TF to wait for her and go on into the house.

I follow everyone into the living room. Outside is a pool and beyond that the yard drops off to expose the city and river. It's just amazing and I wonder how TF could ever afford to buy such a place.

OK, I know Wade, of course. Then there's Isaac. It looks like Dusky, Jules, I, and whoever TF is bringing in right now are the only women here today.

"Excuse me," TF clears his throat. "This is Amanda, Wade's cousin."

Is this Amanda the church organist that had an affair with Pastor Bill? It can't be-- she's too young to have ever consented. I can't help but wonder what really happened to her with that pervert Senior Reverend Pastor William?

Actually, she seems awfully nice and I feel an immediate bonding most likely through suffering the same type of betrayal as the rest of us.

I catch Wade's eye and shoot my eyebrow up while nodding at Amanda, "Yes," he whispers. She catches me nodding and rather than get embarrassed, I just walk over and give her a hug. She doesn't seem that much older than my own kids.

"I'm Dawn. That's my sister Dusky with her husband, John. That's my husband, Josh. And these are my kids Jules and Ray—Jules's the one without a goatee." Ray really didn't have a goatee but he hadn't bothered to shave for a couple of days and there was something on his chin. Not manly whiskers but a dark area nonetheless.

Amanda is bouncing on her heels, flapping her hands in the air, "Oh-oh-oh, I know you." Now it's her turn to nod toward Wade. "This is Super-Streak Ray and the Brawler Family."

Ray has a nickname?

We look at Ray who is repeating, "I'm Super-Streak Ray. Move over Brawlers, I need room to remove my clothes."

I start to groan about the laughter hoping that it's not the hilarious attacks we've been getting. Thankfully, it's not.

TF takes over the introduction and quickly moves beyond Ray's clothing threats.

"Why don't we meet everyone else now? Let's see, Amanda is finishing up her Master's Degree this year at Portland State University."

"Wade is a Detective with the City."

"John is an electronics engineer for HP specializing in scientific equipment."

"Josh is a health care developer and general contractor. He's just finishing up a large project in West Linn."

"Jules is sophomore in high school. Ray is a senior."

"Isaac is a marketing consultant and is currently working on a marketing plan for a start up national chain of restaurants."

"I don't think the rest of you know Markos." TF points to a man in his mid 50s on his right. He looks almost familiar...it's as if I would know him if he were dressed differently or under other circumstances. He is wearing a dark green baseball cap with a very long bill that keeps his eyes in the shadows. It would be an understatement to say he is interesting. Even though he's sitting he looks like he's pacing...kind of like a caged tiger of unreleased energy. "Markos is a fairly well known author who goes by the pen name of Cornelius Brown—anyone heard of him?"

We all had heard of him. Cornelius Brown wrote amazing faith building books and Bible studies that are used in churches across the nation, maybe across the world. Why would he be here? We all sneak more looks at Markos.

"The last person invited today, and I want to say now that I did intend to invite you Wade, so it was good that Dawn beat me to it. Anyway, the last person," TF points to a man of indistinguishable age…he could be in his mid 70s to over 100 years old, who knows? "This is my old friend and former professor, Lee Heisler."

"You can call him 'prof,'" TF adds.

"No, you cannot," responds Lee. "Call me Lee."

Everyone paused for just a second. The reprimand was barely polite but not biting. This is something important.

TF explains, "I think everyone now has heard me talk about the principle of equality in the Bible?" Regardless of whether anyone wanted to respond, TF goes on, "Call no man father, shepherd or pastor, or teacher? Lee has dropped the title professor."

Lee takes over, "First, we're all sinners except by the grace of the blood of Christ. So, no one is greater than another."

"Second, it's the most humble who get to be close to Jesus. I'd rather be known for the kid in me because children get to be close to Jesus. To me, any title means a separation from Him. If you were building a brick wall to keep me from Jesus, I'd want to kick down every brick. When TF put a brick of a title between me and Jesus, I kicked it down."

We all knew now why he reacted so quickly.

"But," I hesitate to take on the limelight, "can we really be that egalitarian when in fact there are people who have degrees in theology and really know more than I do?"

"Lee introduced me to these concepts about six months ago. I now teach courses on it. However, we don't necessarily agree on every little detail and rely on the Holy Spirit in each other to lead us. That took a little bit of experience with each other, something the whole group here hasn't had yet, so we're going to approach this first through Lee's leading."

TF finishes and turns to Lee, "Let her rip."

Before Lee could take his cue, Markos interrupts, "I'd like to offer a prayer, first." Then without anyone's consent, "Father, we come before you as one body to seek your spirit just as Jesus had your spirit in His body. We commit ourselves to your Word, your 'logos', which is Jesus our Christ. Let every veil fall, let every doctrine be shut up, let only your word as you mean it be revealed in our hearts. Let the I AM spirit be in us now and ever more."

We're caught off guard at this prayer. Finally, Lee roars, "Amen."

We shout "Amen" in response.

I feel like we're starting to get comfortable with each other and there seems to be an intimacy here.

A cell phone rings the tune from Phantom of the Opera. It's Isaac's. "Really?" he says before he turns to us to explain. He tries to say more both on the phone and then as an explanation to us but he's so choked up he can't. We wait for him to get control and tell us what's going on.

"My ex-wife is in the hospital from a suicide attempt. She's asked me to come pray for her. It looks like I may not be a part of this group after all," he says sighing.

This seems to me like someone was just culled out. I don't know why and consider it in silence.

Isaac leaves and Lee pauses for some time then looks one-by-one each of us in the eyes until he reaches me. The quiet connection has us entranced. "I was seminary trained, I have a PhD in Divinity from a prestigious school," he's making this point to me, "yet all I'm about to tell you I never learned in college or church."

"But, before I start sharing, I need your help." John was gazing intently on Lee. This was the first time he had heard any of this and it seems to be making a big impression. Lee notices and turns to John, "tell me you're most disappointing treatment by a church you attend now or in the past."

The suddenness of the question caught John with his guard down. He didn't even pause.

"It was before I met Dusky. I lived in Salem for a couple of years while working for IBM. I attended a Baptist-style church, just a little church of 85 people.

"For several years they had a drive on to collect funds for expanding their church. After a year they asked me to join the Building Committee. I did, but wasn't that thrilled about it."

"For one thing, the Committee's goals were not very realistic. They wanted to build an addition for 250 people but they didn't have plans to add on any more classrooms. In fact, the church had never had more than 87 people ever even though capacity was 150.

"My first night there and the Committee came to order under the direction of Edward Mae and his wife Claire. These people were very dictatorial and I soon found out they were the original establishers of this church and ran it like it was their own. The Pastor told me, 'Lots of bodies lay strewn behind them in their conflicts over the years.'

"The first meeting started with Edward and Claire introducing me. They asked me if I had read the past minutes and if I had any questions? I said I had read the notes and I only had one question. I think having only one question they took as a compliment of how orderly they ran things.

"I asked them to describe for me the typical new member they see attending the new addition. When I looked over the board members, I was the only one besides the pastor who was under 75 years old.

"Edward at first seemed kindly entertained by the question but when he looked around the Committee and saw that no one had an answer, he got confused. Then he got irritated and gruffly asked me, 'What does that have to do with anything?'

"Well, if you're going to have a lot of young families come in it changes how we need to prepare support services and there may not be enough classrooms.

"I then asked if there were any marketing classes available for start up and growing churches so we can establish the answer to how and who to prepare for when we grow.

"Claire saw this as an opportunity to shut me up and told the Committee how the denomination had a marketing seminar coming up soon and why don't they send me?

"I did go and it was great. The seminar was led by a couple of pastors out of Portland who grew huge black community churches in just a very short time. To this day they're still successful churches.

"I came back from the seminar all charged up and started implementing outreach recruitment. From door hangers inviting the neighbors to postcards for the congregation to mail out, within six weeks we had 130 members. Everyone was shocked at how quickly we grew. They even had an emergency Building Committee meeting.

"I went into that meeting feeling pretty good about the successful recruitment. In fact, I had no clue about the toes I had stepped on.

"Edward called the meeting to order. Without any preliminaries he turned to me and said, 'Why are you ruining our church?' I was expecting a pat on the back, maybe even a thank you trophy of some kind. This I was not expecting.

"I still had more of a temper in those days and it came out as sarcasm. 'Eddie, you don't like the people the Lord has brought into His house?'

"'The Lord had nothing to do with bringing into this church crying kids, adults who challenge our authority, and new people playing music we don't approve of,' Edward corrected me. 'In fact, we don't want your presence in this church anymore.'

"I got up and walked out without saying a word. The pastor ran after me and caught up with me in the parking lot. 'I warned you about Edward and Claire,' he whispered.

"Yes, you did. The question is why are you still here knowing what they're like?

"'I get my PhD in three months. After that I'm out of here. Please don't hold it against me for failing to stand up for you. I would have been fired and I don't know if I would ever be able to finish up the doctorate in that case.'

"You know, if they'd been honest with me and answered me that first night by telling the truth—that they wanted people who are seniors like themselves, then all the recruiting could have been that way. Instead, they took building funds from people and made them believe that they wanted kids, youth, and younger adults. It's really fraudulent what they've done.

"Statistically, they'll all be dead within five years and this church will go on the way the Lord wants. All of their manipulation and control will only work for just a couple of more years.

"I heard from the pastor a year later. He was at a church in the Puget Sound area. He got his doctorate and then got out of Salem immediately. He told me before he left and without his knowledge, Edward and Claire had a church business meeting where they called his wife before them and told her how she didn't act like a proper pastor's wife. So, she quit going to church the last two months he was there.

"Edward died of a heart attack a year later. Without him, Claire had little authority at the church. Within five years, they built a new addition with lots of classrooms. Not one of those people in power currently has a position in the church.

"I moved on to other churches but never trusted the hierarchy again. In fact, I've turned down several church positions because I don't need the politics. In fact, I'm convinced the organizations are evil."

❖

I don't know if Dusky had ever heard this whole story before but I had not. No wonder John had always stayed out of church politics. We thought he was shy or just not comfortable taking on the responsibility but now we understand. John had already experienced his Reverend Senior Pastor years ago.

Lee is sitting forward in a kitchen chair looking down at his feet. Without looking up, "John, I'm truly sorry for you. To be condemned for doing what is right and being successful at the goals set for you had to be confusing at the very least.

"Since most of you have come out of one church and know each other's stories, I want to stick to asking people from other churches…so, Wade, what's your church experience?"

Again, the unmanipulated and personal interest so earnestly felt by all causes Wade to unfold without any defense or hesitation.

"I grew up in Laguna Beach, California. My next door neighbors were Greeks—the Koulakis family. Great people. Six boys, some around my age, and one gorgeous daughter who turned 12 the same year I did. I suspect now that had more to do with wanting to go to church with them than any spiritual direction inside me." He smiles with remembrance. From his face, we all see how beautiful the daughter must have been.

"I hadn't gone to church much; my parents didn't attend at all. But, when I did go, it was to the kind of Protestant services most of you know. However, the Koulakis family went to a Greek Orthodox Church. Do you know the term 'high church?'?" Wade is looking quickly around the room. John is shaking his head "no" so Wade explains.

"'High church' is the practice of liturgies and rituals that have been passed down for ages. Although the Catholic Church claims to be the original church, history pretty well proves that it was the Greek Orthodox Church that was established by the apostles in different places and ruled for generations by Archbishops."

"Wait," John interrupts. "I have read some history about this and they said there wasn't even a pope until the

600s AD. If so, how can the Catholic church claim to be the original church?"

Lee quickly interrupts, "These are matters of theology and history. It's the kind of issues that have turned Christian brothers against each other for centuries. They argue over whether the Holy Spirit was sent by Jesus or by the Father. What it eventually led to is that Christian brothers did not support a Christian empire and the Muslims conquered what is now called Istanbul. Muslims carried on warfare in Eastern Europe for centuries afterward. The warfare we've seen in our lifetime in these areas is a continuation of this sin done by Christian brothers to Christian brothers.

"As we progress, you'll see me focus away from theology and history. Our focus is on the Holy Spirit and it is a direct connection with God that we're going after. Now, I've lectured too much, please continue Wade."

Wade didn't continue but instead asks Lee, "Is that why you don't allow anyone to call you a Christian?"

I could tell by the faces of the others that I'm not the only one a bit shocked.

"Brother, I love you! Wahoo, you put it direct." Lee then answered, "Mostly, I don't make an issue out of the term Christian but I am conscious that people have used that name to do all kinds of horrific things to others. Just look at the things the Christian Catholic Irish and the Christian Protestant Irish have done to each other—how is Christ in any of that? The Apostles themselves only said they were followers of 'The Way.'"

"The Way," I mumbled not sure if I understand correctly.

"Yeah, 'The Way.'" Lee adds, "I always thought it funny in Acts when Paul is sent out to find the followers of 'The Way' to put both men and women in prison in Jerusalem, that he instead finds 'The Way' for himself."

"I do understand why you find the term "Christian" so prejudicial," Jules speaks up. And as if it were a signal to Wade, he picks up where he left off.

"Beyond the high church liturgy," Wade picks up where he left off, "the Greek Orthodox church has 2,000 years of mature thinking and reasoning. There's even an element of mysticism. For example, the icons seen in the churches represent a state of meditation. Even the most illiterate person of the centuries could focus on the meditative aspect to grow closer spiritually with Jesus."

"Icons or idols?" Ray asks.

"I don't claim to be an expert on this but it's my understanding that the church believes the images painted or sculptured are icons. Now some of these are saints which is a foreign concept to Protestants but the Orthodox priest explained it to me like this: If you knew of someone who successfully went through the same trials that you were going through, wouldn't you go to them and ask for prayer and support? To the church, whether that person is on earth or in heaven doesn't matter. When you ask for help, they stand with you before the throne of God. It's not their authority to resolve your problem, they just stand with you."

"That makes sense totally. I always misunderstood and thought people were praying to idols in a pagan way." Ray is obviously fascinated by the fact that a long time Protestant prejudice could be toppled so easily.

"The name of the Orthodox priest who taught me is Alexander—a brilliant man who is only about 15 years older than me. That was a lot of age difference when I started going to church there at 12 years old but not so much when I was in my early 20's."

"While I loved church, I loved the Koulakis daughter even more. Her name is Arête and I was told it means 'virtue' in Greek. I spent more time at the Koulakis family house and they saw how much we two were in love. It seemed like they were relieved when I got accepted for a Masters Degree in Oceanography at Oregon State University. They'd never heard of Corvallis, Oregon, but seemed happy I was going to be in another state.

"Arête and I were in love. Within a term, she too moved to Corvallis. Her parents would have been very upset that we moved in together, so we didn't tell them.

"I wanted us to get married but she said until I formally became a Greek Orthodox that she couldn't do that to her family. All those years of attending church and I never went through the training or baptism. So, I secretly started the process at the church in Eugene. I didn't want her to see me at the Corvallis church.

"I was down to one week of training left when she told me she was pregnant. We both wanted the child, we both wanted to get married. I decided that a week was not so much time to wait and still wanted to surprise her with my baptism.

"Arête had a lot of anxiety over the pregnancy, our relationship, and how we were living together without her parents knowing. She felt guilty every time her parents called, especially when they started asking questions like how far away I lived.

"It was the day before I finished up my training and was to be baptized. Alexander, the priest from California, and the oldest Koulakis brother, Gus, were knocking on our door. They're van was parked on the street and they must have driven all night to get here like this. We didn't have a clue who was knocking and threw the door open standing in our bathrobes."

"Arête started crying immediately. Gus started shouting and took a swing at me. Alexander quickly stepped in and pushed Gus away. Pandemonium is the word that comes to mind.

"Alexander seemed to be acting reasonably and took me aside while Gus was still shouting. He asked me if they could have a couple of hours in the house without me being there. That obviously, there is a family issue that needs to be settled.

"I turned to Arête and said, 'They want me out of here for a couple of hours. Do you want me to stay or go? She said, 'Go.'

"So, I went to my classes. I stayed away for three hours but made sure my beeper was on. At that time cell phones were too large to carry and too expensive for college kids. I didn't know if it were a good sign or bad that I hadn't heard from her. For the first time in my life, I felt fear as I drove into the driveway and the van was gone.

"I ran into our townhouse apartment, 'Arête, Arête', each time calling louder. But, no one was home. I don't even remember running up the stairs to our bedroom. I just stood there in amazement.

"The bedspread was gone. So were all of her clothes and everything of her's in the bathroom. They must have dumped it on the bedspread and hurried off with her. Would she do that to me?

"It was campus housing so I called Campus Security. Fortunately for students today, Campus Security is a lot different. Back then, it was made up of washed out or burnt out cops. They know how to fill out a report, but it was obvious they wouldn't do anything about it.

"A three hour start on me, I knew I could never catch up to them. So I decided to cut them off. I went to the airport in Eugene and got a flight to the John Wayne airport in Orange County. I thought I'd beat them by almost a day.

"I got to John Wayne, rented a car and then drove to Laguna Beach. My Granny still lived then on Catalina Street and I went to her house.

"I loved my Granny very much. We never had a secret between us and I quickly told her what had happened. I admit I was crying uncontrollably by the time I finished the story. I was just exhausted and she sent me upstairs to bed promising to wake me for dinner. She didn't. Maybe it was the ocean sounds from three blocks away or maybe it was the emotional exhaustion, but I was out like a like a light. I slept through to 4:30 AM the next day.

"I quickly showered but didn't shave and got dressed. I was out in the rental car within minutes of waking and headed up the hill to the Koulakis house.

"I kept playing over and over in my mind what I would say. I decided the best thing to do was have them talk to the priest in Eugene. Perhaps if we settled the church membership thing we could resolve this conflict quickly? After all, they had always treated me as if I were one of the family.

"I wound my way up the hill seeing places from my youth. The first familiar place was the bus stop where I had to walk from after school because none of the drivers wanted to go up that steep of a hill. The avocado orchard where my cousin and I would have avocado throwing fights in spite of the sign that said anyone picking them would be fined $5,000. There's only the cement left from the old Countrymen Estates sign. But none of these pleasant memories could overcome the dread I felt.

"I drove down the crowded little street to the Koulakis house. They used to have a great ocean view but people built across the street and blocked most of it. The streets were put in sometime in the late 1950s and were way too small now. Basically, with all the parked cars there was only one lane open. A half block up there was an open space to park.

"I pulled in and got out to check if the van had arrived yet. It was still dark enough no one could tell who I was and I felt safe walking down to their house.

"Their garage extended almost to the street. On top was a patio and the house entrance was reached by stairs. At the bottom of the stairs I paused at the gate. As kids Arête and I used to stand on this gate and swing back and forth.

"No van. I looked inside the garage door windows but it was like I always remember it being—full of everything except cars. The six brothers must have moved out by now but there were their six surfboards stacked in a row. The old fashion giant kind—too tall to stand upright in the garage, they lean out taking up a third of the garage."

"I went back to my rental car and leaned the seat back to relax but went to sleep. I hadn't eaten since the airplane and didn't really count that as a meal.

"I woke up stiff and sore. It was after noon but still no van. This worries me because they should have been here by now…unless they went to a brother's house instead. A Chevy Suburban pulled up and stops partly in the driveway. Tom, one of the brothers, honks his horn and leans out his window. Mother comes out on the deck and shouts down to him, 'have you heard from them yet?'

"'No,' he shouts back. 'They should have been here by now. Did they stop in Sacramento?'

"Mother shouts back, 'I don't know. They said they would call if they did and I haven't heard anything.'

"I wanted to thank them for the update but they were oblivious to me. It made it easier to just eaves drop for now. I waited for Tom to drive off before I got out of the car. I walked around the block in the opposite direction from the Koulakis home.

"On the other side of the block is where I grew up. Our backyards were just one house away. I remember when Pop Koulakis found a snake in his burn pile how he was about to pick it up and remove it before lighting things on fire. I stopped him and told him it was a young rattlesnake. He didn't believe me. I grabbed his shovel and shoved it in front of the snake's face and it coiled, shook its little tale, bared its fangs and tried to bite the shovel. I chopped its head off then its tail and showed Pop the rattle buds on the tale. He really owed me his life for that one. That's probably why he started asking me over to their house.

"It was a great place to grow up. The hills were mainly barren then with few houses. Other than scorpions and rattle snakes, it was a safe place. I looked over to the water tower where the Koulakis brothers and I would sneak in and swim.

"I was just getting too weak without food and decided to risk driving back to my Granny's. She'd made me a big breakfast thinking I was still upstairs asleep. Although it was cold, it was wonderful. I'll never forget her fresh squeezed orange juice. She got the fruit from the neighbor's tree.

"I told Granny what I had overheard. She didn't like the sound of it either. After talking it over with her, I decided to go back and confront Pop and Mother and just get to whatever point they had. That was a decision easier made than implemented but I finally got the nerve up and went to my car."

"This time there were no fond reminiscings. I just kept rehearsing in my mind how to tell them I was the father of their grandchild, how I was about to be a church member, and how we wanted a church wedding. That had to be a good thing, right?" Wade wasn't really asking for any of us to comment. He doesn't seem to be aware of our presence was he continues.

"This time I didn't even hesitate at the gate but walked right up the stairs and rang the door. Mother answered and shouted for Pop. Pop in turn shouted at me, 'What disgrace have you brought to my family?'

"Somehow I got out the story of taking classes and being ready for baptism. I told them of how we planned a church wedding but didn't want to tell them until I was officially a member. They asked me why Arête hadn't told them of this and I explained I was keeping my baptism a secret until today—that if I were in Oregon, I'd be baptized right now. They seemed skeptical.

"So, I called the priest in Eugene and put them on the phone with him. I think that was effective, at least they seemed to now be acting different.

"Pop said, 'We need to tell Gus. This makes a big difference.' He tried to call Gus's cell phone while at the same time explaining, 'We haven't been able to reach them for 24 hours now. It makes us nervous.'

"It made me hysterical but I didn't let on.

"Tom came back and when Pop and Mother explained things to him, he seemed nice to me. But, you could tell he was worried as well. Something is wrong for them to be gone so long.

"Finally the phone rings. Pop puts it on speaker phone. I got the feeling he used the speaker phone a lot to compensate for his hearing loss. It was Alexander's voice.

"'Where's Gus,' Pop asked.

"'Gus can't make this call,' answered Alexander. We all knew whatever followed was not going to be good.

"'Arête,' wailed Mother.

"Alexander went on. 'When we were packing Arete's stuff, Gus accidentally dropped it on the apartment stairs. Arête fell over it. She fell hard but didn't seem hurt. Well, she was already crying so much we didn't understand she was in physical pain as well. He just pushed her into the van and we took off.'

"'By the time we got to Sacramento, it was obvious to her that she was having a miscarriage. There was blood everywhere in the back seat.'

""Gus drove to the closest hospital. Arête was in a coma by the time we got there. We didn't call because the doctor was optimistic and we thought she'd be better by now.'

"My heart sank. I understood that instead of better there was something far worse going on. I shouted at Alexander, 'Is she alive or not?' Everyone gasped at me—they hadn't yet thought that traumatic of a jump.

"'She died just a few minutes ago.' And that was the end of my heart."

Wade stops for a second and repeats, "That was the end of my heart.

"My love and my child died because of their kidnapping rather than allowing someone who wasn't Orthodox to marry her. They didn't even know I was hours away from being Orthodox.

Wade sobs desperately after getting this story over. Our hearts ache for him. We finally understand why he never got married. We probably even understand a depth of his feelings over his niece being with Reverend Senior Pastor William. "No wonder he became a cop," I muse.

Lee is still looking at his toes. The emotion he feels comes through in his voice, "Let's pause for the communion. We've got a lot more to talk about."

TF brings in a bottle of wine and a baguette loaf. Instead of reciting the last supper, Markos in silence pours us each a glass of wine then passes around the bread taking off a piece first for himself. Markos did this with a quiet grace of someone who deeply believes and who has done this many, many times. Our silence has a deeper meaning than ritual and you can see it on each other's faces.

8
THE SHADOW RE-APPEARS

THE LONG SUMMER NIGHTS ALWAYS CONFUSES MY SENSE OF TIME BY LATE AFTERNOON. I see a clock on the living room mantle, it's not quite Five. From the flush count, I'm guessing we all were ready for a break but it hardly seems like any time has passed since we first started. I get up and walk outside by the pool. Ray is standing there and I see Wade come up behind him.

"No skinny dipping," Wade warns.

"Do you think my reputation will always be smeared over one little mooning?" Ray down plays his humor as if he's really troubled.

Amanda walks up behind Ray and says, "As long as you have your sister, your reputation is at risk."

Ray's a little embarrassed by her attention. I saw his face when Amanda came in and though she's too old for him, he is a male and he does like what he sees. Only at his age, it makes him tongue tied.

"Detective Wade," Ray's basking in Amanda's attention and milking it for all it's worth, "what's the criteria for justifiable homicide?"

Wade pauses as if he was going to answer but he's really waiting for Jules. She is sneaking up on the other side of Ray and lightly pushes him towards the pool. Caught off guard, he almost does fall in.

"Way to go, sister," Amanda winks at Jules.

"These two go at this kind of stuff night and day," I say to Amanda and Wade. "I've resolved myself to this since by experience I've learned if they're not doing it to each other..."

They look at each other and in unison say, "Then we're doing it to Mom."

"That's the plight of loved Moms everywhere," I proclaim. Dozens of times every day one of them jumps out of the storage closet, sneaks up behind me and taps me on the shoulder, presses the ring tone on the portable and hands it to me as if someone had called…the list goes on. Yet, they keep telling me how much they love me. Of course I tell them it's very twisted love but that's not how they choose to see it. In fact, Ray is always saying, "we can live with it Mom." The unspoken question is whether I can live with it?

Ray asks Amanda, "Would you like to hear the story about Mom's bladder?"

Before I could shout at him not to tell that one, Amanda answers loudly, "No bladder stories. No bowel stories. No fart jokes. And, you've got to promise to keep your pants on."

Jules laughs, "Don't know what else he'll have to say but it is better if he doesn't talk."

As the kids tease each other, John comes up to me and quietly leads me aside.

"How are you?" he asks.

"John, I've never been as well as I am now. I'll bet there's a big change in me since you saw me last?"

"Dawn, you haven't spoken to me for about a year now. At first I thought you were mad at me but then Dusky said it was some kind of depression. Every time she went over to your place, she came back depressed as well."

"Well, I'm fine now. Thanks for your patience. What do you think of all this?"

"I'm excited. I've got a Bible verse that came to mind and I'll share it when we all start again. I see Lee is coming for us now."

"Next time we wear swimsuits and do this in the water," Lee deadpans. I've never met anyone quite like him.

He's articulate, probably in his early 70s but still very youthful acting, and so intelligent without any pretension. "If we can tear Amanda away from Ray, let's get started again."

Truth is Amanda wasn't near Ray right now but Ray loved the jibe. I'm sure this is created some kind of kidding precedent.

As we start back into the house a set of bongo drums bang loudly from the backyard of the house below us. First, it is a single heavy beat like a heartbeat. Now another drum set joins in, and another, and another. A full drum circle beats from below growing like a brush fire and coming right at us.

We can't make out what is being chanted. It isn't in English. It almost sounds African. The chanting gets louder with the drum beats.

The beats not only get louder but speed up as well.

Everyone inside the house now joins us on the patio. We're all staring intently into the backyard below us. TF goes over to the far side of the pool and stands tippy-toe trying to look through the foliage into the backyard.

"Bruce... BRUCE," TF is shouting at his neighbor below. The drum beats and chanting just keep getting louder and faster.

Lee motions for TF to come over to the porch with the rest of us. He shouts, "Let's go inside and close the doors to talk."

TF rounds us up and closes the sliding glass door behind us.

None of us can ignore the drums and chants but we can at least hear each other now. Some sit down at the kitchen table and the rest of us gather around them.

Lee leans over the group, "I've heard these chants and beats before in Haiti. I want each of you to understand right now that we are under spiritual attack."

"TF," Lee looks to him, "Do you know your neighbor well enough to know if he's a Satanist or into voodoo?"

"We've spent a lot of time together," TF acknowledges. "We've fished together, we've exchanged dinner parties, and we've both done each other favors over the years. As far as I know, he's a good Episcopalian Christian."

The crescendo of drum beats dramatically ceases—is that a human scream or animal?

Josh is out the door and down the backyard hill in a heartbeat. Ray and John are not too far behind. TF catches on and starts after them pausing only to pickup his portable phone from the kitchen bar. Wade follows only so far choosing to stay close to the house with his gun drawn. Lee stays with us women and barks, "Pray."

That's what we do. We pray standing, we pray sitting, we pray kneeling, but indeed we pray.

A gun shot from below.

Another different sounding gun shot from towards the street.

Wade is on his cell phone calling for backup. He's not going to leave us if he thinks we're the ultimate target.

"Look at all the blood," screams Josh. I start to run out after them to make sure it's not Josh or Ray's blood but Lee puts his hand on my shoulder and shouts again, "Pray."

"It's a goat," Jules says. And then, as if we share one mind, Amanda and I see the mental image of a goat head severed and on a post in the backyard below. We share that image in our minds; our eyes have yet to see it.

Ray calls up to TF and Wade, "They sacrificed a goat. We saw a guy run away towards the street; he stopped and shot at someone out there. That person shot back and knocked the gun from his hand. Both of them are gone now."

TF was on the phone to the police from the minute he went out there. At the same time, the police were trying to tell him that Detective Wade had already arrived at the scene. "Of course he has, he's been here the whole time!"

Wade over hears his call and fills in his people what's going on. Meanwhile, we hear the police cars coming.

Josh, Ray and John walk up to TF and Wade while we're coming out of the kitchen towards them. Josh says, "We didn't jump the fence back there but it seems like there are symbols and voodoo curses written out all over that backyard."

TF just shakes his head, "That's just not right. That's not at all how Bruce is. Let me tell you, Bruce is..."

Wade interrupts, "Guys, the squad car is at the house below and wants us to come down now. Are you up to it?" They nod.

Turning to us, "Lee, please keep the ladies here and safe until we come back." I think he really means that we would be sick to see what all is in the backyard but we've already seen an image in our mind. However, none of us needed coercion to avoid the reality of it.

Wade, TF, Ray, Josh and John walk through the house to go out the driveway and down the street to the house below. The door closes behind them only for Ray to open it quickly and shout out, "When you get a chance, come look at our cars." Then he closes the door and we hear his running steps to catch up with the other guys.

Lee looks at us and says, "Well?"

We all get up at once and go out to the driveway. Six cars and each of them have an old yellow lacey cord hanging from the antennas. I immediately thought of our front door and then of our mailbox.

"What?" Lee says as he strokes the cord hanging from his Jeep.

"Who is what you mean," I say to Lee.

"OK, 'Who?'"

"I think his last name is 'Dunamis'. At least that sounds like what he said. I didn't get his first name."

"That's not a name," Lee replies.

"Wait a second, where's Markos...that Cornelius Brown guyed?" I ask.

Amanda answers, "I haven't seen him since we had Communion." She looks at Jules.

"I saw him go out front when everyone was going to the bathroom but assumed he was getting something out of his car."

"There were six cars when we came here and there are six cars now. Which one belongs to Markos?" I ask Lee.

He looks around and says, "Is that your car, Amanda?" She nods. "And, that's your car, Dusky?" She nods.

"That's our car," Jules points out.

"That's Uncle Wade's car," Amanda nods at ugly Ford that's obviously a Detective's vehicle.

"The Nissan pickup and Maxima belong to TF. That's six cars and everyone accounted for except Markos." Lee pauses for a while thinking back about when Markos arrived. "I don't remember him driving a car."

Dusky speaks for everyone when she says, "Who is this guy?"

"Do you think TF has any Cornelius Brown books inside the house?" now Jules is the detective.

"Let's go take a look," Lee leads us back inside the house.

TF's library originally was designed as a bedroom. It would have been a large bedroom. My guess is its 15 feet by 12 feet. What had been a clothes closet is now a desk alcove. Every wall and above the door has shelves. Each shelf is filled with books, some shelves over run with books. It's an amazing library. Some of the books appear very old if not ancient.

Lee directs, "All those in that corner are too old to touch. Those may be ancient scrolls, so don't touch them. We're looking for books on this wall, "he points directly in front of him, "somewhere in this area."

The area he's pointing to covers a couple of shelves. The colors are much brighter-- these books are obviously newer.

Dusky drops to her knees and says, "I'm taking the bottom shelf."

Jules drops beside her, I'm taking the second to the bottom shelf."

Amanda says, "Third shelf."

"I'll take the fourth," I say to Lee.

He responds, "I'm going to go check out the shelves in the living room."

"Come get us as soon as the guys come back," I ask him as he leaves the room.

It seems like I've barely started when Dusky stands up with one book in her hand. She points at it, "Got one. I'll do the fifth shelf."

Jules is going slower but she's got two books in her hand.

Amanda stands and says, "Nothing. I'll check the top shelf."

I find two books. Dusky finds another. Amanda finds one. Jules only found two books total.

I hand mine to Jules, "That's all I found." Jules collects Dusky's books as well. She stands there with her arms bent straight down and her hands in a 'U' shape. Amanda adds her books to the stack. Jules is now holding seven books.

Jules heads off to the living room and we follow.

Lee is going through several shelves of books on the mantle wall of the living room. There's something very homey about a living room wall with a fireplace in the middle and shelves of books on either side.

"We found seven total," Jules calls out to Lee.

"I've found that many out here, Lee points to the couch where he's obviously just thrown the books he's found.

"Don't mistreat the merchandise," Amanda points at the books. Lee is slightly embarrassed by this...he wasn't really thinking about what he was doing.

"You're right," he says and comes over to where Jules is dropping her stack on the couch beside the other books.

"What are we looking for?" Lee turns to us.

"Let's start with the copyright dates and we'll organize the books in a row on the couch by those dates." Amanda offers.

We really don't know what we're looking for but a little order couldn't hurt. Jules opens the first book, "August, 1958."

We put that book on the left assuming that would be the first book in the chronological order we were after.

Lee holds up one of his books, "October, 1968." He hands the book to Amanda who puts it on the right of the first book.

Dusky is shaking her head holding her book open to the copyright notice page, pointing at it for Jules to read, "1924".

We all look at Jules. 1924 cannot be right. Lee grabs the book for himself and repeats what Jules said, "1924."

"How would that be..." I start to ask.

Dusky finishes for me, "...that's impossible."

We are totally confused. We don't know what to do.

Lee hands us each another book and nods at me, "What year?"

"1893," I respond in disbelief.

"I don't find a copyright for this book," Jules holds her book up.

"1805," Dusky offers.

"1791—that would be one year after the first major copyright laws were passed. Although the US Constitution mentions such rights in Clause 8."

"How do you now this?" I ask Amanda.

"I work part-time at Grinnel's Bookstore. We're required to know about the history of book publishing as part of our training."

"So," Lee asks Amanda, "we won't find any copyrights older than 1790?"

She shakes her head as she puts the 1791 book to the far left.

I pass Lee and walk over beside Amanda in front of the couch. Of the 14 books, 10 have wrap around covers. I quickly take those 10 and turn them over to see the back.

Of those 10 books, eight had the picture of the author. As I take those eight and lay them side by side, Amanda goes through the back inside pages of the other books. She opens to the back page from the 1893 book; this includes an author's picture as well.

There is no doubt: All the author images regardless of the year depict Markos but named Cornelius Brown. In each picture he looks the same age—somewhere in his 50s but youthful, vital, energetic.

"It's the same person and I know where I met him. He is The Shadow." The words coming out sound strange even to me. Before I can read the response on their faces, the front door comes open and the guys spill into the room.

TF looks to the books on the couch, "Guess you want to know about Markos?" The guys don't have a clue and ignore him instead telling of their story.

John, as usual, walks straight up to be by Dawn. "Honey, we got down there and it was the same squad car that responded to Josh's house the other night. The cops groaned when they saw him and said, 'not you'. Only they shut up when they saw Wade with us."

TF takes over, "They asked me to go to the front door with them. I did. We rang but no one answered. While we were talking on the front door step, Bruce pulls up in his car. Only he can't get into his garage around the cop car so he gets out and comes over and asks what's up."

"The cops are taking notes when I tell Bruce how the drumming started, how they're had to be ten or more drums and people chanting. The cops interrupted and asked him if he has a musical group that meets at his house. Bruce laughed at that."

"As I'm still telling the story, Bruce waives us around and we follow him into the backyard. There was blood everywhere. A goat had been quartered and the pieces arranged to the four directions of the compass at the bottom of his tiki pole light. The head was hung from the pole only upside down."

"There were parchment scrolls everywhere, stretched out to read but the writing looked like some kind of scribbling. I saw it is used in Haiti for voodoo curses."

"Blood was sprinkled on dolls with pins sticking out of them…there was a doll for each of us. Our names in English were pinned on a doll representing us. "

"Bruce about fainted. Even the cops could see it was nothing of his doing."

"I told them about the two shots," Ray adds. "Whoever it was did not shoot at me, they were shooting at someone on the street. I looked in that direction and I did see a black figure, almost like a shadow. He fired back and hit one of the drummers. The last thing I saw of that was a dark limo coming down the hill, slamming on its breaks and skidding to a stop to pick up The Shadow. The drummers roared off in a van and The Shadow seemed to be pursuing them."

"The officers turned to me and laughed as if this were some kind of joke. If I had not been here, they would have refused to take the report. As it is, I walked them out to the street. There were fresh skid marks by a very long vehicle—longer than a SUV. The oak tree across the street had a huge splinter were I bet one of the shots landed. I ordered the guys to get the bullet out of the tree for ballistics tests." It was easy to see that Wade is upset with these two officers.

"We heard a shot returned and could see a trail of blood where one of our drummers got hit. Before we came back here, one of the officers found a neighbor who saw a group of guys get into a light green van and leave. There was blood to the curbside and it appears the bleeder got into the back of this van from where the trail stopped."

"The neighbor described the group as 'dressed for Halloween'. His idea of Halloween dress is that these guys were dressed as 'African witchdoctors'. The guys are still trying to get out of him what that means."

"No one heard the drums. No one heard the shots. No one heard a big car skid to a halt. But, the same neighbor who saw them get into the van says he saw a long black car in the road behind them. When the car halted briefly the back door opened as if it were a shield. A man stood behind on the street behind the door wearing a dark colored baseball cap as if he were taking charge. This man was holding a gun. He couldn't tell if he was forcing them into their van or providing protection for them." Wade stops the police reporting-style and takes a breath.

"Markos, the description kind of sounds like you," Wade says out loud thinking Markos is still present with us.

I look to Lee who jerks his head towards Wade as if to tell me to explain about Markos.

I look to the guys and then specifically to Wade who is waiting for Markos to reply. "Markos left us sometime after Communion but before the drama from below." I didn't purposefully make my words dramatic but I'm sure from now on, we'll call this 'drama from below.'

Ray turns to TF, "Who is that guy really and how did you get to know him?"

TF is puzzled. "I've never met him before today. He walked up and said he was here for the meeting. As an introduction he handed me a book with his picture on the back. I've got some of his books and recognized the picture."

Dusky interrupts, "We pulled out all your books we could find by Cornelius Brown and laid them out on the couch. Would you like to come see?"

Dusky waives John over with the crook of her finger and they lead the way inside the house.

Amanda moves in front of the couch like a tour guide and takes over.

"We first organized the Cornelius Brown books according to the copyright notice date." She looks to TF to make sure he's not upset about going through his books and taking over his couch this way. He's not.

"Then we selected out those with either an authors depiction in the book itself or on the book wrap." Amanda holds up the 1924 book and points to the last page. "This picture of Markos looks like it was taken this morning."

She hands the book to Wade. He looks to the front section and finds the copyright date. "But, this copyright says 1924. Is this a reprint with an updated book wrap?" Wade looks to TF since it's his book.

"Look at the inside front page," TF directs Wade. "See the inscription?"

Wade reads what he finds, "To J.W. Farmer, thank you for the kind words. Truly yours, Markos. December 24th, 1924."

Amanda takes over, "We missed the inscription. But do look at the copyright again; you'll see that there is only one print date. I don't believe there was an updated date or that the wrap with his picture comes from a later time."

"But, that's impossible. Isn't it?" Ray asks out loud.

"Is this the oldest with a picture of Markos?" Wade inquires of Amanda.

"No. The oldest picture is inside the book pages themselves on this book." She hands him another book. Wade is intently examining the picture. It's not as clear as the others but there is no mistaking Markos. He looks up to Amanda.

"1893," is all she says.

Josh looks at me with the most astonished look I've ever seen on him. I just nod.

"I'm pooped," TF announces. "How about a barbecue here tomorrow night, 7 PM? I've got hamburger enough for all. You bring drinks and other stuff."

Everyone nods in agreement. We've got a lot to discuss and no energy left.

We start filing towards the front door and Ray jambs up the line by stopping and shouting back to TF, "Hey, what book did he give you tonight?"

TF hurries to the front of the line and there by the door in the side window sill is a small book. "Here," TF hands it to Ray, you read it and tell us about it tomorrow night."

Ray takes the book and resumes walking out the door with all of us behind him.

We quickly say our goodbyes and get into our car.

The ride home is silent but inside our heads we're all busy. Just too much to process.

Inside our house Ray goes to the kitchen to enter the alarm code. Jules goes upstairs; I turn out lights and lock the front door.

Josh meets me at the bottom of the stairs and we look up to see Ray lingering at the top step.

"The title of the book," Ray tells us without turning around, "is **THE FAITH OF GOD**."

9
LESSONS BEGIN

A HECTIC DAY AND WE'VE ALL BEEN SO RUSHED THAT WE HAVE HARDLY TALKED TO EACH OTHER. Now we're back in the car and headed towards TF's house for dinner.

Jules breaks the silence, "He did say hamburger and not goat meat?"

Everyone groans at that. Sadly, she takes this as encouragement. "Has everyone been practicing their conga dance routines?"

This time our groans turn to laughter.

Except for Ray who sits glued to his portable computer screen.

Josh looks in his rearview mirror and sees Ray.

"What's up, Einstein?" We call each other than whenever someone is lost in the computer space-time continuum. We know with our family, anyone who says they'll be five minutes more at the computer means anywhere from 25 to 55 minutes. If Einstein were alive today, he would have to create a whole new subcategory of Cyber-Time Relativity.

Ray grunts back.

We all wait for him to start speaking but he doesn't.

"Ray," I turn to him, "what are you so lost in?"

"I'm reading that book, **THE FAITH OF GOD**, and I'm cross referencing the Bible verses to Strong's and seeing if the meanings are really there."

"And?"

"On one hand some of the stuff in the book seems so simple that I don't know why it's here. On the other hand..." Ray drifts off while staring at his screen.

"He's lost," I wave my hands above my head to emphasize he's in space.

Ray ignores me and writes sticky notes putting them on the back of his computer. High tech meets low but even a techie like Ray admits there are no sticky note replacements.

The driveway doesn't look any different than yesterday except John and Dusky are already here.

Dusky comes out of the house to greet us. I look down at my watch, no, we're not late. Everyone else was just early.

"We were so tired but couldn't sleep a wink last night, what about you?" Dusky asks me.

"I slept pretty well. In fact, I was the last one up this morning," I recall for Dusky.

Adorable Amanda is once again in front of the couch. She's going back through the stack of books. I look over her shoulder and see she's writing the names of the publishers and printers. I look down the list and see that while the printers have changed, the same publishing company has always produced the Cornelius Brown books.

"Very good, Amanda," I say pointing to the publisher's column.

Josh joins TF, John, Ray, Lee and Wade. "Sweetie," he calls to me, "do you mind if I tell the guys your story about the black limo and meeting The Shadow at the mailbox?" I wave for him to go ahead.

"What story," Amanda asks and I realize I haven't told her the story either.

Before the voodoo drums, goat sacrifice and gun shots, my story seemed kind of spooky. Now as I hear myself re-tell it to Amanda, it just doesn't seem to hold comparison to last night.

"Do you think it was him?" Amanda wants to know. I do think it was him, that is Markos or Cornelius Brown, but I can't say that from recalling his face.

I explain, "Did you notice yesterday that you couldn't really see his face?"

"I saw him," Jules offers.

"OK, describe his eyes."

She looks at me for a while and says, "I see what you mean. I have no idea—they burned brightly, his eyes made him seem very smart, I think I saw caring in his eyes, but I can't tell you for sure the color." She thinks more about it and adds, "I don't know, were they close together or far apart? I don't remember glasses but do remember they seemed sunk back farther than normal. Weird?"

"Even on these pictures," I point to the book wraps each showing a black and white photo of Markos, "see, the sockets are created by blackness, there is no real detail of the eye." Indeed, from the 1893 picture to the 1968 picture, not one showed any real definition of the man's eyes.

Ray walks over and picks up one of the books. "Do you have a scanner?"

TF nods yes and motions for Ray to follow him to a back room where he leaves him.

TF starts talking to me even before we see him, "Dawn, what was on your ribbon left the first night you saw 'The Shadow'?"

"Fear Not," I hold up my hand with the first finger extended. "Faith of God," I now hold up two fingers. "And All Things Are Possible," I hold up my third finger showing that all three things have been said.

"**FEAR NOT** is one of the books I read this morning. It's only a couple of hundred pages," TF shares.

Josh explains, "**FAITH OF GOD** is the book you gave Ray last night. I think he's read it all. I know he's been researching on it."

Amanda and Jules are talking and seem to be carried away with their new find.

"What's up?" Dawn asks them.

"OK," Amanda nods, "we've got something good here. Regardless of the year, the publishing company is the same name."

Lee can't believe she stops at that—"and what is that name?"

Amanda was enjoying this too much and makes Lee wait a few seconds before saying, "Anastasis Dunamis Limited. They even have the same New York City address throughout the years."

I gasp.

"The Shadow told me on the sidewalk that his name was something Dunamis. I didn't get the first word then but believe it was 'Anastasis.'"

Lee clears his throat, "Do you know what 'Anastasis Dunamis' means?"

I shake my head.

"It's ancient Greek. 'Dunamis' is power. The same root word we get 'dynamite' from. So, it's explosive, unstoppable, blow the way open kind of power."

"Anastasis?" Jules wants to know as badly as the rest of us.

"'Anastasis' means 'Resurrection'. Actually, that doesn't do it very much justice; it's often used for a specific act. We've lost this meaning in our Protestant backgrounds but I bet Wade's Orthodox training can help us." Lee is really asking Wade who can't help nodding through this explanation.

"Can we use the dining table to sit down and talk about all this," Dusky asks TF.

"Actually, the dining table is filled with our dinner. Let's go eat and then we'll discuss." TF leads the way.

TF defers to Lee and sits him at the head of the table. The rest of us just sit where we want. John sits on the left next to Lee. Beside John sits Dusky. I sit beside Dusky with Josh beside me. Wade sits at the other end of the table between Josh and Ray. Jules, Amanda, and TF sit to the right of Lee.

The hamburgers are great. Ray eats two before thinking of asking if he took too many. "I anticipated your appetite," TF assures him.

The potato salad is store bought but it is fresh and tastes great. Probably better than what I would have made.

I've always thought potato salad is too much work compared to what you can buy it for in the store.

Amanda and Jules are laughing at Ray's face. He's got mustard on his chin and has no clue. He looks at me as if to ask why he's getting picked on. Dusky tells him, "Ray, you either have the ugliest makeup or mustard on your face."

Ray has been taught well. At our house, whoever cooks is exempt from clean up. He takes his plate, silverware and milk glass to the sink, rinses them, and then loads them into the dishwasher. Then he goes to the bathroom to remove his organic makeup.

Amanda is impressed watching Ray clean up. "I have a room mate that he needs to train." No one likes picking up after others and that's clearly to seen on Amanda's face.

We each follow Ray's lead and one-by-one the kitchen table is clean and we assume some kind of order as Lee, the last of us, returns from the bathroom.

"TF," he asks, "do you have the Communion?"

TF has on a large platter the wine glasses and a baguette loaf waiting in the kitchen. He quickly gets it and brings it back.

Lee says, "Most of the time I like to have Communion before our meal but Ray looked weak tonight."

It's always smart to feed a teenage boy before you start anything.

"Does anyone feel led to pray over this or say anything before we start passing this around?" TF is a good host and turns his head to each one of us.

John speaks up, "If our experience so far was based on what we prayed for, none of us got what we prayed for. I feel like we're being led, if not herded, into something beyond our understanding. So, my prayer is this: 'Lord, teach us what we don't know so that we will know you.'"

"Amen." We all say that in unison and we mean it.

Ray has been so wrapped up in studying all this that I'm surprised that he has left his computer in the living room. When he starts speaking now, I expect for him to talk about FAITH IN GOD. Instead, he says, "The Shadow seems to have directed our first study to 'Anastasis Dunamis'. Let's focus there to start—ok?"

"Yes, let's get to the 'Anastasis,'" agrees Wade. This seems very important to him.

Lee asks, "Are you ready to lead us on this?"

"I'll start us, but I think the Holy Spirit will lead us all into providing understanding about it. Kind of exciting that this is the first time we really get to start. Until this point, we've been harassed by churches for even trying to learn. Lord, lead us on and everyone else feel free to interrupt."

"Can you imagine if we were in church doing this?" I laugh. "I can't tell you how many times I wanted to interrupt Pastor Bill and pepper him with questions. Now Wade invites me to do so!"

"Thanks for the worst possible comparison," mocks Wade as if he is hurt. Then he smiles and starts.

"'The Anastasis' involves a place. A place not taught well or really understood in Protestant churches. So, we're going to take a trip to Hades. That's the Greek word. The Hebrew word is Sheol."

"Why don't you just say we're going to hell AND BACK?" Ray emphasizes as we all laugh.

I can't imagine where all this is leading because I've never had an open discussion where everyone is eager to seek the truth without debate. So, I'm excited as Wade continues.

"I'm not sure what all the belief's are here so share your's if it's different than how I summarize things." We nod for Wade to continue.

"First, the foundation of our belief is that Jesus Christ defeated death. As Christians, we share the certainty that the dead will be resurrected." Ray pulls his index card of notes out from the back of his Bible which is now before him. "Ray," he hands over his Bible, please read 1 Corinthians 15:12 through 22."

While Ray is opening the Bible and finding the verse, TF hands out Bibles to everyone. We're all going to be participating on this.

Ray reads, "[12] But if it is preached that Christ has been raised from the dead, how can some of you say that there is no resurrection of the dead?

[13] If there is no resurrection of the dead, then not even Christ has been raised.

[14] And if Christ has not been raised, our preaching is useless and so is your faith.

[15] More than that, we are then found to be false witnesses about God, for we have testified about God that he raised Christ from the dead. But he did not raise him if in fact the dead are not raised.

[16] For if the dead are not raised, then Christ has not been raised either.

[17] And if Christ has not been raised, your faith is futile; you are still in your sins.

[18] Then those also who have fallen asleep in Christ are lost.

[19] If only for this life we have hope in Christ, we are to be pitied more than all men.

[20] But Christ has indeed been raised from the dead, the firstfruits of those who have fallen asleep.

[21] For since death came through a man, the resurrection of the dead comes also through a man.

[22] For as in Adam all die, so in Christ all will be made alive."

"What is Paul telling us?"

Amanda quickly answers, "He is saying that without the resurrection of the dead, we would be the most pitiful of all people on the earth due to a worthless faith. But because Jesus lives, our faith is based on evidence." Amanda knew how to choose her words to make her Uncle Wade happy. More than that, it's obvious she truly believes.

Dusky now joins in. "This isn't exactly about Hades or Sheol but it is related. Whenever we start talking about the resurrection of the dead it opens up the discussion for the wild and wacky questions as well as such theological distinctions of soul, spirit and body. I admit I still get confused over soul and spirit so don't want to talk about that. Let's talk about the wackier stuff—it's more dominant on television and something we will each be asked: 'how many times do we live?'"

Wow, she really knows how to bring up an issue!

Lee takes this one. "I think I can help. Let me state the answer first, but whether me or anyone else, don't accept the answer until or unless we can prove it in the Bible. The simple answer and I'm going to emphasize this, "he says raising the tone of his voice to just below a shout, "MAN ONLY LIVES ONE LIFE."

He continues while lifting his Bible closer to his face and looking for the exact verse he's after. "The Bible is very specific about this. We can avoid a lot of discussions and deceptions by knowing simply that man lives one time. Turn to Genesis 3:1 through 6. Please read it Dusky."

Dusky reads, "1 Now the serpent was more crafty than any of the wild animals the LORD God had made. He said to the woman, "Did God really say, 'You must not eat from any tree in the garden'?"

2 The woman said to the serpent, "We may eat fruit from the trees in the garden,

3 but God did say, 'You must not eat fruit from the tree that is in the middle of the garden, and you must not touch it, or you will die.'"

4 "You will not surely die," the serpent said to the woman.

5 "For God knows that when you eat of it your eyes will be opened, and you will be like God, knowing good and evil."

6 When the woman saw that the fruit of the tree was good for food and pleasing to the eye, and also desirable for gaining wisdom, she took some and ate it.

She also gave some to her husband, who was with her, and he ate it."

Dusky looks to Lee. This doesn't answer the one life he's talking about. She knows he has more to say.

"Here we have the first lie in human history...and it is a lie that is still repeated today: 'You will not surely die...'. One of the problems we have when we read the Bible in English is the imprecision of our own language. In the Hebrew, the word die is 'muwth' and the meaning is larger than we could use in one word in our language. It could just as easily be translated as 'death sentence' and is certainly meant that way. We know that Adam and Eve did not die immediately but they did live under a death sentence from this time forward. Every one of us since then stands under this same condemnation from this first judgment at Eden."

Lee sees that we're trying to tie this all back to the question of one life. "I'll bring this all together in just a minute. Consider this, those who believe in multiple lives are essentially arguing against a single death. They may choose to believe that the soul lives on to occupy other bodies, but that is not what the Bible says."

"Look up Job 14:5," Lee says to me.

I find it quickly and start reading, "Man's days are determined; you have decreed the number of his months and have set limits he cannot exceed."

"According to Job," Lee points out, "not only do we have one life, but we have limits we cannot exceed. No matter how many times a day you chant. No matter how many vitamins you take. That's not to say we are not responsible for the quality of our lives by what we do, but there is an inherit limit to our life span. Even more than that time limit appointed to us, we are restricted to only one life.

"You had an easy one, look up another...Hebrews 9:27."

Whoops, I started to look for Hebrews in the Old Testament but find it quickly in the New. I read, "Just as man is destined to die once, and after that to face judgment..." I stop there now fully convinced of Lee's position.

Lee's not done explaining, "Our life and death are tied to the judgment that all of us face. If we kept coming back in multiple bodies to redeem ourselves, then wouldn't that mock the sacrifice that Christ gave in His death? Man cannot achieve perfection and that is why Christ had to redeem us. That inability to save ourselves applies to everyone."

This time Lee reads his own verse. "Psalms 89:48 What man can live and not see death, or save himself from the power of the grave? Selah."

"Having one life is not only foundational to humans, it is also true for animals. The Greek philosophers argued endless about the difference between "being" and "becoming". The "potential" verses the "reality". In the Bible we get the kind of hard practicality that is startling in clarity. See what Solomon said about death."

This time he turns to Jules, "please read Ecclesiastes 9:4."

Taking time to look up Bible verses is not disruptive. If anything, I'm more involved and anxious just to hear what Jules reads.

"Anyone who is among the living has hope -- even a live dog is better off than a dead lion!" I see Jules' disgusted face and know she's thinking of the stupid poodle next door. But, the point sinks in.

"The Bible is clear—we all live once, die once before facing judgment (except those alive at Christ's coming), and are raised from the dead to face judgment. Yet, there seems to be a continuance of man's consciousness, what we call "spirit", even after the body ceases. Christ referred to this. Josh, please read Luke 20:37-38 ."

Josh doesn't normally like to read in groups but from the flush on his face, he's as excited as the rest of us. "[37] But in the account of the bush, even Moses showed that the dead rise, for he calls the Lord 'the God of

Abraham, and the God of Isaac, and the God of Jacob.' [38] He is not the God of the dead, but of the living, for to him all are alive."

"Amanda is working on her Master's Degree right now. She probably understands this better than I do. Think about this-- since God the Father exists in all times and everywhere at the same time, even when a person is dead, the Father is present with them while they lived."

Lee has put a lot of time and research into this. We all feel privileged to be in this study. "Second, the Bible teaches us that the spirit of a person continues on waiting for the Day of Judgment. Is the spirit just a different life or is it part of the one life allotted? Let us see what happens to the spirit."

"Many churches believe in a doctrine that when a person dies their spirit dies with them. They claim that as soon as the spirit leaves the body then that person's being is dead until the resurrection. Wade, please look up and read Ecclesiastes 9:5 since this verse is most often quoted for this position.

We can tell by Wade's face that he's still wondering how all this will tie back to how he started to explain 'The Anastasis' but he's as enthralled as the rest of us and starts reading, "For the living know that they will die, but the dead know nothing; they have no further reward, and even the memory of them is forgotten."

Lee expects for us to keep up and we barely are. "The Hebrew word, 'yada', for 'know' is interesting—it means more than just knowledge, it means the cessation of learning by experience, the inability to reveal or make known, and even the lack of revealing one's self. It does not necessarily mean the absence of existence but instead a meaninglessness to their condition or what they are now—there is no further reward for them and there is nothing they can do to change their situation.

"The first time we read about a person after they are dead has to do with Samuel—the wise Judge of Israel. The

Bible describes an event where Samuel's spirit is called "up". We'll get into where it's up from shortly. Right now let's note that the following story does not say that this is a satanic deception or a fake appearance; it claims that a spirit was called from another place of existence and appeared. John, please read 1 Samuel 28:3 through 25."

No one hesitates now, we're eager to study this. John starts reading immediately, "[3] Now Samuel was dead, and all Israel had mourned for him and buried him in his own town of Ramah. Saul had expelled the mediums and spiritists from the land.

[4] The Philistines assembled and came and set up camp at Shunem, while Saul gathered all the Israelites and set up camp at Gilboa.

[5] When Saul saw the Philistine army, he was afraid; terror filled his heart.

[6] He inquired of the LORD, but the LORD did not answer him by dreams or Urim or prophets.

[7] Saul then said to his attendants, "Find me a woman who is a medium, so I may go and inquire of her." "There is one in Endor," they said.

[8] So Saul disguised himself, putting on other clothes, and at night he and two men went to the woman. "Consult a spirit for me," he said, "and bring up for me the one I name."

[9] But the woman said to him, "Surely you know what Saul has done. He has cut off the mediums and spiritists from the land. Why have you set a trap for my life to bring about my death?"

[10] Saul swore to her by the LORD, "As surely as the LORD lives, you will not be punished for this."

[11] Then the woman asked, "Whom shall I bring up for you?" "Bring up Samuel," he said.

[12] When the woman saw Samuel, she cried out at the top of her voice and said to Saul, "Why have you deceived me? You are Saul!"

[13] The king said to her, "Don't be afraid. What do you see?" The woman said, "I see a spirit coming up out of the ground."

[14] "What does he look like?" he asked. "An old man wearing a robe is coming up," she said. Then Saul knew it was Samuel, and he bowed down and prostrated himself with his face to the ground.

[15] Samuel said to Saul, "Why have you disturbed me by bringing me up?" "I am in great distress," Saul said. "The Philistines are fighting against me, and God has turned away from me. He no longer answers me, either by prophets or by dreams. So I have called on you to tell me what to do."

[16] Samuel said, "Why do you consult me, now that the LORD has turned away from you and become your enemy?

[17] The LORD has done what he predicted through me. The LORD has torn the kingdom out of your hands and given it to one of your neighbors--to David.

[18] Because you did not obey the LORD or carry out his fierce wrath against the Amalekites, the LORD has done this to you today.

[19] The LORD will hand over both Israel and you to the Philistines, and tomorrow you and your sons will be with me. The LORD will also hand over the army of Israel to the Philistines."

[20] Immediately Saul fell full length on the ground, filled with fear because of Samuel's words. His strength was gone, for he had eaten nothing all that day and night.

[21] When the woman came to Saul and saw that he was greatly shaken, she said, "Look, your maidservant has obeyed you. I took my life in my hands and did what you told me to do.

22 Now please listen to your servant and let me
give you some food so you may eat and have the
strength to go on your way."

23 He refused and said, "I will not eat." But his men
joined the woman in urging him, and he listened to
them. He got up from the ground and sat on the
couch.

24 The woman had a fattened calf at the house,
which she butchered at once. She took some flour,
kneaded it and baked bread without yeast.

25 Then she set it before Saul and his men, and
they ate. That same night they got up and left."

Lee takes over again, "What we read here is that after Samuel's death, his spirit was recognizable and existed. And while Samuel's spirit had nothing to share that could save or help Saul, he did tell Saul that he would see him and his sons shortly in the place Samuel's spirit dwells. The referral of this place where there is some kind of continuing existence is not just in the Old Testament. Christ Himself told about a place where spirits were sent and existed. But, most people dismiss this as a tall tale. Dusky, your turn again. Read Luke 16:19-31 only from this version." I'll have to ask later why the different version.

I've never seen Dusky find Bible verses so quickly.
She reads, "19 "Now there was a certain rich man, and he
habitually dressed in purple and fine linen, gaily living in
splendor every day.

20 "And a certain poor man named Lazarus was
laid at his gate, covered with sores,
21 and longing to be
fed with the crumbs which were falling from the rich
man's table; besides, even the dogs were coming and
licking his sores.

22 "Now it came about that the poor man died
and he was carried away by the angels to Abraham's
bosom; and the rich man also died and was buried.

[23] "And in Hades he lifted up his eyes, being in
torment, and saw Abraham far away, and Lazarus in his
bosom.
[24] "And he cried out and said, `Father Abraham,
have mercy on me, and send Lazarus, that he may dip
the tip of his finger in water and cool off my tongue; for
I am in agony in this flame.'
[25] "But Abraham said, `Child, remember that
during your life you received your good things, and
likewise Lazarus bad things; but now he is being
comforted here, and you are in agony.
[26] `And besides all this, between us and you there
is a great chasm fixed, in order that those who wish to
come over from here to you may not be able, and that
none may cross over from there to us.'
[27] "And he said, `Then I beg you, Father, that you
send him to my father's house—[28] for I have five
brothers—that he may warn them, lest they also come
to this place of torment.'[29] "But Abraham *said, `They
have Moses and the Prophets; let them hear them.'
[30] "But he said, `No, Father Abraham, but if
someone goes to them from the dead, they will
repent!'
[31] "But he said to him, `If they do not listen to
Moses and the Prophets, neither will they be persuaded
if someone rises from the dead.'"

Scratching his eyebrows and with his eyes closed, Lee ponders, "Before we move on to discuss the place of existence, let's take a moment to note that we are told here the Word of God is living and speaks to us beyond what any dead person could ever say. While this Lazarus-- not the same person as he that rose from the dead-- wanted to return to the land of the living long enough to warn his brothers, the Lord said his testimony was irrelevant in comparison to the Scriptures. That should be part of our foundational belief as well—if something is contrary to scripture, then it has no authority."

We all say "Amen." This is one of our new tenants of shared belief. I can't help but wonder if we're a new church, a new religion, or just where all this is going.

"On the other hand, to restrict our mindset to what we have been reared as believing is scripture-based will deny us the revelation the Holy Spirit provides during diligent study and prayer. Our growing relationship with Jesus Christ requires revelation of the scriptures we study. The Bible is the love letter, Jesus is the loved one." Lee makes a great distinction. I saw a church deacon run across a room and dive under a falling Bible as if the Bible were sacred. Yet that man swore like a trooper and his relationship with Jesus was not high up on his list.

"Yet, people who do not believe the Bible or who believe in things only if with scientific data go to the extreme to test such things as spirit. Those people have long sought to verify the existence of the spirit in some measurable way. The most famous attempt is still in our popular lexicon today: 21 grams or approximately a half ounce."

Ray interrupts Lee, "I remember the movie by the same name. But, isn't 21 grams the supposed weight loss when someone dies? It's supposed to be the spirit leaving the body?"

Nodding to Ray, Lee continues, "Having a spirit is not a matter of science. It is a matter of faith. Not faith in what we believe, but faith in what the Bible tells us. We take a stand in faith when the Bible provides us information because to have faith in the Word is to have faith in the Lord. From what the Bible says, even in direct quotes from Christ above, we see that spirits continue some type of existence and in some particular place."

"Wade, I've stepped in too long. I know you're prepared for this. So why don't you take us to the references to that place of existence."

"Shoot, you really are going to tie this all together! I thought you got lost for a little while." Wade seems surprised. "Let's start with the terminology."

"There are several terms for the same place: Sheol, Hades, Hell, The Pit, The Grave, and Death. Dusky already read to us where Christ talked about this as a location. David also provides it as a location when talking about his son with Bathsheba dying. Ray, please read 2 Samuel 12:23."

Ray reads, "But now that he is dead, why should I fast? Can I bring him back again? I will go to him, but he will not return to me."

"The implication here is that it is a place."

Ray asks as if on cue, "If it's a destination, then wouldn't we find a name for it?

Wade nods, "This destination does indeed have a name. We see another event where people went directly to a place called Sheol.

"Buddy, look up Numbers 16:23 through 33 for me."

Ray does and reads, " [23] Then the LORD said to Moses,

[24] "Say to the assembly, 'Move away from the tents of Korah, Dathan and Abiram.'"

[25] Moses got up and went to Dathan and Abiram, and the elders of Israel followed him.

[26] He warned the assembly, "Move back from the tents of these wicked men! Do not touch anything belonging to them, or you will be swept away because of all their sins."

[27] So they moved away from the tents of Korah, Dathan and Abiram. Dathan and Abiram had come out and were standing with their wives, children and little ones at the entrances to their tents.

[28] Then Moses said, "This is how you will know that the LORD has sent me to do all these things and that it was not my idea:

[29] If these men die a natural death and experience only what usually happens to men, then the LORD has not sent me.

[30] But if the LORD brings about something totally new, and the earth opens its mouth and swallows

them, with everything that belongs to them, and they go down alive into the grave, then you will know that these men have treated the LORD with contempt."

31 As soon as he finished saying all this, the ground under them split apart

32 and the earth opened its mouth and swallowed them, with their households and all Korah's men and all their possessions.

33 They went down alive into the grave, with everything they owned; the earth closed over them, and they perished and were gone from the community.

"The Hebrew word for 'grave' that Ray read in verse 33 above is "Sheol", the same destination Christ talked about. It is a place where souls are kept—these evil men did not even die first—they literally went straight to hell. It's interesting to note that while you can't take your possessions with you to heaven, these men took them to hell. In heaven we will have better things but in hell, they already had the best they'll ever get."

Jules quips, "The good news is you can take it with you. The bad news is, as long as you're going to hell?"

Wade chuckles and goes on, "We have been discussing the foundations of our Christianity. Sheol is more that that—it is part of the foundation of this world…that is this planet. In addition to the description Christ gave, we see verses in the Old Testament that tell us Sheol or Hades is beneath or in the earth. Jules, look up Ezekiel 31:15 through 17."

That's a good idea, I think. Keep her busy before we hear from her again.

Jules reads, "15 Thus says the Lord God, 'On the day when it went down to Sheol I caused lamentations; I closed the deep over it and held back its rivers. And its many waters were stopped up, and I made Lebanon mourn for it, and all the trees of the field wilted away on account of it.

[16] 'I made the nations quake at the sound of its fall when I made it go down to Sheol with those who go down to the pit; and all the well-watered trees of Eden, the choicest and best of Lebanon, were comforted in the earth beneath.

[17] 'They also went down with it to Sheol to those who were slain by the sword; and those who were its strength lived under its shade among the nations.'"

Wade adds, "'Sheol' is one of three words translated as 'hell' in the King James Version. The New International Version translates Sheol and its descriptions more exact to the original language. For example, the Hebrew word 'Sheol' in Deuteronomy 32 describes a 'realm' which means kingdom, territory—a definite place for the dead located below the living—below the surface of the earth. Amanda, read Deuteronomy 32:22."

"For a fire has been kindled by my wrath, one that burns to the realm of death below. It will devour the earth and its harvests and set afire the foundations of the mountains." Amanda reads somewhat dramatically but this description requires a little drama.

"The idea of depth—of being below is brought out in Job as well. The word translated as 'grave' is 'Sheol'. Stay with me Amanda and read Job 11:7 to 8."

Amanda's dramatic voice is perfect as she reads, "[7] Can you fathom the mysteries of God? Can you probe the limits of the Almighty? [8] They are higher than the heavens--what can you do? They are deeper than the depths of the grave --what can you know?"

As if to answer, Wade says, "In Isaiah we see that Sheol, a place below or of descent, is also insatiable. I love your reading, Amanda read Isaiah 5:14."

"Therefore the grave enlarges its appetite and opens its mouth without limit; into it will descend their nobles and masses with all their brawlers and revelers."

"Regardless of the location, God is present and ruler of Sheol as much as of heaven and earth. He literally is the God of the dead—Abraham, Isaac and Jacob even when they were in Sheol. I'll get into them being in Sheol in a minute. First, let me read from my King James Bible Psalms 139:8."

Wade reads, "If I ascend unto heaven, thou art there. If I make my bed in hell, behold, thou art there."

"The meaning of Sheol incorporates what we would describe as the grave, the underworld and the state of death. Historically in the countries of the Bible the dead were thought of as existing below the earth in a kingdom of the dead. For example, in Babylonia, this place was called 'aralu'. Unlike the pagans around them who believed such places were ruled by their own gods, as we already read from David, the Israelites believed there was only one true God who was present in Sheol as much as in heaven.

"Jacob understood that he would be gathered to his family in death and gave specific instructions that relied on this. Read Genesis 49:29 through 33," Wade directs Amanda again.

"29 Then he gave them these instructions: "I am about to be gathered to my people. Bury me with my fathers in the cave in the field of Ephron the Hittite,

30 the cave in the field of Machpelah, near Mamre in Canaan, which Abraham bought as a burial place from Ephron the Hittite, along with the field. 31 There Abraham and his wife Sarah were buried, there Isaac and his wife Rebekah were buried, and there I buried Leah.

32 The field and the cave in it were bought from the Hittites."

33 When Jacob had finished giving instructions to his sons, he drew his feet up into the bed, breathed his last and was gathered to his people."

Wade notes, "In addition to the gathering to his family in Sheol, it is interesting to wonder if the cave of Machpelah may have been considered a type of entrance to the underworld... there is a tradition that Machpelah is the burial site of four famous couples—Jacob and Leah; Isaac and Rebekah; Abraham and Sarah; and, Adam and Eve."

"Unlike Genesis, Job does not refer to a gathering of family. Instead he emphasizes Sheol as a place of gloom, disorder and darkness." Again Wade looks to Amanda, "Job10:20 to 22."

Amanda reads, "[20] Are not my few days almost over? Turn away from me so I can have a moment's joy

[21] before I go to the place of no return, to the land of gloom and deep shadow,

[22] to the land of deepest night, of deep shadow and disorder, where even the light is like darkness."

Wade explains, "The term "shadow" means that there is some similarity to life but not real life. Isaiah describes a new arrival's welcoming scene similar to what would be expected in real life but it lacks any joy for this is a place without joy." Without looking up Wade says, "Isaiah 14:9 to 10 and Amanda starts to read.

"[9] The grave below is all astir to meet you at your coming; it rouses the spirits of the departed to greet you-- all those who were leaders in the world; it makes them rise from their thrones-- all those who were kings over the nations.

[10] They will all respond, they will say to you, "You also have become weak, as we are; you have become like us."

"Especially in the Old Testament we see that life allows us the opportunity to serve God—that it is in life we can hear His word, provide Him sacrifice and glory, and learn from His intervention. All that stops upon entering Sheol. God is present there, but people are cut off from Him."

"Amanda, I'll pick on someone else after this. Please read Psalms 88:3 to 5."

We love Amanda's voice and hope he continues calling on her. She reads, "[3] For my soul is full of trouble and my life draws near the grave.

[4] I am counted among those who go down to the pit; I am like a man without strength.

[5] I am set apart with the dead, like the slain who lie in the grave, whom you remember no more, who are cut off from your care."

"While we are alive, we experience the opposite of being cut off.

"Now who shall I call on to read?"

Ray answers for all of us, "Amanda." Even TF and Lee are nodding. Wade gives in.

"Amanda, read Psalms 16:9 to 11."

She knows she's doing a great job and starts, " [9] Therefore my heart is glad and my tongue rejoices; my body also will rest secure,

[10] because you will not abandon me to the grave, nor will you let your Holy One see decay.

[11] You have made known to me the path of life; you will fill me with joy in your presence, with eternal pleasures at your right hand."

"David can rejoice because he is not abandoned to Sheol. In Sheol, there is no way to glorify the Lord. Psalms 88:10 to 12."

Amanda goes on, "[10] Do you show your wonders to the dead? Do those who are dead rise up and praise you? Selah

[11] Is your love declared in the grave, your faithfulness in Destruction ?

[12] Are your wonders known in the place of darkness, or your righteous deeds in the land of oblivion?"

Wade pauses. We've laid no ground work out or any boundaries of what to present and how. So far, we've read different versions of the Bible without prejudice. Wade pulls out a printed document folded up in the back of his Bible.

He unfolds it as he talks, "While the Old Testament does not specifically state that Sheol has layers or division, by the time of the Septuagint translation, this seems to be understood. Books incorporated into the Septuagint that were later accepted by the Catholic Church but not by most of the Protestant churches are called the Apocrypha. One of the Apocrypha books is the book of Enoch. Books not included in the Septuagint but claim to be lost books of the Bible or undiscovered gospels are known at the Psuedographia. Let's take a look at how these describe Sheol. I'm reading from Enoch 22:1 to 14."

"1 From there I proceeded to another spot, where I saw on the west a great and lofty mountain, a strong rock, and four delightful places.

2 Internally it was deep, capacious, and very smooth; as smooth as if it had been rolled over: it was both deep and dark to behold.

3 Then Raphael, one of the holy angels who were with me, answered and said, These are the delightful places where the spirits, the souls of the dead, will be collected; for them were they formed; and here will be collected all the souls of the sons of men.

4 These places, in which they dwell, shall they occupy until the day of judgment, and until their appointed period.

5 Their appointed period will be long, even until the great judgment. And I saw the spirits of the sons of men who were dead; and their voices reached to heaven, while they were accusing.

6 Then I inquired of Raphael, an angel who was with me, and said, Whose spirit is that, the voice of which reaches to heaven, and accuses?

7 He answered, saying, This is the spirit of Abel who was slain by Cain his brother; and who will accuse that brother, until his seed be destroyed from the face of the earth;

[8] Until his seed perish from the seed of the human race.

[9] At that time therefore I inquired respecting him, and respecting the general judgment, saying, Why is one separated from another? He answered, Three separations have been made between the spirits of the dead, and thus have the spirits of the righteous been separated.

[10] Namely, by a chasm, by water, and by light above it.

[11] And in the same way likewise are sinners separated when they die, and are buried in the earth; judgment not overtaking them in their lifetime.

[12] Here their souls are separated. Moreover, abundant is their suffering until the time of the great judgment, the castigation, and the torment of those who eternally execrate, whose souls are punished and bound there for ever.

[13] And thus has it been from the beginning of the world. Thus has there existed a separation between the souls of those who utter complaints, and of those who watch for their destruction, to slaughter them in the day of sinners.

[14] A receptacle of this sort has been formed for the souls of unrighteous men, and of sinners; of those who have completed crime, and associated with the impious, whom they resemble. Their souls shall not be annihilated in the day of judgment, neither shall they arise from this place. Then I blessed God."

Wade unfolds another piece of paper and says, "This comes from 2 Esdras 7:36."

"Then the pit of torment shall appear, and opposite it shall be the place of rest; and the furnace of hell shall be disclosed, and opposite it the paradise of delight."

"The Assumption of Moses 10:10 reads,

'And the earth shall tremble: to its confines shall it be shaken:'"

Most understand "confines" to be these hellish regions.

"Judith 16:17 says, "Woe to the nations that rise up against my people! The Lord Almighty will take vengeance on them in the day of judgment; fire and worms he will give to their flesh; they shall weep in pain for ever."

Wade has researched this out better than I ever thought possible. In fact, I had always assumed the Bible was kind of contradictory about hell.

He continues, "The descriptions here appear very similar to the parable of the rich man and Lazarus in Luke. In Luke 16:23 the Greek 'Hades' used in this passage represents the underworld in the clear context of how it is described in Greek literature. This is the New Testament version of the Hebrew word 'Sheol'. For those denominations that believe in the Anastasis, this word substantiates the idea."

I'm glad to hear 'Anastasis'. I forgot that we were going to end up this study there and somehow hope we get some understanding into Markos.

"Amanda, please read Acts 2:27 then Acts 2:31. Wait, do we have a Living Bible?" TF passes her a Living Bible.

She nods to Wade and starts with Acts 2:27, "because you will not abandon me to the grave (Hades—the underworld), nor will you let your Holy One see decay.

Without pausing she goes to verse 31, "Seeing what was ahead, he spoke of the resurrection of the Christ, that he was not abandoned to the grave (Hades—the underworld), nor did his body see decay.

Explaining, Wade says, "The referral in Acts is really a prophecy from Psalms. David is obviously not talking about himself. Let's revisit Psalms 16:9 to 10—use the first Bible version."

Amanda takes the cue and starts reading, "9 Therefore my heart is glad and my tongue rejoices; my body also will rest secure,

10 because you will not abandon me to the grave, nor will you let your Holy One see decay."

"Another prophecy is that the gates of Hades will not prevail against the Lord or His People. An ancient kingdom was protected by its and the gates. The Bible talks of two gates: the gates of Zion; and the gates of Hell."

"We sticking with Amanda?" Wade asks us all. Everyone just nods. "OK, Psalms 9:13 to 14."

"13 O LORD, see how my enemies persecute me! Have mercy and lift me up from the gates of death,

14 that I may declare your praises in the gates of the Daughter of Zion and there rejoice in your salvation.

"A kingdom's strength depends on the ability to keep their gates shut. The gates of Hades cannot be kept shut because Christ holds the keys to the locks."

"Read Revelation 1:18."

Amanda does, "I am the Living One; I was dead, and behold I am alive for ever and ever! And I hold the keys of death and Hades."

"I know there is a lot of confusion about the areas in Hades. We already read in Christ's story about someone being in an area of Hades called 'Paradise'. The word 'paradise'-- in Greek `paradeisos'-- occurs in only three instances in the New Testament. Let's look at the first one in Luke 23:43."

Amanda reads, "Jesus answered him, "I tell you the truth, today you will be with me in paradise."

"This text is somewhat problematic for those who believe that paradise only means heaven. For Christ clearly said after His resurrection that He had not yet returned to heaven and told Mary not to touch him. That would mean if paradise meant heaven, the Jesus lied about being with the thief in paradise that day they died."

Wade tells Amanda, "John 20:17 ."

"Jesus said, "Do not hold on to me, for I have not yet returned to the Father."

"So the paradise promised that day to the thief on the cross was not heaven—it was one where Christ would be that very day... that's what He said. The paradise described was the same one Jesus described Lazarus the beggar going to—it was a place good people went immediately after their death. This paradise was a place in Hades but not a place of punishment."

Wade is doing well describing some pretty theologically heavy ideas and yet every point is clearly in the Bible. I'm really learning a lot.

"The word `hell' is `ghenna' and it is a transliteration of the Hebrew `Ge-hinnom'. Hinnom is an actual place that is a valley with steep, rocky sides located southwest of Jerusalem, separating Mount Zion to the north from the hill of "evil counsel" and the sloping rocky plateau of the plain of Rephaim to the south. The idolatrous sinners sacrificed their children in fire to Molech in this valley. The city burned its filthy rubbish here. The potter's field, the Aceldama-- purchased by the priests from the money Judas returned to them and the place where Judas died is in this valley. This place is an image or type of the hell in the underworld of Hades. The `hell' Amanda is going to read in Matthew 5:22 is in the original this word 'ghenna.'"

Amanda tells us, "But I tell you that anyone who is angry with his brother will be subject to judgment. Again, anyone who says to his brother, 'Raca, ' is answerable to the Sanhedrin. But anyone who says, 'You fool!' will be in danger of the fire of hell."

"Christ describes two kinds of death in 'ghenna' or hell: body and soul. Those who kill the body can only send someone to Hades. Those who kill the soul go to `gehenna.'"

"Read Matthew 10:28."

Amanda reads, "Do not be afraid of those who kill the body but cannot kill the soul. Rather, be afraid of the One who can destroy both soul and body in hell."

"So, we see there are distinctive places in hell. One place is Paradise. Another place where the distinction of a fiery place of hell is in Mark. 'Hell' here is the Greek word `gehenna.'"

"Amanda, read Mark 9:43 to 48. Everyone should know that in the NIV, verses 44 and 46 are blank. In the King James both these verses read the same: 'Where their worm dieth not, and the fire is not quenched.'"

Amanda just shrugs and begins, "43 If your hand causes you to sin, cut it off. It is better for you to enter life maimed than with two hands to go into hell, where the fire never goes out.

44

45 And if your foot causes you to sin, cut it off. It is better for you to enter life crippled than to have two feet and be thrown into hell.

46

47 And if your eye causes you to sin, pluck it out. It is better for you to enter the kingdom of God with one eye than to have two eyes and be thrown into hell,

48 where "'their worm does not die, and the fire is not quenched.'

"Luke also quotes Jesus in His distinction of a place translated as `hell' but is again `gehenna.'". Without even acknowledging her, "Luke 12:4 to 5."

Amanda knows she's supposed to continue and does, "4 I tell you, my friends, do not be afraid of those who kill the body and after that can do no more.

5 But I will show you whom you should fear: Fear him who, after the killing of the body, has power to throw you into hell. Yes, I tell you, fear him."

"James has a little different insight about this fiery place. Where before Christ warns us it is better to lose body parts to this place than to lose our soul, James says the tongue can come from hell. Read James 3:6."

"The tongue also is a fire, a world of evil among the parts of the body. It corrupts the whole person, sets the whole course of his life on fire, and is itself set on fire by hell."

"Moses told us what the Lord said about this fiery place. He said it was a place of His wrath." Wade looks up at Amanda, "You still with me?" She smiles and nods. "Good, Deuteronomy 32:22."

"For a fire has been kindled by my wrath, one that burns to the realm of death below. It will devour the earth and its harvests and set afire the foundations of the mountains."

"Peter also describes hell as being a place of confinement and punishment. He provides us the insight that this punishment is prior to the judgment. This hell of Peter's is not 'gehenna' but is 'tartaros' which is a region—a location. 'Tartaros' used here is not only the place of punishment referred to in Greek classical literature, but here it is a specific place for the angels who have fallen. Read 2 Peter 2:4 to 9."

"4 For if God did not spare angels when they sinned, but sent them to hell, putting them into gloomy dungeons to be held for judgment;

5 if he did not spare the ancient world when he brought the flood on its ungodly people, but protected Noah, a preacher of righteousness, and seven others;

6 if he condemned the cities of Sodom and Gomorrah by burning them to ashes, and made them an example of what is going to happen to the ungodly;

7 and if he rescued Lot, a righteous man, who was distressed by the filthy lives of lawless men

8 (for that righteous man, living among them day after day, was tormented in his righteous soul by the lawless deeds he saw and heard)—

[9] if this is so, then the Lord knows how to rescue godly men from trials and to hold the unrighteous for the day of judgment, while continuing their punishment.

"I hear in church after church that sinners will be punished on the day of judgment. That's not what Peter says—he says that they are continually punished until judgment. That's a scary distinction!"

"As we have already seen, Hades is a place in the underworld, below the earth, where all souls went. Hell is a region in Hades and it includes fiery punishment. Paradise, the place the Jesus promised the thief and where we found Lazarus the beggar, is a place in Hades where the righteous go. Or, at least they used to go there. The question is whether they-we-me still does?"

Wade admits, "That's probably not good grammar, but you know what I mean."

"Peter wrote above that the righteous are taken out from being with the wicked. Paul did not expect to go to Hades upon dying, but instead said that he would immediately go to be with Christ."

"Amanda, read Philippians 1:23 to 24."

"[23] I am torn between the two: I desire to depart and be with Christ, which is better by far;

[24] but it is more necessary for you that I remain in the body.

"We know that Paul did not believe that being in Christ's presence would be in the body because he said elsewhere that he would be physically resurrected when Christ returns. Paul expected until the resurrection for his spirit to dwell with Christ."

"I'm a cop. I've seen so many people get through the loopholes of our justice system that I had to study all this to find some kind of perspective of what's just. I found it in how the Bible describes hell and who is there and what they suffer. But that doesn't help us get to the Anastasis."

"Let's get back to that by asking a question. What about those who died before Christ? During His life, Christ described the paradise place for Lazarus the beggar and promised the thief on the cross that he would go there with Him. There is a historic Christian belief not specifically stated in the Bible but based on the assumption of Christ literally going to Hades. For if the righteous now are with Christ, then how did they get from Hades to Heaven as Paul looked forward to? Or, how would the righteous dead return as we read about in Matthew 27:50 to 54?"

Amanda looks up the text and reads, "[50] And when Jesus had cried out again in a loud voice, he gave up his spirit.

[51] At that moment the curtain of the temple was torn in two from top to bottom. The earth shook and the rocks split.

[52] The tombs broke open and the bodies of many holy people who had died were raised to life.

[53] They came out of the tombs, and after Jesus' resurrection they went into the holy city and appeared to many people.

[54] When the centurion and those with him who were guarding Jesus saw the earthquake and all that had happened, they were terrified, and exclaimed, "Surely he was the Son of God!"

"That is the reasoning behind the Anastasis— that on Jesus death He immediately descended to hell, kicked the gates down, and released 'many' of the holy people who were raised to life. The Bible doesn't say 'all' the holy people leading some to think that Paradise in Hades most probably still exists. Their reasoning is that only those who die in Christ are described as going to Christ. Personally, I believe Paradise in Hades is empty and all those souls are in heaven."

"What happens when someone who believes in Christ dies now? We know from the New Testament that the soul of the good no longer goes to Sheol. According to Paul, the righteous soul now immediately goes to the presence of the Lord. Read 2 Corinthians 5:6 to 10."

Amanda does. "6 Therefore, being always of good courage, and knowing that while we are at home in the body we are absent from the Lord

7 —for we walk by faith, not by sight—

8 we are of good courage, I say, and prefer rather to be absent from the body and to be at home with the Lord.

9 Therefore also we have as our ambition, whether at home or absent, to be pleasing to Him.

10 For we must all appear before the judgment seat of Christ, that each one may be recompensed for his deeds in the body, according to what he has done, whether good or bad.

"Christ on earth had authority to command even the demons to go to Hades including a special area called the Abyss—in the Greek called the 'abussos'—it is the deepest part of Hades reserved for demons. Read Luke 8:26 to 33 ."

"26 They sailed to the region of the Gerasenes, which is across the lake from Galilee.

27 When Jesus stepped ashore, he was met by a demon-possessed man from the town. For a long time this man had not worn clothes or lived in a house, but had lived in the tombs.

28 When he saw Jesus, he cried out and fell at his feet, shouting at the top of his voice, "What do you want with me, Jesus, Son of the Most High God? I beg you, don't torture me!"

29 For Jesus had commanded the evil spirit to come out of the man. Many times it had seized him, and though he was chained hand and foot and kept under guard, he had broken his chains and had been driven by the demon into solitary places.

30 Jesus asked him, "What is your name?" "Legion," he replied, because many demons had gone into him.

31 And they begged him repeatedly not to order them to go into the **Abyss**.

32 A large herd of pigs was feeding there on the hillside. The demons begged Jesus to let them go into them, and he gave them permission.

33 When the demons came out of the man, they went into the pigs, and the herd rushed down the steep bank into the lake and was drowned.

This time Amanda comments. "I think I get it. While it makes no sense for the death of Christ to change where evil people and demons go until the judgment, especially since Peter says their punishment continues until the final judgment, it does make sense that the righteous would now go to the presence of Christ."

Wade answers, "So 'The Anastasis' is a very important type of power—it's the power over hell. There's a very famous depiction in the Chora church in Istanbul that shows this on a ceiling painting. Jesus stands on top of two gates, the gates of hell kicked down, underneath the gates is a bound Satan. Jesus holds out one hand to Eve, the other to Adam, and drags them from the grave. All the saints hold hands leading back to Adam and Eve and are being pulled out with them. 'Anastasis Dunamis' is the Messianic power of Jesus over hell, over Satan, over death. That's what our Shadow friend whispered."

Lee stands, "As the elder spokesman of our group, I think it's time to call a bathroom break?"

I know I'm with him on that one.

He adds before he rushes down the hallway, "Let's come back in 15 minutes. I have more to wind up from this."

Dusky and I met each other outside on the patio. "What do you think?" I ask.

"I've learned more tonight than in 20 years of going to church." I just nod to what she says.

Jules, Amanda and Ray join us. We walk over and around the pool to see the Portland view. The moon is not full yet but between it and the city lights that contaminate the sky, not many stars are visible.

Ray observes, "No drums, no goat heads, what's with the floor show tonight?"

Sure enough, no drama. We all listen intently. All we hear from below is a muted Sinatra tune. What is that? "We Got High Hopes?" That seems appropriate for us tonight.

The guys come out and John asks, "Any shooting going on?"

We forgot about that and step back from the edge.

"Did I tell you we found a ballistics match?" Wade goes on, "Same gun used in a shooting last month. Very strange since what usually happens after a shooting is the gun goes into the river. Someone wanted to tease us about this case."

"Pleasant thought," chips in TF. "I talked to my neighbor down below again this morning. He's got no clue to who was there. He was invited to a fashion show a month ago and that's where he was at. Then he got a headache and came home early. He would have been home earlier too if it hadn't been for a flat tire."

"That flat tire probably saved his life," said Wade.

Lee amazes us by singing Amazing Grace. We all join in, at least the first verse. Can't say I remember the rest of the song. But, it sounded beautiful on this quiet night.

"Are we ready to wind down or do we need to pick another night?" Lee asks.

We all feel revived and beat him back to the table.

"All of what we've heard is so important and I feel I've never had all the pieces before," Lee admits. "Part of what is still missing that we need to explore are the different types of judgment. Evil beings, and I mean people and demons, are judged unto death. Righteous people are judged according to their rewards. For the righteous, the death sentence judged at the Garden of Eden is satisfied by the death of Christ on the cross. The righteous do not have to be judged that way again."

"Allow me to get back to reincarnation for a little bit. Let's get a little better understanding of what all we've discussed. At the time of Christ, people believed that the soul of a dead man stayed near his body until the third day. Then the soul was irretrievably sent to Sheol. The fact that Lazarus, the dead friend, and Christ were not raised until the third day had put them beyond hope of any resurrection as far as the disciples were concerned. They knew that their souls had literally gone to Hades. Presumably, to the part of Hades known as Paradise, but still they were irretrievably in Hades.

"Whether resurrected with Christ or for those brought back to life on this earth either in the Old Testament or the New (like Lazarus), the question remains whether these people then died again here on earth. If they died here again, that would be a type of reincarnation. This is rather hotly debated among the various denominations. We're going to see that dying more than once is restricted in the Bible. Amanda, you back as our reader?"

This time she shook her head, "How about sharing some of the joy with Ray?"

"OK, Ray, look up Hebrews 9:27 to 28."

Ray clears his throat and reads, "27 Just as man is destined to die once, and after that to face judgment,

28 so Christ was sacrificed once to take away the sins of many people; and he will appear a second time, not to bear sin, but to bring salvation to those who are waiting for him."

"How would you summarize that, John?"

"To live multiple lives would mean multiple deaths required of Jesus."

Huh? Maybe I didn't get it.

Lee clarifies, "interesting but I think the main point is man is destined to die only one time and be judged for that life only. Am I reading too little here?"

TF adds, "I've never considered what John said but believe it's true. At the same time, I concur with you—these are not exclusive ideas."

I can't help myself, "I've got something to add. I don't think that the judgment talked about here is the same as the final judgment. To live a life then face judgment ties in with what Peter said about punishment in hell before the final judgment. If there were only the final judgment, then there would be no punishment now in Hades as Peter describes."

"It took me years to get to that point," admits Lee. "We have seen that there seems to be many reasons and corresponding areas in Sheol—sometimes punishment, sometimes abandonment from God, but always a place to stay before judgment.

"We have also seen how the demons did not want to go to the Abyss—a place where we already read in Peter that angels are kept until the final judgment.

"There is another inhabitant in the Abyss part of Hades that we only find described in Revelations. It is a type of being similar to locusts but with faces and hair like humans who now dwell in the Abyss. They will be loosed in judgment on the earth but only have the power to harm the unrighteous. Interestingly, there is no description of them being sent back to hell after their five months of power is up. I can't help but wonder what on earth will that be like with these hellish beings running around with regular humans? Do you know who I'm talking about?" Lee asks Jules in particular.

She shakes her head "no".

"Then you read for us Revelation 9:1-4."

Jules quickly finds it and reads, "1 The fifth angel sounded his trumpet, and I saw a star that had fallen from the sky to the earth. The star was given the key to the shaft of the Abyss.

2 When he opened the Abyss, smoke rose from it like the smoke from a gigantic furnace. The sun and sky were darkened by the smoke from the Abyss.

[3] And out of the smoke locusts came down upon the earth and were given power like that of scorpions of the earth.

[4] They were told not to harm the grass of the earth or any plant or tree, but only those people who did not have the seal of God on their foreheads."

"Everyone who is evil gets punished before the final judgment. Those who die get punished in Hades. Those alive at the time Jesus comes will be punished by these beings."

Lee keeps explaining, "There is also a king of these beings, an angel who dwells in the Abyss, who is set loose with them. In the following verse we find the only known name of a fallen angel that is now in hell. Jules, read about him in Revelation 9:11."

Jules does, "They had as king over them the angel of the Abyss, whose name in Hebrew is Abaddon, and in Greek, Apollyon."

"In the Hebrew 'Abaddon' means `death' and in the Greek 'Apollyon' means `destroyer'. This is a person, a being who has charge over Sheol or Hades. `Death' is a being who carries out the death sentence pronounced in the Garden of Eden. Jules, good work, read Revelation 6:8."

She does. "I looked, and there before me was a pale horse! Its rider was named Death, and Hades was following close behind him. They were given power over a fourth of the earth to kill by sword, famine and plague, and by the wild beasts of the earth.

"Before Sheol is destroyed, it will have another infamous inhabitant. Satan himself will be held there for a period of time before the final judgment. Read Revelation 20:1 to 15."

Jules follows the directions and reads, "[1] And I saw an angel coming down out of heaven, having the key to the Abyss and holding in his hand a great chain.

2 He seized the dragon, that ancient serpent, who is the devil, or Satan, and bound him for a thousand years.

3 He threw him into the Abyss, and locked and sealed it over him, to keep him from deceiving the nations anymore until the thousand years were ended. After that, he must be set free for a short time.

4 I saw thrones on which were seated those who had been given authority to judge. And I saw the souls of those who had been beheaded because of their testimony for Jesus and because of the word of God. They had not worshiped the beast or his image and had not received his mark on their foreheads or their hands. They came to life and reigned with Christ a thousand years.

5 (The rest of the dead did not come to life until the thousand years were ended.) This is the first resurrection.

6 Blessed and holy are those who have part in the first resurrection. The second death has no power over them, but they will be priests of God and of Christ and will reign with him for a thousand years.

7 When the thousand years are over, Satan will be released from his prison

8 and will go out to deceive the nations in the four corners of the earth--Gog and Magog--to gather them for battle. In number they are like the sand on the seashore.

9 They marched across the breadth of the earth and surrounded the camp of God's people, the city he loves. But fire came down from heaven and devoured them.

10 And the devil, who deceived them, was thrown into the lake of burning sulfur, where the beast and the false prophet had been thrown. They will be tormented day and night for ever and ever.

11 Then I saw a great white throne and him who was seated on it. Earth and sky fled from his presence, and there was no place for them.

12 And I saw the dead, great and small, standing before the throne, and books were opened. Another book was opened, which is the book of life. The dead were judged according to what they had done as recorded in the books.

13 The sea gave up the dead that were in it, and death and Hades gave up the dead that were in them, and each person was judged according to what he had done.

14 Then death and Hades were thrown into the lake of fire. The lake of fire is the second death.

15 If anyone's name was not found written in the book of life, he was thrown into the lake of fire.

"The last two things destroyed include Death and Hades—which I believe are one being. No being will ever have such power or authority again. All who have been held inside Sheol or Hades will now be released to judgment."

Lee looks to Josh, "Why don't you read Revelation 21:1?"

Josh does, "Then I saw a new heaven and a new earth, for the first heaven and the first earth had passed away, and there was no longer any sea."

"Note that the former earth had a Hades, not true of the new earth. For, there is no more judgment to come and no need for Hades."

"We're all in synergy here—trying to arrive at foundations since what we have been taught is such failure. The foundation of our belief is the reality of our death and resurrection. The unrighteous will have a resurrection to judgment; the righteous will have a resurrection to life. We have people now who claim the resurrection has already taken place, but that also happened to Paul and he warned us against such people. Did you know that?" Lee still talking with Josh who shakes his head "no". "Look up 2 Timothy 2:17 to 18."

Josh does, "[17] Their teaching will spread like gangrene. Among them are Hymenaeus and Philetus,
[18] who have wandered away from the truth. They say that the resurrection has already taken place, and they destroy the faith of some."

"Our faith is in a bodily resurrection yet to come. That resurrection has purpose: the judgment and then new creation."

Lee is back to rubbing his eyes. He looks tired but I just had a thought I can't suppress. "Wait a second. If our spirit goes to heaven when we die, then that means it would have to come back to earth with Jesus to be reunited with our bodies…is that right? Does the Bible say that anywhere?"

Lee is revived by the question. "Yes, it does. I'm not sure anyone has ever asked me about it that way, but that's exactly what the Bible says. I'll read it to you."

"1 Thessalonians 4:13-14: [13] Brothers, we do not want you to be ignorant about those who fall asleep, or to grieve like the rest of men, who have no hope. [14] We believe that Jesus died and rose again and so we believe that **God will bring with Jesus those who have fallen asleep in him.**"

"I understand that perfectly now…Jesus brings with Him the spirits of those who died believing in Him because they now live with Him. He brings the spirits to be united with their bodies at the resurrection during His return. He wouldn't have to bring them with Him if they were still here."

Josh says, "Way to go, Sweetie," as if I thought this up. Then the full impact hits me—at the Second Coming, Jesus is going to be surrounded by angels and other heavenly beings described in Revelation, and all the spirits who died believing in Him. I have a feeling we will see billions of beings present…hard to imagine.

"We still haven't finished talking about judgments. But I'm pooped. Today's Tuesday, we need a break. How about back here on Friday?" Lee is really looking at TF to see if that's OK. It is.

"I'd like to tell you something TF and I are doing that we've come to love. Every morning instead of breakfast, we're doing Communion."

"It might be hard to do that with Ray in the house," he's talking to Josh, "knowing how he likes the sacramental wine and how much he eats..."

Ray walks over and pushes him slightly as if to threaten him.

Dusky can't leave it without summarizing, "Fine, Friday, same time, Dawn and I will bring the food."

"I want to help," adds Amanda.

"Come to our house at 5 PM," offers Jules. "Give me your email and I'll send you a Mapquest link."

Rays seems happy about that.

We hear Wade calling from outside the front of the house. Thankfully, he doesn't seem concerned.

We all go out front to our cars. There on each car, Wade points out, is another yellow lacey cord hanging from the antenna.

Josh asks Wade, "I've never seen a ribbon or cord or whatever it is like this. Can you take your's to work and find out what it is? CSI Portland-style?"

10
THE STORM BEGINS

TO ME IT SEEMS SCHIZOPHRENIC HOW NORMAL LIFE IS BETWEEN THE PARANORMAL. Yesterday and today seemed calm and normal, even boring. Tomorrow we go back to TF's house but here I am in bed watching the news while Josh is locking up downstairs. "It's like a strobe light on the dance floor," I consider thinking how one second life is normal and the next we're being tossed out of a church or someone's doing voodoo spells against us.

I hear Josh pause part way up the stairs. Why? Then I hear it as well-- the distinctive sounds of that dark car's big engine. The Shadow is back.

I'm more suspicious than others and I can't tell whether The Shadow is pretending to be good or is he instigating these problems? We never had things like this happen before he showed up.

The creepy feeling I'm having right now makes me think he's not so good.

I get up and go out to the top of the stairs, "I hear him, too."

Josh just nods as he wonders what to do. When in doubt, get the bat. And, that's what he backs down the stairs and grabs.

I look back down the hall and see the lights are out in the kids' rooms. Hopefully, that's good.

Josh has the bat in his right hand and starts to open the door with his left hand. He leaves the chain on the door so he can open it without someone barging in.

"Don't open the door," a vaguely Mediterranean sounding voice orders Josh. I recognize it as Markos.

"You're safe inside. Try to sleep and you'll find out what's going on in the morning."

Josh tries to talk more, "Markos, is that you?"

"Yes. We will talk more another time. Please go in where it's safe," and then he pulls the door closed on Josh.

Josh turns to me, "Sing me the theme from the Twilight Zone."

He is probably kidding but Dusky and I use to memorize TV theme songs. "There is a fifth dimension," I use my deepest voice as I recall the words, "beyond that known to man…it is a dimension as vast as space and as timeless as infinity…if is the middle ground between light and shadow…" The words now mean more than ever before and I stop reciting. I turn and head back to bed. The strangeness now almost seems routine. We truly live in the Twilight Zone.

Josh goes into the bathroom to get ready for bed. I call out to him, "Honey, you haven't said much about work lately. Anything going on?"

I hear Josh stop brushing his teeth. Then he rinses and comes back into the bedroom before answering.

"Yeah, I didn't want to worry you. The construction company and the West Linn project are coming along fine. But, our partners are worried about an IRS audit going on."

Now he's sitting on the bed beside me, "They just told me a little bit about it—remember that I don't do anything with those companies but collect our partnership distribution? But, I saw how concerned they are."

"Do you know what year or what the issue is?" I ask.

"I know it was four years ago. I didn't think the IRS could go back more than three years but evidently there was a semi-secret clause in the 2004 omnibus act about saving jobs that eliminated all audit time limits. The IRS can now go back to when you were 16 and didn't claim your student summer wages. That's a scary abuse of power right there.

"The other part of the law that changed is how they make the CPAs accountable. Basically, the CPAs now work for the IRS. It was one of the partner's CPAs that started the audit.

"From what I've been told, the audit may change deductions for that year. Since those deductions offset other company income, we may end up owing taxes. Right now I don't know enough about it to even guess." Josh shrugs.

"Anything unusual happen four years ago?" I ask because I remember something different going on then.

"I don't know if it's coincidental or not, but seems to me that was the time when Anderson-Anderson, the big accounting firm, sent out their Denver specialists to show the partners how to get the maximum write offs."

The name Anderson-Anderson brings chills to me almost as much as The Shadow. A once dominate worldwide accounting and marketing company, they went down in flames and were charged criminally over fraudulent accounting on that big Texas utility company.

Any business that had a tax filing with the Anderson-Anderson name on it is getting audited.

"Well, maybe," I'm trying to offer some hope, "they did something with Anderson-Anderson's name on it and that triggered an audit. As long as everything was above board, we shouldn't have to worry, right?"

"I'm not smart enough to worry," Josh smiles.

The loping exhaust sounds of the big limo speed up and we hear it drive off.

"Want to go check out there?" I ask knowing that Josh is smart enough to say "no."

"Sure," but to the contrary he's shaking his head "no" and climbing over me to his side of the bed.

"Should I put a note on the kids' doors not to go outside until we're with them?"

Josh covers himself and rolls over mumbling, "What happens whenever you tell them to 'not' do something?"

Now I turn off the light and hunker down under my blankets.

"That's the first thing they do. You're right, we'll tell them in the morning."

I feel a storm brewing over us. I don't know if it's the IRS or partners or Markos, or what. I'm just too exhausted to worry about it any more.

❖

I wake, Jules is screaming. Usually in the summer the kids sleep in until 9ish but I see on the alarm it's 6:30.

Josh jumps up and is out the bedroom door heading down the stairs. Jules' voice is coming from the driveway.

Ray's right behind Josh.

I can't find my slippers... then I remember I left them downstairs. As I hit the bottom of the stairs I hear Jules, "That's so GROSS."

Josh yells, probably to Ray, "Don't touch them."

Forget the slippers; I'm out the kitchen and about to hit the sidewalk when I see something long and brown across it-- a snake.

Jules is hysterical pointing around the house. It sinks in. There are hundreds of dead snakes all around our house.

"What the hell is this?" Ray turns to Josh. "Are they all dead?"

Josh had his baseball bat in his hand and started moving the snakes from in front of Jules and Ray to clear a path to where I am.

"They all appear dead." Ray says while kicking them out of the way.

Detective Wade drives up and parks on the street. He talks to us as he walks closer, "I got a call that I'm guessing was from The Shadow. He asked me to come here. What is this freak show, anyway?"

He looks around and sees dead snakes hanging in the bushes, in the roses, and all over the sidewalks and lawn. "Freak show" is the perfect description.

"None of them are moving," Wade calls back to Josh.

"If they do," Ray returns, "be ready to shoot. See those 'V' shaped heads? That means they're venomous."

"I grew up with rattle snakes in my backyard. I can tell they're venomous." Wade is now bent over some on the sidewalk.

Josh walks over and joins him, "Now what?"

"I don't want to make this official. I definitely don't want to write up reports on this. We know we're in some kind of battle by an unnamed evil. What can you tell me about last night?"

As Ray starts telling Wade about the short conversation with The Shadow, I motion the kids inside the kitchen.

"We've had at least two possible fatal events directed at us, yet I don't feel like we're going to be killed." Ray walks over by Jules who is seated at the breakfast bar, "Do you feel at risk?"

"I hate snakes. I hate snakes. I hate snakes." Ray leaves Jules chanting and walks over to me.

"Mom," he says putting his arm around my shoulders, "do you feel at risk?"

"I feel like we're being attacked at many levels. I'm not sure what all is happening. Your Dad has some stuff going on at work as well. If evil is after us, it will be on many levels and in many ways."

"But, do you feel at risk?" Ray never lets go of what he's after.

"Not really...I'm not even sure what that would feel like. Sometimes I feel like we're being led, sometimes I feel like we're being blocked and misdirected. I don't like the feeling of manipulation. Whether it's good for us or bad for us—why not just tell it like it is?"

Although I'm not done, Josh and Wade come in the door and Josh asks, "Coffee on, yet?"

I made up the coffee last night but haven't turned it on yet. I punch the switch and say, "Right up."

Wade explains to Josh, "That's a lot of poison out there. We've got to get those things out of here before a dog runs off with one or some kid starts playing with one."

Ray offers, "Call Dennis."

"Who?"

Josh answers Wade, "Dennis is a professor friend of mine. He works up at Oregon Health Science University."

Wade likes that idea. OHSU trains doctors, nurses, pharmacists, lab techs, etc. It's probably the only place in the city that could actually use the venom.

"Will he keep it quiet?" Wade says what's on all our minds.

Josh shrugs, "Let's ask." He picks up the portable phone and walks off into the living room while he talks.

I hand Wade a cup of black coffee. "Want any cream in that or do you take it like a man?"

"Cream, please."

I get the creamer out of the refrigerator, "Didn't mean to tease you about the cream." He just smiles as he pours some into his cup and hands it back.

"Thanks."

"Your welcome…wussy."

Wade just laughs.

The kids have been staring into the cabinets for a few minutes now. That usually means they either can't decide what they want or they want me to fix something. I take the cue and ask, "Omelets?"

"Yes please." They turn and sit at the bar with Wade.

I pull out the omelet pan just as Josh comes in.

"Detective Wade, I've just solved your case for you."

"Do tell."

"One of the assistants that works under Dennis is in charge of the herpetology lab. This is they keep the poisonous snakes. Care to guess where ours came from?"

Wade shakes his head, "But there are hundreds out there."

"That's why they've been so slow about calling in a report. Who would want hundreds of snakes? They've had people scouring the facilities trying to figure out if the snakes were taken or just let loose."

"Oh," Wade interrupts, "I remember last month they had a bunch of rats let loose by the animal rights activists. Did they think the same people would let snakes loose?"

"You know they probably would," Josh answers. "Actually, they didn't know what to think about who took them or who let them loose—they just wanted to make sure no one was at risk. They've called in extra security to search the grounds. The last thing they wanted was to encourage the activists or put anyone at risk."

"Does he have a proposal for getting the snakes out of here?" I want them gone now and get to the point.

"They're on the way, dear. They're just going to bag them up and take them back and tell everyone they got out of their cages and had to be killed. They don't need them alive to do what they're doing, anyway.

Jules asks the sane question, "Why would anyone want that many live poisonous snakes?"

"Dennis said they were flown in yesterday from Egypt. They're Egyptian Asps—think Cleopatra. OHSU got a big cash grant awarded with it. But, no one wanted the live snakes. It was just part of the package."

I have the first eggs beaten and pour the first omelet. Now all eyes are on me. Nothing like a little adventure to stimulate the appetite.

"Here," I hand Wade the first omelet. "Who knows if you'll want to eat after you help get those snakes picked up?"

I'm off to the next omelet and Jules is getting the toast for everyone. We work as a good pair. She's already a great cook. So is Ray.

I hand Josh his omelet as he and Wade are discussing the possibilities of whether an Egyptian official were involved in what ultimately ended in a rather sinister act.

Ray and Jules listen to the discussion. We're all involved in stuff that makes no sense, has no logic, and all we've got are feelings. None of us like the feeling of hundreds of dead Egyptian Asps around the house. Especially if The Shadow killed them for us, which would mean that they were supposed to be live Asps when we woke up.

"Why Egyptian Asps?" I wonder. Again, what we've been going through has no reason. I'm sure somewhere there is a connection but basically, it's just another attack.

I just get Jules' omelet done when a van pulls up in front.

Josh, Wade and Ray head outside. I'm not going anywhere until I get an omelet and Jules would rather finish eating than go play with snakes.

"Guys are weird," Jules says about how they ran outside.

"Want to move into the living room and see what they're doing?" She's right, guys are weird. I've always found it fascinating to watch them, however. I must have been warped by all the Three Stooges movies I watched as a kid.

Jules finishes her omelet and grabs a half empty glass of orange juice heading for the living room. I follow holding my plate up close to my mouth shoveling my food in.

Jules opens the drapes and we see four guys from the van, each with big canvas bags, sticks with long hooks on the end, pulling the dead snakes up and dropping them in the bag. Sometimes they were getting five snakes at a time.

Dennis drives up in his bright red Prius. We don't hear much of what he's telling Josh and Wade but we do hear, "Please, please don't tell anyone about this."

Ray's coming out from the side of the house. He must have just finished checking the backyard out. One of the four guys is with him. They're just shaking their heads— I take it he means there are none back there.

The last of the bags are loaded and it seems like the green traffic light is on and people are now out on the street. Kids are out playing, people are walking on the sidewalk but no one knows what happened. They wouldn't have believed it anyway.

Josh and Ray come in waving goodbye at Wade.

"See you tonight," Ray calls out.

Josh says, "You won't believe it... every snake had its head crushed!"

"He will crush your head...that's what God said to the snake in the Garden of Eden." Ray seems joyous about this.

We all wonder what's in store at TF's tonight.

11
The Storm Grows

DUSKY AND I OFTEN PUT TOGETHER FANTASTIC DINNER PARTIES ALL OVER TOWN. The dinners are even better now that Jules is old enough to contribute. The thing is, what do you want to eat with Communion? And, what do you want to eat when all you really want to do is get to work?

We settled on chicken fajitas. I'm still not sure how that goes with Communion. Earlier at my house Dusky made the meat and vegetables and now they're ready to serve. I have chips, fresh salsa, and bean dip—all homemade today as well. Jules made the rice. Everything was easy to eat and easy to serve.

Amanda joins us in the TF's kitchen. She met up with us earlier and made her contribution—a melon salad. Jules was just putting it out and Amanda put a serving spoon into the bowl. "Something to take the fire off the Mexican food," she winks at Jules.

Amanda opens the pan top of the fajita meat and asks, "Fresh snake meat?"

"Yuk," says Jules. "You wouldn't have thought it funny if you had been there."

"I'm sure it tastes like chicken," Amanda teases. "Uncle Wade told me about it. I'm glad I wasn't there. So far, nothing weird has happened to me. Knock on wood," Amanda says this as she taps Jules on the head.

In spite of the nine year age difference the two of them really do get along well.

"There," Dusky says as she puts the last dish on the table. "Done in 20 minutes."

"Eaten in ten minutes or less," Ray circles through like a shark beginning an eating frenzy. I've actually seen him eat whole meals in seconds.

"Can you believe Amanda asked if the meat were snake?" Jules didn't really expect for Ray to answer.

Amanda checks the table and since it is ready she walks to the edge of the dining room closest to the living room, "Snake's on the table and ready to eat."

That's not the kind of announcement that I would have made but it gets the guys in here. They assume the same seating arrangement as last time.

Lee brings the Communion platter over and passes around the wine glasses as he fills them. "Anyone want to say anything before we start communion?"

To everyone's surprise I say, "Yes. We have experienced unusual if not deadly events. Yet, I feel like we're being herded and protected at the same time. I love the feeling of being protected but find I'm kind of resenting the manipulation at the same time? Why should it happen at all?"

We all looked at each other without an answer. Finally Lee breaks the silence.

"Father, we're ready to share in the Communion of your Son but have confusion about our conflict. We want to appreciate your support and protection but don't understand what's going on. None of it makes sense. So, we ask for your guidance in this. We do not want the natural feelings of resentment that manipulation causes if you have a higher purpose in all this. Amen."

We all say "Amen" after Lee.

Ray's on the food in a flash but barely ahead of Wade. I'm guessing Wade doesn't get many home-cooked meals.

"Anyone want a cerveza?" TF asks if we want beer. I just don't know what to expect later in the night and would rather not. No one else takes him up on it either.

Ray was right—ten minutes was about all that it took for everyone to get their fill. He, again, was the first one to finish his plate and take it to the dishwasher.

Dusky and I stored the leftovers back in their carriers but we leave a lot for TF and Lee.

"Um, I'll bet that mixes well with an omelet," Wade points to Dusky's container of meat left over.

"I'll bet your right," Dusky answers and fills a bowl for him to take home.

Meanwhile, TF has just wiped down the table while everyone else is taking turns in the bathroom.

Dusky and I take our turns and return to a table with everyone ready and Bibles all around.

"As you have seen, this kind of Bible study is fast paced, especially when we all start adding what the Spirit has revealed to us." Lee pauses before saying, "I hope every one of you participates as the Spirit leads you. Without your sharing, we will only get part of the message."

"Believe it or not," Lee looks to Wade for affirmation, "I didn't coordinate with Wade last time. We just spoke as the spirit led us."

I love this. Can you imagine anyone in any church anywhere saying this? I commenting on this last time but I just appreciate it so much.

Lee picks up, "Alright, last time we left off in Hades and tonight we're going to the resurrection. We're going to talk about the role of the two primary judgments to come: the judgment of who lives eternally; and the judgment of rewards. The judgment of who lives means who lives eternally since we're all already condemned under the Judgment at the Garden of Eden to die and most have at this point, hence the Resurrection.

"I don't think we have to look it up, but if you do look at the judgment of life in Hebrews 6:2, you'll find it is called the "eternal judgment". This is one final, ever-lasting, judgment with no appeals, no mistrials, and no hope of leniency. This is the final dissolution of the old creation. But, there predates this final judgment certain types and methods of judging that impact the final judgment."

We're all a little lost but willing to hang in there. We know Lee has grappled with these issues and is going for something important.

"Many Christians do not realize ALL of the ways in which we will be judged. For example, we may think nothing of passing on worthless jokes or teasing others dismissing such action by saying, 'I was only joking.' Yet, the scriptures are very clear about this. Ray, read Matthew 12:36-37 "

Ray picks up his Bible and reads, "[36] But I tell you that men will have to give account on the day of judgment for every careless word they have spoken.

[37] For by your words you will be acquitted, and by your words you will be condemned."

"Crap," Ray says, "I say things all the time in joking. Double Crap, did just saying 'crap' now count?"

"Personally, I don't think it's talking about all kinds of kidding. But, if you've been careless in what you say, like passing on secrets or offending people regularly, I'll bet that's something we have to answer for," Lee responds. "Humor is not the issue, but the content of that humor can be. Passing on a joke we know is either a waste of time or inappropriate is not acceptable. Humor itself can be most effective when correcting manners, eliminating fear or building someone up. I think that's how you use humor Ray and I appreciate it."

Ray smiles.

Lee gets back to his agenda, "While we tend to think of judgment as only applying to overt acts of evil, the Lord looks at how we allow things to impact our lives and relationships. For example, the Lord told us that angry name calling would subject us to judgment. We tend to think of anger as an excuse but according to the Lord, it's not an acceptable excuse. Jules, please read Matthew 5:21-24."

Jules reads, "[21]You have heard that it was said to the people long ago, 'Do not murder, and anyone who murders will be subject to judgment.'

[22] But I tell you that anyone who is angry with his brother will be subject to judgment. Again, anyone who says to his brother, 'Raca, ' is answerable to the Sanhedrin. But anyone who says, 'You fool!' will be in danger of the fire of hell.

[23] "Therefore, if you are offering your gift at the altar and there remember that your brother has something against you,

[24] leave your gift there in front of the altar. First go and be reconciled to your brother; then come and offer your gift.

Lee waits for a comment to come from Jules but it doesn't come.

"The Lord judges us by what goes on in our minds. He knows that for the sake of our own reputation we may curtail the outward demonstration of what we inwardly feel. Amanda, your turn, Matthew 5:27-28."

We all love hearing Amanda's voice again and she reads, "[27]You have heard that it was said, 'Do not commit adultery.'

[28] But I tell you that anyone who looks at a woman lustfully has already committed adultery with her in his heart."

"I'll be a little blunt and hope it doesn't offend the women here tonight. Most guys whether in church or not have struggled at one time or another with pornography. There are many people who refuse to believe that computer pornography is adultery, yet that is not what the Bible says—lust is adultery. I'm an old fart and I still get clobbered with targeted porn email just because I'm a guy."

This is definitely something that causes discomfort. The guys look slightly embarrassed and we gals just don't want to know about it. But, he's right, I caught Josh looking at computer porn one time and I felt like it was adultery.

"The above verses are just two examples of how we will be judged by what we allow our minds to dwell on. If we allow our minds to dwell on adultery and indulge in images that worship it, then we have committed adultery in our hearts and against our spouses. Let's make clear that we are not being judged for being tempted—Christ was tempted. But, Christ did not allow His mind to dwell on those temptations. He did not do as some of us and make time or take efforts to be exposed to temptation but instead refuted each one. That's our role as well—not to be he-man strong enough to stand up to temptation, no one can do that, but instead to avoid it. John, read Matthew 6:13."

John is eager to understand and quickly starts reading, "And lead us not into temptation, but deliver us from the evil one."

"If we're delivered from temptation, then we're also delivered from the judgments of God." Again, Lee pauses waiting to see if we have any questions. No one does but I don't yet fully understand where he's going.

"The various judgments probably do not constitute different events but instead different methods in which we will be judged. Some of these judgments described have special significance in how we are to act now. Let us review these types of judgments as they contain important information for us personally. Josh, Matthew 7:1-2."

Josh reads, "1 Do not judge, or you too will be judged.

2 For in the same way you judge others, you will be judged, and with the measure you use, it will be measured to you.

"Now read Luke 6:37."

Josh continues, "Do not judge, and you will not be judged. Do not condemn, and you will not be condemned. Forgive, and you will be forgiven."

"What these two verses tell us is that at least one method of the judgment will be about 'like kind', The difference between them is that Matthew tells us it is how we will be judged as a process and Luke tells us it is how we will be condemned with the only escape being through how we forgive."

"Does everyone see this? Lee asks. "This is consistent with what Christ told us."

"Dusky, please read Matthew 6:14-15."

Dusky told me she's not sure if she likes reading like this or not but tonight she sure seems eager and finds the text quickly. "[14] For if you forgive men when they sin against you, your heavenly Father will also forgive you.

[15] But if you do not forgive men their sins, your Father will not forgive your sins."

"Wade, I want you to read three verses that relate to the "judgment of the cross". For those of us who claim the sacrifice of Christ, every curse against us was cancelled with the judgment Christ suffered on the cross. As if that were not enough, every blessing granted to Abraham has now been granted to us. Abraham did not get these blessings after he died, he got them while he was alive. So, too, is this our blessing because of Christ's condemnation on the cross."

"First verse, Wade, is Galatians 3:13 and 14."

Wade hesitates for a second trying to remember where Galatians is then finds it. "[13] Christ redeemed us from the curse of the law by becoming a curse for us, for it is written: "Cursed is everyone who is hung on a tree."

[14] He redeemed us in order that the blessing given to Abraham might come to the Gentiles through Christ Jesus, so that by faith we might receive the promise of the Spirit."

"The following verse focuses on our humbleness after being released from our curses because our blessings come only from the cross and sacrifice of Christ. Wade, read Galatians 6:14."

Almost immediately Wade reads, "May I never boast except in the cross of our Lord Jesus Christ, through which the world has been crucified to me, and I to the world."

"This last verse tells us that righteous law that righteously condemned us was taken away and canceled by the cross—the judgment upon the cross by Christ has superseded our unrighteousness. Read Colossians 2:13 and 14."

"[13] When you were dead in your sins and in the uncircumcision of your sinful nature, God made you alive with Christ. He forgave us all our sins,

[14] having canceled the written code, with its regulations, that was against us and that stood opposed to us; he took it away, nailing it to the cross.

"Thank you, Wade."

"There is another way that we avoid judgment by God: when we judge ourselves. Self judgment is part of our continuing life of repentance and starting over again where we previously allowed damage to our spiritual self. It is always in our best interest to be our worst critic and take accountability before the Lord."

"TF, I always forget about asking you to read. Please read 1 Corinthians 11:31."

TF reads, "But if we judged ourselves, we would not come under judgment."

"Wow," I say. "I've never heard that before—judgment itself is optional?"

"Seems so," Lee answers.

"Paul talks about a judgment for everyone but in Corinthians he specifically tells us of a judgment for believers that happens after we die. This occurs before the judgment seat of Christ and it is about rewards not life and death. However, it appears that even believers will still have to answer for their bad deeds."

"Dawn, read 2 Corinthians 5:8-10."

I read, "[8] We are confident, I say, and would prefer to be away from the body and at home with the Lord.

[9] So we make it our goal to please him, whether we are at home in the body or away from it.

[10] For we must all appear before the judgment seat of Christ, that each one may receive what is due

him for the things done while in the body, whether good or bad."

"This does not appear to be the same final judgment concerning life and death that Daniel describes. This judgment is about life or death and which book each person's name is written in. Daniel 7:9-10."

I think he means for me to continue reading and do, "9 As I looked, "thrones were set in place, and the Ancient of Days took his seat. His clothing was as white as snow; the hair of his head was white like wool. His throne was flaming with fire, and its wheels were all ablaze.

10 A river of fire was flowing, coming out from before him. Thousands upon thousands attended him; ten thousand times ten thousand stood before him. The court was seated, and the books were opened."

"These could be the same judgments but I don't think so. Whether they are or not is somewhat immaterial. Our goal is to stand as clean as we can before the Lord."

"Not everyone the Lord accepts into eternity will be treated the same. The traditional view is that the "sheep and goat" judgment are the terms for the Jews and Gentiles. Both will be accepted but they will be identified differently. Whether this is literal or symbolic, both the sheep and the goats end up at the side of Christ. Read Matthew 25:31-33."

I continue reading, "31 "When the Son of Man comes in his glory, and all the angels with him, he will sit on his throne in heavenly glory.

32 All the nations will be gathered before him, and he will separate the people one from another as a shepherd separates the sheep from the goats.

33 He will put the sheep on his right and the goats on his left."

I can't help myself, "Do you really think the sheep and goats are a type of discrimination or judgment on their own?"

"Thanks for that question. So many of our English words do not say what the Bible really says. The Greek word for 'nations' is 'ethnos', the word we get 'ethnic' from. Church doctrine aside, I think what the Lord means is we'll have as diverse of races and cultures in heaven as on earth and He wants to be in the middle of it all."

"I like that," quips Amanda.

"Good, let me go on. Another judgment that may be symbolic or may be literal has to do with the separate judgment of Israel. Those who accept this as a literal judgment tend to believe that Israel during the Millennium will remain on earth while Christian Gentiles will be in heaven. This is confusing but deserves to be mentioned."

Wade speaks up about this, "I hate to get into discussions with Jehovah Witnesses about this since they seem to believe we're in the Millennium."

"OK, then you volunteer to read Ezekiel 20:33-44."

Wade does. "33 As surely as I live, declares the Sovereign LORD, I will rule over you with a mighty hand and an outstretched arm and with outpoured wrath.

34 I will bring you from the nations and gather you from the countries here you have been scattered--with a mighty hand and an outstretched arm and with outpoured wrath.

35 I will bring you into the desert of the nations and there, face to face, I will execute judgment upon you.

36 As I judged your fathers in the desert of the land of Egypt, so I will judge you, declares the Sovereign LORD.

37 I will take note of you as you pass under my rod, and I will bring you into the bond of the covenant.

38 I will purge you of those who revolt and rebel against me. Although I will bring them out of the land where they are living, yet they will not enter the land of Israel. Then you will know that I am the LORD.

39 "'As for you, O house of Israel, this is what the Sovereign LORD says: Go and serve your idols, every one of you! But afterward you will surely listen to me and no longer profane my holy name with your gifts and idols.

40 For on my holy mountain, the high mountain of Israel, declares the Sovereign LORD, there in the land the entire house of Israel will serve me, and there I will accept them. There I will require your offerings and your choice gifts, along with all your holy sacrifices.

41 I will accept you as fragrant incense when I bring you out from the nations and gather you from the countries where you have been scattered, and I will show myself holy among you in the sight of the nations.

42 Then you will know that I am the LORD, when I bring you into the land of Israel, the land I had sworn with uplifted hand to give to your fathers.

43 There you will remember your conduct and all the actions by which you have defiled yourselves, and you will loathe yourselves for all the evil you have done.

44 You will know that I am the LORD, when I deal with you for my name's sake and not according to your evil ways and your corrupt practices, O house of Israel, declares the Sovereign LORD.'"

Lee says, "I don't have a summary for you about whether there is a separate treatment for Israel verses the Gentiles, I just want you to be aware that some see it that way."

We're all nodding our heads in appreciation. This is a thorough study.

"Both Paul and Jude tell us that the fallen angels will be judged. Jude tells us how they are held until that judgment. Let's stick with Wade-- Jude 1:6."

Wade reads, "And the angels who did not keep their positions of authority but abandoned their own home--these he has kept in darkness, bound with everlasting chains for judgment on the great Day."

"Paul tells us that we will be the ones who judge these angels. The final judgment will involve us believers in the process. As we already read in Daniel 7, there will be other thrones set up beside the Ancient of Days for that judgment. Evidently, that is where we will be seated."

"Princess Jules, please read about whom you will judge in 1 Corinthians 6:3."

Jules reads, "Do you not know that we will judge angels? How much more the things of this life!"

"The role we have in judgment is assigned to us during the thousand year Millennium. Before a jury makes condemnation, the judge takes time to instruct them on their duties. Can you imagine what we will be instructed before this judgment? Wade, read Revelation 20:1-10."

Wade does, "[1]And I saw an angel coming down out of heaven, having the key to the Abyss and holding in his hand a great chain.

[2] He seized the dragon, that ancient serpent, who is the devil, or Satan, and bound him for a thousand years.

[3] He threw him into the Abyss, and locked and sealed it over him, to keep him from deceiving the nations anymore until the thousand years were ended. After that, he must be set free for a short time.

[4] I saw thrones on which were seated those who had been given authority to judge. And I saw the souls of those who had been beheaded because of their testimony for Jesus and because of the word of God. They had not worshiped the beast or his image and had not received his mark on their foreheads or their hands. They came to life and reigned with Christ a thousand years.

5 (The rest of the dead did not come to life until
the thousand years were ended.) This is the first
resurrection.
6 Blessed and holy are those who have part in the
first resurrection. The second death has no power over
them, but they will be priests of God and of Christ and
will reign with him for a thousand years.
7 When the thousand years are over, Satan will
be released from his prison
8 and will go out to deceive the nations in the
four corners of the earth--Gog and Magog--to gather
them for battle. In number they are like the sand on the
seashore.
9 They marched across the breadth of the earth
and surrounded the camp of God's people, the city he
loves. But fire came down from heaven and devoured
them."

"Before the people of this earth receive their final judgment, it is preceded by the execution of Satan. Both Daniel and John in Revelations tells us about this. Daniel 7:11."

Wade reads, ""Then I continued to watch because of the boastful words the horn was speaking. I kept looking until the beast was slain and its body destroyed and thrown into the blazing fire."

"Now read Revelation 20:10."

"And the devil, who deceived them, was thrown into the lake of burning sulfur, where the beast and the false prophet had been thrown. They will be tormented day and night for ever and ever."

"My pardons to Flip Wilson," Lee says without noticing that the kids have no idea who that is. "No one will get the chance to point at the devil and say, "he made me do it". The final judgment is known as the "White Throne Judgment". When this occurs for sure is not described exactly. Whether we judge Satan during the Millennium or whether the Lord has already condemned him before the final judgment, we do know that there is no further plea on his behalf just execution."

"Wade, please continue reading Revelation 20:11-15."

"[11]Then I saw a great white throne and him who was seated on it. Earth and sky fled from his presence, and there was no place for them.

[12] And I saw the dead, great and small, standing before the throne, and books were opened. Another book was opened, which is the book of life. The dead were judged according to what they had done as recorded in the books.

[13] The sea gave up the dead that were in it, and death and Hades gave up the dead that were in them, and each person was judged according to what he had done.

[14] Then death and Hades were thrown into the lake of fire. The lake of fire is the second death.

[15] If anyone's name was not found written in the book of life, he was thrown into the lake of fire."

Wade questions, "I wonder if the 'lake of fire' is the sun? Revelation says the sun is done away with in the new creation."

"I think you're right," Ray agrees.

"We may need to do a separate study on the three heavens but let me sum it up quickly. Paul talks about going to the third heaven and if there's a third, you can bet there's a first and second. Personally, I believe all creation is one of three parts of the heavenly sanctuary and we're in the first part. One the reasons I believe that is we are told that the first heaven is removed at the White Throne Judgment along with the first earth. The area that was the Outer Court, that is our world and heaven, now becomes and functions as the Most Holy Place—a place where God dwells."

Ray, your turn, Revelation 21:1 to 3."

Ray jumps on it. "[1] Then I saw a new heaven and a new earth, for the first heaven and the first earth had passed away, and there was no longer any sea.

[2] I saw the Holy City, the new Jerusalem, coming down out of heaven from God, prepared as a bride beautifully dressed for her husband.

[3] And I heard a loud voice from the throne saying, "Now the dwelling of God is with men, and he will live with them. They will be his people, and God himself will be with them and be their God."

Ray notes to Wade, "So the sun would be gone after this point. That would mean an end to time as well as seasons."

Lee continues, "After the final White Thrown Judgment, there is no more death, no more curse, and no more sin. Our soul, spirit and body are inseparably one in a new type of body. We are no longer made of the dust of this world but instead have heavenly bodies made of the same substance of Christ's risen body. Our abode is in the Most Holy Place. Those who enter the Most Holy Place are priests and that is our destiny in Christ. It was His intention for us on this earth—John told us that we have already been made priests and kings."

"Already?" Amanda asks.

"See for yourself. Read Revelation 1:4 to 6."

Amanda reads, "[4] John, To the seven churches in the province of Asia: Grace and peace to you from him who is, and who was, and who is to come, and from the seven spirits before his throne,

[5] and from Jesus Christ, who is the faithful witness, the firstborn from the dead, and the ruler of the kings of the earth. To him who loves us and has freed us from our sins by his blood,

[6] and has made us to be a kingdom and priests to serve his God and Father--to him be glory and power for ever and ever! Amen."

"Our role as priests and kings is applicable both now and in the kingdom to come. And as kings who wear them, we are told to hang on to our crowns. Revelation 3:11."

Amanda reads again, "I am coming soon. Hold on to what you have, so that no one will take your crown.

"But," Amanda follows up, "that's not the kind of authority and power we're all experiencing right now. How do we get to that point?"

TF stands up, "This time I'm the one who is pooped. Same time Sunday night?"

Wade says, "Fine but I'm paying for pizza. I don't have the cooking talents to compete with tonight."

"I just wish they knew how to cook pizza," Ray forlornly points at Jules then me.

Outside the cars we find the anticipated lacey yellow cord hanging from the antennas. "At least nothing more happened tonight," I note as we all get in our cars.

12
Storms From New Directions

I SAW THE CALLER ID AND KNOW IT'S JOSH ON THE PHONE. Things have gone from anxious to full blown worry over the IRS review on what the partners did.

"What's up?" I try to act cheerful but know he wouldn't call during the day unless something is wrong.

He doesn't really give me a clue, "How about lunch at Tanford's?" He knows I love Portland's waterfront area.

"Yaquina Bay and it's a deal," I answer. Yaquina Bay restaurant is out on the piers and I love looking at the boats along the water front.

"OK, but make it 11:30. We need to miss the lunch crowd."

"Alright, lover, see you at 11:30. Goodbye." A month ago I couldn't stand him or myself. Now I can't imagine us being closer. I'm so glad that the dark cloud of despair… depression..spiritual darkness? Whatever it is has left and I feel like I'm genuinely me for the first time in a long time.

The irony in all this is that we've never been under such attacks before. First it was my cloud, then the excommunication, then physical attacks, and now the IRS.

Ray calls from the bottom of the stairs, "Mom, I've got pancakes ready." I just can't believe how grown up both of the kids are this summer. They're handling the most insane situations as if they were adults. It seems like they're my brother and sister more than son and daughter. I know they've got a lot more maturing to do…and I've got a responsibility to help in that. But, I feel the presence of the

Spirit in them and in that we're equals. Now if he'd only do his own laundry.

I'm halfway out my bedroom door and Jules pushes me back in laughing. "Uh-uh, first pancakes are mine." Oh, what a brat but I can't call back to her since I'm laughing too hard.

Sure enough, by the time I get to the kitchen, she's eating the first batch. Ray's just smiling.

"I didn't find the blueberries until after the first batch, so she didn't win anything, Mom." As if I need consoling over being too slow for Jules.

"Ray, didn't you get a letter yesterday from your high school counselor?" I couldn't wait any longer for him to bring it up. Besides, he's finished my pancakes so I can bring it up without sacrificing breakfast.

"Yes, I did. Let's just say the Lord doesn't want me going to Stanford."

"It seems," say I, "that we're having as much or more guidance by what's closed off than what's opening up."

"I guess it's a good time to tell you then that I didn't make the cheerleader squad," sighs Jules dramatically. But she's grinning.

"You never tried out for that, dear," I can tell when my leg is being pulled.

"I'm meeting your Dad for lunch today. What are you two up to? Boating with Sam?" Sam is a friend of Ray's and Jules has had a crush on him forever. We like Sam because he's a very devout Christian boy. That doesn't mean they don't occasionally drink lightly on the boat—something I don't totally agree with but something I did at that age. I don't think it a moral issue but do realize that our laws are pretty tough on kids now. My sister and I would have spent our summers in jail if the laws had been that tough when we were that age.

"I told Sam about our Bible studies…kind of left out the entertainment around them. He's coming over to do a Bible study with us today. We've developed a new way to study."

"How's that?" I really want to know.

"We use the QuickVerse Bible program to search the entire Bible for topics. After we find the texts, we go online to **www.blueletterbible.org** and use their lexicon to look up all the meanings of a word." I can tell Ray is excited about this.

"You see, Hebrew has several different meanings for a word depending on how it is used. It's kind of like if we had five different conjugations for the same word. All the meanings apply, but if you read them all, they amount to a greater understanding than just the one word used in English."

I ask him, "How did you come by this?"

Jules tells me, "We were instant messaging the other night and the three of us started exploring online resources. We just found **blueletterbible.org** to be the easiest."

"Can you give me some examples?"

Jules shares wit no restraint to her excitement. "You know how Jesus said there won't be the kind of marriage in heaven as we have here?"

I nod as she continues.

"It's almost as if there are no females in heaven. All the angels I've ever heard talked about are males. The combination makes you think there are no relationships or sexes in heaven."

I've never understood all this before but agree that seems to be what most churches teach.

I do remember that Solomon in Proverbs calls "Wisdom" a woman several times and even says to make her your sister. Those multiple referrals always make me think he was speaking of a real person… not human but a spirit or heavenly being. But I don't remember anything about women angels.

Every room in our house now has a Bible in it. We're all looking up and verifying what we're being taught. Jules picks up the kitchen Bible.

"Listen to this, Mom. Zechariah 5: 9 'Then I looked up--and there before me were two women, with the wind in their wings! They had wings like those of a stork, and they lifted up the basket between heaven and earth.'"

"Zechariah is referring to women angels! There have always been women in heaven. When Jesus says that there will not be earthly marriages, he's not saying there won't be relationships, they just won't be like here."

"With even Christians having a 50% divorce rate, that's good news," I tell her.

As I finish breakfast, I can't help but continuing thinking about women angels in heaven. Jesus surrounded himself with women on earth and I'm sure that's the same way in heaven. For some reason, I find this makes me feel closer to the Lord. I've always been a little freaked out about a marriage on earth that we enjoy, honor and work at just being tossed aside in heaven. My guess is that there's something better and that would be a good thing. Who knows, maybe that first marriage feast in heaven involves a marriage for all of us?

"What did you find, Ray?"

"I wasn't looking for anything big but I found a lot of little things." I nod encouraging him on.

"Like in the movie the Ten Commandments? Moses comes down the mountain top with these big tablets in his arms? The Bible really makes it sound like he's got small smooth tablets just big enough to carry in his palms—maybe one in each palm. And, the more I researched it, I think both tablets had the all the commandments on each. The law required two witnesses."

"Wow. What made you think of that?"

"I saw the Ten Commandments again and thought there is no way the Israelites would have put something that big in the Ark to lug it around. The Ark just wasn't that big."

When I think about how Cecil B DeMille's version of the size of the Ten Commandments had become church doctrine, I realized that there's too much we just accept as Bible that's not.

That church tower, I recall at the time calling it an obelisk, I wonder how that became almost a doctrine of every church? You'd think churches are required to build a spire. Yet, I'm sure spires indeed came from obelisks and no one says anything about it.

"What are you studying now, Ray?"

He answers me, "I'm trying to find out where the cross symbolism came from. The Bible says Jesus was hung on a tree. It describes Him carrying a beam but not necessarily a cross."

"How far have you got?"

"Far enough to know that the original Christians used the symbol of the fish, not a cross. Do you know where the fish sign came from?"

I don't and just shake my head.

"I wrote it down here," Ray grabs a piece of paper and reads, '**I**esous (Jesus) **CH**ristos (Christ) **TH**eou (God) **U**iou (Son) **S**oter (Savior)] the combination spells `**ICHTHUS**' or the Greek word for `fish.''"

"Do you know how the early Christians referred to themselves?"

Again I shake my head.

"They called themselves followers of `The Way'," he explains. "So the name "Christian" and the image of the cross never came from Jesus or the Apostles."

"Could you imagine a Church without spires, without crosses, and all of them just followers of 'The Way?' That would be awesome," I burst out kind of puzzling the kids.

"I'm trying to research the cross more. There are some who say the 'T' shape stands for Tammuz, the Babylonian god also mentioned in the Bible."

"Ray, I don't remember that." He was ready for me.

"Let me read from Ezekiel 8," and Ray does.

"1 In the sixth year, in the sixth month on the fifth day, while I was sitting in my house and the elders of Judah were sitting before me, the hand of the Sovereign LORD came upon me there.

2 I looked, and I saw a figure like that of a man. From what appeared to be his waist down he was like fire, and from there up his appearance was as bright as glowing metal.

3 He stretched out what looked like a hand and took me by the hair of my head. The Spirit lifted me up between earth and heaven and in visions of God he took me to Jerusalem, to the entrance to the north gate of the inner court, where the idol that provokes to jealousy stood.

4 And there before me was the glory of the God of Israel, as in the vision I had seen in the plain.

5 Then he said to me, "Son of man, look toward the north." So I looked, and in the entrance north of the gate of the altar I saw this idol of jealousy.

"Oh, yeah," interrupts Jules. "That makes me think of Colossians 3:5: 'Put to death, therefore, whatever belongs to your earthly nature: sexual immorality, impurity, lust, evil desires and greed, which is idolatry.' Idols must be the representation of certain specific sinful acts."

"I agree," I add. "Except that idols are more than the act, I think it's the strategy or method for certain demons. That's not quite right," I pause to search for a better way to explain it, "I think idols are the representation or logo of a demon in charge of that act. Let me have that Bible, I remember where to look."

Ray hands me back the Bible and I find Deuteronomy 32:17, "They sacrificed to demons, which are not God--gods they had not known, gods that recently appeared, gods your fathers did not fear."

"Wait, one more," I hold my hand up for just a second as I recall the other text. It's amazing how the verses are coming back to me.

"I remember—Psalms 106:36 and 37: '36 They worshiped their idols, which became a snare to them.

37 They sacrificed their sons and their daughters to demons.' So idols and demons are the same thing. To

worship lust or greed is the same thing as worshipping an idol or demon. Boy, that's never taught in churches."

"Sorry for the interrupt," I apologize to Ray.

"No, that's great. Interrupt me any time. Ok, back to Ezekiel, picking up at chapter 8 verse 6." Ray takes back the Bible and reads again.

"6 And he said to me, "Son of man, do you see what they are doing--the utterly detestable things the house of Israel is doing here, things that will drive me far from my sanctuary? But you will see things that are even more detestable."

7 Then he brought me to the entrance to the court. I looked, and I saw a hole in the wall.

8 He said to me, "Son of man, now dig into the wall." So I dug into the wall and saw a doorway there.

9 And he said to me, "Go in and see the wicked and detestable things they are doing here."

10 So I went in and looked, and I saw portrayed all over the walls all kinds of crawling things and detestable animals and all the idols of the house of Israel.

11 In front of them stood seventy elders of the house of Israel, and Jaazaniah son of Shaphan was standing among them. Each had a censer in his hand, and a fragrant cloud of incense was rising.

12 He said to me, "Son of man, have you seen what the elders of the house of Israel are doing in the darkness, each at the shrine of his own idol? They say, 'The LORD does not see us; the LORD has forsaken the land.'"

13 Again, he said, "You will see them doing things that are even more detestable."

I can't help but wonder what detestable things Senior Pastor Reverend William and his gang are up to in their hidden meetings. Does the Bible teach all churches are frauds? Certainly it was the pious religious leaders who killed Jesus.

Ray keeps on reading, "[14] Then he brought me to the entrance to the north gate of the house of the LORD, and I saw women sitting there, mourning for Tammuz.

"The same Tammuz you're talking about?" I ask Ray.

"Yes, the same one. They associated this god with death and rebirth. I'm really concerned that the 'T' shaped crosses, like some of the idols and images brought into Christianity, really represent this old god."

"What does a cross represent to you," Jules wants me to respond.

"I think of it as the symbol of Christ's payment for my sins." I answer.

"Then how it came to be probably doesn't matter. If idols are emotions or sins, then this cannot be an idol for you," Jules is feeling her way into a great summation.

"Right, we can make an idol out of anything, including going to church!" Ray's got it as far as I'm concerned.

I go load my dishes and say, "Thanks for the wonderful blueberry pancakes," emphasizing "blueberry" and Jules laughs at the dig.

As I head for the bottom of the stairs I detour to the ringing front door bell. With all that's going on I stop first to look through the peephole. It's Sam.

Opening the door, "Hey, Sam, long time since I saw you last."

"Hey, Mom." Everyone who comes over calls me Mom. "You wouldn't believe what I just picked up—a video I ordered from www.baseinstitute.org. These two guys follow the Bible directions to the location of the real Mount Sinai in Saudi Arabia. It's awesome."

I can't believe how these kids have gotten so serious into the Bible. Actually, I can't believe how serious I've gotten into the Bible.

"Will you leave it for me to see later?"

"You bet." Sam walks off into the kitchen being called by Jules who is now cooking him blueberry pancakes.

❖

I have to admit that I get tired of the seven months of Oregon drizzle every year. But these summer days out on the Willamette River make it all worth while. I pull into the public parking garage and look around for Josh. He's not here yet.

I walk out onto the piers leading to the restaurant. Across the river OMSI stands out. I have taken the kids there for years. In front of it is the USS Blueback—a real Navy submarine the kids loved to go through. My favorite OMSI thing has always been the OmniMax domed movie screen. It's huge.

I'm not good at guessing distances, but it must be a 50 foot long boat that is tying up in front of OMSI. I think I'd like to do a boat tour somewhere—maybe the Caribbean. I know there are pirates and dangers, but maybe a safe tourist boat?

Amazing how you can hear on the water. The people coming off the boat are laughing and joking about the captain's inability to tie up properly.

Josh is 15 minutes late which is to say he's on time. Josh is always 15 minutes late. I once set his watch 15 minutes early and he still arrived 15 minutes late. I don't know how he did that but it's just the way he is so I quit fussing about it long ago.

I see his gray Chevy pickup now. I better get us seats.

Inside the restaurant it smells wonderful. I tell the hostess that I want a table for two but before she leaves I ask, "What smells so good?"

"We got in a bunch of fresh crab caught at Newport this morning. The special of the day is crab cakes."

I order for both of us, "Two ice teas, two crab cakes, bleu cheese on the salad—did I forget anything?"

"How about rice or twice baked garlic potatoes?"

"The potatoes," I answer knowing Josh will love them.

Here he comes now, "Scoot over, sweetie, I want to sit beside you."

"What is that smell?" He sniffs the restaurant air.

"That, lover, is the smell of lunch. Specifically, crab cakes fresh from Newport Bay this morning. I also ordered you twice baked garlic potatoes. Does that make you happy?" I pinch his cheek and shake it as if he were a little boy.

"It certainly helps," he answers.

We wait for the waitress to set down our salads before I ask, "What's up?"

"IRS stuff I'm afraid."

"How bad is it?" I'm not really sure I want to know.

"I called Rick Zucker this morning and he told me he can't represent us anymore."

Rick is our attorney. This just doesn't sound right.

"Rick was introduced through the partners and he is also their attorney. Rick created some of the tax documents for whatever they did with Anderson-Anderson and now the IRS has called him on it. Rick says the State BAR told him he has to drop us and the partners as clients and just represent himself."

This doesn't sound good at all.

"I feel like that's a big 'screw you' from Rick," I openly say it.

"Indeed. He referred me to another lawyer and then faxed me a half hour later saying all the things he said by phone. He's scared."

"I asked him if I should be nervous and he said 'yes'. He says that the IRS has determined that the way the merger of two companies impacted the capital accounts amounted to a strategy known as BOSS or Son of BOSS. I don't know what that means. What I do know is that year we were given a 1099 providing us $50,000 of depreciation when the year before we only got $5,000. Every year since then we've had big write offs from that company."

"How big?" I ask.

"We haven't filed taxes yet—thankfully we don't usually do that until September and have a few weeks left before sending in last years. So, we don't have depreciation for last year but the all previous years amount to about $145,000. Before whatever they did, we would have only got about $15,000."

"Did Zucker say what he thought they were after from us?"

"He thought we could do the one time settlement and maybe avoid penalties—that we'd end up paying about $50,000."

"That would wipe us out." I point out. "Can't we go against the partners?"

"I'm about to secure the final loan to replace the construction loan in West Linn. I can't have this IRS claim or it will keep us from getting a loan. And, I don't think the IRS will wait for us to do a lawsuit against our partners."

"Do they want to sell a facility?"

""So far, no one is talking to me. They're all trying to cut their own deal with the IRS. The thing is, if we sell the facilities in the company with taxes due, then there will be capital gains taxes on that sale."

"That's OK as long as there's money to pay the taxes, right?" I'm not sure any more.

"No, it's not OK. They've depreciated those accounts by whatever they did. Now if those accounts are adjusted, they'll be negative. That means even if all the money goes to pay the mortgage and taxes, we're going to be taxed on the negative capital as well. So, we'd pay out every dime of a sale and still have more taxes to pay. We can't sell."

"How about selling West Linn?"

"It takes a year to fill up a facility like that. It won't have any real value until it's full. That will be too late to do anything." Ray just shakes his head, "We're going to have to use our savings and hope no one gets sick and there are no emergencies."

I understand.

The waitress brings our lunch and we stop talking shop. For today, for this minute, we enjoy our meal out. We may not be able to afford any more for a long time to come. Whatever happens, we are together. And that makes the moment sweeter and the meal taste better.

As she cleans up the dishes the waitress asks, "Desert?" We look at each other knowing we want this meal out complete.

"We'll share a hot fudge sundae." I say.

Ray says, "No, we won't. We want two sundaes."

The waitress laughs with me and leaves to get two hot fudge sundaes.

"What time will you be home tonight?"

"What do you have in mind?" he responds.

"I was thinking about asking Lee over for dinner. I'd like to hear what he as to say about this...I guess it's persecution. What do you think?"

"I think I love you...I think I love hot fudge sundaes... I think talking with Lee makes sense...and, most of all, I think I hate leaving you and going back to work."

We walk back to the parking lot together. I got my ticket validated at the restaurant but they only do one so Josh is going to have to take care of his parking.

We kiss in front of the meter before going to our cars. "It's like we're violently being torn away from our old lives," Josh says exactly what I feel. There's a violence to all we're going through and we have no choice to leave the old behind.

❖

Jules cooked spaghetti for dinner tonight. The smell is fantastic. I look around to see if there's anything I can do to help but everything is ready. The dining room table is set and looks great. We're going to use the baguette bread both for Communion and to accompany our meal. The Communion wine glasses are already poured. I don't even have a second thought about the kids drinking communion wine anymore.

Josh ran late from work and is still upstairs taking a shower when the door bell rings. Ray gets it as I fuss needlessly with a couple of the napkins on the table.

"My goodness—look at that wonderful table," Lee says. "And the smell..." I assume he means it's great.

"I forgot about you living with TF—was he upset that I didn't invite him? I didn't mean to snub him."

"We usually eat breakfast together and that's it. We've both got busy lives. Did I tell you he's been setting up home churches?" Lee had not told us that but I like the idea of it.

"Have a seat at the head there, Josh will be down shortly."

"Where do you sit?" Lee asks Ray.

Jules answers, "If he's good, Mom lets him take his meals in the laundry room. Otherwise, it's outside with the rest of the dogs."

Lee winks at Ray, "I have a sister—I can sympathize with your suffering."

Jules flicks a dish towel at Lee catching him on the corner of his arm.

"Ouch." He rubs his arm a little too showman like for any of us to feel sorry.

"Obviously time for Communion," Ray says as he catches the tail end of the teasing entering the room.

We all sit down around the table. The kids on one side, Josh and I on the other, and Lee at the head.

Lee grabs the bread and breaks off a piece, "Is there anything anyone wants to say before we commune?"

"The blood of Christ, the body of Christ, I think we need the consciousness of Christ as well—can that be our prayer?" Jules surprises everyone.

"That's the most mature thing I've heard anyone say," astonishment is on Lee's face.

Dinner goes quickly and Lee makes a show of leading the way loading his plate in the dishwasher. I wash the table off as Ray points out where the downstairs bathroom is under the stairwell.

It's not long before we're all seated again.

I take the lead, "Lee, we've all been going through some tough times. Poor little Jules didn't make the cheerleading team she didn't try out for."

Of course that didn't make sense to Lee but we all laughed. He understands that part is a joke.

"Seriously, Ray got cut from applying to Stanford. Josh and I have IRS problems. Even our lawyer quit on us today. Do you have any insight as to what's going on?"

This is news to the kids and they are shocked but wait to hear it all out.

Lee doesn't respond at first. We wait for him.

Ray sees what's going on first and gets up and puts his arm around Lee who is just shaking. Now he's crying hard without making any noise. What in the world is going on?

"I'm so sorry for what you are going through. It's brought back some unpleasant memories for me. I don't have an answer but I will share what I went through."

I'm not sure we're ready for something this bad but don't want him to stop, either.

"This happened some time ago. I was married to my third wife then—I've not been a success at relationships. I was good at getting degrees and lots of titles and positions at the University."

We knew of his teaching at the University and we read about some of his honors in the newspaper.

"My third wife stole the prenuptial agreement from my lawyer's files. What little I had left from the first two marriages was at risk. The judge didn't care...in Oregon the judges routinely refuse to enforce prenuptial agreements.

"What surprised me during the divorce is my brother-in-law. He's a pretty worthless person, hardly ever holds a job, and I can't remember when he's done something productive. But, I treated him well over the years and even loaned him money. I'd go so far as to say he wouldn't have a dime if it hadn't for what I did for him.

"Anyway, the brother-in-law broke into my office at the University and stole my briefcase with my post office keys in it. He and the soon to be ex-wife would go through my mail every day including all my lawyer's correspondence. When I finally figured it out, it was too late. A lot of damage was done including destroying every one of my legal defenses.

"I never could get an eye witness to what happened. I just know my briefcase was missing and that a mutual friend said he saw it at the brother-in-laws. I tried to get the FBI to do something, but no one really cares. As soon as you tell law enforcement that there's a divorce going on, they discount everything you tell them.

"After the final hearing, where she got almost everything I owned—which is why I don't live in my house of 30 years and live with TF now, the brother-in-law came up to me on the courthouse steps and bragged about what he did."

"I couldn't feel lower or further away from the Lord. I decided that I'd get justice either with or without the Lord," he pauses for a second looking at the kids.

"This is going to get pretty graphic. I hope you're not offended. I'm not really this way but was depressed, despoiled, disillusioned, and defiant to the Lord. All those 'D' words that happen when the Devil has control."

We grit ourselves not knowing how bad this will get.

"I went online at Craigslist.com. I put an add out as if I were a gay man and asked people to send me pictures and call me—only I gave my brother-in-law's number and email. I heard that there were at least 50 calls.

Ray started laughing. I hope this doesn't start anything with him—I could see the Senior Reverend Pastor William hotline now.

Lee cuts him off, "What happens next is not so funny."

"Craigslist lets you have an anonymous email referral and I got email through it from a guy who wanted me to have sex with him and his wife."

"Ewww," says Jules.

"I told you it wasn't funny," Lee tells her. "This guy asked me to meet him for a drink. I wrote him back thinking I could use him to show up at the brother-in-laws. I told him I didn't want to be around any white trash. He told me he is a lawyer. That made me curious enough to meet him.

"I met him. His wife came in and said "hi" then left. Seemed almost like a normal guy except he went into all this sexual detail and history. He asked me to email him and tell him that I'd do the things he asked. No, I'm not going to go into those details. The point is he told me two more pieces of information—his first name and where he took his undergraduate degree.

"I recorded the whole conversation. I recorded the email and sent a record to myself. I hate lawyers and I had a chance to take one down. This, I thought, was justice. I felt mean and I was happy.

"I know how to research. I went to www.martindale.com where all lawyers are listed. All I had was a first name, where he got his undergraduate degree and what city he practiced in but that was all I needed. I found out who he was, where he lived. And, I found out he was a judge. Not just any judge, but an Appellate judge, the best known of the Appellate judges.

"I was trying to figure out who to get to this guy. Whether to meet with he and his wife again as he asked or get more correspondence or what? I emailed him more saying the things he wanted to hear but he never wrote back in response. He just kept saying he wanted to meet at a restaurant. I knew if I did that they'd expect for me to go home with them. I wasn't about to do that— to be blunt I wanted to screw him in other ways."

Lee stops short realizing he may be getting too graphic for the kids. "Sorry," he says towards Jules.

"This isn't any worse than HBO," I offer. But, it's real and while Lee needs to finish and I want to hear the story, it is not pleasant.

"I had an assistant who worked with me for years. A wonderful woman. I trusted her completely. I hoped in my heart that someday we'd have a relationship. She had my password and would print off my email so I could read it on my lunch break."

We could all see where this was going.

"I forgot to delete the recordings. She read my email records, she saw the depraved things I wrote trying to trap this judge, and she wrote me a long termination note and slid it under my office door."

"Couldn't you explain it to her," asks Jules.

"I was afraid to tell her not knowing what the fallout would be...I didn't want her to be caught up in some judge's wrath."

"I realized that you can't get into the pig pen without getting pig shit all over you. I regret every moment and every thing I did about all that...and I stopped immediately. As far as that judge knows, I just never showed up at the restaurant.

"As I said, I worried about what that judge could do and it was foolish to think I could have compromised him. I hate that there are those kinds of people in charge and it got me to thinking about our so called 'Justice System.'

"So, I researched it out. Do you know where it came from?" Lee asks Ray then Josh.

"In Roman times whenever a question would arise, people would go to a pagan temple. The priests would cut open a pigeon and examine its entrails to arrive at a decision. Over time, these decisions would be written down and referred to by latter priests. Eventually, these decisions were codified into law. The black robes judges wear today come from the priestly dress of those pagan temples. Our laws come from worshipping the Roman goddess Justicia. Even our courtrooms are designed after these temples. The architect of the Supreme Court building purposefully called it the Temple of Justice."

"That's why the courts uphold abortion?" I ask. Lee nods.

"That's why criminals have rights but victims don't?" Ray questions. Lee nods.

"That's why anything to do with law, whether the IRS or regular law enforcement is used against us—we're no longer worshipping in their temple," Josh proclaims.

"Every person who truly pursues the Lord will suffer in some way from these civil authorities…that's my belief. Maybe by the police, maybe by the IRS, maybe in unfair lawsuits…but definitely at the hands of civil authorities including churches-- you've been witness to that persecution. I think it's a desperate attempt to keep you in their temple system but the Lord Himself is who pulls us out."

Josh semi-quotes the Bible, "Come out My People."

We all sit in silence trying to measure what all this means. It's just over whelming. But I've said that before and it's becoming a common experience.

"What can we do?" I ask.

"Keep praying, keep growing, and see you Sunday."

"We are praying, we are growing and we will see you Sunday," Josh leads him to the front door.

13
Lessons On Maturing

PIZZA IS A GREAT IDEA AND EVEN RAY HAS HIS FILL. I watch him finish eating his seventh piece in less than ten minutes.

We've gotten into a routine now and everyone sits in the same dining chair. TF offers more pop but everyone is full and can't wait to get started. Besides, another Diet Lime Coke and I won't be able to sleep tonight.

Lee leads out, "We're going to talk about maturing in the Lord tonight. I have to say that while there's a lot to cover, I don't feel like we've got all of what we're supposed to study. Hopefully, we'll discover more as we study."

"Let's get going, but as always, feel free to interrupt. If we take two sessions, so be it. Just follow as the Spirit leads."

"I'm going to use an image from something that Josh is more familiar with. Please correct me if I'm wrong, Josh."

As if he needs to ask, I think.

"The wider, taller and heavier a construction is, the more it relies on the strength of its foundation and flooring. Josh, what defines how strong the building materials need to be?"

Josh explains, "A big building like you're talking about usually has a lot of cement in it. How strong the cured material needs to be is defined in the design criteria based on an assessment of risks. For example, projects constructed in seismic zones have far more exacting requirements for the earth preparation as well as for the strength of the concrete."

Lee interrupts, "But, it's my understanding that concrete does not gain strength all at once. How do you know when it's strong? It must look the same on the outside for several days?"

Josh says, "It's not unusual for building specifications to require concrete strength tests at seven days, fourteen days, twenty-one days and the final test at the twenty-eighth day. When the concrete is being poured, some of what is being used in the footings, foundation and floor is put into plastic cylinders. We get at least one sample from every batch from the plant that's used in the building. At testing times the concrete is taken from these cylinders and tested under pressure to find its breaking point on the days specified and correlate that to the specifications."

I didn't know this and I've been around construction for years.

"What is tested at seven days is not expected to be at full strength. What is tested on the 28th day has cured to the point where it should meet the specification needed for full strength. The testing in between tells a builder whether the concrete is on its way to meeting full strength and that allows a reasonable determination about whether to start building on the uncured slab before the final test."

Lee takes over, "Is it fair to say that time for curing competes with time deprived of final use?"

Josh nods yes.

"If the focus is on use of the building instead of the strength, then curing time is resented when in reality it is the most important aspect for the final use. Would you agree?"

"Absolutely," Josh concurs.

"Ray, would you read Hebrews 6:1 and 2? We're going to be focused on this text since it tells us the basic things to do to reach maturity."

Ray gets there quickly, "[1] Therefore let us leave the elementary teachings about Christ and go on to maturity, not laying again the foundation of repentance from acts that lead to death, and of faith in God,

[2] instruction about baptisms, the laying on of hands, the resurrection of the dead, and eternal judgment."

"This verse tells us six things to do and the seventh is the result—reaching maturity. In fact, that's the whole point to the instructions in Hebrews 6:1 and 2-- to grow to maturity. This is our point of strength and it requires curing time which we often resent."

"Amen," I say. I realize that I'm growing through all this but part of me just wants it done.

Lee kindly ignores me, "Yet it is only as fully mature and strong Christians that we ultimately assume a very different role: that of priest and kings. This is the special role that John reveals to us. Let's look again at what John had to say. Ray, you're ready, read Revelation 1:4 to 6."

Ray reads, "[4] John, To the seven churches in the province of Asia: Grace and peace to you from him who is, and who was, and who is to come, and from the seven spirits before his throne,

[5] and from Jesus Christ, who is the faithful witness, the firstborn from the dead, and the ruler of the kings of the earth. To him who loves us and has freed us from our sins by his blood,

[6] and has made us to be a kingdom and priests to serve his God and Father--to him be glory and power for ever and ever! Amen."

"This is exciting stuff. Did you get that it is Christ's will that we rule with Him? Jesus doesn't need us to be kings yet He wants us to partake of His nature as He did of ours. Contrast that with Satan who is a despot and only wants us in oppression and without a voice. Christ wants us on thrones around Him ruling with Him! It's not His intent for anyone other than Him to be over us. And, that means right now—did you notice the tense John used? He said,

"..*has made* us to be a kingdom and priests...". It's already been decreed."

We're getting as excited as Lee about this.

"The question we need to ask is how do we grow from where we are now to being the kings and priests of our destiny? That question, although simple, shakes the very foundation of most churches. It got all of us turned off churches and it's driving us all nuts trying to figure this out."

This time Dusky says, "Amen." I'm glad I'm not the only once.

"Partly, we need to understand the hierarchy Jesus used with his disciples. Let's get back to Josh's expertise. How do construction workers get their training?"

Josh answers, "Apprenticing. It's not unusual in the course of construction to see up to two thirds of the labor working as apprentices. Every master builder had to apprentice at some time. I've got to tell you though that new apprentices do the dumbest things—they're our entertainment, frustration, and conflict but we can't get a project done without them."

Now Josh is laughing, "Sometimes they have just bought their very first tools. Now to an experienced person, multiple tools are used for specific jobs. To an apprentice who only owns one hammer, every situation looks like a nail ready for clobbering."

Josh goes on explaining, "An apprentice doesn't know how to read the plans and it takes a lot of patience to teach them. The big boss, in my case, me, may hire an apprentice, but it's usually the foreman who has to deal with the hands-on learning. Co-workers help out as well since it's in their best interest to train an apprentice enough to keep from being hurt by them." Josh has told me about onsite accidents and they're always by someone doing something dumb.

"By default, every new worker becomes a joint project with everyone else on the job. But the more an apprentice learns, the less likely he needs others teaching him until the point he becomes the foreman and even later becomes his own boss."

Lee asks, "That's a great and thorough explanation. So would you say that the hierarchy of a job organization helps to get the apprentice fully functional?"

Josh nods yes and explains, "Some learn in little time, others take longer. But if an apprentice stops learning, then he is of no value and will soon be replaced."

"The original church was designed to have that same kind of temporary hierarchy. Every position is supposed to be a temporary position until we all reach maturity. Before discussing the role of church offices in relation to training apprentices, let's briefly discuss the role of church apprentices."

We're following this analogy fairly easily.

"If all apprentices are doing is sitting on a pew in church all of their life without maturing, then they are the kind of worthless apprentices that should be replaced. At the same time, it is the church hierarchy that is supposed to be training everyone up to the point of eliminating the hierarchy."

"Ray," Lee asks, "do you believe this?"

Ray shrugs.

"Read Ephesians 4:11 to 13."

Ray reads, "11 It was he who gave some to be apostles, some to be prophets, some to be evangelists, and some to be pastors and teachers,

12 to prepare God's people for works of service, so that the body of Christ may be built up

13 until we all reach unity in the faith and in the knowledge of the Son of God and become mature, attaining to the whole measure of the fullness of Christ.

"Two things here—note we're talking about mature Christians and note that we're all supposed to be building each other up to that level of maturity and there seems to be an orderly process for doing so.

"Most Christians, at least Protestants, usually only think of three official roles designated within a church organization: Pastor, Elder and Deacon. However, this type of hierarchy is for operating efficiency and is not the spiritual hierarchy Christ intended for the church. As we see above, the spiritual authority of the church is in five positions (often referred to as the Five-Fold Ministry of the Holy Spirit). In descending order, these are:

1. Apostles
2. Prophets
3. Evangelists
4. Pastors
5. Teachers."

John's a stickler for details and asks, "Doesn't the Bible say something about shepherds?"

"Ephesians 4:11 is the only verse I know of that uses the term 'pastor'. I think you'll agree with me that 'pastor' is just another name for 'shepherd?'"

John agrees with TF and he continues, "Yet, what do we see taught as submission to spiritual authority? In many pulpits we hear that we are to submit our spiritual authority to our pastor. This is simply not Biblical nor does it make sense that our obligation is to the person only two rungs up from being an apprentice."

John and Josh look at each other in astonishment—they really get the depth of what Lee is saying. So do I.

"Another misconception is the belief that it is Biblical for Pastors to be subject to a board of Elders. Yet, clearly the list Paul gives us shows that Pastors are to be under Evangelists, Evangelists under Prophets and Prophets under Apostles. We have allowed tradition and assumption to define a perpetual church organization that was never intended. Worse yet, many have neglected their apprenticeship duties to mature and instead have become permanently spiritually retarded in a relationship under a human being instead of growing to authority under Christ."

Amanda has been quiet to now, "Spiritual challenged is exactly how I felt, maybe even what I expected to remain. Now it's all changed… how did that happen?" I find it interesting that she used the past tense. She must feel like I do—that we've already grown and are in the process of growing much more.

"Are you asking if the Bible claims any spiritual authority for these positions? Let us examine what the Bible reveals about spiritual authority. Amanda, read 1 Thessalonians 5:12." Lee directs.

Amanda takes over the reading duties, "Now we ask you, brothers, to respect those who work hard among you, who are over you in the Lord and who admonish you.

"Have you heard this quoted to you for reason to be submissive to your pastor? This word "respect" is the Greek word "proistemi" which means to be over someone as a protector or guardian—not as someone who has spiritual dominion over another person. They get the relationship responsibilities backward. A guardian has a duty to their ward only until that person reaches maturity. The role of a guardian is that of responsibility to the person he has been put in trust over. This same type of guardian relationship doesn't just apply to the pastor and church members. It is the same responsibility regardless of the position (i.e. apostle to prophet, prophet to evangelist, evangelist to pastor, pastor to teacher, teacher to believer). We see this same word used in 1 Timothy 3:4 as a way to describe how the children of a deacon should consider their father—it is a word used to describe the training role but it is not a description of perpetual spiritual dominion of one person over another."

"In fact, each position of authority in a church is just another rung in the apprenticeship program. If you are a teacher, then you are an apprentice pastor. If you are a pastor, then you are an apprentice evangelist."

Lee looks around to make sure we're following him and we are.

"Let's see how this works by re-examining verse 12 above: the sole role for these positions is to build up other Christians to be united in faith and to learn the full knowledge of Christ until we are mature. In verse 13, we see that these roles are only supposed to be in place ***'until'*** this happens. For us to grow into being the priest-kings Christ intends we must progress through all of these roles until we reach maturity. The emphasis is on our apprenticeship dedication and efforts—not on serving those people in positions above us. We have a two-fold problem with the five-fold ministry." Lee thinks his line is funny but we're more interested in hearing about the two-fold problem.

"First, those in position often don't understand that their efforts are to make themselves obsolete.

"And, second, and worst of all, we don't accept our responsibility as apprentices to continually grow and learn striving for the next level of responsibility."

We look to each other sharing the conviction we all feel. However, I could see sorrow on everyone's face.

Amanda starts praying, "Lord, we haven't pursued you as you would have us, but here we are now. Please forgive us, lead us, and open our eyes."

"Amen" comes from everyone.

Lee just leads on, "Does our all this mean our ultimate goal should be to become apostles? Could we actually mature to the position of apostleship? We may wonder, "Surely, we are not all supposed to be apostles?" And, it's a good question-- a question that is hotly debated. Yet, there is no doubt that the original apostles constituted the most successful apprenticeship program ever."

Josh says "Amen."

"So, let's start by asking another question: Who were the original 12 apostles and who ended up replacing Judas Iscariot? Look at the list of the original apostles."

"Jules, it's your turn to read for a while, start with Mark 3:16-19."

Jules does, "[16] These are the twelve he appointed: Simon (to whom he gave the name Peter);

[17] James son of Zebedee and his brother John (to them he gave the name Boanerges, which means Sons of Thunder);

[18] Andrew, Philip, Bartholomew, Matthew, Thomas, James son of Alphaeus, Thaddaeus, Simon the Zealot

[19] and Judas Iscariot, who betrayed him.

"OK, now Jules, name the gospels."

"Matthew, Mark, Luke and John—wait, Luke and Mark aren't apostles."

"We'll get to that. What we see named are 12 apostles plus another 70 people we don't know by name but probably include Mark and Luke all of whom were sent out on missions. Out of that group we find only one who drops out: Judas Iscariot. After Judas died, the apostles decided to select another person from the apprentices to fill in the vacancy. Peter defined for everyone what experiences the apprentice replacement needed. Jules, please read Acts 1:20 to 26."

She does, "[20] For," said Peter, "it is written in the book of Psalms, "'May his place be deserted; let there be no one to dwell in it,' and, "'May another take his place of leadership.'

[21] Therefore it is necessary to choose one of the men who have been with us the whole time the Lord Jesus went in and out among us,

[22] beginning from John's baptism to the time when Jesus was taken up from us. For one of these must become a witness with us of his resurrection." [23] So they proposed two men: Joseph called Barsabbas (also known as Justus) and Matthias.

[24] Then they prayed, "Lord, you know everyone's heart. Show us which of these two you have chosen [25] to take over this apostolic ministry, which Judas left to go where he belongs."

26 Then they cast lots, and the lot fell to Matthias; so he was added to the eleven apostles.

Jules wants to know, "This is how the apostles decide who to choose—by gambling?"

"The Bible tells us about people casting lots and the assumption was that the Lord made the outcome. So, they didn't consider it as gambling. But I think you missed the criteria.

"It appears as if they wanted someone that shared the same experiences with them. Here we see a definition for the first time of who qualified to be an apostle: someone who had been with them the whole time from Christ's baptism by John until Christ's ascension. These two events are important to consider because both were attested to by heaven."

Jules, read about Christ's baptism in Mark 1:9-11."

"OK, 11 At that time Jesus came from Nazareth in Galilee and was baptized by John in the Jordan.

10 As Jesus was coming up out of the water, he saw heaven being torn open and the Spirit descending on him like a dove.

11 And a voice came from heaven: "You are my Son, whom I love; with you I am well pleased."

"Now, read about his ascension in Acts 1:9-11."

Jules reads, "9 After he said this, he was taken up before their very eyes, and a cloud hid him from their sight.

10 They were looking intently up into the sky as he was going, when suddenly two men dressed in white stood beside them.

11 "Men of Galilee," they said, "why do you stand here looking into the sky? This same Jesus, who has been taken from you into heaven, will come back in the same way you have seen him go into heaven."

"There initially seems to be a practical side to their requirements-- an apprentice who shared these experiences knew for whom they worked. At Christ's baptism, we see the interaction of the Godhead: Christ being baptized; the Holy Spirit as a dove; and, God the Father speaking. Someone who experienced that knew the intimacy of the Godhead.

"At Christ's ascension we have the testimony of two angels promising Christ's return. The ability for a new apostle to testify to both the historical things accomplished by Christ as well as to the heavenly testimony pronounced over Him seems critical for the apostles to choose a replacement.

"It also makes being an Apostle unique to just a few—no one else could qualify in subsequent generations," the usually quiet TF states.

"You're right," agrees Lee, "all of this makes sense and means that only a few could have ever been called to apostles. It also means that it was a historic position and could not have been passed down to new generations of believers. That is what it could have meant, should have meant, and would neatly end our obligation to mature to that point ...BUT... then along came Paul."

"The Apostle who would not follow the criteria," I chip in.

"Exactly," agrees Lee. "After all these years, Paul is still a bit of a trouble maker. We cannot come to a neat conclusion about the apostle-position because of him. For Saul, later to be called Paul, was not an apprentice. Yet, why do we call him an apostle?"

No one bites so Lee says, "Dawn, read Romans 1:1 to 4."

I clear my throat, "1 Paul, a servant of Christ Jesus, **called to be an apostle** and set apart for the gospel of God—

2 the gospel he promised beforehand through his prophets in the Holy Scriptures

3 regarding his Son, who as to his human nature was a descendant of David,

[4] and who through the Spirit of holiness was declared with power to be the Son of God by his resurrection from the dead: Jesus Christ our Lord."

"Why do we call him an Apostle? We call Paul an Apostle because that is what he claimed to be. Did he meet the criteria laid down by the Apostles when they replaced Judas?" Lee asks.

Ray says, "No."

"Paul never heard the heavenly proclamations over Jesus. He never mentions witnessing the life of Jesus. He didn't even personally know the apostles before his conversion—if he did, he probably would have killed them. Yet, here he claims to be an apostle—actually that he had no choice because he was called to be an Apostle. What kind of an Apostle could he be under the circumstances and given the lack of qualifications previously defined?

"Dawn, read Romans 11:13."

I do, " ..**Inasmuch as I am the apostle to the Gentiles**."

I can't help raising my voice over some of this as I get more excited over the growing definition of being an Apostle. I'm not shouting, just emphasizing what I feel.

Continuing Lee explains, "Paul describes himself as the apostle to the Gentiles. As in capital T, capital H, capital E—THE. Was Paul really "the", as in the only, apostle to the Gentiles (non-Jewish people)?"

He answers his own question, "The Greek can just as easily be rendered without "the" making him one of the apostles to the Gentiles—which would be historically more accurate. After all it is a historical fact that many other apostles reached out to the Gentiles especially after Jerusalem and the temple was destroyed. For example, it is accepted that Bartholomew and Thaddeus founded the Armenian church and lived there until they died. Mark founded the Coptic church in Egypt. The majority of the other churches founded by apostles banded together and defined what became known today as the Orthodox church."

Wade is nodding heavily agreeing from his perspective as well.

"Eventually all the apostles (who lived long enough) ministered to the Gentiles. But, to this day, Paul's voice still speaks uniquely to us Gentiles."

I feel like I still share the floor and ask, "Was there any other criteria Paul claimed for a basis of being an apostle?"

"Yes, Dawn read 1 Corinthians 1:1."

I read, "Paul, called to be **an apostle of Christ Jesus by the will of God**". Again my voice emphasizes the "apostle" position as I internally am getting a clearer picture of what an Apostle means.

"So, by Paul's criteria, his apostleship was not based on being recruited, having an apprenticeship, or experiencing the same testimony as the other Apostles. Instead of these criteria, Paul basis his apostleship on the will of God. And no other Apostle ever challenged that."

Dawn, last verse for a while. Please read 1 Corinthians 9:1 and 2."

I do, "1 Am I not free? Am I not an apostle? Have I not seen Jesus our Lord? Are you not the result of my work in the Lord?

2 Even though I may not be an apostle to others, surely I am to you! For you are the seal of my apostleship in the Lord."

Amanda and I seem to be in sync tonight and she says as if for me, "But, surely there must be common criteria with the other apostles that qualified Paul."

Lee takes that up, "In fact, there is a common criterion that Paul shares: he saw Jesus. That is not to say he met Christ while he was on this earth. Let's revisit what Paul experienced, I'll read Acts 9:1-7."

"[1] Meanwhile, Saul was still breathing out murderous threats against the Lord's disciples. He went to the high priest

[2] and asked him for letters to the synagogues in Damascus, so that if he found any there who belonged to the Way, whether men or women, he might take them as prisoners to Jerusalem.

[3] As he neared Damascus on his journey, suddenly a light from heaven flashed around him.

[4] He fell to the ground and heard a voice say to him, "Saul, Saul, why do you persecute me?"

[5] "Who are you, Lord?" Saul asked. "I am Jesus, whom you are persecuting," he replied.

[6] "Now get up and go into the city, and you will be told what you must do."

[7] The men traveling with Saul stood there speechless; they heard the sound but did not see anyone."

"One personal experience with Jesus and Paul believes he was as called to his apostleship as any of the other Apostles. Being an Apostle was not designated to Paul-- Christ did not tell Paul he was an Apostle. At least we have no record of Jesus saying that to Paul. However, unlike Paul, Jesus did indeed designate the other 12 as apostles in such a way as to provide a greater understanding for what the position means.

"No more picking on Dawn, let's get back to Dusky—after all it is the proper order." Lee thinks he's funny but we've heard this too many times to even groan. "Dusky, read Mark 3:14 and 15."

She reads, "[14] He appointed twelve--designating them apostles --that they might be with him and that he might send them out to preach

[15] and to have authority to drive out demons.

"This designation made by Christ gets at the heart of the meaning of "apostle". The word for Apostle is actually a combination of two Greek root words.

"The first word is "Apo". I got the following definitions from www.blueletterbible.org:

1) of separation

a) of local separation, after verbs of motion from a place i.e. of departing, of fleeing

b) of separation of a part from the whole

1) where of a whole some part is taken

c) of any kind of separation of one thing from another by which the union or fellowship of the two is destroyed

d) of a state of separation, that is of distance

1) physical, of distance of place

2) temporal, of distance of time

2) of origin

a) of the place whence anything is, comes, befalls, is taken

b) of origin of a cause"

The second word is "Stello" and it means:

1) to set, place, set in order, arrange

a) to fit out, to prepare, equip

b) to prepare one's self, to fit out for one's self

c) to fit out for one's own use

d) to prepare one's self, to fit out for one's self

e) to fit out for one's own use

1) arranging, providing for this, etc.

2) to bring together, contract, shorten

a) to diminish, check, cause to cease

b) to cease to exist

c) to remove one's self, withdraw one's self, to depart

d) to abstain from familiar intercourse with one

"That's a long explanation. I understand from Ray that he's been sharing these multiple definitions with his family. They certainly provide more of an idea for the meaning in a foreign word—something our English does not address adequately."

"So, the combined word, 'apostellos' is the act of setting aside and sending someone. That person then is an 'apostolos' which literally means a messenger— that is someone sent by command. Another way to say it is a person who has a mission. In the book of Romans we saw that Paul said he was the 'apostle' that is the one sent to the Gentiles—that was his mission."

"Wait." Amanda interrupts, "if the meaning of an apostle means one sent, then were there other people designated in the Bible as apostles besides Matthias, Paul and the original surviving 11?"

"Great question and the answer is 'yes'," Lee is happy for the interruption. "There are other people who are called apostles. Let's take a look. Amanda, read Romans 16:7."

She does, "Greet Andronicus and Junias, my relatives who have been in prison with me. They are outstanding among the apostles, and they were in Christ before I was."

"So," continues Amanda, "Andronicus and Junias are apostles?"

Lee nods, "Not only are Andronicus and Junias described as apostles, but the implication is that there were more apostles that Paul was referring to since these two were 'outstanding' among the apostles."

"Anyone want to guess who else was named an apostle?

Ray speaks up, "Wasn't Barnabas was also referred to as an apostle?

"Yes! Do you know the verse?" Lee asks but Ray shakes his head. "Try Acts 14:14."

Ray emphasizes the names he reads, "But when **the apostles Barnabas and Paul** heard of this, they tore their clothes and rushed out into the crowd, shouting".

"One of the reasons why we have a hard time with the term apostle is that it's not always translated the same. For example, Epaphroditus was also called an 'apostolos'—but in this case apostle is translated as 'messenger'. Read Philippians 2:25.

Ray reads, "But I think it is necessary to send back to you Epaphroditus, my brother, fellow worker and fellow soldier, who is also your **messenger**, whom you sent to take care of my needs."

"Someone on a mission always has a message—translating apostle to messenger makes sense," Amanda notes.

"I like that," says Lee. "If the definition of an 'apostle' is not so much a title but rather accepted as the description of one chosen by Christ and sent on a mission, then apostles could easily be a role for people today. Our question is whether the definition of one sent, a messenger, really holds up whenever the word 'apostle' is referred to—and I think it does.

I'm beginning to think so as well. What does the future hold for me, for us? Apostle Dawn?

Lee is just getting wound up, "Let's examine one specific Bible text where we find a person called an apostle but they are not chosen by Christ… and neither are they from this earth. We couldn't guess this person because believe it or not, it is Christ Himself."

Ray's jaw drops open at that. "Read Hebrews 3:1."

Ray reads, "Therefore, holy brothers, who share in the heavenly calling, fix your thoughts on Jesus, **the apostle** and high priest whom we confess.

Ray asks, "Christ is an apostle? How could that be?"

TF breaks his silence again, "Going to the literal definition of the word 'apostle' as being 'one sent', Christ does indeed meet the definition of an apostle, the One sent by God the Father."

Lee says, "Let's overlook the other times the Bible says Christ was sent. John, your turn again, read Mark 1:12 to 13."

"[12] At once the Spirit sent him out into the desert,

[13] and he was in the desert forty days, being tempted by Satan. He was with the wild animals, and angels attended him."

"I see that Jesus was sent by the Holy Spirit," John summarizes.

"Check out Mark 9:37."

John reads, ""Whoever welcomes one of these little children in my name welcomes me; and whoever welcomes me does not welcome me but the one who sent me."

Again summarizing, John offers, "Obviously Jesus is saying that the Father sent Him. Are there other times that the Bible says Jesus was sent?"

"Yes, lets read them quickly—try Luke 4:18 to 19."

John reads, "[18] The Spirit of the Lord is on me, because he has anointed me to preach good news to the poor. He has sent me to proclaim freedom for the prisoners and recovery of sight for the blind, to release the oppressed,

[19] to proclaim the year of the Lord's favor."

"Now try Luke 4:43," says Lee.

John reads, "But he said, "I must preach the good news of the kingdom of God to the other towns also, because that is why I was sent."

"John 4:34."

John reads, "My food," said Jesus, "is to do the will of him who sent me and to finish his work.

"John 5:22 to 24."

"22 Moreover, the Father judges no one, but has entrusted all judgment to the Son,

23 that all may honor the Son just as they honor the Father. He who does not honor the Son does not honor the Father, who sent him.

24 "I tell you the truth, whoever hears my word and believes him who sent me has eternal life and will not be condemned; he has crossed over from death to life.

"Now look up John 5:36 to 38."

John continues, "36 I have testimony weightier than that of John. For the very work that the Father has given me to finish, and which I am doing, testifies that the Father has sent me.

37 And the Father who sent me has himself testified concerning me. You have never heard his voice nor seen his form,

38 nor does his word dwell in you, for you do not believe the one he sent."

"John 6:28 and 29."

Again, our John reads, "28 Then they asked him, "What must we do to do the works God requires?"

29 Jesus answered, "The work of God is this: to believe in the one he has sent."

Josh adds, "The criteria for us to do the work of God is to believe that Jesus was sent by Him?"

"Right on, brother," shouts TF.

Lee is not through. "Jesus was an apostle because He was sent by God. He was a messenger and He had a mission. If our role is to emulate Christ, then we must ask: Can we be apostles? There is no reason to doubt that we can be apostles. Because literally, whenever the Holy Spirit directs you to a mission, you too are an apostle. Every day we fulfill that role in many ways but we also have a primary mission. What is our primary mission our Father calls us to? We cannot even be in a relationship with Jesus unless we respond to the call of God. I'm reading from John 6:44."

"No one can come to me unless the Father who sent me draws him, and I will raise him up at the last day.

"Isn't that amazing," queries Lee. "The reality of being called to Christ is that we are sent to Him by the Father. It is only by the Father's direction we find Jesus. Therefore, we all are in fact apostles because we have been sent by the Father. Furthermore, all those called to Christ have accepted His great mission."

TF read Mark 16:15 to 18.

"[15] He said to them, "Go into all the world and preach the good news to all creation.

[16] Whoever believes and is baptized will be saved, but whoever does not believe will be condemned.

[17] And these signs will accompany those who believe: In my name they will drive out demons; they will speak in new tongues;

[18] they will pick up snakes with their hands; and when they drink deadly poison, it will not hurt them at all; they will place their hands on sick people, and they will get well."

"I had TF read that because not long ago he started putting all this into action. He can tell you personally that it is possible to drive out demons and heal people—we know that one house here learned they can pick up poisonous snakes with their bare hands. We are becoming apostles!"

"Amen!" We all say.

"Up until now our spiritual apprenticeship has only led us through verses 15 and 16. Yet, the maturity we are called to exceeds talking and baptizing. We fulfill part of our mission but have lacked the authority of mature faith and the signs that accompany it. Too often we have been told we can't be apostles and if we can't be apostles, then how could we do signs? But, if we indeed can be apostles, then can we really progress to that point of authority?"

Looking at each of us, "Are you ready to pursue that type of authority no matter how many more changes come in your life?"

"Yes," again we say in unity.

"Part of what we are really asking is if we are to be apostles, then does that mean we can be prophets, evangelists, pastors and teachers as well? Of course it does. Everyone who accepts that Jesus is coming again and tells others is prophesying. Every believer has to be a prophet and testify of the judgment day or he is not a true believer. Very few people ever ask the Holy Spirit for the great gift of prophecy but at their heart, every Christian must be a prophet to believe in that which has not happened and cannot be seen."

"But," Dusky desires to know, "doesn't Paul tells us that we are to be zealous for, covet—greatly desire greater gifts and by implication, greater offices or positions?"

"Do you remember where that verse is?" Lee asks her. After she looks for a while and without finding it he reads, "1 Corinthians 12:29 to 31. 29 Are all apostles? Are all prophets? Are all teachers? Do all work miracles?

30 Do all have gifts of healing? Do all speak in tongues ? Do all interpret?

31 But eagerly desire the greater gifts. And now I will show you the most excellent way."

"The word `eagerly' is in Greek `zeloo'. In case we miss the meaning of how we are to burn to grow greater, let me read the blueletterbible.org definition:

1) to burn with zeal

a) to be heated or to boil with envy, hatred, anger

1) in a good sense, to be zealous in the pursuit of good

b) to desire earnestly, pursue

1) to desire one earnestly, to strive after, busy one's self about him

2) to exert one's self for one (that he may not be torn from me)
3) to be the object of the zeal of others, to be zealously sought after
c) to envy"

"I take that to mean that if we are not performing miracles or performing the functions of the next higher office, then we're to be diligently, relentlessly, earnestly desiring and pursuing the next greater thing. For example, if you're a pastor, then be on fire to become an evangelist.

"I really read this as saying Paul will show you the way to do the thing you desire to do in the Lord—that it's all part of what we're to accomplish.

"To get back to the apprenticeship, let's consider being an evangelist. That is the call for every believer as well. Pastors and Teachers administer mainly to those already believing—evangelizing is what we do to recruit new believers. Pastoring and teaching focuses on growing people to be mature enough to evangelize. I tell people all the time, if there are pastors in your church and teachers in your church, then go look in the mirror for the evangelist. That is one of our roles and if you're not fulfilling it, then you are ignoring the commission the Lord gave you.

"As I said before, many churches believe that pastoring is a position of spiritual authority over the church congregation. In fact, the reality is the other way around. The church is supposed to be using its spiritual authority to provide protection for the pastor. So many pastors are left at the whim of their congregation and demanded of to the point where they have nothing left for their own needs."

"Amen to that," TF wants to discuss. "A well known psychological fact is that people who suppress anger are often over weight. Look at the amount of over weight pastors and guess at the underlying anger issue— the issue is how little support congregations provide their pastors and how little consideration they show them as brothers in Christ. I got to the point I wouldn't answer the phone after 6

PM because it was mostly the same people with the same problems that after 6 PM became my emergency."

We knew some of the people who frequently called TF and none of them had emergencies…only chronic problems that mostly were from their own doings.

"For just a second, let us review something we read in previous chapters regarding our role in relationship to pastors. Have you ever studied who provided spiritual authority to the Levitical priests? TF, read Numbers 8:9 and 10."

TF does, "[9] Bring the Levites to the front of the Tent of Meeting and assemble the whole Israelite community.

[10] You are to bring the Levites before the LORD, and the Israelites are to lay their hands on them.

"Pastors, like the Old Testament priests, derive their spiritual offices from the authority granted to them—it is not an authority over people but from people for specific tasks. We don't grant that authority anymore. Our spiritual authority is not transferred to any man or any position but instead is always ours to account for directly between Jesus and us individually. In fact, Jesus told us specifically to not allow any person to be put in positions over us. TF, I know we're getting to something close to your heart, please read Matthew 23:8 to 10."

TF does, "[8] But you are not to be called 'Rabbi,' for you have only one Master and you are all brothers.

[9] And do not call anyone on earth 'father,' for you have one Father, and he is in heaven.

[10] Nor are you to be called 'teacher,' for you have one Teacher, the Christ.

Holding up his hand, TF says, "Let me follow up with John 10:11. 'I am the good shepherd. The good shepherd lays down his life for the sheep.'"

"Wait, now Hebrews 13:20 and 21. '[20] May the God of peace, who through the blood of the eternal covenant brought back from the dead our Lord Jesus, that great Shepherd of the sheep,

[21] equip you with everything good for doing his will, and may he work in us what is pleasing to him, through Jesus Christ, to whom be glory for ever and ever. Amen.'"

"This is important teaching," I feel like I'm interrupting but quickly add, "but I have two points to make." Tonight has gone on at such a fast pace with such detailed information that I haven't known how to break in without interrupting. I've got everyone's attention.

"My first point to make is about what Jesus said to Peter after the resurrection…He asked Peter three times, 'Do you love me?' Peter denied him three times before Jesus was killed and now Jesus lets him say three times back that he loves Jesus. Right after that Jesus tells him to "feed my sheep." That's how Peter was to love him—by taking care of His flock not being the new shepherd."

Lee nods, "That's in John 21:17. You're right, Jesus makes it clear that others may feed but He alone is the Shepherd. What's your second point?"

I can see that everyone suspects something much more profound. I hate to pop that bubble but just out right say, "My bladder is about to bust."

Just reading Bible texts for so long has been interesting but almost impossible for me to concentrate on any more over a full bladder. I stand up to go to the bathroom and Dusky puts her hands on my shoulders pushing me back down.

"After me, you're next," Dusky whisks past me down the hall. Jules looks at me and laughs. "She's pretty good at that. Must have been a challenge growing up with her."

John says, "It's still a challenge."

We all stand up and stretch. We sense we're in the middle of a great learning experience but at the same time we are hesitant to pause, we're also protective about keeping a high level of focus.

Lee disappears into the kitchen and returns with bottles of water for everyone. He doesn't even ask and just puts them out on the table in front of each chair. Josh and John are talking about spiritual authority and the way that Pastor Bill has abused his position. Jules and Amanda quietly listen in. Ray ducks out the back door and behind a tree. I swear, that kid will pee on a tree any chance he gets and here we are in downtown Portland.

"Your turn," Dusky pats my shoulder. I laugh and take leave.

Coming back into the room I see that everyone is sitting down and we're ready to resume. Good. Even though it's a long night, I'm not ready to leave. This study is too important.

TF clears his throat to get our attention and takes over for awhile for this truly is his issue. "A shepherd is essentially the same name as pastor—that is the literal translation in both Hebrew and Greek. If Christ said do not call anyone "Rabbi" (reverend), "Father" or "Teacher" because those titles belong to Him and the Father, then what do you think He wants us to do about the term "Pastor" when only He is the Good Pastor? Of course we are not to be using this term or elevating people to some special type of holiness or ungodly spiritual authority over us. We have the Good Shepherd and that is our **ONLY** pastor."

"TF, you persuaded me some time ago about this, but I think there's something even more powerful about this than you're stressing," John barely can interrupt TF's fast pace. "I don't know what it is, yet, but keep going, please."

TF needs no encouragement, "When we renounce all spiritual authority except for what is directly from Christ, then we are free to grow to be apostles under Christ's direction. Teachers, Pastors, Evangelists, and Prophets do not have a duty to control believers but instead have a duty to develop believers to mature to become apostles. What good does that do-- what did apostles do that was different from other positions?"

Lee takes back over, "Allow me to read a couple of verses that explains the role of apostles. Let's start with Mark 3:14 and 15."

"[14] He appointed twelve--designating them apostles --that they might be with him and that he might send them out to preach

[15] and to have authority to drive out demons.

"Now I'm reading Luke 10:9-- Heal the sick who are there and tell them, 'The kingdom of God is near you.'"

Lee is not turning the conversation back over to TF and continues, "We see that Christ before He died had the apostles drive out demons, heal the sick, and tell the people that the kingdom of God *"is near"*. Not in a location such as around the block "near" but instead, it was a statement of time as in "nearly here".

I've never got that before. They're right, the English language just doesn't capture the intent of the Bible very well.

"While generations of Christians have been waiting for the pending kingdom of God, we have abdicated our authority in that kingdom by thinking it is delayed. It is not delayed, it is now. Those who think the kingdom of God is waiting for Christ's return to earth simply do not understand what the Bible says. The best way to understand that is to ask, 'where is Christ right now'?"

"So, Amanda, let me ask you, 'Where is Jesus right now?" Lee pauses for Amanda to think about it.

"I've heard some preachers say He is in the heavenly temple offering His blood for us as a perpetual High Priest. I have a friend who tries to tell me that since a certain date He's been in the Judgment room judging us." She stops and says, "I really don't know."

"Then read Ephesians 1:17 to 21" Lee directs.

Amanda reads, "[17] I keep asking that the God of our Lord Jesus Christ, the glorious Father, may give you the Spirit of wisdom and revelation, so that you may know him better.

[18] I pray also that the eyes of your heart may be enlightened in order that you may know the hope to which he has called you, the riches of his glorious inheritance in the saints,

[19] and his incomparably great power for us who believe. That power is like the working of his mighty strength,

[20] which he exerted in Christ when he raised him from the dead and seated him at his right hand in the heavenly realms, [21] far above all rule and authority, power and dominion, and every title that can be given, not only in the present age but also in the one to come.

"Then Jesus is in the throne room ruling now with God?" Amanda wants clarification.

"You got it! Paul in Ephesians states that Christ is in heaven in this present age—in other words, right now. What is Christ doing in heaven right now?" Lee asks Amanda to read again, "Colossians 3:1."

"Since, then, you have been raised with Christ, set your hearts on things above, where Christ is seated at the right hand of God.

Lee nods his thanks to Amanda and says, "The image here is not that of someone in his Lazy Boy recliner, just sitting in heaven. No, this is of a king on a throne—in fact, THE KING OF KINGS. What do kings do on a throne? They rule. Look again at the place where Christ sits, it is a throne. Read Hebrews 8:1."

Amanda is still the designated reader, "The point of what we are saying is this: We do have such a high priest, who sat down at the right hand of the throne of the Majesty in heaven,"

Ray breaks in, "I have a favorite verse about this. It's Hebrews 12:2." Ray reads, "Let us fix our eyes on Jesus, the author and perfecter of our faith, who for the joy set before him endured the cross, scorning its shame, and sat down at the right hand of the throne of God.

Lee looks at TF and smiles—Ray is on to where they are going. Lee continues, "Thanks, Ray, great verse. Now we know one of Christ's heavenly activities while ruling over us—He is actively authoring and perfecting our individual faith. Jesus is actively involved in our salvation. In fact, that is the whole goal of His reign—to bring salvation to its fulfillment. And when salvation overcomes all the obstacles of this world, it leads us directly to His side. That's where He wants us, it is what He continues to work for, and that should comfort us all. Ray, read Revelation 3:21."

"To him who overcomes, I will give the right to sit with me on my throne, just as I overcame and sat down with my Father on his throne."

"But," Jules is trying to choose her words delicately, "I've always been taught that Jesus won't rule until he comes again. That's not what we've read tonight."

"You're right," it's not what the Bible says but it is what's taught as church doctrine. To sum up what the Bible says, Christ is on His throne. He has taken up His kingdom and will never, ever relent from ruling. Right now, Christ rules in the middle of his enemies. But, there is coming a time when God will put all the enemies under Christ's feet and we saw that at the final judgment the last great enemy to die is death."

"What do you think about that?" Lee asks Jules. She doesn't answer so he says, "Read Psalms 110:1 to 2."

Jules reads, "1 Of David. A psalm. The LORD says to my Lord: "Sit at my right hand until I make your enemies a footstool for your feet."

2 The LORD will extend your mighty scepter from Zion; you will rule in the midst of your enemies."

"Now read 1 Corinthians 15:21 to 26." Lee tells her.

She does, "21 For since death came through a man, the resurrection of the dead comes also through a man.

22 For as in Adam all die, so in Christ all will be made alive.

23 But each in his own turn: Christ, the firstfruits; then, when he comes, those who belong to him.

24 Then the end will come, when he hands over the kingdom to God the Father after he has destroyed all dominion, authority and power.

25 For he must reign until he has put all his enemies under his feet.

26 The last enemy to be destroyed is death.

Jules comments, "Then Jesus is ruling now?"

To answer, Lee nods and says, "So, if Christ is ruling, then the kingdom is not just near as John the Baptist cried out: instead it is NOW. Christ ruled before He came to this world and He returned to rule His kingdom as only a victorious king may. If He had failed, then like any king, He would not have His kingdom. But, He did not fail because by His power He overcame."

"I think what Jules has not been saying is this—the Christianity we've been raised...I mean reared with..." Ray stops to find the right words.

I remind him all the time that animals and vegetables are raised, people are reared. Glad to know that it is sinking in but wonder what he's struggling to say.

"Crap, there's no good way to say this. The Christianity I've been taught is weak, wishy-washy, and doesn't have the power of God. Even what Mom and Dad are going through now, where is the power of God?'

Not everyone knows what we talked about with Lee today. He looks at Josh and says, "That has been my stumbling block as well—to believe that the power of God is postponed or not effective. When you believe that, then the only alternative is to believe that the control in your life rests in your own hands. And, that's a miserable lie to live with and leads to doing miserable things." I feel the pain from what he confidentially told us earlier.

Lee's chin is trembling and his eyes are filled with tears. He can't go right now and TF senses that and takes over directing Ray, "Read 1 Corinthians 4:20"

"For the kingdom of God is not a matter of talk but of power."

Ray shouts out, "That's what I'm talking about!"

TF continues the conversation, "And, if the kingdom is now, then why don't we each have the power of miracles? Is it because we have failed to become mature Christians that can be used as apostles for God appointed missions? Can you see that we give up spiritual authority when we place ourselves under the authority of another person, like a teacher or a pastor? If we fail to become mature and reach the fullness of Christ as we are directed to do, then how can we have the authority of Christ? In short, if Christians were today driving out demons, healing people, and explaining that the kingdom of God is now here, would there be a beneficial impact on this world?"

John has something to say, "We, that is Dusky and I went to a faith healing meeting when a national TV evangelist came to town. You see him knocking people on the TV stage all the time—pretty dramatic."

Dusky never told me about this. I didn't tell her about making fun of pompadour hair healer when he was on TV.

"We saw people in the audience all around us being healed. There were 17,000 people in the stadium— all praying and the results were pretty amazing. But, that wasn't what was going on the stage—all of that seemed choreographed. And, there were endless calls for offerings. So, right in the middle of what felt like manipulation were true healings and genuine prayers. It was very confusing."

"I've been to those meetings in Seattle and Portland. I know exactly what you're talking about." TF agrees, "It is confusing. The one thing I thought of later is that if all those people had been taught to heal and carry on the works of Jesus, then can you imagine how society would be changed? 17,000 people leaving the stadium and healing 17,000 more before the day was out, Then the next day those 34, 000 people heal 34,000 more? What a shame to neglect the apprenticeship duties to grow on!"

"Is it possible," John still has the floor, "for us as sinners to have healing powers?"

John still has doubts about what we're learning.

"Let me explain about the indwelling of God." TF responds. "You wonder whether we are supposed to be exercising Christ's authority today... should we really be driving out demons and healing people? Let's take a look at what Christ said about this. John, please read John 14:12 ."

John reads, "I tell you the truth, anyone who has faith in me will do what I have been doing. He will do even greater things than these, because I am going to the Father."

Lee rejoins and asks John, "Who does Jesus say will do what he's been doing?"

John feels like there's some kind of trap or trick answer. He re-reads the verse silently before stating the obvious, "Anyone."

"Anyone?" Lee asks. "Even 50 generations and 2,000 years later—us '***anyones***'?

This is starting to really sink in to us all and we all nod.

"That's what Christ said. And, He said it is '***the truth***'. I'm emphasizing 'THE TRUTH' because what is it He says is true? That truth is: Anyone of us can be doing what He did—water to wine, disease to health, demons cast out, leprosy to vitality, death to life—"anyone" of us can do that. But how? How do we get that kind of power?"

We all are paying attention now. We're all tired of having our butts kicked by evil. How do we overcome?

"The first misunderstanding to correct is that we do not get that authority by seeking power separately from seeking Him. Whatever gifts we strive for must be in connection with serving Him more and more. Seeking power separate from the relationship is a stumbling block for Christians trying to grow to maturity. As we mature, we find that God the Father does not impart His power to us—instead, He puts His kingdom inside us—He dwells inside us so that He in us does what He did in Christ. That's the source of our authority—His indwelling. That's why we must mature in Christ so that He can rule within us and without the confusion and sabotage of our earthly nature. That is why we must continually seek greater and greater gifts and growth in authority because we are in reality seeking for Him to expand in us." Lee turns to TF and asks, "Please read John 14:23."

TF reads, "Jesus replied, "If anyone loves me, he will obey my teaching. My Father will love him, and we will come to him and make our home with him.

Lee looks suddenly looks tired. This day has been very emotional for him.

"I forewarned you that we might not get through all this tonight. We're only about halfway through and I'd like to stop now."

The rest of us are not that tired but I say on our behalf, "Lee, we appreciate how you've been teaching us. Ray always double checks your scriptures."

Ray's a little embarrassed but adds, "And you've been right on every time."

"You learn a lot by double checking, don't you?" TF wants to know from Ray.

He shakes his head, "Oh, yeah. More than I ever learned in Sunday School."

Josh notices it first. I see him looking at it and turn to find what he sees.

It's a bright pink balloon half filled with helium bouncing up against the sliding glass door. Even from here I can see the yellow lacey chord tied around the bottom with a piece of paper tucked in.

TF notices what we're looking at and quickly walks over, opens the door and retrieves the paper from the balloon.

Now everyone is watching, "What does it say?" Amanda asks for all of us.

"It says, 'Four days until a time of testing.'"

Wade abruptly cuts in, "I've had the lab look at those ribbons or chords, whatever you want to call them. They're old—like maybe even 16th century old. Probably from Belgium—guess it was a specialty for them at the time. The guess is that the original color was white. But, I haven't been able to figure out any meaning for these things. This is no accidental use—but why?"

"I don't know, but let's not get away from the four day notice. Can we meet again in two days?" I'm worrying because everything about The Shadow seems threatening.

Lee answers, "Can't do in two days. TF and I are meeting with a home church for the first time. How about Wednesday?"

There's no stopping us for Wednesday. We want to finish learning the next half before the warning kicks in.

Lee prays for us before we stand to leave, "Father, Jesus, come dwell in us, live in us, be the power in us and through us. Allow the works of Jesus to continue to praise you by what He does through us. Amen."

14
WHAT ROLES DOWN HILL

WE'RE NOT IN NORMAL ROUTINES ANYMORE. Instead of watching TV, Ray has installed a copy of QuickVerse on everyone's computers and we're all studying the Bible more and more. That's not to say we're doing this in isolation. Instead, we're talking more than we ever have. Since we all have portable computers with WIFI connections, we're even doing our computer research together in the dining room. That was Ray's idea but I suspect the proximity to food is a criterion for him.

Tonight we go back to TF's for dinner. I plan on asking he and Lee more about the home churches they're starting up today. I'm not sure how home churches would differ so much from regular churches but want to learn. However the big thing on my mind is that tomorrow is the fourth day. I wonder if the warning means something bad will happen on the fourth day or if it means after the fourth day? Dusky and I had the same dilemma as kids—did we go on the count of three or after the count of three? Countdowns bring anxiety.

I recall The Shadow when he was out at the mailbox. I remember feeling this power about him but still wonder if it's all good, all bad, or if he's just screwing with our lives at a time we're vulnerable?

The kids think he's someone good. But why would he hide behind the same images over the years? Obviously, it can't be the same person so he's taken a lot of effort to look like the same person. That alone seems sinister to me.

I sit in front of my laptop and search Google for the New York Secretary of State's website. I find it. One of the listings says, "Corporation Division" and I go to that. On the left side of the screen is a choice to "Search The Corporation/Business Entity Database." I choose that.

Could it be this easy to find out who Markos really is? Just trace down his publishing company?

The search screen wants to know what name to look for and I enter, "Dunamis." Seven names come back but none of them are what I'm after.

I try again and enter "Anastasis." This time I get the following on screen:

NYS Department of State
Division of Corporations
Entity Information

Selected Entity Name: Anastasis Dunamis Co.

Selected Entity Status Information

Current Entity Name: ANASTASIS DUNAMIS CO.

Initial DOS Filing Date: March 21, 1860

County: New York

Jurisdiction:

Entity Type: FOREIGN BUSINESS CORPORATION

Selected Entity Address Information

DOS Process (Address to which DOS will mail process if accepted on behalf of entity)

Herbert Johnson
199 White Street
New York, New York, 10038

Registered Agent

NONE

NOTE: New York State does not issue organizational identification numbers.

"What am I supposed to think about that?" I wonder.

I decide to find out who Herbert Johnson is. I call up **www.dexonline.com** and try entering his name under the Business Search. I suspect he's a lawyer.

Nothing turns up under Herbert Johnson.

I try the Residence Search and find a half dozen Herbert Johnsons but nothing that necessarily ties them to the business address.

So, I call up a separate window for Mapquest.com and enter the address in it. I find the office location quickly. It's in a business district in Manhattan. That's not going to help. I thought I might be able to look through the Residence Category and find an "H Walker" living nearby. I found over a hundred 'H Walkers' but nothing to suggest by location who the company man would be.

I started calling the private residence listings. I printed off the names and stop for just a second to rehearse, "Hi, are you the Herbert Walker representing Anastasis Dunamis?"

That seems too long. I try again. "Hello, is this where I reach Anastasis Dunamis?"

That's better—simple, direct, if it's not Walker then maybe someone will direct me.

I call the first name and get a message asking me to leave my name and phone number. I didn't think about whether I want to do that or not and just hang up.

The second Walker answers and says, "I have no idea what you're talking about." I thank him and hang up.

The third Walker hangs up on me. Guess it's an example of those famous New York manners.

The next call the man simply says he can't help.

This time a woman answers but she can't help either.

I'm thinking about calling back the first number but decide to first to call the last number on the list. I tell him the same thing, "Hello, is there where I reach Anastasis Dunamis?"

This time a long pause.

"Who are you looking for?" the man asks.

"I'm looking for Markos."

"Where did you meet him?" the man persists.

"We met in Portland..." then I remember in New York they may think I main Portland, Maine so add, "Oregon."

"He's legendary, you know?" the man asks. "I've never met him but we exchange email. He didn't say I couldn't share his email. Do you want it?"

I try and contain my excitement, "Sure, why not?" Judging by the tone of my voice, I should never play poker.

"Markos@bristolfiber.com. Sometimes he doesn't get his email for a couple of days," he adds.

I know I'm pushing but ask as innocently as I can, "My husband and I plan on being in New York soon—would we be able to drop in at the 199 White Street office?"

"No, that's just where I pick up the mail for the company," the man tells me. "Goodbye."

I think he knows I was fishing about the office but that helps me knowing it's just a mail address.

"Just a sec," I barely catch him before he hangs up. "Is there an emergency number I can reach him at?" I don't want day four or day five, whatever is going to happen, to catch me off guard if he's got more information.

"A printing emergency?" the man laughs and just hangs up.

I'm not giving up this easily. I call the New York Corporate Division and ask them if there is a way to find out who the foreign owner is for this company.

"Sure, what's the initial DOS filing date?" the clerk tries to help out. But, when I tell her March 21, 1860, she just laughs. "There's no way to tell on those old companies. We had no requirements for disclosure back then and obviously a company that old isn't owned by Al Qaeda. We can't help you."

Not distinguishing one government agency for another I think, "Sure, you can tell every dime some partner screwed up the IRS with but you can't tell me who owns a 146 year old company?"

Josh calls and I'm glad to put this down for awhile. "I'm coming home for lunch," he says.

"Is that good news or bad news?" I ask.

"I haven't heard from the IRS but I did hear from our new lawyer. I'll tell you about it in 20 minutes when I get home."

"Thanks, lover." I am grateful for how he keeps me informed even if I'd rather be the ostrich with my head in the sand.

The kids are in their rooms but I hear their keyboards clacking. We're all so busy. But is it just a goose chase?

I fix Josh his favorite sandwich—tuna fish using bleu cheese dressing instead of mayonnaise. He loves for me to finely chop up baby garlic dill pickles and mix in. When Walla Walla sweet onions are in season, I thinly slice those on top. Today local tomatoes will have to do. Of course it all goes on toasted sourdough.

Thankfully the kids left him his favorite potato chips—Maui sweet onion. This plate will make him happy. Just in time I'm done.

Josh walks in, "Nice lunch."

"You're so simple to please. If we only had Oreos, you wouldn't go back to work."

"I'm not going back to work anyway," Josh looks tired. "Too much to think about."

"Unload some of that thinking on me."

He does. "I hired a new lawyer for us. His name is Dan Piper. As far as how he looks or talks, he's cut from the same cookie cutter as any other lawyer."

I think, "Which means he's barely tolerable."

Josh explains more, "His specialty is in tax law. He even used to be an accountant. Before I left, he called the IRS agent. It was someone he's known for years and they're going to get together next Monday. But, the IRS agent gave him a range depending on what they find in the audit."

I held my breath waiting. Josh knows I'm always asking him for best case-worse case scenarios. That's how I think.

"Best case, we pay $50,000. Worst case, we get 30 days to come up with $100,000."

"How can we come up with $100,000 in 30 days?"

"Piper is used to this kind of thing. He called a broker friend of his who said they'd loan up to $100,000 on the equity of our house. It's a little higher than bank rates but they'll fund immediately."

"Our house?"

"Yes. That makes me nervous as well. Especially after Piper said as private lenders they don't have to give us all the notice and payment rights that banks do."

"Does our mortgage allow us to get a second loan?"

"Sweetie, I need your help on this," Josh implores. "Please get out a copy of the mortgage for me to drop off tomorrow at the broker's office. He said if the loan doesn't allow a second, they may buy out the first. But, that would take longer and that means it's critical to know."

"What are the partners doing? How are they going to handle this?" I don't know if that even matters but it seems logical to ask.

"I said I wasn't going back to work but I'm not staying home either. I will go visit their office after lunch. They're not even returning my phone calls."

"Did you talk to Rose?" Rose is the bookkeeper for the partners and she knows everything. They all want her to keep things from each other but Rose ignores them and tells everyone exactly as it is.

"That's who I'm going to go see after lunch."

I feel better now. I've always felt like the partners were a bit too slippery. We get our checks fine but they're always asking Josh to pad a construction cost or put the cost for one site into another project. He doesn't and that's made for some tense times in the past. Except for that's what bonded he and Rose. She's exactly the same way—everything has to be accounted for with her."

"Any other stops along the way?" I'm not sure why I ask but wonder whether he'll be back on time for dinner at TF's tonight.

"I don't have anything set up but I thought I'd stop at the old accountant's and talk to them about this."

The old accountant's were B.L.U. Accounting. A great bunch of people. We were concerned about the partners switching over when they did but they thought the prices had grown too high. And, B.L.U Accounting wouldn't go for any kind of aggressive tax strategies. In hind sight, maybe we should have stayed with B.L.U.

"Great idea. If not today, then tomorrow. I'll come with you if you want," I offer.

Josh hasn't really talked about my depression much and kind of surprises me, "Guess I got out of practice asking you after being turned down for a year." That's not recrimination in his voice. "Thank God you're back."

Josh leaves and I put sandwiches out for the kids. I'll tell them to come eat when I go back upstairs. First, I want to get an email off to Markos.

Using the email I just got from New York, I write:

"Dear Markos, our family is under attack from every direction. Please help, even if it's only to give insight. Sincerely, Dawn."

If he's hanging around here, he already knows Dawn-who.

Just anxiety has me so tired I can't keep my eyes open. I go upstairs and lay down promising myself it will only be for a few minutes. It seems like I've only rested my eyes when Josh is back waking me up. I haven't had a nap like that for awhile and feel pretty good.

"Have you been asleep the whole time?" Josh asks.

"Umm," I'm still waking up, "guess so."

"Good for you," he takes his shoes and socks off and plops on the bed beside me. "Want to know what Rose said?"

"Definitely!"

He hands me a copy of a document. "That's what the partners were supposed to get me to sign at the time they secretly voted on doing a tax strategy. They told us that they had to combine two companies to have enough assets to get a loan for the second building. I think that's true but what they did also ended up in this strategy that the IRS is on them for now.

"This is a disclosure notice waiving our rights to go against the partners and the CPA firm if there's an audit," I've read far enough to get the gist.

"According to Rose, we need to take this to Piper and see about whether this constitutes fraud. She thinks the IRS may settle without penalties under the circumstance."

"There goes the partnership," I exclaim.

"Really, how could we stay in that after all this anyway? Besides, Rose says the partners are all turning on each other. They're only talking through their lawyers. Word is that they're trying to divide the assets in a way to get rid of each other forever."

"What about us?"

"Talk is that they want us to take West Linn and in return give up everything else." Josh kind of shrugs.

"What's that shrug mean?"

"Its high risk but it might be a very profitable thing for us to do. Get rid of 10 small ownerships of different facilities for one we own by ourselves. It's just that we're facing the end of the construction loan and I'm not sure how we'd qualify for the permanent loan. But, it could be a good thing. Especially good considering that we don't know if the partners screwed around with any of the other accounting."

"Notice how we can't even say something is bad or good anymore? We're living in an unknown state. I like the possibilities of good things. Just still creeped out about the 'fourth day' warning." I haven't told him yet of the search for the illusive Markos let alone emailing him.

"Don't you have to prepare dinner for tonight?"

"No, Amanda called early this morning. She's made lasagna for tonight." I don't know how Josh does it but he makes a grin like Garfield the cat.

"Lasagna," he starts to dribble out of the corner of his mouth.

❖

TF stops us from attacking the lasagna that smells so wonderful.

"Let's start first with Communion. I'm not going to ask if anyone has something to share because we're all going through strange times."

TF passes the Communion to John. We're all sitting in the same places and the wine glasses are quickly distributed followed by the broken bread.

"Amen." We repeat after TF. Somehow, I feel closer to these people after Communion.

The lasagna barely gets passed around the whole table before Ray is asking for more. Even Lee, who never takes seconds, is going for another round.

Jules is up taking the serving dishes from the table. I can tell she's eager to finish the second half of the teaching we started last time. We all follow suit and the table is clean with everyone returning quicker than usual.

I look around—no balloons this time. I can't hear any drum beats. No shots. Dear God, let's get going before something does happen.

No fear about Lee starting things up. He immediately begins where we left off.

"Last time I read, 'Jesus replied, "If anyone loves me, he will obey my teaching. My Father will love him, and we will come to him and make our home with him.'"

"Let's start up at that thought. If Christ and the Father are dwelling in you, what can any man, demon, or Satan himself do to over power them? If you allow Christ in you to command, then what demon can fail to obey? If the Father in you shields you, then what power in the universe can come against you? That's the power we have by faith in Christ: the indwelling of the Father and Son."

Ray's almost rude in breaking in, "But that's not anything I've every experienced!"

"That's what we're getting ready to experience. Look, Ray, I'm like you. I hate the weak crap I was taught in Seminary. But now we're moving on to something better."

"Who gave the Apostles their authority?" Lee is asking Ray but none of us have a quick answer. "Did Christ just delegate authority to the Apostles? No, the authority the Apostles had came from their faith. How do we know that? Because we are told that before the Apostles performed miracles they first asked for their faith to grow."

"Ray, have you ever asked to perform miracles?"

"Never…didn't even think that was something we should ask."

Lee says, "Read Luke 17:5 and 6."

Ray reads, "[5] The apostles said to the Lord, "Increase our faith!"

[6] He replied, "If you have faith as small as a mustard seed, you can say to this mulberry tree, 'Be uprooted and planted in the sea,' and it will obey you.

Ray prays for us all, "Lord, increase our faith as you did for the disciples."

TF points at him, "You say it, brother!"

Lee continues, "To have the fullness of Christ, we need to first ask for faith. We also have to understand what faith is: first, it is <u>not</u> about our resolve."

Lee pauses to see if anyone has questions and then continues, "Second, our faith is about being in a relationship with Jesus where His presence in us passes on His power. It's not a formula whereby His name has magic powers…I've seen too many people who act that way. Our faith must be in the historical fact that the man Jesus they crucified is now alive as the Christ and His kingdom rules. Our faith is in the faithfulness of Christ. Faith has nothing to do with belief in self."

The usually reserved John surprises us, "That's what I'm talking about! The faithfulness of Jesus is something I can have faith in...I finally understand faith!"

Lee laughs at John, "Then you read Acts 3:16."

He does, "By faith in the name of Jesus, this man whom you see and know was made strong. It is Jesus' name and the faith that comes through him that has given this complete healing to him, as you can all see.

"So, who healed this man in the first post-Jesus miracle by the Apostles? Peter? John? No, it was Christ who healed the man because of faith. That is how any miracle is done—Christ may work through a believer, but the power is His. Healings do not come about by any person, they do not happen because of any person, healing only happens through the agent of a person when the Lord indwelling in them exercises His authority over the situation."

John says something like, "'Eloi' something-something." Is that tongues I wonder? Is he really speaking in tongues? I think he is and it seems natural.

We all notice it except John himself who is now quiet.

This doesn't stop Lee, "But, is it not just enough to have faith in Christ and not be laboring at belief or distinguishing our selves from the world? The answer proposed by James is that the faith Christ calls us to demand deeds."

"Jules, you read James 2:18 to 24."

I can't believe how much she's grown up in the last month. With confidence and a sincere heart, she reads, "[18] But someone will say, "You have faith; I have deeds." Show me your faith without deeds, and I will show you my faith by what I do.

19 You believe that there is one God. Good! Even the demons believe that--and shudder.

20 You foolish man, do you want evidence that faith without deeds is useless ?

21 Was not our ancestor Abraham considered righteous for what he did when he offered his son Isaac on the altar?

22 You see that his faith and his actions were working together, and his faith was made complete by what he did.

23 And the scripture was fulfilled that says, "Abraham believed God, and it was credited to him as righteousness," and he was called God's friend.

24 You see that a person is justified by what he does and not by faith alone."

Lee is getting relentless now, "According to James, the kind of faith without deeds is the same kind of faith that the demons have…and that does not seem to be working too well for the demons and in us it leaves us without authority."

Not surprisingly, Ray interrupts, "But that's exactly the kind of faith we've all been raised—reared to believe—the faith of demons. I couldn't describe it any better than that."

Lee continues, "Luke tells us in Acts a story both of how healing works by God through an individual and what happens when people have the faith of demons. Ray, please read Acts 19:11 to 17."

Ray is excited to read, "11 God did extraordinary miracles through Paul,

12 so that even handkerchiefs and aprons that had touched him were taken to the sick, and their illnesses were cured and the evil spirits left them.

13 Some Jews who went around driving out evil spirits tried to invoke the name of the Lord Jesus over those who were demon-possessed. They would say, "In

the name of Jesus, whom Paul preaches, I command you to come out."

Ray looks around to make sure no one has questions before proceeding. "[14] Seven sons of Sceva, a Jewish chief priest, were doing this.

[15] One day the evil spirit answered them, "Jesus I know, and I know about Paul, but who are you?"

[16] Then the man who had the evil spirit jumped on them and overpowered them all. He gave them such a beating that they ran out of the house naked and bleeding.

[17] When this became known to the Jews and Greeks living in Ephesus, they were all seized with fear, and the name of the Lord Jesus was held in high honor."

"Ray is right," Lee admits. "We've all been taught to practice the faith of demons. Problem is the faith of demons is ineffective. Yet, how many church pews are filled with people who have demon-faith? They sit week after week with lives indistinguishable from the unsaved. Churches can grow with these kinds of believers but they do not thrive. We need to be beyond the faith of demons."

TF interjects, "I've seen the results. Personal debt, marital problems, gambling and shallow spiritual studies reflect in the church operating budget deficits. The kind of faith Christ calls us to must have evidence, it must take action, it must be sincere and it must be generous. The faith we are called to must absolutely have the presence of Jesus to do the work of Jesus—the same work He did while on earth. That's how I'm convicted and I failed my own test. That's why I had to make such radical changes."

"Ray, let's keep you involved for awhile. Please read for us how Christ dwells in a person in Ephesians 3: 16 to 19."

Ray reads, "[16] I pray that out of his glorious riches he may strengthen you with power through his Spirit in your inner being,

17 so that Christ may dwell in your hearts through faith. And I pray that you, being rooted and established in love,

18 may have power, together with all the saints, to grasp how wide and long and high and deep is the love of Christ,

19 and to know this love that surpasses knowledge--that you may be filled to the measure of all the fullness of God."

"Let's break this down and see certain requirements for Christ to dwell in us. Lee reads from an index card he's kept in his shirt pocket until now.

"1. We have to be strengthened by the Holy Spirit so that in faith Christ can dwell in our hearts—we already learned that even when Christ was present, the Apostles had to ask for an increase in faith
2. We have to be rooted in Christ's love
3. We have to be filled with the fullness of God"

Putting the index card back in his shirt pocket he continues, "Interesting requirements and none of which are achieved due to any action of our own other than asking. These requirements are things we desire, which is why Paul told us to "eagerly desire the greater gifts" and did not tell us just to go work hard and earn them.

"This was an important point for me and TF," Lee emphasizes. "As humans, we tend to get goals and desires mixed up. So, let us define the differences. Goals are a series of events where we take action that determines a final outcome—these are all under our control.

"Desires are outcomes beyond our determination. We want the outcome yet there is nothing we can do to make it happen. So, what does God invite us to do? TF, read Psalms 37:4."

TF reads, "Delight yourself in the LORD and he will give you the desires of your heart." He adds, "That's one of my favorite verses."

"Mine too. It's the only promise I know of to make our desires come true. When we desire in the Lord, it is always a situation beyond our own capacity for things beyond our own ability to achieve. That's where the Lord wants us to meet Him. This kind of lifestyle is faith and faith is a gift."

"Christ's love is a gift. To be filled with the fullness of God is a gift. These gifts are the desires of our heart. To be filled with Christ means we have to have a heart for Christ and that happens only by desire, not by our achievements."

Everyone says "Amen".

Lee says, "I'm reading Matthew 5:8. 'Blessed are the pure in heart, for they will see God.'"

"Now the Greek word for "see" is "isoptanomai". It actually means "to allow oneself to be seen". A more literal meaning here is that if we open our hearts, the Lord will be seen in our hearts."

"Wow, that would be the total opposite of demon faith because you don't see any heart difference with demon faith," Ray comments.

"Yes," Lee nods, "So, when we talk about the fullness of Christ in us, we are talking about how He fills our hearts. The same Greek word for dwell, 'katoikeo', is used for both inhabiting the heart, such as the Lord's presence in the temple, or for those who reside in a city like Jerusalem. The Lord wants to inhabit our hearts. And, if He is in our hearts, then when we allow Him to act through us, and those actions have His authority. 'If God is for us, who can be against us?' Paul asks us in Romans 8:31."

"Ray, please read Colossians 2:9 and 10."

Ray reads, "9 For in Christ all the fullness of the Deity lives in bodily form,

10 and you have been given fullness in Christ, who is the head over every power and authority."

"You 'have been given'—past tense, already done?" Ray asks.

"Yes, we have already been given the fullness of Christ but it is our lack of maturity that keeps us from implementing it. That is why the author of Hebrews implores us to make a resolution about maturity, 'Therefore let us leave the elementary teachings about Christ and **go on to maturity**'. If we are mature, then the five roles of apostles, prophets, evangelists, pastors and teachers will be fulfilled and there will no longer be a need for them. That is our goal the goal of our apprenticeship: maturity for all so that Christ may indwell in each of us."

Josh surprises me with his comment. "Is there a step beyond being an apostle?"

"Good question," Lee lauds Josh. "The Apostles had the indwelling of Christ but is apostleship our final destiny? If not, where do we grow to after being apostles? What is the ultimate design that Jesus has in mind for us and when will He make it happen?"

Without waiting for anyone to answer, Lee goes on, "In fact, apostleship is not the final office for a mature believer. We must understand that the apprenticeship roles of teacher, pastor, evangelist, prophet and apostle are not designed to make us apostles but to take us another position one step beyond. Let me say this plainly, it is Christ's will that we are His priests and kings. He wants us to be like Him.

"This is something TF and I studied this morning so I'm going to have him read for awhile. Revelation 1:6, only read it from the King James Version."

TF reads, "And hath made us kings and priests unto God and his Father; to him be glory and dominion for ever and ever. Amen.

"Ray caught this earlier in another verse. Note the tense—He has already 'made us to be' these positions. Every other position is an apprenticeship training to fulfill this role of being kings and priests. This is what even the original apostles were training for and Christ told them they would have their own thrones. Matthew 19:28."

"Jesus said to them, "I tell you the truth, at the renewal of all things, when the Son of Man sits on his glorious throne, you who have followed me will also sit on twelve thrones, judging the twelve tribes of Israel."

TF mocks, "Here we see that 12 of the original followers will judge the 12 tribes of Israel—I think that means we will be judging the Gentiles? I know we'll be judging angels. But how can we be kings and priests?"

Lee picks up the mocking, "We can't be priests! Is that what you are saying? The evidence we have been taught seems to speak against this. After all, we are not Levites and according to the law all priests have to be Levites. But, if we can't be priests than neither can Jesus. After all Christ was not a Levite yet He is our High Priest. How can that be? Hebrews 5:4 to 10."

TF reads, "4 No one takes this honor upon himself; he must be called by God, just as Aaron was.

5 So Christ also did not take upon himself the glory of becoming a high priest. But God said to him, "You are my Son; today I have become your Father."

6 And he says in another place, "You are a priest forever, in the order of Melchizedek."

No one stops him so TF continues, "7 During the days of Jesus' life on earth, he offered up prayers and petitions with loud cries and tears to the one who could save him from death, and he was heard because of his reverent submission.

8 Although he was a son, he learned obedience from what he suffered

9 and, once made perfect, he became the source of eternal salvation for all who obey him

10 and was designated by God to be high priest in the order of Melchizedek."

Lee explains, "Just as Aaron was designated a high priest, so God the Father designated Christ as our High Priest. Jesus did not become the earthly high priest subject to the Levitical laws—or He would not have qualified under those laws to be our high priest who offered His own blood as a final and perfect sacrifice on our behalf. By that same token, we are not called to be kings and priests under the Levitical laws or we would be excluded. Read Hebrews 7:11 and 12."

TF does, "[11] If perfection could have been attained through the Levitical priesthood (for on the basis of it the law was given to the people), why was there still need for another priest to come--one in the order of Melchizedek, not in the order of Aaron?

[12] For when there is a change of the priesthood, there must also be a change of the law."

"There are many who would argue that the law always existed. However, that is NOT what Paul tells us. We see that the law was introduced 430 years after Abraham and never replaces the promises of grace, but instead is used to fulfill those promises in Christ's sacrifice. Read Galatians 3:16-18."

"[16] The promises were spoken to Abraham and to his seed. The Scripture does not say "and to seeds," meaning many people, but "and to your seed," meaning one person, who is Christ.

[17] What I mean is this: The law, introduced 430 years later, does not set aside the covenant previously established by God and thus do away with the promise.

[18] For if the inheritance depends on the law, then it no longer depends on a promise; but God in his grace gave it to Abraham through a promise." TF's voice rings with promise.

"Before Abraham and to whom Abraham was subject was Melchizedek whose priestly order preceded the Levitical order and has now superseded it. Before the law was given to Moses there was Melchizedek. After the law was fulfilled by Jesus, Christ is our Melchizedek priest. That is what allows us to become kings and priests. In fact, we see that the Levitical covenant is considered obsolete. Read Hebrews 8:13."

TF reads, "By calling this covenant "new," he has made the first one obsolete; and what is obsolete and aging will soon disappear."

"What is the subsequent text after 8:13 referring to being now obsolete? What's obsolete is the way in which the former law called for worship?"

Ray's excited and Lee sees it, "OK, Ray, you read Hebrews 9:1."

Ray reads, "Now the first covenant had regulations for worship and also an earthly sanctuary."

"Ray, why did the way of worship have to change?"

Ray answers, "If the first covenant were still binding, then Christ would have to be on earth in the earthly sanctuary to be our high priest."

"Exactly. Change was necessary because the heavenly sanctuary, like the pre-Levitical Melchizedek priesthood, existed before the Levitical laws. Because we are not under the Levitical covenant, we indeed can be priests and kings with Christ. Under the old law, no one but the high priest could enter the Most Holy Place. Now that we qualify as the under the Melchizedek priesthood we are due the privileges this priesthood has, we have access to the Most Holy Place."

"Dusky, you've been too quiet tonight, read Hebrews 10:19 to 22."

Truth is, like me, she's just been trying to keep up. This type of Bible study is challenging but she's glad to participate. We're learning real life spirituality!

Dusky reads, "19 Therefore, brothers, since we have confidence to enter the Most Holy Place by the blood of Jesus,

20 by a new and living way opened for us through the curtain, that is, his body,

21 and since we have a great priest over the house of God,

[22] let us draw near to God with a sincere heart in full assurance of faith, having our hearts sprinkled to cleanse us from a guilty conscience and having our bodies washed with pure water."

"Ever think what the results would be if we did go back to the Levitical laws? We would lose our access to Jesus and the Father who are in the Most Holy Place. Too many denominations argue endlessly over issues such as Saturday or Sunday Sabbath keeping. What is implicit in that argument is that we are still under the Levitical covenant law. If we are under that law, then we are not qualified to be the priests and kings that we are declared to already be. In fact, under the Levitical law, Jesus as a non-Levite is not qualified to be a priest either. We have no hope and never did under the law."

"There are people and congregations that hold tight to the law. For those people they read the following and exclaim that there is no way that the law has been made obsolete. Dusky, please read Matthew 5:17 and 18."

She does, "[17] Do not think that I have come to abolish the Law or the Prophets; I have not come to abolish them but to fulfill them.

[18] I tell you the truth, until heaven and earth disappear, not the smallest letter, not the least stroke of a pen, will by any means disappear from the Law **until everything is accomplished**." Dusky emphasizes the last four words.

"You've already got the issue," Lee nods to Dusky, "The real issue here is if "everything is accomplished" and whether Christ did indeed fulfill the law. The law called for sacrifice for sin—Christ fulfilled that. The law called for living a perfect life—Christ fulfilled that. Once it is fulfilled, it cannot be abolished. If a house mortgage is paid off and the obligation fulfilled, do we keep paying the mortgage? Of course we do NOT continue paying the mortgage... because the contract is fulfilled. But, neither do we abolish the mortgage because what's fulfilled is completed, not done away with. In this same way, the old priesthood and its covenants are valid but fulfilled."

"Amanda and I were talking about a particular denomination earlier but there are many denominations that create a burden of the law and teach that what we can't achieve in the law on our own goodness-- that the blood of Christ will continually be used to make up the on-going deficit. This keeps us and Christ bound to the Levitical law. But what the Bible tells us is that we died with Christ and are no longer under the law. There is no on-going deficit because the law is completely fulfilled by Christ. Amanda, you read Colossians 2:20 to 23."

We all enjoy Amanda's voice which has been too quiet tonight. "[20] Since you died with Christ to the basic principles of this world, why, as though you still belonged to it, do you submit to its rules:

[21] "Do not handle! Do not taste! Do not touch!"?

[22] These are all destined to perish with use, because they are based on human commands and teachings.

[23] Such regulations indeed have an appearance of wisdom, with their self-imposed worship, their false humility and their harsh treatment of the body, but they lack any value in restraining sensual indulgence."

Amanda adds, "That sounds like the church I was talking about."

Lee goes on, "Jesus described for us the inadequacies of the law when an expert in the law questioned Him. This is a far more poignant story than what most of us read for it addresses through the characters the Levitical law. Amanda, read Luke 10:25 to 37."

She reads, "[25] On one occasion an expert in the law stood up to test Jesus. "Teacher," he asked, "what must I do to inherit eternal life?"

[26] "What is written in the Law?" he replied. "How do you read it?"

27 He answered: "'Love the Lord your God with all your heart and with all your soul and with all your strength and with all your mind' ; and, 'Love your neighbor as yourself.'"

28 "You have answered correctly," Jesus replied. "Do this and you will live."

29 But he wanted to justify himself, so he asked Jesus, "And who is my neighbor?"

30 In reply Jesus said: "A man was going down from Jerusalem to Jericho, when he fell into the hands of robbers. They stripped him of his clothes, beat him and went away, leaving him half dead.

31 A priest happened to be going down the same road, and when he saw the man, he passed by on the other side.

32 So too, a Levite, when he came to the place and saw him, passed by on the other side.

33 But a Samaritan, as he traveled, came where the man was; and when he saw him, he took pity on him.

34 He went to him and bandaged his wounds, pouring on oil and wine. Then he put the man on his own donkey, took him to an inn and took care of him.

35 The next day he took out two silver coins and gave them to the innkeeper. 'Look after him,' he said, 'and when I return, I will reimburse you for any extra expense you may have.'

36 "Which of these three do you think was a neighbor to the man who fell into the hands of robbers?"

37 The expert in the law replied, "The one who had mercy on him." Jesus told him, "Go and do likewise."

"Thank you," Lee says to Amanda. "Let us review what the Lord is saying. We have an expert in the law asking Jesus about the effectiveness of the law—what makes it effective to achieving eternal life. Jesus replies to him about the ineffectiveness of the priesthood through describing the first person who finds the victim and it is an officer of the law—this priest who turned his back on one in need of saving. The next character is a Levite, those chosen to uphold the law and he does the same thing as the priest. One by duty of office, one through hereditary qualifications both of these two men were bound to be the torch bearers of the law yet they lacked one thing. The Levitical priesthood and those appointed could not provide the one thing that all mankind desperately needs: Mercy.

"Who then appropriately ministers to the soul in need? The Samaritan provided mercy even though he is not part of the Levitical priesthood-- just as Jesus was not a Levite… nor are we.

"You see, the seduction of the law is that it is good for men to act according to it. Society benefits, families benefit, governments benefit by the order and reason of the law. Christ didn't proclaim it evil or say that it was deficit. We are the ones who are deficit—so much so that we cannot ever fulfill the law. So Jesus fulfilled it for us and now its good influence is not in the chiseled logic written on stone, but instead under the new covenant its benefits are implanted in our hearts. Amanda, read Hebrews 8:10."

"This is the covenant I will make with the house of Israel after that time, declares the Lord. I will put my laws in their minds and write them on their hearts. I will be their God, and they will be my people." Amanda pauses, "is that what's happening to us—we're becoming His people?"

I think so but don't say so out loud.

Lee nods, "If a pastor, church or denomination is teaching anything other than the heart issues, then suspect that the written law is incorrectly being promoted. And, under the written law, we are not priests, we are not kings, and therefore can not have access to the Most Holy Place. Unfortunately, that is what so many of the organized religions rob us of—the presence, the power, and the mercy of God. Remember that the Mercy Seat is only in The Most Holy Place. This is why we must know Jesus Christ personally through His word, through His Spirit, and through our own diligent searching. For it is in the drawing close to His throne on the Mercy Seat that we receive His mercy. And, we all need His mercy."

"Ray, do you remember what Jesus told us to actively seek?" Lee asks.

Ray nods yes but adds, "I don't remember the verse."

"Look up Luke 11:9 and 10 and let's look at exactly what He said."

Ray reads, "9 So I say to you: Ask and it will be given to you; seek and you will find; knock and the door will be opened to you.

10 For everyone who asks receives; he who seeks finds; and to him who knocks, the door will be opened."

"Christ tells us "ask". The Greek word here is "aiteo" and it means: "beg", "call for", "crave", "desire", or "require". Lee gets out a pre-printed list and reminds us, "These definitions come from blueletterbible.org."

"The Greek word for "seek" is "zeteo". It means:

1) to seek in order to find
- **a)** to seek a thing
- **b)** to seek (in order to find out) by thinking, meditating, reasoning, to enquire into
- **c)** to seek after, seek for, aim at, strive after

2) to seek i.e. require, demand
- **a)** to crave, demand something from someone"

"Taking all these meanings together, we're supposed to be actively seeking the fullness of what Christ has already designated us to be: priests and kings. That authority, that power, that indwelling only comes from one source. Whose door are we knocking on? From whom are we asking? Who are we seeking? If it's anyone other than Christ directly, then we're at the wrong door, got the wrong number, and looking in the wrong direction."

"Knocking on the door of demon faith," adds Ray.

"Amanda, we all love your voice. Please read John 5:39 and 40."

She happily obliges, "You diligently study the Scriptures because you think that by them you possess eternal life. These are the Scriptures that testify about me,

40 yet you refuse to come to me to have life.

"You notice that we're not doing the usual Bible study," Lee asks us all. "Jesus condemned those who believe the Bible is the answer. There's only one answer and it's the person of Jesus not the Bible."

"That's radical," Jules comments. "But I see the truth."

Dusky adds, "Even Satan quoted scripture to Jesus."

Ray air high fives his aunt's brilliant comment.

Lee proceeds, "We don't go to teachers, pastors, evangelists, prophets or apostles—those are positions we apprentice in, but not our source of authority. They should be reliable guides for us but no human is the destiny of our faith. Only Christ is our destiny and who is the Christ we come to? He is our High Priest in the order of Melchizedek—a priesthood with laws different from the Levitical law that allow us to reign with Him."

"Jules, you read 2 Corinthians 1:20 to 22."

"20 For no matter how many promises God has made, they are "Yes" in Christ. And so through him the "Amen" is spoken by us to the glory of God.

21 Now it is God who makes both us and you stand firm in Christ. He anointed us,

22 set his seal of ownership on us, and put his Spirit in our hearts as a deposit, guaranteeing what is to come."

"Jules, all of you, are you ready to accept the promises and speak now our Amen and be the mature priests and kings the Lord has declared us to be?" Lee waits for us to respond.

"Amen, amen, amen," we all shout.

"One thing that is similar between us and the Levitical priests is the idea of family. The Levites were a family tribe. Consider that for a second.

"Our only example of a fully mature priest-king is Jesus Christ. Jesus is not a position—it is because of who He is that He is our Priest-King. He is the Son of God. However, He is not the Son of God because He is the High Priest. Neither will we assume our positions in the Father by achieving a title. We will achieve the titles because of who we are because we too are the Sons and Daughters of God."

"Remember that while the Father provides titles and positions to us, He Himself is only comprehended by the title 'Father'. If we were to try and define God, then we will quickly conclude we can't do that without calling Him Father. Paul explains this clearly by telling us whether angels or humans, we all have one Father. I'm reading from Ephesians 3:14 and 15. 14 For this reason I kneel before the Father,

15 from whom his whole family in heaven and on earth derives its name."

TF can't help himself and cuts in, "That's what we are called to—not to be a church, denomination or religion, but to recognize that we are part of the Family of God with only one Father. Jesus acknowledged this and told us to pray to "Our Father" in heaven."

Lee takes back over, "When we look at the way Jesus contacted people while He was on earth we see his emphasis on families. First, the man who proclaimed Christ to the world was John the Baptist, a relative of Jesus. We know this from what Luke reports that the angel Gabriel said to Mary. It must have been reassuring for Mary to know that if her relative Elizabeth, who was beyond child-bearing could have a baby, then the Lord could make Mary have one without a human father. Mary was assured in Elizabeth what miracles the Lord could do when it came to having a baby."

"I never thought of that, before," I admit. "The Lord brought into Mary's life an example in Elizabeth's impossible pregnancy."

"Exactly. So, Dawn, read Luke 1:36 and 37."

I read, "[36] Even Elizabeth your relative is going to have a child in her old age, and she who was said to be barren is in her sixth month.

[37] For nothing is impossible with God."

Lee goes on, "John the Revelator tells us about how John the Baptist directed a family member to follow Christ.

"I'd ask John to read this be three Johns in a row is too much. Josh, please read John 1:32 to 42."

Josh reads, "[32] Then John gave this testimony: "I saw the Spirit come down from heaven as a dove and remain on him.

[33] I would not have known him, except that the one who sent me to baptize with water told me, 'The man on whom you see the Spirit come down and remain is he who will baptize with the Holy Spirit.'

[34] I have seen and I testify that this is the Son of God."

Josh pauses before going on in case anyone has questions. None of us are used to this fast paced study style. No one does so he continues, "[35] The next day John was there again with two of his disciples.

[36] When he saw Jesus passing by, he said, "Look, the Lamb of God!"

[37] When the two disciples heard him say this, they followed Jesus.

[38] Turning around, Jesus saw them following and asked, "What do you want?" They said, "Rabbi" (which means Teacher), "where are you staying?"

[39] "Come," he replied, "and you will see." So they went and saw where he was staying, and spent that day with him. It was about the tenth hour.

Again Josh pauses and looks up briefly before he reading on, "[40] Andrew, Simon Peter's brother, was one of the two who heard what John had said and who had followed Jesus.

[41] The first thing Andrew did was to find his brother Simon and tell him, "We have found the Messiah" (that is, the Christ).

[42] And he brought him to Jesus. Jesus looked at him and said, "You are Simon son of John. You will be called Cephas" (which, when translated, is Peter).

"Jesus is interacting with families here. First of all his own family— we're going to look at something few people ever understand. Josh," Lee requests, "Please read from this King James version," he hands Josh a different Bible.

Josh reads, "Now there stood by the cross of Jesus his mother, and **his mother's sister**, Mary the wife of Cleophas, and Mary Magdalene."

"A sad scene. Mary, the mother of Jesus, stands beside the cross as Jesus dies. This verse says her sister is there to comfort her."

I think of the many times Dusky and I have comforted each other through our lives. I know she will always be there for me as I will for her.

"Josh, read, Mark 15:40."

Josh reads, "There were also women looking on afar off: among whom was Mary Magdalene, and Mary the mother of James the less and of Joses, and **Salome.**" Josh emphasizes the last name.

After thinking for a few seconds, Josh exclaims, "That means Mary's sister's name is Salome!"

"I like that," says Dusky. "I didn't realize we knew the name of Mary's sister."

"I think we know more than that," Lee has our attention. "Josh, read Matthew 4:21."

Josh continues from the King James version, "And going on from thence, he saw other two brethren,

James the son of Zebedee, and John his brother, in a ship with Zebedee their father."

"I'm taking awhile to get to the point here. Sorry, but it's a bit obscure and I want you to see each step. Pretty much everyone knows that James and John—that is John the Revelator, are brothers. These two brothers, and there may have been more, we don't know, were called the 'Sons of Thunder'. We might have said they bitched and cursed a lot—or maybe they were just demanding. I doubt it was a nice nickname.

"Josh, do we know who their mother was?" Lee asks.

Josh just says, "We're about to learn, aren't we?"

"Yes, please look up Matthew 27:56."

Lee reads, "Among which was Mary Magdalene, and Mary the mother of James and Joses, and **the mother of Zebedee's children.**" Josh slows way down and raises his voice over the last few words.

Dusky sums up, "So Mary's sister is Salome, the aunt to Jesus, the mother to Zebedee's children including James and John! So, John the Baptist, James the Apostle and John the Revelator Apostle were cousins to Jesus?"

"Yes. John was also known as the 'Beloved' disciple. He rested his head against Jesus at the last supper. He absolutely adored his older cousin—Jesus. Isn't that amazing?"

For some reasons Dusky and I started crying. For me, I am so moved by the fact of how much Jesus cares about families including his own. I remember reading how He came back from the dead and visited James, His brother. No wonder James and his brother Jude were brought into the early church as leaders—they continued the family tradition that Jesus established. This is how families are supposed to relate in the Lord. "Praise God," bursts from my heart.

Dusky responds, "Amen."

"We left off," Lee is not about to stop, "where Luke adds to the description of Peter becoming an apostle. Luke explains about Christ coming to Capernaum and healing

Peter's mother in-law—whether that precluded Andrew's introduction is not known but needless to say, Jesus got to know Peter's family as part of His personal relationship with Peter."

"Dusky, would you please read Luke 4:38 and 39?"

She reads, "38 Jesus left the synagogue and went to the home of Simon. Now Simon's mother-in-law was suffering from a high fever, and they asked Jesus to help her.

39 So he bent over her and rebuked the fever, and it left her. She got up at once and began to wait on them."

"Did this happen before or after Peter was called to be a follower?" Lee asks no one in particular. None of us know.

"According to Luke, it was after this that Jesus called Peter to be a disciple," Lee answers his own question. "Dusky, read Luke 5:1 to 11."

"1 One day as Jesus was standing by the Lake of Gennesaret, with the people crowding around him and listening to the word of God,

2 he saw at the water's edge two boats, left there by the fishermen, who were washing their nets.

3 He got into one of the boats, the one belonging to Simon, and asked him to put out a little from shore. Then he sat down and taught the people from the boat.

4 When he had finished speaking, he said to Simon, "Put out into deep water, and let down the nets for a catch."

5 Simon answered, "Master, we've worked hard all night and haven't caught anything. But because you say so, I will let down the nets."

6 When they had done so, they caught such a large number of fish that their nets began to break.

[7] So they signaled their partners in the other boat to come and help them, and they came and filled both boats so full that they began to sink.

[8] When Simon Peter saw this, he fell at Jesus' knees and said, "Go away from me, Lord; I am a sinful man!"

[9] For he and all his companions were astonished at the catch of fish they had taken,

[10] and so were James and John, the sons of Zebedee, Simon's partners. Then Jesus said to Simon, "Don't be afraid; from now on you will catch men."

[11] So they pulled their boats up on shore, left everything and followed him."

"Great," Lee says to Dusky for reading, "The point being whether with Andrew and Peter or His own cousins, Jesus concerns Himself with families. Even His first miracle at Cana was a wedding celebrating families."

"So," again to no one in particular Lee asks, "why the emphasis on family?"

No one answers—we're too excited waiting for Lee to continue.

"For one thing, we cannot understand the character of God without understanding that He is the Father of us all. The whole point of Christ's redemption is to reconcile us as sons and daughters with Him."

"I'm a Son of God through Jesus Christ!" Ray exclaims.

"Yes," Lee responds, "the whole plan of redemption hinges on our being the children of God—of a family restored. Our position as kings and priests is because of our heritage—with Jesus as our brother, we inherit those positions."

"Ray, read Romans 8:19 to 21."

Ray reads, "[19] The creation waits in eager expectation for the sons of God to be revealed.

[20] For the creation was subjected to frustration, not by its own choice, but by the will of the one who subjected it, in hope

[21] that the creation itself will be liberated from its bondage to decay and brought into the glorious freedom of the children of God.

"Oh, my God! That's who I am? That's who we are?" cries Amanda.

"Yes, and we have the Father's promise to make us His children." Lee is so happy to respond.

"Amanda, read 2 Corinthians 6:18."

She reads, ""I will be a Father to you, and you will be my sons and daughters, says the Lord Almighty."

Amanda looks to Jules and says, "I am a daughter of the Lord Almighty."

Jules looks to me and says, "I am a daughter of the Lord Almighty."

I look to Dusky and say, "I am a daughter of the Lord Almighty."

Dusky looks around the table and says, "I am a daughter of the Lord Almighty."

Lee asks, "OK, guys, who are we?"

The men respond, "I am a son of the Lord Almighty."

"We had demon faith before," notes Ray. "Now we have the faith of God and are his sons and daughters. Who knew?"

"There's a lot that conspires to keep you from knowing," explains TF.

"Wait, there's more." Lee promises. "How do we become a son or daughter of the Father? What happens during the process? It's more than positions but let's review the positions once more to understand the difference between 'being' sons and daughters and filling a position."

"Who wants to read for awhile?" Lee asks.

John raises his hand so Lee tells him, "Re-read Ephesians 4:11."

John reads from the first Bible given to him, "It was he who gave some to be apostles, some to be prophets, some to be evangelists, and some to be pastors and teachers."

"OK, we've looked at how most people stop there and justify whatever position they feel they are in as something perpetual. Yet that's only the first third of that thought. Now re-read Ephesians 4:12."

John reads, "to prepare God's people for works of service, so that the body of Christ may be built up."

"What's the purpose," Lee asks not waiting for an answer. "The whole goal is to assume temporary positions to build each other up. The question then is what happens if we actually succeed at doing this? Ephesians 4:13."

John reads, "until we all reach unity in the faith and in the knowledge of the Son of God and become mature, attaining to the whole measure of the fullness of Christ."

"I realize that this is a quick rehash but I'm trying to emphasize what our goal is-- to be fully like Christ. How do we become the fullness of Christ? Philippians 2:5 only read it from that other version."

John picks up the King James version and reads, "Let this mind be in you, which was also in Christ Jesus."

"So, the fullness of Jesus in us is to have his mind?" John follows up.

"Yes, answers Lee. "The subsequent verses tell us about the characteristics of that mind—it's humbleness, obedience and willingness to be a servant. The point here in what you read is that this 'mind' can be in us. In other words, we are the children of God the Father when we have the same mind as Christ Jesus."

"This sounds like some kind of Buddhist consciousness," comments Amanda.

Wade answers, "The Orthodox church uses language like this a lot. It's just not common to western thinking. There are many eastern religions that get the idea of consciousness much better than western world Protestantism."

Lee doesn't want to get trapped into a definitions discussion and resumes, "Thanks—Wade you're helping us understand the consciousness issue. Let's all agree we know that the Bible is not talking about a brain transplant where we literally get the mind of Christ. We're talking about sharing the same consciousness, attitudes, values—cherishing the same things as Jesus.

"I like that definition," I say. "Using that would apply to how Dusky and I feel—we share the same consciousness about most things and we love the same people."

"Great example," says Lee. "In the Bible the Greek word for 'mind' is 'phroneo' and it means all these things. That's why the New International Version of the Bible says 'attitude' instead of 'mind'. But 'attitude' doesn't do the word justice—for it means actually cherishing the same values as if we were sharing the same brain. I think Dawn did a good job describing that in practice—how she and her sister are one in spirit regarding many things.

"The idea that closely shared feelings is like the shared consciousness of The Holy Spirit, Jesus and the Father—with the same consciousness they are One regardless of their separate entities."

TF interrupts, "I hope you're not about to tackle the Trinity? I've studied all my life and am not even sure the Holy Spirit is a part of the Godhead or just an expression of Jesus and or the Father."

"Thanks for being that provocative," Lee is not really thankful. "If it's OK with everyone, we won't get into the Trinity tonight other than to say this, no where does the Bible say our salvation is in understanding the Trinity. Our only focus is on Jesus Christ and whenever you feel the presence of the Holy Spirit, regardless of who you believe He is, His efforts are all about us understanding Jesus. Can I go on?"

Actually, none of us seem to be aware of this issue. Maybe their theology has got them screwed up over something the rest of us are better off without. We all nod for Lee to proceed.

"We're lucky to discover something about ourselves in life, not everyone really knows who they are, but the Trinity know Themselves so well that their consciousness is one and the same. Under different circumstances, we often become different people...sometimes even surprising ourselves. But the Trinity is always the same and always One and never changes for how could perfection change?"

Lee sure knows how to get back on track and continues, "When Christ was on earth, He had the consciousness of a man. He said "I" and everyone knew He meant the person inside his skin. He was fully man with a man's conscious so He was subject to temptation. He didn't succumb to temptation but He was tempted—that's what the Bible says—He **was** tempted." No one challenges this and Lee goes on.

"John, read Matthew 4:1."

John reads, "Then Jesus was led by the Spirit into the desert to be tempted by the devil."

"Amanda, excuse me if this sounds too Buddhist for you, but Christ also had a God consciousness. He told us that He and the Father are One—obviously not one in body... after all He occupied a human body at this time...but one in consciousness. We're called Christians because we have characteristics of Christ in us—that's His consciousness that defines us and gives us those qualities. It's a pervasive consciousness all over the world that regardless of the culture and country, a Christian has certain shared characteristics because of Christ's consciousness in us. "

"Amanda, do think that's a fair summary?" Lee asks.

"I think it's right on but I've never considered it before. Let's forget the whole Buddhist comparison...I just never heard the Christian use for 'consciousness.'"

"Actually," Lee turns to TF, "we didn't understand it until fairly recently. What we do realize now is how few people believe that they and Christ are one like Jesus said of Him and the Father. Yet, that's the identity that, although diminished from lack of recognition, is really going on to even call us Christians. We have this latent and retarded relationship that we're failing to develop into being the fullness of Christ but at the same time still have certain shared ideas that come from Jesus."

Lee continues, "When Jesus spoke on earth, He didn't say that what He said were His words coming from His man of this earth consciousness. No, He made it distinctly clear who was the source. Read John 14:10."

Ray and John start to read at the same time but Ray defers to John. "Don't you believe that I am in the Father, and that the Father is in me? The words I say to you are not just my own. Rather, it is the Father, living in me, who is doing his work."

"Ray,"" Lee directs this time, "read John 14:24."

Ray reads, "He who does not love me will not obey my teaching. These words you hear are not my own; they belong to the Father who sent me."

"This is so very important, please pay close attention," Lee intones. "Jesus also made it clear that He did not do the miracles. The Jews at the time understood that Jesus said the Father was in Him and they considered it blasphemy and wanted to stone Him. This is what Christ told them in response. I'm reading from John 10:32."

Lee reads, "but Jesus said to them, "I have shown you many great miracles from the Father. For which of these do you stone me?"

"In case they missed the point, Jesus made it even plainer that the miracles come from the Father within Him. What is within Him? Not the body of the Father but the consciousness of the Father. I'm reading John 10:37 and 38."

Lee reads, "[37] Do not believe me unless I do what my Father does.

[38] But if I do it, even though you do not believe me, believe the miracles, that you may know and understand that the Father is in me, and I in the Father."

"We're incredible people. We even lie to ourselves. What credibility could we bring to Jesus, to the Father or to their Kingdom?"

"None, on our own," answers Ray.

"Believe it or not," says Lee, "Jesus the man said he didn't bring credibility either. What brought credibility through Jesus is what His Father did in Him. The point of the miracles was to bring knowledge and faith to the fact that the Father is in Jesus and vice-versa. When Jesus went to be with the Father leaving this earth for heaven, then who is left to carry on this testimony? Let's see what Jesus had to say about that. Read John 14:12 and 13."

This time Ray reads, "[12] I tell you the truth, anyone who has faith in me will do what I have been doing. He will do even greater things than these, because I am going to the Father.

[13] And I will do whatever you ask in my name, so that the Son may bring glory to the Father."

"We've studied this verse before and know we're one of the 'anyone' mentioned." Lee stops for comments but we're all just agreeing with our head nods. "This is the position we are supposed to mature to—this is the fullness of Christ and where we become true sons of God. If the apostles were apostles before Christ died and before the Holy Spirit came upon them at Pentecost, then what were they afterwards? As I understand it, they grew beyond the office of apostle and become sons of God, brothers of Christ. Read Romans 8:29 and 30."

Ray reads, "[29] For those God foreknew he also predestined to be conformed to the likeness of his Son, that he might be the firstborn among many brothers.

[30] And those he predestined, he also called; those he called, he also justified; those he justified, he also glorified."

Lee continues, “That’s the work going on in us—the Father wants us all to be His sons—brothers to Jesus. If we were fully matured now, there wouldn’t be positions of teacher, pastor, evangelist, prophet or apostle-- and there won’t be in heaven— we’re all supposed to be brothers and sisters of Jesus, sons and daughters of God the Father. In fact, just as Jesus practiced on earth that consciousness is available to us now. Read John 14:23.”

Ray reads, “Jesus replied, "If anyone loves me, he will obey my teaching. My Father will love him, and we will come to him and make our home with him.”

Pointing at the second Bible in front of John, Lee says, “The King James Version says ‘keep my word’. The Greek word translated for `word’ and `teaching’ is ‘logos’. It’s the same word we get the business graphic name for a corporate `logo’. Its meaning is not just about what was written or what is taught—it’s about the essence of the teacher. Many incorrectly believe this verse to say keep the Ten Commandments—that’s belief in the law and not in Christ.”

Lee is shakes his head and emphasizes, “That’s **not** what is said. Let’s look at another example of how it is used to get a better idea of its meaning. Read John 1:1 to 3—this time Amanda.”

Amanda reads, “[1]In the beginning was the Word, and the Word was with God, and the Word was God.

[2] He was with God in the beginning.

[3] Through him all things were made; without him nothing was made that has been made.”

“In each of the three referrals to “Word” it is the Greek word ‘logos’. It’s meaning here is much like I already referred to when using a corporate logo that represents the company—Jesus is the representation of the Trinity. The Greek word is ‘pros’ for being with God and the God referred to here is ‘theos’ which usually means the Trinity. Literally, Jesus was part of the Trinity—and John makes this clear by saying “the Word was God”—that is ‘theos’ or part of the Trinity. The spoken Word of God, the written Word of the Bible, the Spirit of God in us that molds us to His character is the logo—the logos or likeness—the consciousness of Christ in us. Our lives as Christians not only represent our savior but also our fellow brothers and sisters. We are called to assume the role of the logos."

Amanda likes to summarize, "There really isn't any difference between having the consciousness of Jesus verses being the likeness of Him—they're the same?"

"Exactly. That's the same role Jesus modeled for us between He and the Father. It was Christ's role as the spokesperson of the shared consciousness that the power of the Father worked through the Son and by which all things were created. That same creative power of the universe that healed people on earth is alive today. Read Hebrews 13:8."

"Jesus Christ is the same yesterday and today and forever," Amanda reads.

"That's right, Jesus is still the same healer, still the same miracle worker, still the same creator-- whose greatest creation is yet to come when He replaces the first heaven and first earth-- and He is still the same Son of God. This is the fullness of Christ's consciousness in us—that we may be and do what Jesus did. Not on our own—for no man can do that—but by Christ in us and the Father in Him, all things are possible. We know this because Jesus prayed a specific prayer not just for the apostles but for those of us in successive generations who simply believe in Him. John 17:20 to 23."

Amanda reads, "[20] My prayer is not for them alone. I pray also for those who will believe in me through their message,

[21] that all of them may be one, Father, just as you are in me and I am in you. May they also be in us so that the world may believe that you have sent me. [22] I have given them the glory that you gave me, that they may be one as we are one:

[23] I in them and you in me. May they be brought to complete unity to let the world know that you sent me and have loved them even as you have loved me."

Lee goes on, "The people of Christ are diverse and have different gifts and understanding but we also have unity in Jesus—not uniformity (we're not the same) but unity of spirit. The fact that Christians in China, Ethiopia, Russia, and Belize and in every country around the world shares this same spirit testifies of the consciousness of Christ. But, it's only the beginning…ask the Holy Spirit for more. For the consciousness of Christ in us still desires to testify of the Father only Christ is no longer on earth. Christ's consciousness leads us and delivers His power through us so that we can continue to glorify the Father for Him. Jesus was so urgent about us continuing this testimony that He made us an all inclusive offer if we seek in His name to honor the Father. John 14:13."

Amanda reads, "And I will do whatever you ask in my name, so that the Son may bring glory to the Father.

Without slowing down, Lee drives on, "'Whatever' in Greek is 'hostis'. It means whoever, whatever, however, whichever—there is no limit. Are you asking Jesus to be in you and work through you to bring glory to the Father? I think that's why we've been led to this place, this house, this discussion. I think that's why we've been under such demonic attacks."

We all say, "Amen."

"Amanda," directs Lee, "read James 1:22."

She reads, "Do not merely listen to the word, and so deceive yourselves. Do what it says."

"I know he's a controversial guy but remember those who recently judged and condemn you with great joy. So don't judge him. I'm talking about the guy whose movie, PASSION OF THE CHRIST, re-taught the world what the word 'passion' means—it means to 'suffer'. In suffering we become passionate—we change our awareness and for us

Christians, it is a time to change into the awareness or consciousness of Christ. Suffering leads us to search for meaning and meaning ultimately is only found in the consciousness of Christ. Man has no meaning apart from the Lord. We were created to be part of His family. Christ established His meaning on earth by constantly submitting to and fulfilling the will of the Father. Because the Father dwells in Christ and Christ in the Father, when Christ is in us—His consciousness is our consciousness, then the Father is in us and we have the same burning drive to honor and glorify the Father. Like Christ, our meaning and the fullness of our individuality is completed through our identification with our Father. We can never be the most we can be as individuals unless we are the most we can be as sons of God the Father for that is who we are created to be. Christ died to redeem us to this position of being His family and this is the passion of our lives—to understand, to accept, and to ceaselessly and with every effort seek, knock, ask for Jesus to be in us and dwell in us and work through us. It's not our right to say, *'We can't do that'*. Our role is in every situation we are in to seek to bring the absolute maximum amount of glory to the Father—it is the prayer that Jesus said would allow Him to bring glory to the Father." Lee isn't even looking at us, it's as if he's looking into heaven while he talks.

"This is a growing revelation during the process of maturity and not everyone will get it. Partly because it is difficult to explain 'consciousness' of Christ but yet we subliminally rely on that consciousness even to define the characteristics of Christians. Without knowing it, we believe in it. It's the knowing and believing that gets difficult. Let's pray for every believer to become fully mature starting with us individually and our families."

Josh takes this as a direction and says, "So be it Lord."

We respond by nodding in agreement.

"I'm going to lighten up a bit to make a point. I'm hoping Amanda jumps in because her Bachelors Degree is in English and I think she'll help me since it's not my strong area."

Amanda agrees by nodding.

"Many colleges require reading certain standard English literature works. Because people tend to write about what they experience, these Classical Works express a lot about the history of their time."

"One of the writers often studied is a man by the name of Samuel Pep-ehs."

Amanda interrupts Lee. "Although his name is spelled P-E-P-Y-S, the correct way of pronouncing it is Peeps—at least that's the way he reportedly said it."

"I knew I could count on you," Lee says to Amanda and continues. "Pepys didn't write any novel, poem or usual literature-type document. He wrote a dairy. OK, for you macho men," he points at Ray, "that believe girls write diaries and men write "journals"—we'll call it whatever you want , but Pepys wrote about what he felt with great details."

"Yes," Amanda adds, "His experiences are something we would have no historical details about because he wrote about every day living a time long ago."

Lee continues, "Now that could be boring but he lived in the interesting time of the mid-1600s. For example, let's see what he wrote about the plague—the last great out break of the plague in Europe, in 1665." Lee pulls out from the back of his Bible a print out ready to read.

"June 7th

... it being the hottest day that ever I felt in my life, and it is confessed so by all other people the hottest they ever knew in England in the beginning of June - we to the New Exchange and there drunk whey; with much entreaty, getting it for our money, and would not be entreated to let us have one glasse more. So tok water, and to Foxe hall to the Spring-garden and there walked an hour or two with great pleasure, saving our minds ill at ease concerning the fleet and my Lord Sandwich, that we have no news of them, and ill reports run up and down of his being killed, but without ground. Here stayed, pleasantly walking and spending but 6d till 9 at night ...."

Ray's laughing at how hard it is for Lee to read this. Lee hands him the document to read. "Oh, this is written the way he spelled or misspelled...no wonder you were having a hard time reading it."

"Never mind, smarty," kids Lee. Just read it.

Ray reads, "This day, much against my Will, I did in Drury-lane see two or three houses marked with a red cross upon the doors, and "Lord have mercy upon us" writ there - which was a sad sight to me, being the first of that kind that to my remembrance I ever saw. It put me into an ill conception of myself and my smell, so that I was forced to buy some roll tobacco to smell to and chaw - which took away the apprehension."

"There's a note here that I'm going to read, "*(Houses infected by the Plague had to have a red cross one foot high marked on their door and were shut up - often with the victims inside. Tobacco was highly prized for its medicinal value, especially against the Plague. It is said that at Eton one boy was flogged for being discovered <u>not</u> smoking.)*"

"I got spanked when I was nine for smoking a cigar—guess I would have got away with it if only there had been a plague going on," Ray shares to my embarrassment.

Lee says, "Pepys saw many events and people from Oliver Cromwell—a Protestant, rebelling and killing the Catholic King Charles the First to replace the monarchy and then the re-establishment of the monarchy after Cromwell's death. These events and people impacted the present consciousness of Britain to this day. In fact, much of what is felt currently about the times comes from the consciousness expressed in the writings of men like Pepys."

We understand that Lee is trying to give us an example of "consciousness."

"Pepys was a vain man who gained some notoriety and influence—most of the influence was through his friend, Earl of Montague also known as Lord Sandwich—that's right, the man who invented sandwiches and for whom the Hawaiian islands were originally named the Sandwich Islands."

The kids pay attention because they love Hawaii… we've taken them there several times. They also know it's history and that what Lee is saying is true.

"We read the journals today and we see insight into Pepys—he was vain, conceited, and prideful—he had adulterous affairs of which his wife found out about only one and she died in depression shortly thereafter. We know about Pepys's consciousness because of what he wrote."

Pausing for a little while, Lee ponders, "So, you know where we are going with this... If we know about the consciousness of Pepys by what he wrote, what do we know about the consciousness of Jesus by reading the Bible?"

Without allowing anyone to answer, Lee goes on, "When we read Pepys, we can choose to read about the knowledge and historical content and that can be very satisfying. If we read at that level, we really don't learn much about the person of Pepys—his consciousness. But, if we choose to read, search, and ask about the man, we begin to put together the most intimate of details and know as much or more about him than his closest of friends. That's how we learn his consciousness."

"We talked about this earlier. Jesus warned people about just reading scripture for knowledge. That was never his intent. People argue endlessly over issues such as Saturday Sabbaths or fully immersed baptisms—and those details are not the person of Jesus. Righteous facts are what allowed the dreaded crusades where thousands of Orthodox Christians were raped and killed by thousands of Western Christians who went on to torture thousands of Muslims as well. Or just look at the religion-based partisan fighting in Ireland today. If it were facts that saved us, these arguments would have been laid to rest long ago. The only fact we have to know is Jesus—and we have to know Him as a person."

"Amen," says TF.

"TF, let's re-read John 5:39 and 40."

TF reads, "39 You diligently study the Scriptures because you think that by them you possess eternal life. These are the Scriptures that testify about me,

40 yet you refuse to come to me to have life."

"We, right now, are learning the consciousness of Christ through two ways. The first way is through His word—studying it not for facts but for Him. When we read the Bible this way, the Holy Spirit reveals truth and provides us understanding that cannot be found otherwise. Some call this type of learning is called Gestalt—a fancy word that really means when a person goes "aha". It's a revelation beyond the facts of what we've just learned creating a new meaning. When you experience this, it is the consciousness of Jesus through the Holy Spirit and the wonder of it is that He is talking directly to you no differently than He did face-to-face with the apostles. This is something everyone can experience IF they study to seek Him and IF they are being led by the Holy Spirit."

"Which is what we're doing right now," interrupts Jules.

"Exactly," says Lee. "There are Bible teachers, you've talked about Sunday School teachers, and they often only teach **about** the word. But, that is not how we learn about the consciousness of Christ. There is only one teacher for that. John 14:26."

Jules assumes reading, "But the Counselor, the Holy Spirit, whom the Father will send in my name, will teach you all things and will remind you of everything I have said to you."

"But, how can we be sure that the Holy Spirit is for us? That we can have this teacher?" asks Lee. "Read Luke 11:13."

Jules reads, "If you then, though you are evil, know how to give good gifts to your children, how much more will your Father in heaven give the Holy Spirit to those who ask him!"

"So, follows up Jules, "all we do is ask?"

"Yes," says Lee, "by the goodness of our heavenly Father, we have the right to ask for and receive the Holy Spirit in our lives. We can and should doubt our own goodness and our own qualifications, but Jesus said it was by the Father's goodness that we receive the Holy Spirit."

"Ohhh, I'm asking now!" Jules says.

"A revelation for us to personally understand is that the Holy Spirit is the part of the Godhead that dwells with us now. It is His presence--the Bible describes Him as a Him...," he stops and looks at Lee. Evidently they argue over this point.

Lee continues, "...it is the Holy Spirit that claims us as part of the kingdom of God—that provides us the characteristics of the Christ-consciousness of the Godhead. We tend to think in two parts of our Christianity—what it's like now and what it will be like after Jesus comes and creates a new heaven and new earth—but that doesn't apply to the Holy Spirit. For the Holy Spirit is a personal gift to us from the Father and the Holy Spirit is given to us forever—He never separates from us even in the new heaven and new earth. Jules, read John 14:16 and 17."

Jules reads, "[16] And I will ask the Father, and he will give you another Counselor to be with you **forever—**

[17] the Spirit of truth. The world cannot accept him, because it neither sees him nor knows him. But you know him, for he lives with you and will be in you."

"I wonder if that means He, the Holy Spirit, is stuck on earth now or if He is also in heaven?" Ray asks innocently.

Lee tells him, "Ray, that's another big doctrinal issue in many churches. Let's avoid that and appreciate how He interacts with us. Let's put some of this together because there are powerful results from what we know."

"First, we know that we can have not just the Bible but an understanding of the Word--the logos—that is of Jesus. We get to claim the Word—Jesus-- for our own. Agreed?"

We all shake our heads "yes."

"Then second, we get to ask for and expect to receive the Holy Spirit—due to the goodness of God the Father and no other reason. We should be assured that we cannot disqualify ourselves from the Holy Spirit because He is an unearned gift from the Father. Agreed?"

We all shake our heads "yes."

Lee continues, "The Greek word for 'spirit' as it describes the Holy Spirit is 'pneumatic'—we get the term pneumatic power tools from this word—the description being the forceful power of unseen air. The Hebrew word of spirit is 'ruwach'...kind of an explosive sound that emphasizes the 'ach'. You can kind of feel the power of the air when you way that word."

"Josh, let's look at Psalms 33:6."

Josh reads, "By the word of the LORD were the heavens made; and all the host of them by the breath of his mouth."

"What this really says in the Hebrew is not breath but instead by the 'ruwach" or Spirit through His mouth. This is the power of combining the Word of God with the Spirit of God. This is how prayers are answered and miracles are performed—when the Word—that is the consciousness of Jesus in us is combined with the Holy Spirit in our lives, the same creative power of the universe works through us. This is the state that a fully mature Christian will be led into if we truly persevere and strive for in our desires. This is how the promise Jesus gave us will be fulfilled—actually, must be fulfilled according to what Jesus said. Re-read John 14:12 and 13."

Josh reads, "[12] I tell you the truth, anyone who has faith in me will do what I have been doing. He will do even greater things than these, because I am going to the Father.

[13] And I will do whatever you ask in my name, so that the Son may bring glory to the Father."

"Again, the word 'name' is 'logos'—whatever we do being in the consciousness of Christ—the state of Christ, the fullness of Christ, the representation of Christ—that's what will accomplish `anything'. By being in that consciousness, it is not us but Jesus who brings glory to the Father by what we do. When we have the consciousness of Christ, then we long to bring glory to the Father by doing the works of the Father. Those works continue the testimony that Jesus and the Father are one. This is the priesthood we are called to—the continual offering of prayers and testimony to glorify God the Father through Jesus Christ by the works of the Holy Spirit in us."

No one interrupts Lee and he continues, "This consciousness of Christ in us is the 'logos' of Jesus and the way in which we become the sons and daughters of the Father. This is the fullness of maturing in Jesus and the purpose of our faith. And, because we are sons and daughters of the Father, then we are granted the offices of priest and kings like Jesus."

Now Ray interrupts, we all expect him to, "When does this become real? When do we see this in our lives?"

Lee answers, "The Lord has already declared this to be and waits for us to take action. Read Psalms 2:7."

Ray reads, "I will proclaim the decree of the LORD: He said to me, "You are my Son; today I have become your Father."

"That means it's real today?" Ray asks.

"That is my understanding," affirms Lee. The position we mature is that we're God's children with Jesus

Christ. That's why Jesus wants us to do even greater things than He did—so that the Father, Our Father, will be honored ever increasingly. This is our heritage, this is our destiny, and this is the design for our lives."

"We're in the same position that the apostles were in prior to Pentecost—we can do some good but not yet fully powered. When I ask if it's real today, I mean can we do what Jesus did right now?" John picks up where Ray left off only he is not about to back down without getting to the kernel of truth.

"I think we continually call upon the Holy Spirit and are provided the fullness of what we are to do and grow from there." Lee is succinct.

Josh says, "I'm sure it's not an over night thing, but your answer doesn't seem complete. I can't put my finger on what's missing."

I think I feel what everyone else feels. We want to be completely the daughters and sons of the Father. We want to do what Jesus did simply to honor the Father, not for personal power. We want to do it now. TF has led out in healing people but it seems like he's not one 100% sure what all led to that. The fact that it's Christ's consciousness that empowered those healings, I agree on. But, what led to the activation or taking over by that consciousness seems missing or unexplained.

Josh senses it too and asks, "Do we have a follow up meeting?"

"Let's meet every Wednesday," offers Lee. "I'll even cook for the next one."

We agree and both TF and Lee follow us out to our cars. We're kind of lingering as if there's still something left that needs to be said when I saw it—another yellow chord this time tied onto the outside of the house entry door handle.

"We missed it," I point.

TF turns around and unties it stepping back into the entry light to read better what's on the backside.

"It says," TF isn't sure whether to go on but does, "Have Courage Tomorrow."

"At least you know," Josh turns to me, "that it's the fourth day and not after the fourth day."

"I'm not sure I want to know," I respond.

One thing we all know is that there is a reason we've been gathered together and appreciate our mutual relationships. Whatever understanding is still missing, I'm sure this group will discover.

PART III

THE ATTACK

15
KIDNAPPED

A SHARP BEE STING AND I WAKE TRYING TO SHOO IT OFF. A car alarm blasts out on the street or maybe that's inside by head? I am dizzy. Something strange is going on.

Wait, a bee sting woke me? I try to rub my arm where it hurts but I can't reach it. The bee is holding my hand. A big faded orange bee and he's laughing. I know this can't be right.

"Help," I scream to Josh thinking this must be a nightmare. Josh doesn't answer.

I twist around to see him with two big orange bees on him. My brain puns, "The bees are after my Josh honey."

"Oh, no," fear in me cries out. "This is real."

One of Josh's bees yells to another, "Hit him again—it's not enough." A third orange bee enters the room with a syringe and sticks it into Josh's arm as the other two hold him.

Josh throws one to the floor and kicks him in the face, "Leave her alone."

He's defending me. Two of the bees are smirking at him but the one on the floor is bloodied—he won't be smirking anyone. But even he's letting his guard down now.

A syringe dangling from Josh's arm taking. Right in the middle of another kick he falls over passed out from whatever they gave him.

I fight the sleep but I'm also scared and my adrenalin is pumping. I shake my head trying to focus on the closest bee. Only this is clearly no bee. I notice a symbol on the orange jumpsuit he's wearing…it's the same symbol that was all over the voodoo sacrifice area.

I hear the kids yelling and turn to the noise.

Our bedroom door is open and the hall light is on. I can't see but do hear them dragging Jules from her room. Her screams aren't loud. They must have a gag on her.

I see them drag Ray by my room. He's got a pillow case over his head and his arms are bound behind his back.

The closest bee or guy, whatever he is, jerks me to my feet. "Wish we had time to play," the orange bee says to me as he squeezes my left breast. "Guess we'll just have to have fun with the kids." The other bees start laughing in such a sick way I want to puke.

Instead, I can't stop the blackness and fall backwards across the bed.

❖

Another sting and I wake to a talking black bee.

Black bee says, "Narcan. You'll be awake soon."

I feel the blackness unwind from my nervous system as I sober up. Kind of like a snake slithering down my spine.

"They gave Josh two injections," I mumble. "And, what's Narcan?"

"Oh," is all black bee says as he stings Josh a second time as well. Then he turns back to me, "Narcan takes away the effect of the drugs they gave you."

Josh wakes now but like me, it's slow and a matter of waiting for the first shots to clear out. He's shaking his head, "Dawn, you OK?"

"Yes, but they have the kids."

Black bee is on our phone now. We're just waiting in silence for our minds to clear. Who knows if a black bee is really any better than an orange bee?

Black bee says, "Get dressed and come down to your car. There's a long drive ahead of you tonight. Wait for Wade."

Black bee leaves. We hear him in the kitchen doing something. I'm still foggy but am getting clearer. Finally,

Josh gets up to his feet and comes over to help me. He extends his hand down grabs mine and pulls me up.

Repeating what I said earlier, "Come on, they've got the kids."

Wondering about the black bee but not wanting to say something while he's around, I quickly get dressed and head downstairs with Josh.

In the bedroom and now along the stairwell, I see the symbols drawn, maybe it's some kind of brand, and it's everywhere. On the walls, on the stair railing, we saw it on the doors. It's as if they wanted every part of the house claimed. Josh stops to look at one on the stairwell wall tracing his finger over it as if to figure out what it means.

"They had these on their jumpsuits as well," I'm sure he didn't see that the way they attacked him so quickly.

Before we start back down the stairs the coffee smell comes to us. "That's what black bee was doing in the kitchen?" I ask.

"Black bee—because of the syringe sting?" Josh gets it. "I thought more like a mosquito—what kind of coffee would a black bee make? Honey flavored?"

"What kind of flavor would a mosquito make?" I counter back.

He must still be under the influence as much as I am. Those orange bees have a potent sting.

I grab the coffee thermos and two cups, Josh grabs water bottles and granola bars. This is a habit I've seen over the years whenever he goes to one of his construction site. "You never know how long it takes," he's said to me too many times to appreciate. But, it's a good idea now.

"How much gas do you have in the Tahoe?"

"Half tank—how about your pickup?"

"Full tank, let's take it." Josh points to the Tahoe, "Get your cell phone."

Our counters got too cluttered long ago and we decided no more cell, Game Boy or PDA chargers in the kitchen. We leave our cell phones in the cars. The kids have their's upstairs in their rooms with their Game Boys. The

PDAs get parked beside our computers. Now if I could only get Josh to put his keys and wallet somewhere else.

The Mom in me pops out, "Before we load up, everyone go to the bathroom." I look around forgetting that we are everyone. Still, good advice and I take it. So does Josh.

While he's finishing inside the house, I put the thermos and cups in the truck. Josh joins me as I get my keys out of my purse to go back to the Tahoe when I remember, "I think Ray left his laptop in the Tahoe—I'm going to grab it as well."

While inside the car I notice that Ray has a special charger cable and grab it as well. Just to make sure we have everything we need, I look through the glove compartment and grab my flashlight. I know Ray has one too but I might need my own. I haven't told Ray yet, but I bought some pepper spray a couple of days ago. "That's definitely coming," I think as I reach for it.

Josh has organized the supplies and now sits behind the wheel as I return and settle in. Both cups of coffee are poured. He has Wade on speed dial, "Wade…Josh. Are you about here?"

Wade sounds awfully worked up, all I hear is "Amanda."

"They've got Amanda?" I ask and Josh slowly nods his head in confirmation.

"No, no, ***no***… what are these bastards after?" Josh doesn't answer me. His chin quivers, his eyes are filled with tears. I know he doesn't intend to respond because he has to stay focused. I honor that and hold back the scream I feel.

He just clears his throat and shakes his head. I understand. There's a time to let go and a time to stay focused. Finally, he breaks silence and says into the phone, "OK, I see your lights now." Putting the cell phone down in the console he turns and hugs me. That's all that needs to be said right now.

Wade pulls in behind the Tahoe, grabs his bag from the backseat of his car, and quickly opens the rear door of the pickup's extended cab climbing in while pushing his bag across the seat. "Let's go in your car."

I'm wondering if Wade's got something too dangerous on his mind to be seen in a police car. Josh doesn't ask, he just backs up the truck and takes off down the street.

"Got any idea where we are headed?"

"No," Wade answers me, "but Lee is in touch with Markos and is supposed to call us in directions."

"I can't tell if Markos is good or bad," I tell Wade.

He just shrugs, "Who helped you tonight?"

I wonder that as well. It wasn't Markos but the black bee dressed like him and had a bit of an accent like him—I'm guessing they're from somewhere in the Mediterranean area.

"Probably someone who works with Markos," I admit answering after an extended pause. Still, I hold back some conviction until I see my kids. Until then I remain suspicious.

Wade has set up a connection with Lee that comes through as an instant radio connection. I nicknamed the service Rude-Tel. I hate eating in a restaurant and hearing those things beep through. It's like every person who has one thinks that they're on par with an on call brain surgeon and that the entire world needs to hear their communications. I wish it were legal for restaurants and theaters to turn on an electronic barrier to keep them from working. I was surprised to find out there's a law against that. Another perfect answer ruined by a stupid law.

I'm happy to hear Lee break through on Wade's phone. Even though we're only two blocks from home, we need to know where we are going. So far, Josh is just headed for the nearest freeway.

"Go down to Naito and take the bridge over to get on I-84," Lee directs. I always get which bridge screwed up but nothing is stopping Josh. He knows the way well since we've often gone out to the airport the same way.

Wade just nods at the cell phone.

"Wade, at least say 'yes,'" I can't help but prompt him.

He weakly smiles, "I'm just so worried about all three kids." To her uncle, Amanda will always be a kid.

"I know," barely whispering I start crying.

"Dawn," Lee barks through. These phones are rude.

Wade passes me the cell phone.

"Which button do I push to talk?" He shows me.

"I'm here," I say finally getting the right button.

I wait for Lee to talk and after a little bit Wade says, "Don't hold the button down—only when you talk."

I let up and Lee comes back, "I know you think Markos could be evil, but he's not. He's helping us right now."

"How's he helping?" I ask wanting reassurance. I need hope that someone somewhere is willing to help us get our kids back.

"That fast fancy car of his you talked about?" I knew he means the long black limo.

"Affirmative," something about this kind of communication reminds me of the old TV show Drag Net.

"He's got people in that car catching up fast on the van the kids are in." Lee adds for Wade, "It's the same van that OHSU picked the snakes up from—maybe the same van that put the snakes there to begin with."

Not so cheery news about the van. But, if any car could make up time, that fast limo can. I'll take whatever reassurance I can get.

Wade takes the phone back, "Any descriptions on the driver or people in the van?"

Lee comes back, "Your favorite two police officers—the guys who went out from Reverend Senior Pastor William to arrest Ray that night after church. Can you believe that?"

I can believe it and tell Wade, "I know they're the ones who planted the snakes. I told Josh so at the time.".

"Yes, you did." Josh looks to me as he agrees. I just motion for him to keep his eyes on the road. He's blowing through every red light along the way so he needs to pay attention.

"I wouldn't even be surprised if they're not real cops," I tell Wade.

"They won't be for long," threatens Wade. I know he means it.

Josh motions for the phone and Ray hands it to him, "Lee, are you in constant contact with Markos?"

"Pretty much. He's calling through TF's phone so that allows me to beep through to you guys. He's leaving the connection open but I don't hear him for several minutes sometimes. I think he's in communication with guys working for him." Lee pauses.

"Wait, he's telling you to go to the Vista House in the Columbia Gorge. Do you know how to get there?"

Josh stops and appears to be searching his memory before answering Lee. We haven't been there for several years. It's one of the most scenic and best known places in Oregon yet we've only been there once.

"No, but I know the direction and Dawn has Ray's portable computer with a map program on it. I'll call you back if we need help." Josh finally responds to Lee.

I didn't know Ray had a map program but take the cue even before Josh passes the phone to Wade in the back seat. I open Josh's computer but it won't start—the battery is dead.

Wade watches me try and boot and says, "Is that cable for a cigarette lighter?" He's pointing at the cable I grabbed.

I pick it up from the console sliding my hand down it to the end. I see it is set up for getting power from the car. I plug it into one of the two cigarette lighter plugs and find the other end and plug it into the computer.

Wade points to a box in the middle of the cable, "What's that?"

"I don't know," I answer truthfully. I do know the portable is coming on.

Josh knows, "Ray got the electronic parts and made a booster for the WIFI. He says it increased the coverage by up to 1,000 times."

"It works," the guys mistake me for saying the computer is on. "I mean the booster works—look," I point at the screen. We're passing a hotel off to the right and on screen I read, "Welcome to Motel 8's Free Broadband Connection."

"I remember Ray telling me about War-Driving. He and Sam do it almost every weekend. They get points from passing certain areas and it's like a big hunt to find all the WIFI tokens. I don't know what they win, but they get pretty competitive."

Wade must think I'm losing track, "Let's stay on focus and get directions to Vista House."

"That map program," I explain, "is on the computer and not online. So I can get to it later. While I'm online, I'm checking Ray's email to see if there are any clues there."

Wade seems to realize that I know what I'm doing and sits back playing with the cell phone.

Out loud I say, "Just one email from Sam."

Long ago we told the kids that we believe the internet is like the front door of our house. We don't leave it open for any stranger to walk in on them and we weren't going to leave the internet open. I have the passwords to both kids' accounts and check regularly for improper solicitations. I've reported many to our ISP.

I check Jules' email messages but she doesn't have any.

I check Josh's email just in case there's a ransom note or something. But there is nothing.

I have two emails. The first one is a response from Markos. I read it out loud, "'Fear Not,' that's all Markos says."

Josh asks, "You emailed Markos?"

"Yesterday. I asked him for help...I hoped he was a good guy." I still hope that.

I return my attention to the computer screen to read the second and last email. "Oh, my God." I cry hard as I pass the computer back to Wade.

Wade reads it for Josh, "We'll send you pictures when we're through. If you're lucky, we'll send you some pieces as well. Satan says to have a good day."

"There just trying to scare you," Wade acts as if that should make me feel better. "We're going to get the kids before they're harmed," he adds and surety does make me feel better.

"Did you see the symbol?" I ask. I have to turn around to see that Wade is nodding. "I think it's Egyptian but not sure." It's just an impression.

I'm fascinated with Egyptian history. Josh and I finally traveled to Egypt several years ago. Part of the trip included a stay on a river boat going up the Nile River. It's an amazing river, full of history and stretches through so many countries. But, I was surprised to find out that it's only about half the width of the Columbia River which is on the left side of the highway now. Josh is making good time.

The scale of nature here reminds me of Egypt as well. We're making good time now but this is no five minute Hollywood chase scene. We've got at least a half hour to go. The Columbia Gorge is huge.

In high school I was taught that the entire Gorge was carved out in about three days. As the ice melted it caused a big dam out in Idaho or Montana. They think the lake backed up into Canada so it was a lot of water. When the dam burst, the water carved out everything quickly. Kind of like what's going on in my life right now.

Lee blasts through my reminiscing across the cell phone, "Markos is pretty blunt how he talks. He specifically told me to tell you exactly how he's describing things. Dawn, are you ready for that?"

Wade passes me the phone.

"Hell, yes," I come back. "Do you think that my imagination isn't going to the worst possible places anyway?"

"Wade," Lee asks and I pass the phone back to him, "are you ready?"

"I know more about these kinds of characters...I've even dealt with some of them. You're not going to tell me anything I don't already know. So, yes, tell us." Wade just wants to get Amanda and I'm sure any information helps him.

"I wish I could send you a picture of their symbol, logo, whatever. I want to make sure Markos is referring to the right people."

"Send it to my email right now and I'll get it," I look on screen and see "The Flying M Station Broadband Welcomes You".

TF knows my email address and within seconds I see the symbol on screen.

I hold the computer up for everyone to see.

"Is that the same symbol?" Lee pauses.

"That's it. They even have it on their orange jumpsuits," I respond.

"Jumpsuits?" Lee puzzles then comes back, "Markos says those are robes they're wearing. Stained in human blood—that's not orange, it's blood."

Now I'm shaking.

He goes on, "The bottom line of the symbol is the top of a crocodile head and the circle is the sun."

I interrupt, "Sobek Re?"

"How did you know?" Wade asks me.

"Josh and I went to Om Kombo in Egypt. Sobek was worshiped there for a couple of thousand years." I recall our tour guide calling Sobek the god of chaos. I remember seeing drawings of him depicted with flint-bladed knives to slay the enemies of Ra. That would probably include kids who believe in Jesus Christ.

"They're from the Temple of Sobek. Tonight is a full moon and their intent is to sacrifice them." Lee certainly is not holding back anything. Yet, I feel like I knew this was the case.

I look at Wade as he responds, "We know that."

I feel like part of me knew it from the first sting.

"Have you found your exit, yet?" Lee is asking but I haven't yet so don't respond.

I pull up the map program and am trying to figure out how to locate us on this.

Josh takes the phone from me and says, "We're coming up on Exit 18…are we getting close?"

I take that as a clue and zoom in on I-84 Exit 18. This is not the exit we want but I can track up I-84 from there. I still can't figure out how to ask the program for directions to the Vista House.

"He says to take Exit 22 to where it dead ends into a road, turn left, there are signs pointing the way to Vista House." Lee repeats directions given by Markos.

I turn off and fold the computer down now that we have directions.

"If we're pulled over for speeding, do you have an alibi ready?" I've wondered the same thing for the last half hour. Every time I look, Josh is doing at least 85 mph. Wade just motions for him to keep driving.

"Corbett, Exit 22," I read from the sign coming up.

We can't be far and Wade is getting ready. I turn to see him open his gun, check the bullets, and put them back.

I pick up the pepper spray I dropped on the floor earlier and hand it to Josh, "I think you might need this."

He asks without taking look, "What is it?"

"Pepper spray."

He takes it and tries a quick peek but the road is too demanding. So, he just sideways nods at me as if this is just the answer needed. He's being brave so I can cry and I do, but not too much.

"I didn't remember this road being so curvy," Josh is apologizing to Wade who just got thrown against the door.

Lee comes on, "Can you guys still hear me?"

Josh passes the phone back to me and I pass it back to Wade.

Wade answers, "Yes, I'm surprised we've got reception, but we can still hear you."

"How far away are you from Vista House?" We're not sure if it's Lee who wants to know or if it's Markos.

"Minutes," Wade answers with one word.

"Markos says Ray is there but the girls are not." Lee is trying to be careful how he says this, "Do you have a first aid kit?"

I cry.

Wade catches Josh's eyes in the rear view mirror.

"Just under your seat should be my first aid bag. We're required to have it on construction sites." Josh's voice is quivering.

Wade nods. He knows that Josh won't be able to handle it. I suspect that he's trained better anyway.

"What the hell?" Josh says as we lurch into a four inch drop off. Literally one side of the road is dropping off. Josh quickly gains control.

"Ask Lee if he knows about this?" referring to the road.

"Lee, you or Markos know anything about half the road giving way?" Wade waits for Lee to come back.

"There were traffic barriers around that earlier. The Sobek people must have cleared it out to trap you."

"Markos says," TF continues, "that these guys will do anything to slow you down or kill you. We'll talk more about it but you're just about there now, right?"

Josh is trying to drive 85 mph even on these winding switchback mountainside roads and the lurching is getting to all of us.

There's the Vista House not far ahead. This octagon shaped building with the fantastic views up and down the Columbia Gorge has been in more movies than any other part of Oregon. Tonight it looks sinister.

Josh drives us up to the base of the stairs at the front door. Every stair is covered with votive candles. The stench of the incense is gagging.

The doors are open and torches light up the inside. The gothic stained glass windows seem to be crawling with the torchlight.

"Malevolent," is the only word that comes to mind.

Wade says, "Wait," and gets out of the truck first. His gun pulled, he walks all the way around the building. We practically hold our breath waiting. Thankfully, it's not that big of a building.

Josh lowers his window, "Anything on the backside," he whispers too loud to pretend we're not here.

Wade emerges from the far side shaking his head, "A bunch of dead snakes."

"What do you know about the interior?" Wade is now leaning in Josh's window.

I lean forward to be seen around Josh and offer, "The bathrooms and shops are downstairs." Basically, that's all I remember about this place but they're both important to me.

"How do we get to those stairs?"

I tell Wade, "You go in through the front door and there are two sets, one on the left and one on the right. Both meet downstairs across from each other."

Last time we were here there were 50 or more people on site. Parking was impossible to find. In this darkness there's not a sound or person around. Between the silence and flickering firelight, well, there' still no better description than sinister.

Wade says to Josh, "Got your pepper spray?"

Josh nods.

"OK, you and Dawn take the stairwell on the right, I'll take the left. Dawn, where are the bathrooms?"

"Men's at the base of the stairs on the left, women's at the base of the right stairs," I inform him.

"Then you two take the women's restroom—turn on the lights if possible, open every stall door, check the trash for clues or whatever and meet me back at the base of the stairs as quickly as possible."

"Got it," Josh says as he takes the pepper spray out of his shirt pocket.

"Should I bring the first aid kit?" whatever condition Ray is in worries me. Actually, I'm closer to panic than worry. I have to fight off the hysteria and just assume he's alive. The best way to do that is to be prepared to care for him.

Wade opens the back door up and gets the first aid kit for me. He hands it to me across the seat as Josh gets out of his door. I get out and catch up with them at the entry stairs. We stop at the base for just a second before going for the front door.

"Should we say a prayer?" I ask at this pause.

"Who hasn't been praying all night?" Wade wants to know. He's right—this night has been and I suspect it will be one long prayer.

"Jesus," is all Josh prays but it's all that needs to be said.

We walk through the votive candles. I cough a little at the incense and wonder if it's patchouli. I always thought that stench is obnoxiously demonic. Even patchouli can't stop me now.

There are two upright torches on the floor under the middle of the high domed ceiling. They're in a brass stand sitting in the middle of a bright white tarp. The tarp has the symbol for Sobek painted in the middle. It's painted with blood.

"It's Ray's blood," I think but don't say.

Before I start crying at the sight, Josh grabs my hand and pulls me to the right stairwell. He knows I'm tormented.

We halt at the top of the stairs waiting for a cue from Wade. He looks at us and just nods before starting down the stairs. We follow practically running down them. At the base on the right is the Women's restroom. Josh runs in and I stop and flip on the lights. The white marble reflects the lights harshly.

Josh begins at the farthest stall and I at the nearest. We throw the doors open for speed, not silence. I hear Wade across the way doing the same.

I hold the first aid bag over my shoulder ready to clobber someone. The irony of hurting someone with a first aid bag isn't lost but right now isn't funny either.

"No one here," Josh says. I run and look inside a waste basket, he looks inside the other.

Both are empty and we run out to meet Wade.

Wade is trying to open a door to the left of the bathroom.

"That's the main store," I tell him.

"Is there another door?"

I nod and motion for he and Josh to follow me down the side hall. I try the back door but it's locked as well.

"What's that door?" Wade points to the opposite end the side hall.

"It's a coffee shop," I tell him as he pulls on that locked door.

Two rooms we can't check and I don't like that. On the other hand, I don't sense Ray in either of these rooms.

There's a lower set of stairs but I see there's nothing hidden down that way. Wade motions back up the stairs and Josh follows me up the same stairs we came down.

We meet under the domed area upstairs and I point to the sides, "Those stairs go up to the outside lookout deck."

Josh remembers as well and grunts.

Wade points back to the left stairs, "OK, I'll go up mine, you go up your's and we meet on the lookout front facing the river." Wade turns and runs up the steps catching us off guard.

We run as well. I'm not far behind Josh.

The old marble steps are steep but the torchlight reflects well off the white marble and it's easy to see where we're going. Josh hits the door hard. It bangs open.

We go to our left and I scream, "Ray, Ray, where are you?"

No response.

We run into Wade at the front of the lookout facing the river. I'm in shock. Where is Ray?

The moon shines brightly down on us and the Columbia River below flickers with the light. This would be beautiful under any other circumstance.

I cry, "Where is he?"

The guys start talking and I start backtracking. I'm check every inch of this lookout right now. I want Ray.

I retrace where we came up but I'm not stopping there. I start to encircle the entire building. I'll climb up on the dome if I must.

I sense him before I see him.

Ray is tied up on a cross facing the parking lot. The cross is fastened to the building. He must have been watching us the entire time. He's got duct tape across his mouth.

Josh calls, "Dawn, where are you?"

"He's here," is all I get out as I try and undo how they tied him up. I can't find the knots.

There's only the candles below and the moonlight, not much light for details, but I see the blood all over him.

Wade is on the other side with a pocket knife and just cuts through the ties. He throws the knife to Josh.

"They're plastic snap ties—just cut through them," he tells Josh.

While Josh cuts through, I hand Wade the first aid kit. He cracks open the sterile water bottle first and start's washing Ray's stomach. I pull the duct tape off his mouth.

Ray tries to steady himself while Wade cleans him up. Josh takes a flashlight out of his pocket and hands it to me. I turn it on for Wade to finish washing him up.

Thankfully, the cuts don't look very deep. This was done for psychological torment.

The water washes away the blood enough that I see the Sobek logo cut into Ray's stomach.

Ray's shaking as Wade cleans him up. Josh just keeps him focused on his eyes talking as if we had all the time in the world.

"Is that your blood downstairs on the tarp?" Josh asks, his voice low and normal. I think he's concerned about how much blood Ray has lost.

"No," Ray assures him. "They had a bucket of blood with them."

Wade says, "Other than a lot of pain, you're not in too bad of shape. Did they beat you?" Wade's got the flashlight looking closer at the now clean cuts.

"Only until the cuffed me…I beat the crap out of a couple of them and they hit back hard," Ray recounts. I see from the bruises on his face what they did. I hope he got them good.

"Good for you," Josh says as he starts leading Ray towards the stairs.

"Dad, you got one, too," Ray tells him. "I heard this guy swearing about how you kicked the crap out of him and his nose will never be the same. They had to go to an emergency room and drop him off. Everyone was yelling at him for making them late."

Wade repeats, "'making them late'—is that what you said?"

We cough our way through the incense and candles back to the truck. Josh clears out the seat behind picking up the drinks and energy bars for Ray to get in.

So far, tonight has been more like a scary movie than real life. However, Josh says something that again makes me think of the difference between us and some Hollywood chase scene, "I don't know where we're going or how far. Anyone want to use the bathroom before we go?"

No one reacts to the bathroom call. While we don't know how far we have yet to go, we all are driven to get from this place as soon as possible. Even if it means our bladders bust later.

Without saying a word, we all get in. Josh hands us each a bottle of water and a granola bar. It's a good way to clear the seat for Ray but it's probably not a bad idea either.

Wade thinks of something and pounds his pockets until he finds the cell phone. "Lee, you there?"

"Yes, how's Ray?" he asks.

"OK, more in a bit. First, where do we go now?"

"Hang on and I'll ask Markos." The phone is silent as we buckle up and Josh starts up the engine.

"Son," Josh says to Ray, "There are a couple of clean shirts I keep in here—probably under Ray's seat."

"You don't want my blood on your seats?" Ray dead pans back.

"You're shivering," I tell Ray. And, he is. Uncontrollably and he doesn't even know it. He finds one of the shirts from under the seat and painfully pulls it on.

Wade interrupts Josh and Ray, "Did you get that?"

Josh shakes his head "no." We both were watching Ray instead of listening.

"Take the road straight ahead and we're going to get onto I-84 again at Multnomah Falls," directs Lee. "We're going to Stonehenge."

I don't think that most people are aware of the full scale Stonehenge replication in the Columbia Gorge. But, Josh and I have been there.

"Stonehenge?" Josh repeats. "That's an hour away."

Lee comes back, "Markos said there's more…we are going to be under attack along the way. He says, don't stop and don't slow down."

Josh speeds off down the hill on the back side of Vista House and on down the back roads towards Multnomah Falls. We're all getting bounced around on the tight corners, bad road, and hair pin turns. I'd usually be screaming if Josh drove like this but now I'd be screaming if he didn't.

"Wade, ask him what kind of attacks," Josh grits as he's trying to see the dark road beyond the headlights.

We understand the silence is waiting for Markos to explain the attacks to Lee.

This old bridge ahead looks small. More like a lane and a half than two lanes. 'Latourell Falls' I read a sign we quickly pass.

Lee comes back on. "Markos says the first type of attack will not be real. If we see animals jumping out in the road ahead of us, these are mental projections. Do not stop. Whatever you see, do not stop."

We live in Oregon. We've all seen cars that do not stop for jumping animals and invariable they have half a deer sticking out of them and people hurt or dead inside. I don't like this.

"And rocks, big boulders," Lee goes on. "These are real so avoid them. They really will try and kill us with them."

Great, kill or let our girls be killed. "Not an option," I think. Josh just drives faster.

This road would be very slow if other drivers were out. But there are no other drivers and Josh sincerely believes there are no speed limits.

"There may be speed boats shooting at you around Biggs," Lee warns. "Markos is almost there with his boat and he thinks he'll get them all out before you arrive."

Wade says, "Lee, can you hold up with Markos for just a second. I've got a question that we really need to know the answer to—like right now!"

I didn't know I had a question that needed answered right now. What's Wade getting at? Whatever it is, I know it's important.

Lee simply says, "Go ahead."

"They told Ray," Wade says, "that they have a schedule. Does Markos know what the schedule is?"

"Yes," Lee is reluctant. "The witching hour, the time of the sacrifice, it's scheduled for 3 AM."

We all look to the truck dash. Right now it's a quarter before 2 AM.

"We can make it," determination is in Wade's voice.

"You don't get it," Lee snaps back. "They don't need to kill you, although they might. All they need to do is delay you—flat tire, punctured radiator, that sort of thing."

Josh gets it and just goes even faster. I know he means to allow no delay.

"Markos says he knows they have a major ambush planned for you. Be careful."

As we come around a bend in the road at Wahkeena Falls, a deer jumps into the road. I automatically yell, "Josh."

Josh speeds up and says, "Remember what Lee said?" We go through the deer like driving through fog. It's not real.

"So the devil can make us see things?" Ray asks weakly from the back seat.

Wade says, "Way to go," patting Josh's shoulder in congratulations.

"How much further to the Multnomah Falls exit?" Josh points to Ray's computer for me to pull up the map.

I pass it back to Ray, "Get to work, lazy."

My kids don't usually appreciate my sense of humor and tonight is no exception.

Ray is sore but I see that he wants to do something and as he gladly accepts the computer.

"Is this it?" I ask about the wide parking on both sides of the road. This must be Multnomah Falls but I don't see a sign. Maybe I missed it?

Ray hasn't had time to look it up and Josh is going to fast too slow down. We quickly pass the parking and a turn off.

When every second counts, the boot time on a computer seems like forever. Finally, Ray has the map program up and is zooming in on where we are. "Call out the next sign you see, Mom."

A few minutes later I find another sign and read to him, "Horsetail Falls."

"Crap, you missed it," Ray tells Josh.

That open area I saw had to be Multnomah Falls.

"Does this road get us there?" Josh asks.

"Yes, connects I-84 at Ainsworth."

"Ainsworth?" Josh repeats.

"Dad, that's where we put in fishing with Richard last year…where you caught the ten foot long sturgeon?" Ray didn't have to add that but Josh has been bragging ever since. He remembers.

"Is it quicker to turn around and go back to Multnomah Falls or go straight?" Josh is trying to decide what to do.

"Go straight, we'll hit the highway shortly," Ray assures him.

I wish the road were straight but hopefully there's not much more bouncing to do. That last bounce threw me hard into the door and I'm rubbing my shoulder.

Wade decides to tell Lee about our detour, "Lee…are you there Lee?"

No answer.

"Probably no coverage," Wade explains.

We drive on in silence, cut off from direction and off course, but making good time.

"This is it," Ray leans forward pointing across Josh's shoulder to the road going to the right. "Oh," he grabs his stomach from the pain.

"You OK?" I ask him and he just shakes his head.

Wade had thrown the first aid kit on the floor. He picks it up going through it using his flashlight to find something. Finally he holds up an aspirin bottle, "Take three of these." He hands them to Ray.

Josh slows down to get on the on ramp.

Before we reach the highway, two cop cars going in the opposite direction pass us with their lights and sirens on.

"Wow, there in a hurry," Josh looks down at the speedometer. "I'll bet they're doing well over 100."

The truck has stiff springs and the side road has been bumpy. I settle back now that we're on the smooth highway. I see Ray is doing the same. I turn to look at Wade and don't like what I see on his face.

"What's up, Wade?" I ask him.

"You don't want to know," he tries to shut me out. But, that makes me really want to know.

"What aren't you telling us? This is no time to hold back anything," I badger him.

"In the 90's," Wade begins reluctantly, "I was on a task force about missing children. We had special training from an expert FBI agent on satanic cults. I didn't believe most of what they told me at the time. I didn't use to think it mattered... a crime is a crime regardless of why it was done. I was wrong."

Wade stops to clear his throat but I can still hear the quiver in his voice.

"The task force grew to include people from Washington State. Over a period of time, it focused on a group out of Goldendale."

"Wait," I interrupt him. "The FBI trained you about Satanism? What do you mean?"

"There's been a lot of back tracking since then. A group out of California, for example, even sues people who post internet information on how they were reared in these cults. They call it false memory recall but the victims I talked to never had a memory lapse. They always knew what happened to them. Anyway, it's gotten so bad that many of these victims won't come forth and speak like they used to because of the persecution and privacy violations that goes on with these self proclaimed scientific groups. In reality, every one of these cults I've read about are led by educated people, often lawyers, doctors, college professors sometimes police chiefs. It's not surprising they've got defenders. However, this isn't about science."

"We're at least 40 minutes away," Josh says looking in the rearview mirror trying to catch Wade's eye, "start from the beginning."

We start through a tunnel that I remember comes up quickly on the fish hatchery on the other side. Out of habit Josh honks as he has always done and always does in tunnels. The sound seems to emphasize for Wade to start talking.

"Elephant," Ray screams pointing down the road to the far face of the tunnel.

I turned from paying attention to Wade to see where Ray is pointing. I've never heard anyone yell 'elephant.'

An elephant stands in the middle of the road covering two lanes of traffic.

"Elephant?" Josh says as he starts to swerve. At this speed and where the elephant stands, there's no hope to swerve without crashing into one of the tunnel walls.

Josh starts to brake.

"It's not real," says Wade.

"Help me, Jesus," Josh cries out and accelerates. Josh has a theory about car wrecks. He's told me many times, when you know it's going to happen for sure, accelerate. I don't remember why and never believed him anyway.

There's no hope to reach Lee and get confirmation from Markos even if we had time, we have no connection.

That's a big elephant. I want to close my eyes but can't.

I hear Ray praying in the back seat but don't know what he's saying. Sounds like he's speaking in tongues or maybe I'm not hearing in English.

Josh starts honking.

Wade leans forward and puts one hand on my left shoulder and the other hand grasps Ray's knee. He's praying loud and fast as well.

I see the elephant's eyes widen.

I think we may die.

We're close enough to see the long hairs on the elephant's legs.

The front legs disappear and we whiz by the elephant behind us now standing upright on two legs. Hi-ho Silver upright and holding there.

We all turn and look back.

"Watch the road," I yell at Josh.

Ray asks, "Did you see it rear up like that? I didn't know an elephant could move that fast?"

"It's not a real elephant," answers Wade.

"For a mirage, it was awfully detailed. Look at it still in the road." I point.

We round the next bend and I can't see the elephant any more.

Josh is shaking but never slowed down. "It looked so real."

"Now what?" I ask pointing at the upcoming turn in the road. There sat two cars with their lights out facing us. If it weren't for the moonlight, I wouldn't have been able to see them. This can't be good.

"What is it?" Wade leans forward between Josh and me trying to assess the situation.

No time to show him so I just jerk the wheel to the right as I say, "take this off ramp."

There's a short piece of highway here with some kind of off ramp. Maybe it was the original highway. It runs parallel to the main highway and appears to rejoin it.

Thankfully, the road is smooth. Jerking the wheel like that could have caused a crash otherwise.

Josh recovers from it and says, "Thanks."

The two cars figure out that we are bypassing them on the inside through the ramp. They don't turn their lights on but we see them starting to move towards us. It's too late for them to cut us off.

The cars speed up but have to go in the opposite direction for a ways to get back to the off ramp entrance. That extra time Josh puts to good use and speeds up even more.

I dimly see a small reflector in the headlights.

"Something up there, get way over to the left." I direct Josh.

He drives over to the left, sees that he can actually cross the remaining area and gets back on the highway.

The reflector is from a boat and trailer parked in the middle of the off ramp. I see that the front of the boat trailer is resting on a camper refrigerator and the left rear wheel is missing.

The chase cars are coming up on us fast. Without any lights on, it's hard to measure their speed and how close they're getting. In the moonlight they look like dark clouds.

I see it and hear it at the same time.

Just driving by moonlight probably isn't enough light to see the boat reflector. The first car slams into the boat shoving it off its trailer and debris spills across the other side where the second car is coming up.

The first car flips and rolls. I see it spinning over the ramp into the highway and right into the road barrier.

The second car hits the boat debris and swerves to the right and off the main ramp. I remember seeing the sign warning about boulders but didn't see any in the moonlight. Neither did this car. It has to be a boulder it hit.

The car flips end over end and lands upside down skidding out across both lanes in the highway behind us.

"Praise God," Ray says still watching the last car.

We all say, "Praise God."

"A disappearing deer, a rearing elephant, and two unlit cars that crash to pieces… wonder when the excitement begins?" quips Ray. Like his father, he tries to sound brave and reassuring. It's a good attempt.

"How about a giraffe?" I answer back pointing along my side of the highway. Sure enough, a large giraffe stands there looking at us.

"At least it's not in the road," Wade is grateful.

"Does make me wonder what's around the corner," Josh notes and for the first time slows down as we go around a bend.

There's a huge over turned truck and trailer in the road. Because Josh slowed down, we're able to brake and drive on the highway shoulder around the wreck.

"No time to stop," Wade reminds him.

Ray is looking out his window and is the closest to the wreck. "It's a circus truck," he tells us.

"What?" I'm confused.

Josh catches on quickly, "Then the elephant was real?"

"Josh, Josh," a singsong kind of voice calls as if he were trying to get Josh for a long time.

Wade grabs his phone telling us what we already know, "It's Lee."

Great, we've got reception.

"Lee, bring us up to speed," Wade tells him.

"You guys at Hood River, yet?" Lee asks.

Ray holds his fingers from one hand up, "Five minutes."

"Minutes away," Wade answers back to Lee.

"Markos says you missed the ambush," Lee starts explaining. "You must have gone through Multnomah Falls earlier than they thought."

"The Sobek people set up two vans across the parking lot and when a car came through, they shot it to pieces killing the two guys inside."

"A State Trooper came up and saw it, called for backup. It's on the news right now. A huge shoot out with several cops responding. They killed the shooters. They're showing the Sobek logo asking people to call in with information. They've identified two of them as the cops we talked about."

I'm not surprised about the two cops, but a shoot out? That's why we saw those cop cars traveling so fast back towards Multnomah Falls.

"How did you miss all that?" Lee prods Wade.

"'Lead us not into temptation but deliver us from evil...' that's how." Wade explains, "We took the wrong turn and missed the Multnomah Falls exit."

"God is leading you, huh?" Lee asks.

He's right. There are no accidents tonight.

"Look, you've got about a half hour more to go. Markos says when you get down close to the river, watch out for gunmen on boats. His guys got three boats but they think one may still out there."

Lee is interrupted by TF grabbing his phone who says, "I just want you to understand you're not alone. Dusky and John are here with us praying."

He holds up the phone and we hear both Dusky and John saying, "We are praying for you and know you'll bring back the girls."

Lee comes back on, "Wade and Josh, Markos says that your involvement in the rescue is critical."

They nod.

"Markos says that there is a Biblical principle about authority to redeem. That only a kinsman could redeem someone. We're not talking about salvation, we're talking about redeeming people from things like debt and slavery."

I'm thinking, "This is no time for a Bible lesson" but the guys are listening closely.

"He'll tell you what to say when it's time, but you've got to go with Markos right into the center of things and claim the girls back by your kinsmen authority and in the blood of Jesus. Will you do that?" Lee didn't need to ask, it's obvious that these guys are dedicated to going to hell and back for the girls.

Ray motions to Wade for the phone and asks Lee, "Can you upload me directions? My program says we turn at Biggs and I've never heard of that place."

On both sides of the road through Hood River Ray is picking up internet access. If we're going to get any email, now's the time to send it.

"Great," responds Lee, "I'm sending you a screen capture on the exit right now."

Ray says, "Not now, Sam. Can you believe he's trying to IM me right now?"

"What's he saying?" I ask. Sam shouldn't be up at this time.

"He says he woke up in a panic afraid that I and Jules are in danger and is praying for us." Ray goes on, "I'm not going to respond but that's a good friend."

Ray picks the phone back up, "Lee, got the map. What's the other attachment?"

"It's a lay out of Stonehenge. Markos wants you all to be familiar with it before you get there. Can you share it with your Dad and Wade?" Lee doesn't have a clue how easy it is to pass the laptop back and forth.

"Anything else I can send you?" Lee is really trying to be supportive.

"Dad's driving so fast we're beyond internet connections now. If you think of something, I might be able to retrieve it when we go by The Dalles." Ray tells him.

Several minutes pass before Wade takes the phone back, "Any other warnings?"

"Markos says they'll only attack for about 15 minutes more then everyone leaves for Stonehenge. Once they're there and the ceremonies begin, their defense is in the outer ring around the altar."

"Fifteen minutes more of rough stuff," I remark.

"Markos says don't be relieved by the lack of attacks," Lee acts as if he can hear me. "The altar defense is impossible to get around. The best thing to do is get here as fast as you can."

I look at the speedometer and Josh is doing almost 100 mph now. The road is vacant. Unless the police stop us, we'll be there soon.

Usually it takes a lot longer to go from Hood River to The Dalles, but not the way Josh is driving. We sweep past the Columbia Gorge Discovery Center on the river side and come quickly through town.

Ray confirms, "Got the map. At this speed, Biggs is not far." He folds up and puts away the computer—no more anticipated connections now.

Minutes out of town and now a headlight explodes.

"They're shooting at us," I cry out.

Josh speeds up to 110 mph as we go down a small hill.

"That's not from any boat," Ray says.

Wade has his gun drawn. I don't know what he thinks there is to shoot at but I like that he's ready.

Josh points up ahead, "River coming up."

I look and see the road goes by the water. It looks like there is water on both sides so if there's a boat attack, this would be the place.

"God, save us," Ray says as if he were blessing us. I think that is what he's doing.

All we can do is wait as we close in on the water.

"Wade, should we roll down the windows to keep glass from going everywhere," I don't know how Josh thinks of these things.

Wade shakes his head, "No, it's safety glass, it won't cut us."

This seems like a ridiculous conversation to me. I wonder if they forget about the bullet part of the situation.

We're here. Water to the right, water to the left. Not a soul out on the highway in either direction. I see the road easily even with only one headlight. Around us the moon lights up the water brightly. I search for movement.

There's not one electric light in sight.

It's as if time stands still and we're just racing through another dimension.

Nothing happens.

Still more nothing happens.

We're beyond the water now.

I wonder where we are and see a sign coming up and read it out loud to everyone, "End Of Columbia Gorge Scenic Area."

I look at the desolate hills and agree. Ever since we left The Dalles the vegetation gets skimpier. Hood River had Douglas fir trees and lots of vegetation. By The Dalles all I saw were a few pine and scrub oak trees. Now there's no growth—just the glisten of far away hills reflecting bare rock in the moonlight.

"They didn't need to tell us it was the end of the scenic area," Ray comments from the back seat.

No more attacks, we're beyond that time. Not too long from now we'll be there. And, I can't stand the waiting.

"Wade, finish telling us about your task force," I remind him.

"I'd hoped you forgot that," his honest reply is sincere.

"We're going to go nuts waiting to get there, tell us what we're dealing with," I know I'm really demanding.

Josh backs me up, "Buddy, I'm going into the hell storm with you. I've got to know what we're dealing with."

Wade is not sure if he wants to tell us, perhaps he's reluctant to say it in front of Ray. He knows he really has no choice but to tell us.

"When I was on this task force in the 90's, there was a famous case involving a Washington man who pleaded guilty to sexually abusing children. He said at the time that it was ritualistic and part of his worship of Satan." We wait for him to go on.

"I have no doubt in my mind that was the case. I talked with some of the kids then and I correspond with two still. They've never changed their story."

The way he said that makes me think someone changed their story. "Did the guy change his story?" I ask.

"Yes, and he's tried to appeal his case. There's been a lot of national debate about Satanic cults and these kinds of claims are not so readily accepted any more."

"Why?" Ray asks simply.

"Because most of the claims have certain characteristics wherever they're made. For one, that judges, cops or some authority is involved and hush things up. That kind of automatically makes the enforcers skeptical."

"Two, the large majority of these claims are from what we not too politically correct call the W-4F… White, Fat, Forty, Flatulent, Female. Suddenly, their memory appears and they make accusations against a long list of people starting with their parents."

"Third, that they witnessed several sacrifices of babies or runaway teenagers. Sometimes the bodies were ground up and fed to them as meatloaf. Others claim the bodies were burned and the ashes spread out over miles or dumped in the ocean. However, no won can find any evidence to back up these claims."

He explains, "There's been a lot of debunking about how memory is recalled and whether it's reliable. The summary is that in the 90's people believe memory recall was possible and today it's not very widely accepted."

"What did your task force believe?" I ask.

"We didn't talk about it much but I never believe totally in any witness. People who see the same crime committed come up with widely varying degrees of details and sometimes none of them are correct. That's why it's common for police on the news to say their looking for a possible 'black suspect'... chances are in a group of white people they're going to say the perpetrator is black whether he is or not. We don't like to admit that, but it's true," Wade makes his point.

"Some of the claims get so exaggerated," he wants us to understand. "For example, some claim up to 50,000 people a year are sacrificed. Our crime statistics are that as horrible as our society is, we don't have more than about 23,000 murders a year. They claim thousands and thousands of runaways go unaccounted for and are the victims but I doubt if there are more than an average of 52 a year we don't eventually find."

"But, we're dealing with the reality of Satanism right now," as if Wade needs to hear that from me.

"I know what's real. There's always been a significant truth that the two extremes bury. There are Satanist. Whether judges, lawyers and cops are leading them or not, the very system they serve provides a protection for them. And, I believe Lee is right about the justice system being a demon-based type of worship, so those people wouldn't even know what they're serving."

"They're so self-righteous about what they do, they wouldn't want to know what spirit they're under," I add.

"You talked about Goldendale earlier," Ray prompts Wade back on track.

"One of the leads the task force got from the child abuse ring led us to a group in Goldendale. I was in on the first interview but I was asked to participate on a follow up interview of a 16 year old girl. This is one of the girls I still am in touch with...I guess girl isn't the right description. She's 26 now and has a kid of her own."

"Who was the group?" but he ignores me.

"I can't tell you things like that," Wade says. "Some of the people accused were innocent, others weren't. One I'd like to kill myself."

Pretty strong talk coming from Wade. I sense that he literally means it.

"I know the case I worked on is real but the similarities to the false memory cases can't be ignored. I think that's the insidious way the truth gets buried.

"From the time this girl was seven months old she was raped by her step-father. From what her mother later confessed, it was part of the Satanic rituals she and her husband followed at the time."

My skin crawls and I just want to puke. I don't want to hear this but any piece of information could be valuable for what we face.

I've turned to watch Wade talk and now he looks at me, "You OK for me to go on?"

I nod. Josh puts his hand on my knee briefly for reassurance. He's driving too fast to leave it there and I place it back on the wheel.

"By the time she was 14, she was taking heavy drugs and had already had an abortion. She claims that the Satanists took the aborted baby and used it's blood in their rituals. I do know that when I researched the hospital records, they had lost the baby and no one ever knew where it went."

"She's the one who told me about Stonehenge. On the Winter Solstice and the Summer Solstice, they would strip her, drug her, and place her on an altar in the middle of the circle. The drugs were hallucinogens and while she was dazed like that, they would sprinkle her with blood and take turns having sex with her. Sometimes they would tell her it's cat blood, other times the blood of babies. Her medical records showed extensive scarring compatible with forced sexual assaults over a very long period of time."

Wade is shaken recalling these details. Ray is angered.

"I asked her if they ever sacrificed runaways and she said that they would kidnap runaways hitchhiking. They'd always drug them and sexually abuse them, but as far as she knew, they never killed anyone." He thinks for a second, "In fact, she never saw them kill a baby or even possess a fetus."

That's little comfort to me.

Josh asks, "Does that mean they don't intend to kill our girls tonight?"

"I can't comfort you there. I don't know anything about activities on a full moon in August, so don't know the purpose. And, what I do know isn't helpful."

I ask Wade, "What is it that you do know?"

"These runaways they drugged and sexually abused… most of them died early from drug over doses, STDs or suicide. They didn't want to kill them because they considered what they did to them a death sentence…they would die from it in time."

"Who was it you wanted to kill?" Ray remembers.

"The step-father." Wade recalls, "He bragged about how he hadn't done anything wrong…that he made the girl a superior being by the attention and training he provided her."

"What happened to him and the mother?" I can't hide my curiosity.

"The mother committed suicide before her trial came up. The father is in jail at Walla Walla. He'll never get out but it's still too good for him." Wade's anger is obvious. His speaking and breathing is slow and heavy. His face is red.

"There's a part of the story even the task force doesn't know about," he's not through sharing. "The girl had a cousin spend the summer when she was 15 and the cousin was 14."

"The girl was so happy to have company but worried about what would happen to her cousin. At 15, she didn't want to admit all that had been done to her but at the same time wanted to protect the cousin."

"Did she?" Ray interrupts.

Wade swallows and takes his time, "No. They drugged them both but over dosed the cousin. She wasn't awake during all the things that they did to her. It was a blessing to the cousin but not to the girl who watched it all. She said she felt like she was getting tortured twice having to watch what they did to her cousin and feel what they were doing to her at the same time." Wade is crying now.

"To this day, the cousin..." now he's really crying and just sobs for a while.

"That is to say, Amanda doesn't know what happened to her," Wade finishes.

"That's so unfair," I say thinking of how lovely she is and how she doesn't deserve it.

"Is it true about her and Pastor Bill?" Ray asks.

I can't think of him as Pastor Bill anymore, all I see is Senior Reverend Pastor William the elevated ass.

Wade speaks so softly we can barely hear him above the high whine of the tires speeding down the road.

"She was in counseling with the pastor and told him about the dreams she kept having. She didn't know that those dreams really happened. Pastor jackass convinced her to drink some wine to calm down. I think to this day he drugged the wine because she only recalls drinking one cup. He raped her and then tried to convince her that she seduced him and it was all her fault."

The enormity of that violation overwhelms me. It must for Ray and Josh as well, they sit in stunned silence.

"I didn't find out about it until much later. She begged me not to get involved. She quit going to church there." Wade's silence betrays the intensity of his anger. No wonder Pastor Bill cowered from the threat of Ray's alibi over the communion wine—he must have known Wade was behind it.

"What's the connection between what happened then and what's happening now?" I'm assuming there is one.

Wade gets out his phone again, "Lee, does Markos know that Amanda has a pre-history with this same or a similar group in this area?"

"I'll ask him. First, how far are you from Biggs?"

Ray has been watching the road signs and answers, "Less than five minutes."

Wade tells Lee, "Ray says under five minutes."

Lee responds, "Markos says the exit sign reads Biggs and Wasco, exit 104, at the top of the ramp you turn left, go north over the river on Highway 97. When you get over the bridge, there's a long sweeping turn to your right. Before you come out of that turn there's a road on your right. A sign out front says Pear Park Camping. Stop at the wine tasting shop right there. One of Markos guys will meet you. Got that?"

"I know the spot," Wade confirms. "But, did you ask Markos about the connection."

"Yes, he's looking into it. I'll be back shortly when I hear."

We see the Biggs junction coming up. It won't be long now.

"Markos wants to know if you know the leader—his name is Jack Daymon?" queries Lee.

I thought, "Daymon like the word demon?"

"Yes. He changed it on purpose. I was on the task force that put him in prison for life." Wade lets the button up and says just to us, "This is the step-father I was telling you about."

"He was let out on parole three months ago. Markos says he's the guy in charge of the Sobek cult. Does Amanda know him?" Lee couldn't have a clue about the pain I see on Wade's face. I'm turned facing him and can't take my eyes off of the torture before me.

"The short story," Wade searches for words, "is that Mr. Daymon drugged and abused an unconscious Amanda in front of his group ten years ago. She doesn't have a conscious memory of it but that's the link."

16
COUNTER ATTACK

NEARLY THRE, THE TRUCK BOUNCES HARD AS JOSH VEERS OVER AND STARTS SLOWING DOWN ON THE OFF RAMP. He cuts our speed in half to make the left hand turn necessary to go for the bridge. I still worry over how fast we're driving with this hard turn coming up.

We're skidding but the truck isn't out of control. Josh must think it's faster to skid than turn. He's already made the corner and accelerating again. Now it's a straight shot over the bridge.

The two lane bridge seems wide enough when there's only one car on the road. The moon lights the bridge and the river brightly. The waves below us break the moonlight into diamond shapes. I see a wheat barge upstream about a mile. That's the first electric light I've seen for miles and it looks very small.

We're off the bridge and starting through the corner.

"Remember to stop at the wine tasting shop," Lee breaks in.

"Also, I told Markos about Amanda. He thinks it good news, that they'll probably not drug the girls. Daymon won't want her to be unconscious again." Lee explains the dark reasoning.

That doesn't seem like good news to me.

"Why Jules?" I ask Wade meaning for him to ask Lee but Josh is slowing down for the hard right turn in front of the wine tasting shop.

A flashlight blinks across the windshield indicating where Markos' man stands off my side of the truck. He runs over to the back door and motions for Wade to move over before jumping in. Josh doesn't even come to a complete stop before the guy is in.

"Stay left," the stranger demands while using his hands to direct us. He's dressed in a black sweat suit, hood up, and dark shoes. There's not enough of his face exposed to really see who he is but I'm guessing that's what he wants. At least he's on our side and I'm grateful for that.

"How far?" Josh asks wondering how fast to drive this little road.

"Over a mile," he answers.

Josh speeds up to 60 but there are houses and dogs around. He probably doesn't feel safe going any faster on a two lane road.

"Up here at the stop sign, park across the street on the left. That's the community church." Josh is slowing down and heading where the stranger leans from the back seat across the front and points.

I see the big black car that Markos owns in front of the church. Josh heads for the side parking lot and comes to a complete stop.

I jump out as quick as I can but the guys are already out. People are dressed in black outfits like the guy we picked up. Two stand on each side of Markos with flashlights in their hands.

Markos extends his hand to Wade, "Unfortunate chain of events. I'm sorry."

Then he turns to Josh and shakes hands before turning to me and Ray saying, "I'm so sorry about Jules. You must wonder why she's involved?"

I do but I want her, "Can we go get her first?"

"We have to wait five more minutes. Part of their ritual is taking drugs and we want those to kick in. After the drugs take effect, they usually have an orgy among themselves before the sacrifice. We want to be there when their attention is on each other." He's talking to me as if this was all logical but I just want Jules.

"Your Pastor Bill has a brother. It seems that this brother assisted Jack Daymon when he assaulted Amanda years ago. The brother recently got your name from Bill's tirades about you. That's the link." Markos seems to feel we need to know.

"Is the brother why Amanda ended up at that church?" As long as I must wait, then I want the whole story.

"Pastor Bill's brother told him about Amanda, Bill called her parents and asked them to come to church there. It seemed to them like divine intervention." Markos doesn't seem surprised by all this. I too have seen my share of gullible Christians.

"Instructions," Markos continues cutting off any more questions from me.

"First, Ray you and your mother stay here. They have a psychic link to you now and will sense you if you get any closer. We need to surprise them. I want you over with the communication center in the back of that van. If we need you, we will call. You too, Dawn." There's no arguing about this so I just nod.

"Second, Lee told you about the Biblical authority you have as kinsmen-redeemers. You follow me and each of you go to your girl. Shout out, 'In the logos and by the blood of Jesus Christ, I claim my kinsman.' Do not take weapons," he motions for Wade to give his gun to Ray. "I'll do the rest but you must shield the girls with your bodies. Do not look at me when I'm addressing them. Do you have that?"

Wade says, "Yes."

Ray is nodding as he tosses me back the pepper spray from his shirt pocket.

They may not be able to use weapons but I'm glad to have one.

Markos waves to an assistant behind him, "Bring them sweatshirts." He points at Josh and Wade.

"You need to put on black sweatshirts like my men," Markos explains. "We want to be unseen and we need to know who our guys are."

Josh sees the sword hanging from the assistant's back. "Are we going to get swords?"

"No, your duty is spiritual, not physical. My guys will handle anything physical." Markos points around at the 20 or more guys now coming in to get ready.

"I thought once they got set up the perimeter ring is impenetrable?" Wade is testing the attack plan.

"It is impregnable," concurs Markos. "But, we're not going through the ring."

"This isn't the first time we've been here," confides Markos. "The first time something like this happened, the builder, Sam Hill, contacted us to drive them out. He showed us the passage we're going to use tonight."

Another assistant brings over black stocking caps and starts putting one on Josh.

"What's this?" Josh isn't sure if he wants it.

"It's for stealth and it has a camera in it. Ray and Dawn will be able to see how you're doing through the video cam in the communication van." I feel relief to know what's going on but scared for Josh.

"Me too?" Wade asks as he picks up then puts on his stocking cap.

"Yes, now it's time to get going," Markos motions for another assistant to set everyone up.

The assistant brings over what looks like a beefed up Segway. "Our version goes faster, farther and over rougher terrain than the commercial versions," Markos brags.

Soon 22 Segways are out. I see Markos showing the guys how to use them while I walk over to talk to Ray.

"Are you mad you can't go?" I ask.

"No, they know what they're doing and don't need me." But I can hear the regret in his voice.

I put my arm around him and we walk to the communications van. The back doors open and we see enough geek gadgets to make Ray jealous.

"I'm Rufus," a dark complexion is barely seen under the black stocking hat and above the black sweat outfit. Ray shakes his hand.

"Let me talk you through this," he offers.

We're still standing outside the van and I see the Segways head up the road. "Those things go fast," I comment.

"Over 40 miles an hour, perfectly quiet because of the electric motors, and it can climb ten inch tall stairs or boulders. Look at what they see," he's pointing to a somewhat greenish glow on screen.

"Night vision, cool," Ray likes it.

I see that Wade and Josh are not at the head of the pack. They're protected in the middle. I'm glad and turn my attention back to the van equipment.

What comes on screen now is a bright glow. We hear drum beats. I recognize them as the same ones from below TF's house. Ray looks at me to tell me the same thing.

"What's the glow?" I ask.

Rufus says, "They have a big fire before the altar. Look at this screen. We've got a guy on the north side shooting into the center of Stonehenge. We call this our 'altar cam'. This screen comes from our 'crowd cam' set on top of a gift shop. It covers the parking lot and outer ring of people."

The altar cam shows what looks like a stone slab. I suck in my breath recognizing the girls bound on the slab.

Between the columns the camera doesn't pick up all the fire but it's huge. And everywhere are people.

"How many people are there?" I ask.

Rufus flips some buttons and crowd cam zooms back and forth. Every inch of what must usually be a parking lot is full. Cars everywhere but people are standing on their cars to get a better look. Many are stomping their feet to the drum beats.

"Sound?" Ray asks.

Another flip of the switch and we get what sounds like hysterical wailing mixed with the heavy drum beats. The wailing sounds of hundreds of people is eerie.

Ray points back to the screen showing our guys. They've jumped the culvert and are taking their Segways up the side of the hill facing the river. We see Markos ahead pointing towards a rock outcropping where he goes.

The guys stop at the rocks just behind Markos. They're following Markos while we see the other guys fanning out.

"The other guys aren't going in?" Ray asks Markos.

"They only go in if Markos fails and needs to be extracted," Rufus shrugs as if that could never happen.

Whatever Markos touched, or maybe he has a remote control…two of the hillside boulders open up for an entrance. Markos steps in first and motions the guys to come. The doors close behind them shutting out the drum beats and moans from above. Now we can hear the guy's voices coming through the monitors.

Markos says, "We're coming up inside the circle and will step out through two of the columns. Remember that the layout is like a triangle. First, the altar, which is a slab about two feet high and ten feet long. In front of the altar is one column and then behind that are two columns with a beam at their top. We come out of the two columns which face each other. Thankfully, the first column hides us from the altar. Understand?"

I know I don't and doubt that they do but I hear them say, "Yes."

"Here's the stairs. Wade you go on the left side, Josh you follow me on the right. When I step out, you two step out directly behind me. Wait for me to signal. I'm going to confront Daymon while you two find your girls and make your kinsmen-redeemer claims immediately."

"Then what?" Josh asks.

"Anastasis Dunamis," Markos responds as if it's obvious.

Josh must be watching Wade because the camera is on him. Wade appears to be looking up at the top of the stairwell because his screen is just dark. We hear Markos say, "Now."

Josh turns his head up to look at Markos and we see on camera Markos pushing against the column wall. It easily gives way and the light floods the camera. Markos kind of appears like a shadow now with all the light flooding him.

Wade's camera shows the door opening and Markos is already in position. We see Josh coming up to Wade and the two of them stand behind Markos.

"Is there anyway to get that altar camera to focus in on them?" I want to see everything that happens.

"We think it's positioned correctly now," Rufus tells me but it's obvious he doesn't want any more questions. He holds his finger up to his lips like a librarian.

Markos is waiting for something. I think I know what.

The moans of the crowd is rhythmic…there's a pattern like an ocean wave. He's waiting for the next lull.

Josh and Wade are drilled in on Markos. They're not even looking around. I imagine they're even breathing when he breaths.

We see Markos holding his right hand up above his shoulders. Both the guys are watching it. One finger goes up. Two fingers go up. Three fingers and Markos disappears around the column toward the altar.

I look at the altar camera and see him confront Daymon who doesn't know what to do. As Markos rips off the headdress that Daniel's is wearing, I see Josh and Wade run out.

I look at Josh's camera—it's jumping up and down as he runs up to Jules.

I see Wade's camera doing the same. Jules' head is at one end of the altar and opposite is Amanda's head. Wade has a few more feet to run than Josh.

Markos must have given them scissors or knives, they're cutting through the plastic ties that bind the girls.

I look at the altar camera again and I see that most of the crowd is lost in their trance and still moaning and drumming. They don't have a clue what's going on. But, now there seems to be a disturbance or response up closer to Markos.

Wade's camera is showing the best lit images and it looks like Amanda hasn't been harmed.

Josh is facing the fire and the image is getting washed out. I think Jules is looking OK but she's not responding.

Rufus says, "They did drug them after all. Your guys will have to carry them out."

The guys were supposed to make their kinsmen-redeemer claims immediately before cutting the girls loose. They forgot but I see them do so now.

We can't hear them say it but we see them hold the girls tight and turn their heads towards heaven.

Their video cams just show a bright full moon.

The altar cam shows them with their heads uplifted, each with their girl in their arms, shouting at the top of their voice.

The crowd camera shows people stopping. The drumming ceases. For just a split second, everything is quiet. We can even hear the roar of the flames.

Wade's camera shows Josh picking Jules up and heading for the column entrance. From the way the camera is jerking around, Wade must be running with Amanda right behind him.

The altar camera doesn't show either Wade or Josh any more. They must be in the secret passage by now.

All we see now is the crowd starting to act as one again. They're howling. The howling of demons. I shudder.

The crowd camera shows cars starting up for a chase. Engines revving like beasts ready to prey. But, no one knows where to go after the sacrifices.

Those inside the circle and closest to the altar start to make for Markos. Outside the circle the crowd continues howling ever louder. Inside the circle it's the quiet grunting of demanding pigs who think they're about to eat and Markos is the menu.

I can't believe how strong Markos is—he seems superhuman. He's got Daymon gripped in front of him. But the crowd moves in.

"Get him out of there," Ray says to Rufus. "Tell your guys to get him out of there!"

Rufus smiles and says, "You're just getting to the good part. Watch."

I watch as Markos reveals his strength. The altar cam shows him picking up Daymon over his head and throwing him 20 feet into the crowd.

"Amazing, but he can't take on the whole crowd?" Ray's not sure.

"He won't. Keep watching." Rufus still smiles.

Markos stands straight. He's talking to the crowd but we can't hear. "What's he saying?" I ask knowing no one knows.

Two men lean forward through the crowd and grab Markos. A woman pulls out a long knife. Evidently, these two would have helped during the sacrifice.

There's a loud popping sound and a flash of light--one guy is down.

The popping sounds more like thunder now and two flashes of light precede three people going down including the woman with the knife.

"What's that?" I'm not sure how to even explain it.

Rufus says, "Psalms 91:11 and 12. For he will command his angels concerning you to guard you in all your ways; they will lift you up in their hands, so that you will not strike your foot against a stone."

Now the thunder roars as more lights move to protect Markos. There must be hundreds of lights and every person is on his or her face. The lights glow brighter than the fire. I feel the light from here.

I hear another van taking off from the parking lot for the hill.

Wade's camera shows Josh coming out into the light still holding Jules.

Josh turns around and we see Wade holding Amanda now. "We made it, buddy!" Josh sounds surprised.

We see his camera go from Wade to the bright lights above. Stonehenge looks lit up like a football field on Friday night only hundreds of times brighter.

Wade's camera turns to see it as well.

"What is that?" Wade can't figure it out either.

We hear the van driving up to the guys but don't see it until Josh turns around and one of Markos' men comes into view.

"Put the girls into the van. We need to go get the drugs out of them."

Both the guys run the girls over to the back of the van and jump in with them. The van turns around but we can tell from the camera movement that the guys want to keep looking at the light.

I look at the altar cam and the light is so bright I can't even see Markos any more. Everywhere the people are lying on the ground as if unconscious. I'm sure that's what happened.

I look at the crowd camera and everyone in the parking lot is the same—on the ground and unconscious. The car engines are turned off. The thunder sounds have ceased and there's a deadly silence everywhere.

Then the light is gone. As if someone threw the switch, every ounce of light is gone. No car lights. Even the huge fire is snuffed out like a little candle. Only the moonlight and it's not showing anything on the cameras.

On the ride down the hillside the guys must have pulled their stocking caps with cameras off. Nothing now except blank screens. I hear their van approaching and grab Ray's hand to run out for them.

Rufus runs up behind us and I yell back, "Is Markos OK?" He doesn't answer me. I look back and see he's nodding. What's with all these guys nodding instead of saying?

Four of Markos' men beat us to the van and open the back doors. Wade and Josh hand off the girls to them and they rush them in the back door of the church. I grab Josh's hand and help him get out of the van. Wade follows.

Ray beats us to the church and we follow.

The church has got to be more than a 100 years old. The pews the girls are laying on must be original.

One of the men appears to be a medic. He's giving the girls an injection. I recognize him as my black bee. Good thing Jules is out of it—she hates shots.

"Narcan?" I ask black bee remembering how quickly it sobered me.

"I'm surprised you remember," he moves from Jules to Amanda.

Josh tells him, "Thank you for your help." He must recognize him from earlier as well. Josh adds, "And thanks for the coffee." He does remember him.

Ray is standing over Jules, "You alright?"

Jules tries to come around, "Turn that damn music off." I'm guessing she's still hearing he drum beats. She doesn't usually swear but in this case, it was indeed 'damn' music.

Ray laughs and walks over to Amanda.

She groans, "I see the light."

It's going to be a little while before they talk coherently.

More guys in black sweat outfits come in and with the back door open, I hear the sound of the Segways on the gravel. Everyone should be back now but I still don't see Markos.

I walk over to my black bee, "Are they going to be alright?"

His face is very kind and he reassures me, "They're going to be fine. Nothing was done to them other than being drugged and that's wearing off fast. They'll be up and walking in five minutes."

"Do you know if Markos is OK? We've got to thank him." I really do want to talk to him before he leaves.

"He's probably helping the guys round up the equipment and get everything back to the boat. Don't worry, he's OK and won't leave until he gets a chance to talk with you."

He turns and starts to walk away. I grab hold of his hand to shake it, "May I ask your name?"

"Cephas, and you're welcome. We are on the same side, you know?" His grin is large and voice sincere. He waves one more time before going out the door.

Josh and Ray are hovering over Jules who is now sitting up. Wade is kneeling beside Amanda who is still lying down.

PART IV

WHAT'S MISSING

17
REVELATIONS

"YOU WANT TO KNOW," I JUMP NOT REALIZING THAT MARKOS IS STANDING QUIETLY BEHIND ME, "WHAT ANASTASIS DUNAMIS MEANS?"

He doesn't bother waiting for an answer.

"It means 'Resurrection Power.'" We nod knowing that already.

He adds, "You know the words but you do not know the power. All this attack is because you are a threat to Satan. He knows you're close to knowing the power, not just the words." Markos looks at us as if we're not getting it.

"You saw the power tonight!" he's excited. "That same power is yours."

"What did we see tonight?" Wade still isn't sure.

Markos answers, "You saw Matthew 26:53 'Do you think I cannot call on my Father, and he will at once put at my disposal more than twelve legions of angels?' Jesus used His authority to send His angels.

"I heard your Bible studies, I know you're pursuing the truth. You have been called out from the lies of Satan. Now it's time to enter the truth and live in the power God means for you. Are you ready?" The dark eyes stare into us as a challenge. I find his eyes searching my soul but there is encouragement as well.

Jules and Amanda stand up and say, "Yes."

I'm surprised by how easily they now move.

Ray, Josh, Wade and I say, "Amen."

"How long have you been fighting... opposing these followers of Sobek?" I feel compelled to ask. After all, the authority and power he's talking about we just saw, so where did it begin? How long does it take to get—power like that can't come over night?

"You want to know how such authority came into my life?" Markos understands. "The power really doesn't have much to do with them I do have a personal history with the followers and the demon known as Sobek."

"I love Jesus very much. I'll tell you shortly about my history with Him but let me start first with Sobek in Egypt. It's pertinent to tonight.

"I went to Egypt as a missionary. This was long ago. Those churches and one of the schools I established became well known. The school trained many people which you would recognize."

I look intently at Markos' face, he doesn't look more than 55 years old but I remember the old photographs. So, I ask him, "How old are you?" It's probably rude to interrupt but there's something so indistinct about his age. His energy and the way he moves makes him seem much younger.

"That's part of my story," he kindly winks at me and then proceeds.

"Most of my work was done in Alexandria. It was such a beautiful city. I haven't been there since so I don't know what it is like now. But part of me still misses it.

"Many brothers and sisters converted but there was a lot of prejudice about The Way. The worst attacks came from the Priest in the temple of Sobek.

"As it is today, so it was then—religions and money were the same thing. If you challenged a religion, you challenged the craftsmen making money off of idols, you challenged the butchers making money off of sacrifices, you challenged the bakers making special cake offerings, you challenged the incense makers, you challenged the potters making incense and sacrificial dishes, and you challenged the priests who live off the offerings. Personally, I don't find that much different than the supposed 'Christian' religions of today." Markos knows how to make a point.

"So, it was pretty easy for the Sobek priest to get the followers worked up. The Gospel had cost them a lot of money. They had pressing debts. Some of the lesser priests had already been sold into slavery. None of them knew how or wanted to do something productive with their lives. The answer was to kill me.

"My brothers and sisters didn't want me harmed. They heard about the plot to kidnap me and cut me into pieces with the flint knives of Sobek on the temple altar.

"They were so pained by the very thought of such a threat that I hurt them by not leaving. Finally, it seemed best for me to leave the area for awhile. I appointed one of the brothers to watch over things while I was gone, a great man by the name of Anianus. I went to a refuge the brothers established in Pentapolis."

"The priest of Sobek, he called himself Ahmed-Ra, left the brothers and sisters of Alexandria alone at first. He told everyone that he wanted to kill me—that to kill a cobra it's best to cut off its head. And he literally wanted to cut my head off. There were continual assassination attempts.

Markos interrupts his story and asks, "Are any of you familiar with this? 'And these signs will accompany those who believe: In my name they will drive out demons; they will speak in new tongues; they will pick up snakes with their hands; and when they drink deadly poison, it will not hurt them at all; they will place their hands on sick people, and they will get well.'"

Ray says, "Yes, I think that's in the book of Mark."

"Very good," Markos likes Ray, "and that is what happened. They would poison me through the well water, they would poison me through the produce in the market place, and they even put a live viper in my bread. But the word of the Lord came true and I did not die.

"Instead, I traveled more and taught The Way to remote parts of Libya. One city, Ammonicia, almost the whole population turned to the Lord. It was there that another Sobek priest declared against me and went to Alexandria to conspire against me with the priest there.

"Literally hundreds of thousands of people turned to the way. The whole economy in Egypt changed because of it. The followers of The Way would help each other as brothers and sisters should. This effectively put an end to the usury practiced by the temple of Sobek and that was their last source of revenue. The two Sobek priests working together whipped up their followers to kill me.

"That year, the Passover coincided with the celebration of the pagan god Serapis. Even the followers of The Way had not yet matured and were confused about this god. If you look at a picture of Serapis, you'll see he is the image most people adopted for Jesus. So much foolishness among those that claim to be His. What people worship as Jesus looks nothing like Him... over time, Serapis became the de facto Jesus. So, don't misunderstand how easy it was for the followers then to get confused.

"The pagan festival brought in idol worshippers from all over Egypt. They didn't know The Way. They didn't know what they were really doing. It was easy for the Sobek priests to get the pagans drunk, whip them up into frenzy and come after me. They thought their after lives depended on it.

"The brothers and sisters were so many that we had several Communion services starting from day break on. Thousands came and stood in line for several hours waiting to get into the church to celebrate. By late night the last service was about half full for the first time in 14 hours. The people were tired. None of us were ready for what happened.

"The Sobek priests had spies watching us all day. When they reported that all the followers were gone except for those in church, Ahmed-Ra declared the time to act.

"They led their drunken followers to attack. Coming from every entrance, they swooped in striking many. Some tried to set the church timbers on fire. They're only real goal was to get me and they did.

"They bound me with a rope and dragged me through the streets whose occupants now were only the drunken pagans.

"They tied me as if I were an ox and took great delight yelling to the crowd, "We're taking the ox to his stall.'

"Finally, they threw me in a prison in their temple. I was cut every where from the stones on the streets I was dragged over. I thought I would die and prayed incessantly Psalms 118:17 'I will not die but live, and will proclaim what the LORD has done.'

"Ahmed-Ra had a different plan for me. He and the other priest, I never learned his name, stayed up all night chanting spells and sharpening their flint knives. I was to be a sunrise sacrifice. They purposefully put me in a cell where I could watch them prepare.

"They prayed to Sobek, I prayed to the Father, and the night wore on until 3 AM. Even there and in those times, that was considered the hour of highest power.

"Ahmed-Ra wanted to anoint my body with the oils they had been chanting over. Their body guards opened my cell door for them but I was too bound and too hurt to resist.

"Before they could carry out their ritual, an angel of light appeared. You saw such tonight. First, there was a loud popping sound, then a streak of light and the priests and guards fell as if they died.

"Many who re-tell this story get it inaccurate at this part and I want to tell you what the angel really said. He said, "Slave of God, Markos, your name is written in the Book of Life. You will always be remembered among the holy apostles. You shall unceasingly proclaim the Most High God and His Son, Jesus Christ. The resurrection power is upon you." Pausing to explain, "He said this in Greek so the term was Anastasis Dunamis.

"I had heard about such a thing from a friend of mine so was not taken by surprise to be lifted in a whirlwind and found myself on Malta.

"I heard later that I was supposed to have been taken through the streets the next day for another round of beatings and then sacrificed on the steps of the temple of Sobek.

"I sent word to Ananias that I was alive and in Malta. He came to see me personally and told me what happened.

"One of the brothers secretly worked as a guard for Ahmed-Ra. It was this man who came in and found the guards and priests unconscious with me no where to be found. He thought I had escaped. To cover my absence, he took another prisoner they had beat up, a vile man who had stolen from us as well as from them, and placed him in my cell. When they had beaten that man, they broke his jaw. He could not talk. My face and his was beaten beyond recognition, it was easy to mistake us. He screamed and moaned to protest that he was not me but no one understood him. Besides, their wrath was too great to care.

"In the morning, they took the fake me and tied a rope around his neck treating him like a beast. Thousands of these drunken pagans from out of town lined the streets jeering. They had tortured him so much that he died before they could sacrifice him.

"Ahmed and the other priest got into a terrible fight over cutting up the pieces of his body and who would get the honors to do it. Their followers grew tired of the bickering and took the body to burn.

"As they tried to burn, a rain started and thunder struck all around them. The pagans thought they were under attack and took off running.

"Some of the brothers who knew the real identity of the body came and stole it from the pyre. To hide what they assumed was my escape they told everyone it was me."

"What happened to the Sobek priests?" Amanda asks.

"The same thing that always happens whenever the Lord tells me to go after them. Their followers turned on them. Ahmed-Ra was cut to death using the same flint knives he wanted to kill me with. The guard who killed him wanted his position. He thought the other priest to be a challenge and made it look like that priest did the killing. They held a trial and the second priest was found guilty of murder and sentenced to death—and the guard now the pretender priest got to cut him to pieces with the same flint knives. The pretender was later himself cut to pieces during a fight. Eventually, their temple was closed but that demon shows up and recreates his temple from time to time in places all over the world." Markos explains.

"Is that your mission—to overcome Sobek wherever he shows up?" Amanda persists.

"Wherever Sobek shows up, he does so to confront people who seek the real truth and the full power of Anastasis Dunamis. My duty is to protect and teach those people. That's the way the Lord thinks—in terms of His people not in terms of demons." Markos looks around to make sure everyone understands what he is saying. I do.

"What about those people?" Jules is pointing up the hillside.

"We've already gathered enough information that Daymon's parole is revoked today. He'll spend the remainder of his life in jail—no more hope for parole.

"The others will suffer what's due in the next few months. They'll go through bankruptcies, divorces, diseases, and failures of every kind. Evil has its own rewards on this earth before Hades, then in Hades as well." Jules is assured by this.

Amanda asks, "Why the old chord or ribbon?"

"I thought you would like them and to let you know I was around. They come from an old Flemish monastery where I lived for awhile. They used them for Bible markers. I think you'd be surprised at how valuable they are."

Nothing dramatic about that.

But Wade looks dramatic. He's been very quiet, almost as if distanced from us. He finally breaks his silence and asks with a great deal of respect in his voice, "Are you Saint Mark?"

I laugh. That would be ridiculous.

Markos takes his time to respond, "Do you believe that what Jesus says He means?"

We all say, "Yes."

"Have you ever read a quote from Jesus that says, 'I tell you the truth, some who are standing here will not taste death before they see the kingdom of God come with power?'"

Josh answers, "Sure, but that's not literal, is it?"

"Because you do not know…experience, depend on, interact with Anastasis Dunamis, you doubt the very words of Jesus. People who claim to know Him and love Him dismiss His very words. And, it's not just this one thing."

We can see how vexing it is to Markos how Christians choose what things to believe—I know from the few things we've discussed about doctrine that what we do is not always right.

"I'll give you another text, 'Do you see all these great buildings?' replied Jesus. 'Not one stone here will be left on another; every one will be thrown down.' Yet to this day Christians from all over the world visit the ruins of the Fortress Antonia as if it were the last temple. What they revere is the same as saying Jesus lied."

I think of the conflict over the Temple Mound and no longer wonder how anything righteous could come of it. The conflict is all about a lie.

Wade brings the discussion back to his point, "Are you Saint Mark?"

"Yes," Markos doesn't hesitate.

Wade continues his interrogation, "You quoted from your own writing, the Book of Mark?"

Markos nods, "Chapter 13 about the temple, chapter 9 about that "some" will live until the end of time."

Wade hardly knows how to follow up but years of practice in interrogations leads him on, "How can you live that long?"

"First, Jesus said so of me and a handful of people. So, it is His will to have us witness His continuing ministry until the end of time. Understand?"

I nod "yes" and others say "Amen."

"Second, who says you have to die?"

"But," Wade pursues, "aren't we under the death penalty from the Garden of Eden?"

"A dear brother, who you call Saint John, quotes Jesus accurately in John 8:51, 'I tell you the truth, if anyone keeps my word, he will never see death.'"

"Do you find it easy to believe that Enoch didn't die because of his faith, that Elijah didn't die because of his faith, but that you must die? You just don't understand what to believe in." Markos shakes his head in great sadness.

How much pain is in this world because of not so much a lack of believe, but because we don't believe what Jesus says? I wonder how many things I've dismissed by thinking it impossible?

I don't even know how to express this as a question.

"John also wrote," I'm glad Wade continues his interrogation since I can't, 'I tell you the truth, anyone who has faith in me will do what I have been doing. He will do even greater things than these, because I am going to the Father.'"

"Yes, John 14:12. I love how my brother kept track of what the Lord said. We've talked about how the Spirit brings conversations back to us in exact detail.

"If you're asking why you don't have such authority in your life, I'll tell you. Is that your question?" Markos knows we're all asking this question.

"I was one of the 70 who Jesus instructed and sent out to heal, cast out demons, and tell the good news that the kingdom of God is now. It was exciting. I had not yet witnessed the Anastasis Dunamis and was thrilled by the power Jesus gave us."

Markos says to Jules, "You're what? Fifteen?" She nods. "I was 14 at the time. Can you imagine having that kind of authority in your life now?" Jules doesn't respond but it would be hard to imagine it in my own life at my age.

"I know you're probably thinking it would be easy to have such power if you were trained by Jesus. I had lots of other people who helped me as well. My uncle was Barnabas. My first mentor was Paul. My second mentor was Peter—I was his scribe for the books of Peter. But, my authority as part of the 70 was directly granted me through Jesus. It puffed me up. I wasn't the only one.

"We tried for several hours but could not cure a boy who had seizures. The boy's father asked Jesus for help and He, of course, easily cured the boy by getting rid of a demon. We didn't want to ask in public because the Lord was often blunt in how He said things and we didn't want to be embarrassed. We waited until the crowd was gone and asked him why we couldn't cure the boy."

I remember this story. Markos wrote about it in the Book of Mark.

"Jesus called us a bunch of perverts. You have to understand that means in Greek that we were corrupt. I know I carried a lot of lust in my heart at the time, but it means more than that...we were corrupt in our attentions, puffed up, and corrupt in our beliefs. I believe that correction cured many things in my heart and started me on the road of true belief.

"I'm going to quote from your King James Version because some of the versions leave out the most important part. 'And he said unto them, This kind can come forth by nothing, but by prayer and fasting.' That's chapter 9, verse 29."

"I wasn't praying like I should, like we saw Jesus pray. I was wrapped up in my own power which was really His on loan. But, the answer that changed my life and will help you is to fast."

Josh exclaims, "This is the key we've been missing! TF fasted before he started healing. He just didn't understand its importance."

Nodding, Markos goes on, "No one understands its importance. Why should going without food bring spiritual power? There's a lot of analysis, and some have interesting facts, but the point for you to understand is that Jesus said to do it, Jesus often fasted, and it works not because of science, but because of the faith you exercise when you do what Jesus tells you to do."

"Do you still start up churches?" Ray asks.

"No. I've come to realize that we're all part of Zion, the heavenly assembly. When we gather here as believers, we're really joining the saints in heaven. I worshipped with many of those people here on earth, so I count it as joy to worship here jointly with them in heaven." Markos' fondness for his friends comes through in his voice.

"Who else is still alive—you said "some" will live until the end?" Wade is back to his interrogation but Markos doesn't mind.

"John. I've been to his so called grave in Ephesus but it's empty. No one knows where the body went because he never died. We rarely see each other, but I miss him all the time."

"He comes to this country sometimes but right now there's so much work to do in Africa.

"The Magdalene also usually stays in Africa. I hate to leave her...she's such a loving person. Like John and Mary, you need to know what the brothers and sisters have allowed to happen in Africa is shameful. More believers in Africa have been persecuted in the last ten years than since Jesus died. Personally, try to get more involved," Markos pleas.

"Who else?" Wade asks.

"There are more, but why do you ask? Their mission is to do what Jesus tells them. If they are directed to contact you, they will. We've learned over time that if people find out about us, they often turn us into some form of worship. So, I'm not going to tell you anymore." Markos cuts the conversation off.

I ask, "We're closer to the Lord than ever before but it seems like we've been cut off from His people, or at least the people who claim to be His."

"I think I know where you are going," Markos gets to the point. "You want to know if there's some church, some group or some structure for you?"

I nod "Yes."

"I heard Lee explain about how there are only brothers and sisters—no teacher, no reverend, no pastor—only Jesus and equality among believers. This is true but incomplete." Markos pauses here for a moment.

Rufus walks up to him and says, "We're ready. State police are headed out from Goldendale, we need to leave now."

I don't want Markos to leave. I want to ask him about what Jesus was like. Was Markos really the guy who ran away naked the night they captured Jesus? What about Paul? Was he a bit of a tyrant or was he full of love? And Peter? What was Peter's wife like?

I see everyone else moan as well. So much to know. Where to start?

"I have no time left but one thing to tell you that's very important. You not only have to love what Jesus loves, you have to hate what Jesus hates. One of the things He hates you've already experienced and it's what we're talking about. Usually, I'd have someone read this from the Bible but I'm going to tell you what John heard from Jesus in his Revelation." Markos seems hurried and we don't interrupt. Every second is precious now.

"Jesus talked about people who claimed to be followers of The Way but taught contrary to His teachings—something you've already learned about. He called these people the 'Nicolaitans'. John tells us what Jesus feels about this in Revelation 2:6, 'You hate the practices of the Nicolaitans, which I also hate.'

He stops to emphasize, "Do you get that, Jesus 'hates' the Nicolaitans. HATES THEM. Who are these people?" Markos asks rhetorically and we wait for his reply.

"Theologians," this appears to be a disdainful term to Markos, "try and say the Nicolaitans were a group led by a man who lived later on—they are not named for a man.

"The term means something in itself. In Greek we often combine two words into one that means something slightly different. In this case, the first part of the word, 'nikao', means to 'conquer' or 'overlord.' The second part, 'laos', means 'people' and that is where your word 'laity' comes from. Together these two parts combine into a new word that means the 'destruction of the people.'

"We, all of us who originally were taught by Jesus, understood that this referred to how the arrogant and power hungry organized a priestly order. These same clergy throughout church history created conflict between believers and rule through doctrine and partial truths. The do not have the spirit of unity from the Lord. Everywhere you find them, there is division.

The only way to accurately translate the word would be 'those who prevail over the people.' The Lord hates them, I hate them, and now you must hate them as well." Markos lifts a tremendous burden from me with this message.

I hate Reverend Senior Pastor William. It's not his person it's the spirit of over-lording that dominates him and through him. He used his pastor position to lord over us, that spirit attacked me, my sister, my husband, my children—it's evil and now I know I'm free to hate it like Jesus does. And, I do.

"What do we do now?" Josh asks as he sees the last of the men leave the room.

Markos moves to leave but stops and motions us all closer to him. As we close in he pulls us each into an embrace against him. We stand encircling him. His arms stretch around us squeezing us. Now he purposefully places in turn his hands on each of our heads in a blessing.

"As the Lord put His hands on me, so I lay my hands on you. This was always intended to be the case for every believer—one generation passing on the blessings of the Lord to the next—a continually line of contact from Jesus.

"So, from the Lord to me to you, I pass on His personal claim for each of you.

"Father, I have done your will and your people are safe. Bless them. Give them wisdom. Bring them fully into our family as mature followers with your power and authority as you have always willed." I feel the undeniable power and presence of Jesus Christ upon me.

Whether lights, angels or a lightly colored blue flame, I see the presence of the Lord on each of us. I think the others do as well.

"Amen," is all we can say.

Rufus appears again in the doorway and motions once more for Markos. I know they need to leave. We need to leave, but Markos has one more thing to say and we're not letting go of him until he says it.

"My friends and I started out just like you. At the same place in our growth, we met and prayed. We spent days fasting and praying for the authority, direction, and resources to go do what Jesus did…that's what He says is His will for us. If you do that, Jesus will send the Holy Spirit. He always does." Now he reluctantly lets go our embrace and walks to the door.

Wade can't help but get in one more question, "Was that Pentecost?"

Markos pauses in the doorway and points his finger at Wade, "You know it. Now go have your Pentecost and get the Faith of God."

PART V

WHAT'S NEW

18
EPILOGUE

IT'S BEEN TWO WEEKS SINCE WE LAST SAW AMANDA AND WE'RE ALL NERVOUS WAITING FOR HER TO ARRIVE FOR DINNER. On one hand, it seems ages since we last saw her. On the other, setting the table here at TF's house seems like something we did just yesterday.

Jules and I have most of the table set up just as Dusky walks in bringing her famous black bean soup to go with our salads and homemade bread. A simple meal but it smells almost too good to wait for anyone else.

Ray walks up to Dusky, "I know you want to see it." He pulls up his T-shirt to show the almost healed cuts on his stomach.

Dusky doesn't say anything as she traces with her finger the faint pink outline of the Sobek logo.

Ray volunteers, "The doctor said the scars will go away in about a month. I hate seeing it in the mirror but I can wait a few more weeks for it to go away."

I already talked to the same doctor about plastic surgery if it didn't go away. No matter what, Ray's not going through life with that thing. I am surprised how fast it's leaving on its own.

John joins us just as Ray starts to put his shirt down, "Don't I get to take a look?" Ray holds his shirt up for a few seconds more. "That's going away fast!" John confirms what Ray wants to hear.

Ray walks over and starts pouring Communion wine. Jules gets the bread out and puts it at the head of the table for Lee or TF to start when everyone sits down.

Behind Jules' back Dusky points and mouths to me asking if she's OK. I worry because she claims she can't recall anything. Whether that's a sign of something suppressed or lack of trauma, I don't know. So, I worry. I just shrug back to Dusky. Let her ask Jules whatever she wants.

Jules looks up and says, "She's here." We know she means Amanda.

Wade leads the way in followed by Amanda, TF, Lee and Josh. Between the greetings we all find our usual seats and Lee starts Communion.

We sit silently for several minutes during Communion. Each lost in their own thoughts, expressing their hearts privately before the Lord. But with the meal comes the questions.

Lee asks Josh, "So, what are you guys doing now?"

"We showed the IRS that we never signed off of or gave approval for the tax strategy our partners initiated. They made us pay the back taxes without penalties and are going after our partners and the CPA. Our partners divided up the holdings so that we don't have partners any more. Things are really settling down. Between Dawn and me, we're running things the way we want."

I add, "The biggest issue we've got facing us is the trial against the Sobek people." I kind of lower my voice not knowing if I'm impacting Jules or Amanda.

Ray feels the awkwardness as well and hurries in to explain, "I don't have any further testimony. The guys who attacked me ended up getting shot in the ambush the Sobek people set up at Multnomah Falls for you guys," he points to Wade, Josh and me.

Jules isn't going to be put off and speaks up immediately, "I've been interviewed a lot for this trial but they may not even put me on the stand. I can't remember anything. I know they drugged me…drugged us," she says looking to Amanda.

Amanda takes over, "The only thing I remember are two faces: Daymon and Pastor Bill's brother. I never learned his name and don't want to. I identified both of their pictures to the police. Turns out Daymon died from Markos throwing him."

That surprises everyone except Wade. He must not have had time to tell us before but he adds now, "Seems like his neck snapped when he landed."

Ray asks impatiently, "What about Pastor Bill's brother?"

"He was transferred to the Walla Walla prison where someone knifed him within an hour. They taped his mouth shut, tied his hands behind his back, and let him bleed to death slowly in the middle of the prison exercise area." I get a sense as Wade tells this that he's seen prison justice before.

"So, who is left to try?" Dusky asks Wade.

He shrugs, "We have Markos' video tapes and are going after the three who had the knives and most likely were to sacrifice the girls. Most of the ones we would have wanted to catch got killed in the ambush and car crashes."

I kind of felt skittish hearing that so bluntly said but the girls didn't get upset.

"People are so stupid-- many of them that night were on probation for prior crimes. We have pictures of them drinking alcohol, smoking dope and taking other drugs. A lot of them are returning to jail for probation violations without any trials." Wade seemed happy about that. I wonder if there's a cop left who trusts judges any more?

TF looks to John, "What are you doing for fellowship?"

"We're meeting on Thursdays taking turns at our house then with Dawn and Josh. Ray and Jules already have a handful of kids coming. We want to stay small so we can really be led by the Holy Spirit. Each meeting we learn something new."

"What did you learn last time?" TF isn't relentless; he's just excited by the changes.

John looks to Josh wanting him to answer. We all agreed it would be too easy to sound like condemnation if we talked about this before most people.

Josh takes his cue and says, “We learned that the majority of the time, Jesus doesn’t want us doing public prayers.”

Even now I remember those endless prayer meeting nights at Evangeline Church. How so many times the prayers were just gossip, “Lord, remember the Kings who didn’t come to church again another week.” Or the man who prayed for his father to change his lying ways—making sure everyone in the church knew exactly what he was lying about.

Josh brought his own Bible this time and now was ready to read from it.

“Matthew 6:1-8 ‘1 Be careful not to do your 'acts of righteousness' before men, to be seen by them. If you do, you will have no reward from your Father in heaven.

2 So when you give to the needy, do not announce it with trumpets, as the hypocrites do in the synagogues and on the streets, to be honored by men. I tell you the truth, they have received their reward in full.

3 But when you give to the needy, do not let your left hand know what your right hand is doing,

4 so that your giving may be in secret. Then your Father, who sees what is done in secret, will reward you.

5 "And when you pray, do not be like the hypocrites, for they love to pray standing in the synagogues and on the street corners to be seen by men. I tell you the truth, they have received their reward in full.

6 But when you pray, go into your room, close the door and pray to your Father, who is unseen. Then your Father, who sees what is done in secret, will reward you.

7 And when you pray, do not keep on babbling like pagans, for they think they will be heard because of their many words.

8 Do not be like them, for your Father knows what you need before you ask him.'"

Lee quickly adds, "I remember hearing from a Professor Plies, a gentleman I met at a local Christian college, who wisely added to this public prayer issue a warning not to make this a hard and fast rule. His reasoning was that like most sin, the issue is not public prayer but of ego. All sin eventually boils down to ego. We have prayed publicly here but we did so without ego. From years of experience I can tell you that the Holy Spirit will lead you many times into public prayer. Don't focus on that so much as focus on the criticism that the Lord has for those who serve their egos...especially by seeming righteous before others.

"What about you?" Ray asks Wade. "Have you got anything going on about all this?"

Wade shakes his head slowly, "It's as if it never happened. No one at work seems to know about it. I've talked a lot with the Washington State police but no one local has said anything to me...not even about the two cops who turned out not to be cops. No one cares about a solved case. We've got too many unsolved cases to worry about."

After pausing for just a little bit, Wade continues, "What is different is that every thing I work on now I see the connection to evil. I've never solved so many cases and it's because I've become intuitive about how evil works. If there's confusion, I know there's evil causing it. I just look for the source of evil. I literally feel the presence of the Holy Spirit with me each day telling me what to do and revealing to me the source of evil."

"I've neglected my need for fellowship, though, and plan to meet with them next week," he points at Josh and me.

"I'll be there, too," Amanda commits.

"So will we," adds TF speaking for Lee as well.

"Wade, I still wonder about those ribbons. Did you ever get those analyzed?" TF asks.

"Yes. Interesting story," Wade pauses long enough to make sure everyone is paying attention. "Do you want to hear it?"

Ray throws a piece of bread at him.

"I'll take that as a 'maybe'," and tosses it back at Ray before going on.

"The lab guys got very excited tracing the ribbon down. It was rare for two reasons. The first is that it's made from raw silk. Something we don't see much and made it harder to identify compared to other materials. The second reason why it was so interesting is its history. It came from a Flemish abbey in the 1600s."

"Do you know what abbey?" Ray asks for us.

"Yes. The design is distinct to the abbey of Affligem. Now this abbey was started by six men, former knights, as part of their redemption. The names of the six nights are Tom, Lee, John, Josh, Wade and Ray. OK, I made up the names but it is true about the six men."

TF asks, "Was there something significant about this particular abbey?"

"Just that it became one of the richest and most influential abbeys of its time. Over the years it set up several other abbeys. Eventually it was too rich and the new French Republic grabbed it and all its lands. Now it's known as an excellent brewery."

As Wade wound down his story, Amanda had excused herself. She now returns with a handful of picture frames. In each one is a section of the ribbon Markos left behind.

"I framed a ribbon for each of you," she says as she hands out her gifts. "I think the background story has meaning for us—we're supposed to get ready and reach others."

We sit around talking small talk everyone hesitant to leave each other's company. We're family now.

"Thursday is only a couple of days away," Josh tells Wade as we ready to leave. "Thank you for all you've done. I know, we know," he says putting an arm around me as I walk up closer, "that you've pulled a lot of strings to keep the kids from having to testify more."

Wade just stands there not saying anything. I can tell it's been a long time since he was appreciated.

Amanda walks up and says, "Did I tell you I'm moving in with Uncle Wade?"

"No," I say.

"Yes, he's letting me live with him while I finish up grad school. Now I don't have an excuse to not finish." She's obviously very happy and I suspect Wade wants to watch over her for some time to come.

The ride home has been quiet but now that we're just a few blocks away, Ray thinks of something and breaks the silence. "Mom, do you still have the email address for Markos?"

"Yes, but I doubt he will answer."

"I'm not after him," Ray leaves me in suspense.

"OK, who are you after?"

"I'm thinking if it's like most companies, all I have to do is change the first name on the address." He still doesn't tell me who he's after but I wait for him this time.

Eventually he pronounces his intent, "I'm going to email Mary Magdalene and John the Revelator. These people are as much our brothers and sisters as Wade and Amanda."

Our lives have certainly become more exciting.

QUESTIONS?

The author will do his best to answer questions or discuss topics as time allows.

Please email him at: **AD@MINETFIBER.COM**

Printed in the United States
65293LVS00003B/136-174